COLD DECEIT

COLD DECEIT

TONI ANDERSON

Cold Deceit

ALSO BY TONI ANDERSON

Her Risk to Take (Novella ~ Book #3)

THE BARKLEY SOUND SERIES

Dangerous Waters (Book #1)

Dark Waters (Book #2)

SINGLE TITLES

The Killing Game

Edge of Survival

Storm Warning

Sea of Suspicion

*For my gran, Sue, who introduced me to
Mills and Boon far too young*

...and created a monster.

1

JANUARY 16TH

Zoe Miller crouched in the dirt under a hot Arizona sun, gently cradling a bleached human cranium as a fly buzzed annoyingly around them both. She wiped sweat off her forehead onto the sleeve of her shirt, grateful for her old floppy hat which protected her from the fiercest of the sun's rays. At first glance, the skull looked like that of an adult male. The bone was heavier, thicker, the forehead sloping rather than rounded in the way of most females.

Zoe ran her gloved forefinger over the prominent supraorbital ridge that would have once shaped this person's brow as she considered the empty orbital sockets. More square than rounded —again a male characteristic—but the edge of bone at the upper margin was sharper than she would have expected and more like that of a female. The lower mandible was missing but the mastoid process was large and distinct, again pointing to a male.

Few forensic anthropologists would make a definitive statement of sex based on the cranium alone. Unfortunately, the pelvis was absent from the scene. Perhaps this cranium belonged to the human remains her friends had found a little distance away, scattered by scavengers.

The Pima County Office of the Medical Examiner would

obtain DNA from the bones and compare it to family reference samples of known missing migrants taken by the Colibrí Center as part of the Missing Migrant Program. If they were lucky, they'd find a match.

Zoe carefully placed the cranium in a box beside the small number of other human bones she'd already collected at this site in the hopes there would be enough to build a meaningful biological profile. Estimates of stature, age, sex, population ancestry of this person would be made, which might lead to a positive ID.

All profiles had to be treated with a degree of caution though. Human populations didn't have fixed morphological boundaries —instead they graded into one another. Even within a known population, morphometrics fell upon a spectrum at both population and individual levels. It meant forensic anthropologists had to be mindful of the limitations of the databases they referenced and their own personal experience.

Still, Zoe's gut was telling her this was part of the skull of an adult male.

Weathered gnaw marks suggested animals had long ago foraged on the soft tissue of the body, indicating this person had probably been dead for about a year. Maybe he'd died shortly after the last time Zoe and her friends had visited this area of Organ Pipe Cactus National Monument. Or perhaps they'd missed him, and this person had been left to decay and disintegrate in this harsh but beautiful landscape that reduced fauna and flora back to dust.

The thought of the latter pained her.

Dirt-encrusted clothing was scattered nearby. A necklace lay in the dirt.

She moved toward the string of beads only to realize it wasn't a piece of jewelry, but instead a rosary, complete with a small crucifix. She photographed everything with her Nikon before placing the clothing into a paper sack and adding it to the box in the hopes the items would further aid identification. Every piece of information mattered. Zoe held up the red beads and admired the dying rays of the sun as they shone through the cloudy orbs, the light refracted into a soft ruby glow.

Hope.

The rosary represented hope to some in a dangerous world, but you needed more than a plastic cross to survive a hostile desert environment.

Without a miracle, or good Samaritans providing caches of water and supplies, migrants died. Even with traffickers "helping" them, migrants often became lost in the wilderness and perished.

Or they were betrayed. Forgotten. Sacrificed.

Zoe shook off the feelings of guilt and melancholy. She'd done what she could. It was enough. It had to be.

She and her three best friends had bonded over stainless steel mortuary tables when they'd interned one summer with the medical examiner in Tucson before starting their graduate studies in Phoenix. Over the last six years, the four of them had spent many days scouring the wilderness for the dead. They were familiar and trusted enough by the ME's office that they held affiliate status there and were legally allowed to record and, in cases of fully skeletonized remains or those with only ligament attachments—Body Condition Scales 7 and 6 respectively—carefully collect and transport the remains to the overworked mortuary.

Helping to provide closure for heartbroken families was the reason Zoe had once spent all her spare time combing the desert for victims. And the fact she'd been consumed by her need to constantly search for the dead was the reason she'd finally had to leave.

Well, it was one of the reasons.

Zoe wiped her brow again and looked around at the lengthening shadows. It was early January, but the day had been unseasonably warm even for the Sonoran Desert. It didn't bode well for the upcoming fire season or deadly heat of summer. She took a deep gulp from the large water bottle at her side and then shook the remainder. She was almost out. Out of water and out of time. She needed to head to the pre-arranged meeting point.

She eyed the setting sun with frustration.

The number of remains of Undocumented Border Crossers was increasing to alarming levels. Didn't matter how vilified migrants might be in today's geo-political landscape, their bones spoke of their humanity and their desperation. They didn't deserve a death sentence for their actions, no matter their legal status.

The wave of sadness nearly overwhelmed her as she gently laid the rosary in the box.

This was the end of an era for her. Her last body recovery in this part of the world.

She'd accepted an academic position that forced her to move far away from Arizona. A part of her felt as if she'd given up, failed. But the issue was bigger than one person, bigger than her small group of fellow volunteers who were always at the wrong end of the search. It was a global problem and needed to be dealt with on an international level. Zoe had a lot of opinions on what might help and was determined to do whatever she could to get the message out.

She wasn't giving up, but it sure as hell felt like it when she looked at the bones of what had been, until relatively recently, a living and breathing human being—a person very like the one she stared at in the mirror every morning.

"Zoe!" Her name echoed over the rocky landscape.

"Coming!" she shouted back, swatting at another persistent fly.

For old time's sake, and the fact they couldn't help themselves, she and her friends had decided to spend their last Saturday together in the desert before Zoe began her long solo trek to her new home in Richmond. This was her last victim, and Zoe would show them the respect that they deserved.

A Phainopepla called out with a distinctive "wurp" on the evening air. She looked around for the handsome, red-eyed, black bird that nested in the Sonoran Desert in the spring, but she didn't see the individual who'd made the call.

She'd walked farther than she'd intended. They'd decided to search one of the ribbons of washes, west of the main migrant trail that cut across the 500-square-mile preserve. The area was thick with towering forests of saguaro cactus, magnificent organ pipes, hardy mesquite, and specialized desert grasses. The ground was covered in spiky cholla pods and prickly pear cacti that pierced the footwear of the unwary.

A male Anna's hummingbird with its iridescent green body and magenta head darted past in search of food.

The sun was setting behind the nearby mountains, painting the landscape with vivid reds and golds, so beautiful it almost hurt to look at. As the shadows elongated, the heat was already, thankfully, starting to ease off.

"Zoe!" Karina's voice once again carried on the breeze, and a shiver skittered over Zoe's flesh. She looked around, the sensation of someone watching her filling her with unease.

The dead did not scare her.

This area was considered one of the most dangerous National Parks in the country, and it wasn't only because of the harsh conditions or threats from wildlife.

As if on cue, one of the park's many rattlesnakes shook its tail in warning. The sound was far enough away she wasn't unduly alarmed but she scanned the ground as a precaution. The reptiles should be denned up by now, but the warmer weather meant they were still active.

She packed away her tools and camera, stood, peeled off her sweaty gloves into a ball and brushed at the knees of her pants. She hefted her light backpack onto her shoulders and reluctantly picked up the box. A flash of gold, twenty feet away, caught her eye.

She frowned and lowered the box to the ground again, hurrying now because she was fast losing the light. She bent to see a gold medallion on a chain with a broken clasp, caught on the spines of a prickly pear cactus. She pressed her lips together as she considered it. She used her cell to take a few photographs and then jiggled the necklace into a paper envelope. She marked the GPS coordinates on the front, along with the date.

Unnerved by the sudden silence, she glanced around, and froze as she spotted an expensive-looking black and pink sneaker attached to an unmoving leg. The rest of the body was hidden by foliage.

Sorrow hit her in the throat.

"Zoe!" Fred's voice echoed off the canyon walls, closer now.

Fred, James, and Karina had spread out farther back on the other side of the wash when they'd found something that was likely a human rib.

"Five minutes!" she shouted, her voice cracking. Her friends would be anxious to get out of the desert before nightfall. So was she.

She eased her way past a looming saguaro. The breath left her body as she took in the scene before her.

A woman lay on her front, her head turned to one side. Her jeans were pulled down and completely off one leg, her t-shirt and bra askew. She hadn't been dead more than a week. From the pattern of decomposition, it was likely she'd been assaulted.

Dammit. What was wrong with people?

"Zoe!"

"Gimme one minute!" Her voice was scratchy and raw with tears.

She blinked rapidly and swallowed hard.

Her hand trembled as she used her cell to take a quick series of photographs. Her flash lit up the gathering gloom.

She recorded the GPS waypoint and took a few more shots from different angles in case the medical examiner had trouble locating the exact spot tomorrow. There was no cellular service in this part of the park, but she'd make a call as soon as she found some. It was doubtful anyone would retrieve the body tonight anyway. Resources were always stretched thin and it was hazardous out here in the dark.

She ignored the odor of decomp and buzz of insects. Donning fresh latex gloves, she squatted nearby and took a series of photographs of what was left of the woman's face.

Zoe spotted something pearly white in the dirt. A tooth. She hesitated, then pulled out another collection evidence envelope and awkwardly scooped up the molar, before placing it in her pocket beside the medallion. It was the sort of evidence that could be easily overlooked. Having found this woman, Zoe felt a heavy weight of responsibility settle over her shoulders.

She straightened and stripped off the gloves, turning them inside out and slipping them into the pocket of her field vest reserved for garbage.

"Zoe!" Closer now. Karina's voice was laced with worry because this desert was a dangerous place at night. A no-man's land between poverty and prosperity, hope and despair.

With a last reluctant look at the dead woman, Zoe headed back to the main trail and placed a small, yellow marker from her kit next to the cactus where she'd found the medallion. It should help whoever came out here to locate the body and more easily retrieve it.

She picked up her box of remains as her three friends rounded the corner and stepped into view.

Karina planted her hands on her hips and blew a breath up into her hair. "We were beginning to worry about you."

"Sorry, guys." Zoe tried to regain control of her emotions as she caught up with them. "I found two UBCs. Some vertebrae and a cranium that might belong to your rib bone. And then another victim, a few moments ago, probably only a week old."

Karina sucked in a shocked breath.

Fred's eyes went wide with concern. "Are you okay?"

"Not really. I think there's a good chance she was assaulted and then murdered." Zoe shuddered.

They all stared dolefully back along the track.

"Come on. You can call Joaquin from the road. Someone from Pima County will pick her up." Sympathy flattened James's lips into a thin line as he ran a soothing hand down Karina's arm.

Zoe nodded even as she looked over her shoulder toward where the victim lay discarded in the dirt. It felt wrong to walk away and leave that poor woman for another night alone under the stars. She wasn't suffering any longer though, and Zoe would do her utmost to make sure the authorities identified her and returned her to her relatives as quickly as possible.

Getting justice was probably unattainable, but discovering an ID would be a good first step.

2

"Let's grab dinner at that restaurant in Gila Bend we all like. I'm starving," James declared with forced enthusiasm, turning and trudging back along the path, flicking on his headlamp to help light the way.

Trust him to be thinking of his stomach.

"As long as I can have a beer," Fred added, bringing up the rear.

"And a jug of sangria with a straw." Karina put in her request, obviously attempting to lighten the heavy mood that had descended over them all.

Zoe shivered as the temperature continued its daily plummet. The sense of wrongness with what she'd seen had shattered her sense of satisfaction and accomplishment with the day. Not that she did this solely out of a sense of altruism. It wasn't about her.

The mile-and-a-quarter hike back to where they'd left James's truck felt like ten times that as the aches and pains from the day kicked in. Her feet dragged. Her arms burned from the weight of the box despite the fact it was pitifully light. And maybe it wasn't exhaustion clawing at her, perhaps it was the realization that this was likely her last trip to this part of the world for a long time—possibly ever.

That knowledge brought up an unexpected and soul-deep sense of both relief and regret. But no matter how many times she and her friends came out here, no matter how many remains they helped recover and reunite with loved ones, there were always more tragic endings waiting for more unfortunate souls.

Zoe was burned out.

When they reached the parking lot, they placed the boxes of remains they'd retrieved into the covered bed of James's old but beloved Ford truck, then filled their water bottles from the large plastic container James always carried with him on trips into the desert. When they were finished, James hefted the heavy plastic jug and placed it near a wooden sign marking the head of Brady's Trail. He picked up an empty jug to take home and refill.

Zoe grimaced, wondering what her mother would say if she could see her now. Best not to think about it. She took off her hat and ran her hand through her sweaty hair. She fanned her face for a few moments, knowing it was beyond redemption.

They emptied their pockets of garbage into a plastic sack in the truck. Zoe held onto the medallion and tooth for now. She'd give it to Fred separately, so he'd know they belonged to the new victim rather than the old one. She took the antiseptic wipe Karina offered and cleaned her hands, face, and neck, before climbing into the oven-hot truck and cautiously resting her head against the burning-hot vinyl of the back seat.

They wound down the windows to release some of the stifling heat, welcoming the breeze as James steered them onto the rough dirt track.

"Aren't you going to miss this? The gorgeous scenery, the wildlife, the heat?" Karina turned to face her from the front seat.

"The dead, the danger, the dehydration," Fred added wryly from beside Zoe. He reached out and gripped her fingers in a gentle squeeze.

He was dark haired and handsome. They'd been an item once, briefly, long ago when they'd first met. She'd called it off after only a few weeks because although she'd liked him, there had been no spark, no chemistry, and they were going to have to spend the rest of their graduate lives working closely together. They both deserved more. They deserved what James and Karina had.

"I honestly don't know anymore." She gripped Fred's hand hard for a moment, reminded that good men existed in the world, and grateful for them. Then she let go, staring out of the window, feeling more alone than ever before.

She thought of the violence inflicted on that poor woman who'd been left to decompose in the desert and shivered. It wasn't even the act of cell death or biological degradation that affected her—her training had long ago revealed the mechanisms behind those mysteries. It was the way the woman had been callously dumped like trash. Abandoned the same way the black plastic water bottles were tossed into the pristine wilderness when they were no longer useful.

Zoe knew violence could happen anywhere, but here, in the Sonoran Desert, it felt commonplace.

Many people worked long and hard to identify the victims, but there were so many cases, and so little information, that the task often became overwhelming. It was impossible to find answers for everyone.

"I already miss you," Karina stated with a sniff. "I hate the fact you're moving so far away from your besties." She reached behind the seat and squeezed Zoe's leg.

"I miss you too." She caught her friend's hand. "You should all come visit me. Virginia's cool and I'm excited about my new job."

"Wait till you start teaching," Fred grumbled. "You won't be so happy then."

He worked at the University of Arizona's Southwest Center where the four of them had conducted their graduate work.

James's truck lurched over the uneven, hard-packed earth until they hit the graded dirt road. The journey was bumpy and bone-shakingly uncomfortable—and a hell of a lot better than walking.

As soon as they hit I-85 and had cell service, Zoe called Joaquin Rodriguez who was her favorite investigator with the ME's office down here.

"Hey," Joaquin answered with a smile in his voice. "What's up?"

"We have some boxes for you, one or two UBCs who we originally planned to drop off tonight but it's later than we expected—"

Fred cut in. "Tell him I'll bring them in tomorrow or Monday morning after you've left." Which would save them at least a couple of hours drive time tonight. "Tell him what else you found."

"Monday is fine," Joaquin said patiently, overhearing the conversation. A few more days wouldn't make much difference when the families had already waited so long. "What did you find?"

"A young woman. She's been dead less than a week by my estimation. I'll send you some photographs from my cell. Possible victim of assault." Zoe fought to keep her voice level. "I marked the trail with a yellow tag but it's off the beaten track." She gave him the GPS coordinates from memory.

"Okay." His voice roughened. "I'm not on call today. It's Rosy's birthday, but I know the team were already called out to a house fire in Summit with possible multiple fatalities." Investigators were reluctant to attend truly remote locations at night especially as they often worked alone. "I'll inform the National Park Service and coordinate. I'll send someone down there at first light."

"I have a couple of small pieces of evidence that I was worried might not be found so I documented and collected them. I'll pass them on to Fred before I leave. Whoever attends the scene will need help moving the body. It's over a mile from the nearest vehicle access point and the terrain is rocky."

"My assistant appreciates the heads-up."

Zoe wanted to say she'd meet them there, but she didn't have time. She couldn't explain the pull of this particular victim. She'd discovered dozens of bodies over the last six years and, although she grieved for them all, she'd found that some victims affected her more than others.

But no matter how much she wanted to stay, she couldn't. She had to let it go. She had a long drive ahead of her and needed to get to her new job. She needed to sever this cord once and for all. The dead woman would be in good hands with Joaquin's team. The best hands.

"Okay," she said weakly. "Thanks."

"You guys go have some fun. Life can't be all work, no play, you know," Joaquin admonished. And Zoe thought she heard sounds of childish laughter in the background. "You're all still young. Go get drunk and party."

"You sound like my dad." Zoe smiled reluctantly.

Joaquin snorted. "I feel like your dad, minus all the moolah."

"At least you have hair."

"Well, there's that." Joaquin laughed and said goodbye.

"What did he say?" James asked from the driver's seat.

"That we should go have some fun."

"Fun?" Karina snorted. "What's that?"

"He has a point." Despondently Fred stared out of the window at what little remained of the magnificent sunset. "None of us knows how to relax without a trowel in our hands."

Zoe tucked her phone away and felt increasingly unsettled. Probably because she was going to miss these people so damn much. The move wasn't temporary. She was striking out on a whole new chapter of her life. Nothing would ever be the same for the four of them again. And that realization was scary.

An hour later, they pulled up outside their favorite restaurant in Gila Bend, which catered mainly to tourists. There was an adjacent motel with a pool where they'd often stayed in the past. Zoe could hear people splashing noisily in the water. RVs were parked across the highway.

This town was a magnet for migrants. Traffickers often

arranged to meet those who survived the desert trek on the outskirts before helping them onto the next stage of their journey across the US.

Zoe stretched out her stiff limbs as she climbed out of the truck. She became aware of the intent gazes of a group of men standing outside the motel. They were watchful and suspicious as they scanned her and her grimy-looking friends from head to toe.

One guy in particular caught her attention. Close cropped hair, bad-boy good looks and a body to go with it. He was also armed. Law enforcement or military from the looks of him.

His gaze caught hers and he gave her a dazzling half smile.

Boom.

Her ovaries exploded into a million particles of lust.

"Zoe," Fred said sharply.

The spell was broken, and she snapped her attention back to her friend. Blinked. "Yeah?"

His dark eyes flicked from her to the men and back. "Coming?"

"Um. Yeah." Her mouth was dry and gritty, and she really needed a drink. She forced one foot in front of the other as they entered the restaurant and grabbed a table. Then she went to wash up in the restroom.

She winced at her reflection. Sweat glistened on her brow, and her face was flushed. Her hair stuck up in fifteen thousand different directions. The sun had burned her nose and cheekbones despite the layers of sunscreen she'd slathered on. Her lips were dry and cracked.

Looking good, Zo.

She was amused she'd had the nerve to ogle the hunk outside. His smile had probably been a prelude to laughter or pity. But it was so much nicer thinking about that excellent physical specimen of masculinity rather than remembering the corpses and bones that had filled her day. The stranger reminded her of the joy and distraction of sex, an activity that had been sorely lacking in her life recently.

She wiped a damp paper towel over the back of her neck and then ran wet fingers through her hair, giving up on making it do anything even vaguely controlled.

Back at the table, Karina, James, and Fred were tucking into a plate of nachos and two bottles of lager.

Zoe slid into the booth next to Fred and watched Karina slip her hand over her fiancé's shoulders and kiss him on the cheek. Karina was one of the most beautiful people Zoe had ever met. It always amused Zoe's inner romantic that her gorgeous friend was completely in love with James who was the dorkiest, palest redhead this side of the Atlantic.

Zoe turned to Fred and found him watching her with something in his gaze that she hadn't seen in years.

It startled her.

She surreptitiously moved away a little, enough to create a physical gap. She didn't want to give her friend the impression she might be up to rekindling any old flames. Not tonight. Not ever.

She thought they'd figured their relationship out. They were friends. Nothing more.

After her last disastrous entanglement, she wasn't interested in a relationship. Not yet. She valued her freedom too much. But a passionate, anonymous, no-strings, up-against-the-wall-fuck-me-until-I-come-please? The image of the stranger flashed through her mind again.

Yeah. She wouldn't mind that at all.

But she had no intention of leading Fred on or confusing the issue. She cared too deeply about him to do that.

She and Karina ordered sangria and the moment of awkwardness passed. They ordered more food and when her chicken fajitas arrived, she was so hungry she virtually inhaled them. She eyed the dessert menu with longing, but it was getting late, and they didn't really have time.

Zoe yawned widely. "I guess we should head off."

"Or," Karina said, shaking her finger at her. "We could have a few more drinks and stay at the motel. Head to Phoenix first thing in the morning. You could still be on the road by noon as planned."

Zoe's brows rose. Karina was the least spontaneous person she knew.

"Do they even have any vacancies?" Zoe thought about the group of men she'd seen outside earlier. There'd been ten of them and possibly more out of sight. The motel might be fully booked.

Karina pulled out her cell phone and found the motel's number and then punched it in. She pressed her hand over her ear and stood to walk over to where it was a little quieter. As she did, the same group of guys from earlier walked in and claimed a large table reserved near the back wall.

The guy who'd caught her eye met her gaze again and then his eyes flicked to Fred whose hand rested across the back of the bench behind her.

Zoe's mouth went dry. She was more than a little flustered by her recent fantasy musings.

Karina bounced down onto the soft vinyl seat which let out a gasp of complaint, the phone still pressed to her ear. "How many rooms do we need?"

Fred shrugged and looked at Zoe. Normally she'd have been fine sharing, but she didn't want to give anyone the wrong impression tonight. Her leaving had upset their usually happy balance, and maybe Fred was simply trying to resist that change the only way he knew how.

"Get three if they have them," Zoe said. "I'm so exhausted I thoroughly expect to snore like a freight train all night long."

She didn't miss the glance Karina sent to Fred and suspected there had been some last-ditch matchmaking attempts going on behind the scenes.

Karina made the booking and Zoe covered her mouth in another yawn. They'd been up since five and had worked hard all day.

More drinks arrived and Karina raised her glass. "To all the good times we've had over the years. We love you. We're going to miss you."

Her friend gave her a teary smile and Zoe's throat closed.

"I'm going to miss you all too. You have to come visit like you promised. Cheers."

She took a gulp of sangria and thought of the boxes of bones in the truck and the body of the young woman lying in the desert and was once again struck by the surreal nature of her day.

Her gaze was involuntarily drawn back to the handsome stranger. He was ruggedly beautiful, with perfectly symmetric features, high cheekbones, full lips, heavy brows.

The glint in his eye looked a lot like trouble and that was exactly her type.

She took another drink of sangria and concentrated on her friends. These three people were precious to her, and she treasured their presence in her life. She was going to miss them all like hell.

———

FBI Hostage Rescue Team Operator Seth Hopper had been frustrated and irritated at being trapped in this hot, dry wasteland. Bored out of his mind and confined to the motel all day. Freezing his balls off traipsing around the desert each night. All while his HRT teammates were on the hunt for a sadistic serial killer who'd fucked with the wrong people.

Then the petite, dust-covered blonde had climbed out of that old truck, stretched out her limbs, and stared at him like he was the answer to all her problems—and his whole world had brightened to sunshine and rainbows.

Unfortunately, the guy she was with gave him the stink eye.

Not that Seth was in much of a position to take advantage of the opportunity presented, given he was due to catch a flight into the middle of nowhere in the not-too-distant future.

A guy could dream.

Life had been sorely without reasons to smile lately.

Seth was seated with his back to the wall while the US Border Patrol Tactical Unit (BORTAC) he was working with slouched around on the cracked vinyl seats.

They'd stayed at the motel next door for the last three days now, longer than they stayed most places, but tonight they were moving on. It had been a useful center of operations even though they couldn't afford to let their guard down. Ironically, it was safer in some places this close to the border to pretend to be one of the bad guys rather than to openly declare yourself part of the justice system.

The guys ordered plates of nachos and pitchers of iced water. A beer would have been good, but they needed to stay operational.

"You checking out that cute blonde or the hot brunette?" asked Roger Bertrand, one of the elite team of Border Patrol agents Seth had spent the last week liaising with.

"Admiring the scenery." Seth held Roger's gaze with a cool smile.

Seth and JJ Hersh, one of HRT's Gold team snipers, were theoretically down here on a three-week exchange. Officially they were working with the United States Customs and Border Protection Agency to help conduct some routine drug smuggler arrests. Unofficially they were here to ferret out someone within this particular BORTAC team who was feeding the cartel real-time situational data that had resulted in a significant decrease in drug busts in this part of Arizona over the last six months and posed a serious risk to ongoing operations and security.

"Want me to go ask her boyfriend for some ID?" Roger suggested slyly.

"And cause a stampede?" Another agent sniggered.

"Don't be asses," Arthur, the team leader, snapped from his seat at the other end of the table.

The men sobered fast. Arthur didn't put up with any bullshit. He was built like a tank and knew his way around the desert blindfolded. A good thing considering they did most of their missions at night.

The blonde and her friends ordered another jug of sangria and Seth smiled wistfully. The blonde's girlfriend was tall and slender with pale brown skin, full lips, and sharp cheekbones. She was sitting hip to hip with the guy with ginger hair whose skin was milky-white except for the scarlet patches he'd missed with the sunblock. The guy next to the blonde was dark-haired and deeply tanned. They weren't touching but the way they sat together and laughed suggested they were close. The blonde was beautiful in an unassuming way—very small-town American girl-next-door type which he'd been a sucker for since high school. Not that those girls had ever been interested in a guy like him. Not in public anyway. In private, under the bleachers or in the back of his old Chevy, they'd been plenty happy to get to know him. He'd had a similar issue as a Navy SEAL with groupies wanting to put a notch in their bedposts. It had been fine for a time, dating women who weren't interested in anything besides one night of sexy times, but after a few years it got old.

Now desire was growing inside him like an itch he couldn't scratch. Unfortunately, he was too busy to even attempt a strategy to get the blonde away from the guy she was sitting with long enough to ask for her number.

Would have been fun though.

He could use a little fun.

A scene flashed through his mind of the last time he'd really had fun. Only a few weeks ago at last year's holiday party with all the guys at the bar where they liked to hang out.

A lifetime ago.

He gripped the cold glass in his hand as his throat swelled and emotions rushed him. He'd lost two colleagues in two weeks and everyone at HRT was still reeling from shock.

Grief rose inside Seth, and he forced himself not to reveal an ounce of the pain he was feeling. Except for Hersh, these people were not his friends, and he did not reveal weakness to potential enemies.

"What's the weather report?" Seth asked Arthur gruffly.

"Weather's fine," Arthur answered with a tight smile.

Code for tonight's op being a go.

Seth nodded and hoped Arthur wasn't the rat. Seth liked the guy. It was always awful to be betrayed by someone who was supposed to be on your side. Seth detested double-dealers and those who sold out their colleagues for nothing more than dollars and cents.

Hersh caught Seth's gaze for a moment before looking away. Seth knew JJ felt the same way.

They were eager for this to be over. They wanted to catch this traitor—but they were both itching to get back with the rest of their team.

The blonde went up to the bar, and his eyes followed her. Her nose was slightly burned as if she'd spent the day in the sun. She wore figure-hugging pants and fuck-off hiking boots. Her short-sleeved shirt was lavender and the olive-green vest she wore on top had a ton of useful pockets which he could totally appreciate. She was either an avid hiker, camper, or maybe a wildlife biologist or photographer. Whatever it was about her low-key, competent-looking beauty, he wasn't the only man in the place who'd noticed her.

The boyfriend glared at him. Again.

Fuck.

Seth checked his cell but no update from his boss. Seth tapped his fingers on the table. He wasn't good with inactivity, which generally made HRT a good fit for his inner adrenaline junkie but, after a day stuck in a boring motel room, energy whirled inside him with nowhere to go. He'd go for a run, but he didn't trust that the cartel wasn't watching them, waiting for an opportunity to strike, especially if there really was a rat in their midst.

He rolled his shoulders. "I'm going for a swim."

He stood and walked to the door, Hersh and another guy got

up and followed him. Seth glanced across the bar and the woman once again caught his gaze. He smiled briefly, acknowledging that their eyes seemed determined to act like the opposite ends of two magnets.

He nodded before heading outside.

"You really going for a swim?" Hersh asked him quietly.

"Yeah, why?"

"I'm going to call Liv." The other man's cheeks flushed. The guy was a newlywed and besotted with his wife.

"No worries. I'll give you some privacy." Seth unlocked their room door and threw his clothes onto the bed and climbed into his board shorts. He grabbed a towel out of the bathroom. His gear was packed and ready to go as they were moving out in a couple of hours.

He didn't like being unarmed and was uncomfortably aware of being watched. Technically, as an FBI agent, he was expected to carry at all times, but he couldn't risk some kid picking up the weapon if he left it on the pool deck.

It was unlikely but not impossible that the cartel would attack a group of federal agents. Seth doubted they'd want to bring down the wrath of the entire US government on their heads, not when scuttling under rocks was more their style this side of the border.

The BORTAC team included agents who stayed behind to guard their gear whenever they went out on missions. The drug cartels were more than capable of planting tracking devices on them and their vehicles, so everything and everybody was regularly scanned. The real problem was the cartel already seemed to know where they were going.

Seth strode to the pool which was now thankfully empty of the little kids who'd spent the day practicing their cannonballs. High fences and thick, prickly hedges surrounded the water on three sides. The other side had a safety fence. The pool area was lit with a few wall sconces and pool lights, but they did little to relieve the shadows of their secrets.

He placed his towel near the edge of the deck. Then he executed a smooth dive into the water. It was a little on the warm side, but whatever.

One lap, two. He used an efficient front crawl to eat up the distance while keeping his senses alert for anyone approaching.

His mind slowly cleared of the grief of loss and worry for his teammates and switched instead to trying to figure out which of his current associates was most likely dirty. His money was on Roger as the guy was cocky and sloppy. He hoped it wasn't Paul or Arthur or Ike who seemed like good guys. Still, he wasn't paid to guess.

Agents out of both the Phoenix Field Office and FBI headquarters' Strategic Information Operations Center (SIOC) were conducting surveillance and monitoring financials of CBP individuals. Homeland Security had people in both locations overseeing this operation.

After twenty laps Seth switched to breaststroke and did another twenty. The chlorine was so strong it burned his eyes, but it was probably a good thing under the circumstances. Laughter warned him that someone was headed this way. He immediately swam to the side where he'd left his towel and pulled himself out. He was drying himself off when two giggling women let themselves inside. And, yes, he was disappointed it wasn't a certain petite blonde, but such was life. When it came to women he was used to disappointment.

Boo-*fucking*-hoo.

The women eyed him appreciatively as he wrapped the wet towel around his neck. The swim had taken the edge off his cooped-up energy levels although he still felt antsy. As if something was about to happen.

He gave the ladies a nod as he walked past them and headed barefoot back to his room.

And there, standing outside a door, two down from the pool, was the woman he hadn't been able to keep his mind off since he'd first seen her.

3

She was laughing with her two friends, who were definitely a couple, as they entered the room next to hers. The old red truck was parked out front now.

As if sensing someone coming up behind her, she swung around. From a safety point of view, he wished the friends had hung around until she was securely inside her room before leaving her—but maybe the boyfriend was waiting inside.

"Ma'am." He slowed and nodded, not wanting to freak her out by getting too close.

She tilted her head to one side. Her lips were a soft pink, the delicate shade you found on the inside of seashells. Her eyes a pale blue-turquoise that looked like the depths of a glacial lake.

"Military or law enforcement?" she asked.

He stopped. He couldn't help himself. "Pardon me?"

"I was curious as to whether you're military or from a branch of law enforcement." Her voice was deeper than he'd expected and held warm amusement.

"Currently the latter," he conceded. "What gave it away?"

"Everything." A rueful smile cut through her right cheek and revealed three perfect dimples. She kept her eyes on his face rather than his dripping torso, which he appreciated.

"I hope you're not supposed to be undercover."

He hiked his brows. He actually was undercover but not in the traditional sense.

"I'm pretty sure all the players around here made us for Feds the moment we rolled into town." He nodded toward their dark government-issue utility vehicles.

She followed his gaze and her expression faltered. "Yeah. Nothing screams Homeland Security like black Suburbans with tinted windows."

Her entire demeanor oozed intelligence, but there was a bitterness in the words he hadn't expected. She looked tired. Her smile wobbled.

He wanted to ask for her name or number, but the timing was all wrong given he was supposed to be working.

Fuck it.

He opened his mouth to ask anyway just as the guy she was with stepped out from the restaurant and started heading their way.

Dammit. He didn't want to cause her any trouble, and he let his regret show in his eyes as he took a step to one side. "You take care now."

"You too." Her eyes drifted lower to his torso.

He walked past her, exchanging a glance with the boyfriend that was full of mutual hostility. Seth stopped at his own door and paused before knocking for Hersh to let him in.

He looked back toward the woman with the dimples, sun-streaked hair, and tired eyes. Watched her laugh with her tall companion before they entered separate rooms. Seth was still standing there staring like an idiot when she shot him a knowing smile and gently shut the door.

He wanted to kick himself.

Bruno Ramirez trudged through the desert at the front of a short mule caravan, sweating despite the frigid night air. He carried night vision goggles but didn't bother wearing them. He preferred the light of the half-moon which shone brightly over the arid landscape that he knew better than his own reflection.

He shouldn't be here, but he'd received word late this afternoon that a group of meddlesome *gringos* had been seen in the area. He spat on the ground.

Even with the huge amounts of money the cartel spent on bribes it was risky for someone like him to be spending too much time in this part of the country.

But if his boss ever discovered what Bruno had done, the man would flay the flesh from his bones and feed it to him one piece at a time until there was nothing left to swallow.

Bruno's skin prickled as he got closer to his destination. He swore when a cactus stabbed his arm. After a short distance, he held his fist into the air.

"Stop."

Bruno went to the first mule, removed a tarp, and thrust it at one of the other men. Bruno wore thin leather gloves because you could never be too careful with potential evidence. Another reason he wanted to make sure all traces of his biggest mistake disappeared forever.

He pointed into the darkness.

He'd chosen these men specifically. They were single. They didn't ask questions. They knew how to keep their mouths shut.

With luck, US Border Patrol and the *federales* would be occupied tonight, far away, too busy to be looking for him or anyone else.

Perhaps the timing wasn't so terrible, after all.

His men tied the mules nearby then calmly trudged over to the dead body before rolling it nonchalantly into the tarp. Bruno recoiled from the aroma and didn't get too close.

The men each took one end of the tarp and carried the sagging load to the mule that was not carrying a pack. They heaved it onto the back of the beast who stood nonchalantly chewing on a tuft of desert grass. One of the men secured the body in place with a rope. He went to pull out another, but Bruno forestalled him.

"We aren't going far." Bruno pulled a flashlight from his pocket and held it low to the ground as he scanned the area where the body had lain.

The gap in his lower jaw ached from where the bitch had smashed a rock into his face. The wound had scabbed over and was healing now, but he'd purposely kept a low profile so no one questioned what had caused the injury.

Bruno didn't see anything that might be his tooth.

Meirda.

He heaved a sigh because he didn't have time to search more thoroughly. He had many things to do tonight. He headed out to the trail and spotted something on the ground. Leaned closer and picked up a small, hard plastic marker.

He clenched his fist. It confirmed his suspicion that the *gringos* in the desert today had found the one body in the whole of the Americas that he'd hoped would remain lost forever.

He straightened and hooked the marker into the back pocket of his jeans. Then he started walking. Coyotes yipped in the distance, probably chasing a javelina or a jackrabbit in a nightly fight for survival. After five minutes, he veered off the path into the untamed wilderness and kept walking. Eventually, he found a suitable place and handed each man a shovel.

Neither spoke as they started to dig. Bruno stared at the Milky Way and watched his breath cloud on the exhale. He'd spent the last seven years scouting these hills and washes for the best routes and staging posts to transport drugs from South America to the Promised Land. The desert was a beautiful but harsh mistress.

The sound of a spade slicing through the parched dirt reverberated through the night and made him flinch. He took out a cigarette and lit it. Drawing the smoke into his lungs and immediately feeling the tension in his chest easing.

It was her own fault.

He exhaled.

Her own damned fault.

Thirty minutes later he checked his watch. "That's deep enough."

The two men tossed the shovels aside and wiped their sweaty brows. Then they pulled the body off the mule and started to unroll the tarp.

"Leave it," he snapped.

He didn't want to see her again.

Without betraying any emotion, the two men silently lowered the heavy load into the hole in the ground. It wasn't as deep as Bruno would have liked, but it would have to do. Border Patrol had drones. Human coyotes or ignorant migrants could unwittingly stumble upon them. Bruno didn't want anyone to suspect what had happened in the desert a week ago.

The men filled the grave and patted the top with the spades. Then they put the tools back in the mule pack and the three of them headed to the trail. They snaked east and then south.

Bruno let the other men lead. When they were far from the new grave, he silently pulled his handgun from the holster and shot the closest man in the back of the head. When the second man turned in surprise, Bruno shot him in the chest.

The mules circled in fright. Bruno quickly caught the one with the pack which he still needed. He tied the spooked animal to a short scrubby bush before dragging the dead men off the trail by their feet. He hoped they weren't found for a long, long time.

The howl of an endangered *lobo* made the hair on his nape rise.

A good omen. A blessing. He looked up at the silvery slice of moon and drew in a deep cleansing breath.

Usually no one paid much attention to death in this part of the world—which was exactly how he preferred it.

He tugged on the mule's lead rope. He still had a lot to do tonight.

Seth lay freezing his ass off in the dirt as he listened to gunshots echoing through the night. The shots were several miles east of their current position but didn't bode well for whoever or whatever was on the receiving end.

Seth had spent the previous half-hour staying alert for snakes and scorpions. He wished he'd worn an additional fleece for warmth. Trouble was, when they were moving around, he got hot and started to sweat and that sweat turned to ice when they settled into position for any length of time. And he was left in exactly the same position as right now—shivering, while wondering why the hell he'd volunteered for this particular duty.

But he knew why. Burying himself in work was his de facto method for coping with real life shit. Perhaps not the healthiest way of dealing with things, but better than going on a three-week bender. And if he could shut down some narcos while he was doing it? He smiled grimly to himself. Icing on the freaking cake.

An owl's hoot echoed through the darkness and brought Seth back into his own ball-cracking frozen reality.

The BORTAC team had left the motel and driven to a small airstrip where a helicopter had picked them up and then dropped them in the desert about ten miles north of the Mexican border in the Cabeza Prieta Wilderness. Authorities had received a tipoff earlier that day that a large shipment of uncut Colombian cocaine was crossing into Arizona tonight. The shack that Seth was currently staring at through his night-scope was supposedly the first resting point on the journey across the desert.

Techs at FBI HQ's SIOC were monitoring communications in and out of the area to see if anyone on the team attempted to warn the drug runners that Border Patrol were onto them.

Before leaving the motel, they'd packed their gear into the vehicles and the support team had headed to the next location about twenty miles west. Unfortunately, that meant Seth would never see the pretty blonde again and for some reason that pissed him off more than it should have.

He couldn't have opened his mouth and given her his name?

Introduced himself when she'd been right there in front of him? Of course, she could be a plant by the cartel so real names, addresses, and phone numbers were out of the question. Still. He could've gotten her name and tracked her down when he was finished in Arizona. Conducted a thorough background check to make sure she wasn't a criminal before he invited her out to dinner...

"I have movement," Arthur declared softly.

Seth clenched and unclenched his hands, warming up his trigger finger. The team were spread along the barely visible track that led away from the hut. Something slithered across the dry earth nearby and only Seth's many years of training kept him from flipping out and running screaming into the night.

Snake.

He hated snakes.

"I see two men and two mules." Arthur's words were a murmur on the frigid night air but clear through the personal comms system all the team wore. It wasn't quite the cutting-edge standard of equipment Seth was used to, but it did the job. The team wore matte black infrared markers on their uniforms that glowed through NVGs and allowed them to identify each other as friendlies at night.

"Think there are more coming?" Seth asked in a murmur. Two mules were hardly the substantial haul they'd been promised.

Arthur watched for another long moment before answering. "Looks like it's just these two." He sniffed. "Better than nothing. No one moves until I give the signal."

Seth did not like this situation. The cartel that operated in this region was ruthless. They'd previously been affiliated with *El cartel de Mano de Dios* in Colombia before they'd broken away last summer because of some internal dispute. The leader, Lorenzo Santiago, held a prominent position in the FBI's Most Wanted list, as did one of his underlings, Bruno Ramirez.

Seth rolled his shoulder. Maybe the intel had been wrong. Maybe plans had changed at the last moment. Or maybe the cartel had discovered their informant had been compromised and this whole fucking situation was a trap.

"Something seems off," Seth stated quietly. It was a heads up to Hersh more than anything. His Gold team colleague might not yet realize that Seth felt like a rabbit about to run into a snare and get his neck snapped.

"Wait for my word," Arthur ordered.

Moving slowly, Seth scanned his scope over the uninhabited landscape behind him. He knew his FBI colleagues were watching from above, but the only way he could contact them was by pulling out the sat phone hidden in his pack and asking questions that would immediately compromise his mission.

"I have movement on our six," said Hersh.

"Hold position until I give the word," Arthur hissed.

The sound of unshod hooves scraping over hard-packed dirt told Seth the mule train was close now. The first drug runner passed by so close Seth could smell the man's sweat over the stink of mule as he lay in the dirt. He was surprised to see the target also wore NVGs, but he shouldn't have been.

Despite the old-fashioned method of transportation, today's narco-traffickers were highly sophisticated and obscenely well-funded.

Suddenly Arthur rose out of the ground at the side of the path. "Freeze! Border Patrol!"

The other BORTAC agents jumped up, shouting, and the mules startled away from them, rearing and wheeling. The two suspects didn't try to escape. Instead, they swung automatic weapons from beneath their cloaks and started firing.

"Take cover. Return fire," Arthur shouted.

Seth was already diving to the ground even as he caught the nearest guy with a double tap to the chest with his H&K 416 carbine. He added a third shot to the head to be sure the guy couldn't hurt anyone because if he wore NVG's you better believe he also sported body armor.

The second drug runner lit up the night with an assault rifle, hitting one of the team before being taken out.

More gunfire rang out from behind them and confirmed what Seth had suspected. This was an ambush. He frowned as he rolled in the dirt.

A BORTAC agent trained as a medic began treating his injured colleague while Seth scanned the line. He counted seven infrared patches.

"We're missing someone," he said quickly. Or someone had covered the insignia that marked them as friendly to one another, but as the enemy to the cartel. That someone had betrayed them to be slaughtered in the night.

"Everyone come to me." Seth was in a protected position that was out of visual range of the assholes who were raining fire down at them from the southern ridge.

"Fuck." Arthur crawled next to Seth as bullets kept coming.

Seth pulled out his earpiece and stuffed it in his pocket.

"Don't use comms," Seth told the others who started to curse.

Everyone quickly removed their earpieces.

"Why not?" Arthur asked in confusion.

Seth ignored him. "Who's not here?"

A quick head count told them Roger Bertrand was missing.

"I guess we know who's been feeding information to the cartel, huh?" Seth said wryly.

"What the hell?"

"Are you fucking kidding me?"

There was more cursing and swearing from the rest of the team.

"Ike's dead," the medic said as he crawled a few feet to join them.

"Cover your infrared patches," Hersh told them quietly. "These guys can use them to target us." Shooting at them like fish in a barrel.

"I called for backup but it's at least an hour away." Arthur sounded furious.

They were in a deep gully, and it sounded like there were five or six shooters attacking their position. Plus Roger, wherever that motherfucker had fled to.

Which meant there were only six members of the BORTAC team left to fight back.

"Let's split up into three pairs." Arthur pointed west and east. "See if we can circle around and stop these assholes before they outflank us."

They all nodded and moved in a fast crouch to new positions.

Seth grabbed Hersh's arm. "You thinking what I'm thinking?"

Hersh gave a swift jerk of his head. "Looking for the best place to set up."

Seth pointed to a jumble of rocks on the other side of the trail. Hersh nodded and they moved toward the outcrop at a sprint, the others thankfully pinning down the shooters with cover fire.

He and JJ reached the rock formation that still held the warmth of the day's sunshine and quickly found a path between the boulders.

"I do not want to know what's in any of these crevices," Seth grunted as they scrambled into position. Thankfully, there was enough foliage to shield them and hide their silhouettes. Unfortunately, every piece of foliage wanted to hurt them.

Seth and Hersh set up in position, the other man stretched out with his Remington cradled in his hands. It might not be Hersh's preferred sniper rifle but at this range, and with a marksman as skilled as JJ, some serious damage was about to be inflicted on the enemy before they even knew what was happening.

Seth crouched behind another boulder, spotting with his scope. The tangos weren't hiding. They were simply spraying the desert with bullets like lunatics.

"Two hundred yards, ten o'clock." Seth pointed out the first shooter.

"Got him." Hersh sent the bullet and a surprised grunt rang through the night.

Seth estimated the range of the next target. It wasn't perfect but it was close. "One seventy yards, one o'clock."

Hersh did the rest.

Another man down.

"Feels like old times," Hersh stated grimly.

Seth nodded. They'd spent a lot of time during New Operator Training School—NOTS—paired up and hanging out. Seth had never expected the two of them to be waging war on home soil though. Not like this.

"Two-twenty yards, eleven o'clock."

Hersh fired another shot and once again a man went down. Hersh might have the sweetest personality anyone would ever meet, but he was deadly with a rifle.

"Two left. That I can see."

"Plus, Roger," Hersh bit out.

"Plus, Roger. Not gonna forget that asshole in a hurry," Seth agreed.

The bad guys had gone quiet now. Either out of ammo or realizing death was hunting them in the darkness. This was no longer their empire. They no longer had the element of surprise.

"Think Roger was the only dirty player on the team?" Hersh whispered.

Seth pulled out the satellite phone in his pack and shrugged. "Let's see what Command can tell us."

"They're running," Hersh said quietly.

"They better." Seth smiled grimly.

As FBI agents, he and Hersh were not about to shoot men in the back as they ran away—unless they were still firing at them.

If Arthur's call for assistance had been heeded, hopefully Border Patrol would be nearby waiting to cut off the shooters' escape and scoop them all up. Especially that Judas motherfucker, Roger Bertrand.

Seth would love to be the one to put the cuffs on that guy, although it should be one of the colleagues Roger had callously sold out who got to do the honors. One of Ike's friends.

That would be a fitting justice for a man low enough to betray his own.

———

Zoe lay in bed watching the shadows on the ceiling. The air-conditioning unit rattled noisily in the window. A fly buzzed annoyingly around the room. She'd slept for a short time after her shower, the after-effects of fatigue and sangria dragging her under as soon as she'd crawled into bed.

But something had woken her a few minutes ago and now she couldn't get back to sleep even though it was only 1:01 a.m.

Her thoughts kept straying to the dead woman she'd found today. How scared she must have been knowing there was no one there to help her. How desperate. How alone. How fucking *angry*.

Zoe shifted in agitation and forced herself to think of something else. The lectures she needed to plan for the next academic year. The grants she needed to write. The massive amount of unpacking she needed to do in her new home in Richmond. The excitement of going on a field trip to Namibia this summer.

None of it held her attention. Instead, the image of the man she'd spoken to, oh so briefly earlier flashed into her mind. She wished she'd had the nerve to spend a little more time with the guy, to maybe flirt a little the way the old Zoe would have done.

She didn't even know his name.

Maybe she could use her mother's connections to track him down? Or maybe she should go knock on the door she'd seen him enter earlier or slip her number under it?

But what was the point?

She wasn't into casual hookups and, with her moving out east, what else could this be? She'd had to force herself not to ogle his perfect wet body when he'd come out of the pool. If it hadn't been for her too recent run-in with another guy with a cocky smile and confident swagger, she might have said something, or done something—like dragged him in here for a quickie in the shower...

She hugged the blankets to her chest.

It was a good fantasy.

But he could be married or have a different woman in his bed every night. Or both. Zoe wasn't planning on ever finding out. She simply wanted someone to moon over, to tempt her freaked-out soul into the thought that maybe, just maybe, one day she might have sex again.

A noise outside had her sitting up in bed. A shout. What was that? Partygoers late leaving the restaurant?

She froze.

One of the agitated voices sounded like Karina...

Zoe climbed out of the covers and peered out of the window and saw several figures attempting to break into the back of James's truck.

The boxes!

She'd suggested moving them into her room, but James had waved her away, saying anyone stealing his truck was in for a nasty surprise when they accessed the canopy.

But the last thing any of them wanted was the desecration of the remains they'd collected today. Plus, James needed his truck.

She pulled on a pair of yoga leggings beneath her long-sleeved gray cotton sleep shirt and grabbed her cell, her finger hovering over 911 as she risked cracking open the door.

The appearance of a lethal-looking handgun in the hands of a man who stood off to one side had her stiffening. He planted his foot in the small gap. He wore a hat pulled low and had a bandana covering his nose and mouth. His eyes were black and glittering with sharp intelligence.

Why the hell hadn't she called the cops *before* she'd opened the door?

4

―――――

S he stumbled back into the room and he followed her.

     "Help!" she screamed.

Her room was dark. She shuddered as she remembered what had probably befallen the dead woman she'd found in the desert today.

"Quiet," he barked. "I will kill you right now if you cause me any trouble." The man held out his hand while keeping the gun pointed straight at her. "Give me your phone."

Zoe wanted to put up a fight but didn't think he'd have any issue pulling the trigger. She handed him the phone which he powered off and stuffed in his pocket.

Shit, was this a kidnapping?

"Get all your belongings and put them in here." He kicked her canvas bag that sat on the floor. "Hurry. Leave nothing behind."

She did as he asked, prolonging her actions for as long as she could in the hope help would arrive. It didn't.

Did he know who her mother was? She toed on her work boots not bothering to take the time to pull on socks in case he decided to deny her any footwear at all.

"Why are you doing this?" she asked.

His eyes remained impassive.

"Where are you planning to take me?"

"Enough talking." He raised his hand as if to strike her and she flinched. "Hurry." He strode to the bathroom and grabbed her toiletries bag off the counter.

She eyed the open doorway but even as she prepared to run another man moved into the frame.

"Is that everything?" the first man asked.

Zoe nodded.

He snatched up the handles of her bag. "Outside." He indicated with his gun. "Run away and I'll shoot your friends."

Zoe's eyes widened and her heart thumped frenetically. He was probably going to shoot them anyway.

"What do you want?" Her voice was scratchy.

His eyes traveled down her body and her flesh crawled. "Move."

Outside the room she saw Fred and James both nursing their faces. Blood dripped down Fred's chin from a busted nose. Another man gripped Karina's arm so tight she was squirming in pain.

Zoe looked around in confusion, but no one was coming to their aid. Not even the group of law enforcement officers who'd been staying here earlier. Then she noticed the three large vehicles that had been parked outside their rooms were gone. Had these criminals waited until they'd left? Probably.

Karina's terrified gaze met hers. Zoe sent her a reassuring smile that she didn't really feel. Then she and Karina were shoved into the back seat of a beaten-up SUV while James and Fred were tossed into the back of James's truck, their wrists bound with rope.

"What is happening. Why are you doing this to us?" sobbed Karina.

"Shut up," their captor snarled.

Karina recoiled in fear.

Zoe didn't know what was going on or why they were being

taken. She did know that she had seconds to call for help before they disappeared, possibly forever.

Shielding the glowing face of her smartwatch she pressed a button on the side and then slid her finger across the Emergency SOS button. Not only would it call 911, but it would also, more importantly, send a text to her parents and their security team with her exact location. She prayed the message would connect via the motel's Wi-Fi or the nearby cell tower even without her phone being on.

It was cellular, so it theoretically should.

She hoped her parents understood that something was seriously wrong and to send help urgently. Otherwise, she and her friends were either being held for ransom, about to be trafficked, or killed.

She dragged the watchstrap around so that the face was on the inside of her wrist and it looked like a sweatband or bracelet. She tugged her sleeve lower.

Did they know who she was? Was this all her fault? Her naïveté bringing danger to people she loved?

The kidnapper glanced at her over his shoulder. She set her teeth and met his gaze square-on.

A smile hit his eyes. "I like the spirited ones best, *chica*. They are the most fun to break."

Revulsion uncurled in her stomach and she was grateful not to throw up. She kept the retort she wanted to say locked firmly behind her teeth. She wasn't a complete idiot. She stared out of the window and realized how utterly helpless they were. She twisted around and saw someone else driving James's truck, following them. Another rusted junker bounced over the road behind that.

"Face front, *chica*. Keep your eyes on me." The barrel of the black gun wavered unnervingly between her and Karina. The man had his finger on the trigger.

"Why are you doing this?" Zoe asked.

He gave an exaggerated shrug. "Because I'm a man who

knows how to follow orders." He sent her a hooded gaze. "You'd do well to do the same."

———

Seth crouched in the dirt over the body of the dead cartel member he'd shot on the trail. Arthur and the others crowded around him. Hersh stood back, watching them all, watching the desert. It was always possible there was more than one dirty agent in the group. Seth and Hersh knew better than to let their guard down.

Seth donned nitrile gloves and went through the dead man's pockets. Cash. Cell phone. He bagged the latter. Took a photograph of the man's face, peaceful now aside from the bullet hole decorating his forehead. Seth felt sorry for the choices that had led this man to this place. He didn't regret killing him, but he regretted *having* to kill him.

He blamed the ring leaders. The ruthless cartel bosses controlling their underlings with the promise of cash and the threat of violence. The only way out of that life was either prison or here, lying on the ground without a heartbeat.

Seth photographed the man's tattoos on his neck and forearms. The jewelry he wore. The NVGs and weapons he carried. Seth collected fingerprints. They'd do this for all the dead gunmen but if they could get an early identification, it would help pinpoint which cartel to target with a response all that much quicker.

An elite Border Patrol Tactical Unit had been ambushed and an agent murdered while carrying out his duties. The cartel had to know the US government wouldn't let that go unpunished.

Federal agents were converging on the region closing off the border, scouring the desert. CBP. NPR. US Fish & Wildlife. ICE. DEA. FBI. US Marshals. Seth would be shocked if people from the CIA, DIA and the freaking Texas Rangers didn't turn up at some point.

His satellite phone buzzed in his pocket, and he moved closer to Hersh to take the call. It was ASAC McKenzie out of SIOC who was helping coordinate this op.

"We have a new situation that I need you on, ASAP," the man said without preamble. "We believe the daughter of VPOTUS was kidnapped about twenty minutes ago out of Gila Bend. She was able to send an SOS from her watch at exactly 1:23 a.m. We immediately diverted the drone we had in the sky for your op and picked up three vehicles we believe to be involved, traveling south on I-85 at high speed. We have CBP amassing at Lukeville but it's unlikely they'll try to cross legally."

"Is this a diversion to take away agents south of here?" Seth asked. "To allow Roger Bertrand time to escape?"

"Could be, but how would the cartel know the woman was going to be in the region? My hunch says this is a separate incident. We don't even know if they know who they've kidnapped. Could be they decided to snatch the woman because she's pretty and without protection. They might not be planning to cross the border at all."

Seth's gut clenched. They could be taking her into the desert to rape and murder her.

Bad enough the cartel targeting CBP. This could legit start a war. "Where's her protection detail?"

"She refused the protection of the Secret Service."

Seth ground his teeth.

"We have a fix on the vehicles and I have as many bodies as I can find taking up positions all along the border, but if these kidnappers have some other means of crossing—a tunnel or aircraft—or if they decide to head into the desert or disappear into the heartland…"

Then the woman was as good as dead.

A wolf howled in the darkness and sent cold fingers tip-tapping slowly down Seth's spine.

"A helicopter is on its way to your location. I want you and Hersh tracking these guys."

"Across the border?" Seth murmured so the others couldn't hear.

"If necessary. As long as you don't get caught," McKenzie added quickly. "HRT and SWAT teams across the country are already on standby to track down this damn serial killer who killed one of your colleagues. DEVGRU has been alerted about Ms. Miller's abduction and are mobilizing in case this turns into an international incident. In the meantime, you're it."

If the Naval Special Warfare Development Group became involved it could mean all-out war between the US and the cartels on the other side of the border, which the Mexican government might not appreciate.

Task Force Blue didn't issue arrest warrants.

"I will request agents from Phoenix and Tucson to assist but they are at least ninety minutes behind you and don't have your training. You and Agent Hersh are the closest and best bet we have of retrieving Ms. Miller in one piece."

Preferably before dawn on this side of the Mexican border.

"What about the CBP agents here?" He didn't like abandoning these men. They'd been through hell. Lost one of their own through a backstabbing colleague.

"I can't risk involving them. Backup's on the way in the form of FBI agents to interview them and help process the scene. No hint of any unauthorized communication from more than one device in the group which has since gone dark."

Presumably that belonged to that weasel, Roger.

"As much as I'd like to send them with you I can't."

A slight reverberation pulsed through the night air warning Seth he didn't have long to think about this or make a decision. Not that he was the one giving orders.

"It's a lot of ground to cover." But two men could do it covertly especially if they had eyes in the sky. He looked at Hersh who was crouched beside him in an alert manner. Seth's eyes had adjusted to the moonlight enough to read the man's tense expression. "Don't let the drone lose her."

Seth hung up and the noise of the helicopter grew louder. Arthur glanced nervously toward the aircraft. It wasn't only the good guys who used helicopters for transportation in this part of the world.

"That's one of ours." Seth assured the guy. "Hersh and I have to go. Backup is on the way."

"What the fuck?" said Arthur.

"Sorry. We received another urgent priority call. Keep collecting intel on the attackers here." Seth sent his information to HQ as he spoke. They could share it with the case agent and Homeland Security.

"Anyone have any spare ammo?" Hersh asked, holding out his hands for fresh magazines. Even though he didn't know the details of the conversation Seth had had with McKenzie, he'd picked up enough to know it might involve another firefight. The guys handed over the extra mags they carried and Seth hoped to hell the bad guys were well and truly gone from this area. Although, to be fair, most of them were dead.

"You weren't down here as part of a routine training exercise, were you?" Arthur asked heavily.

Seth shook his head.

"Someone suspected we had a rat."

Seth nodded again and Arthur's gaze went to Ike, the team member they'd lost.

"If we'd known, if we'd been warned…"

Seth pressed his lips together. Investigations didn't work that way.

"They suspected me, too, didn't they?" Arthur asked.

Again, Seth kept quiet. How was he supposed to answer that when the answer was obvious?

"All these years on the job and the government didn't trust me. Ike had a wife and kids and if we'd known we could have been watching each other's backs." Arthur raised his face to the sky and let out a long piercing yell of frustration.

"I'm sorry, man. Support will be here shortly," Seth said quietly.

Arthur's reply was lost in the noise of blowing dust and wash of the rotors of the descending machine. Seth and Hersh jumped into the small bird and the pilot immediately took off again.

They pulled on headphones and Seth filled his teammate in on the new op.

"We have any idea what this kidnap victim looks like?" Hersh asked, checking his weapons.

Seth shook his head and texted McKenzie for a photograph of the VP's daughter, then pulled out a topographical map. Then he realized the copilot held a small tablet showing the drone footage from a thermal camera overlaying a map. Seth held up his water-proof map and took a fix on the general location.

Then he watched as the short convoy of vehicles turned off the road into the desert of the Sonoyta Valley.

This looked bad. This looked really bad.

"Drop us here." Seth indicated on his map to the copilot. The guy nodded. It was close to the border, about six miles north, five miles east of the main road crossing. "We'll hike into this area." Seth again circled the location to the copilot. "And we're taking that with us," he indicated the tablet. He gave the guy their satel-lite and cell numbers on a card and the guy returned the favor. The copilot would be able to watch the drone footage on his cell, but Seth knew if the kidnappers split up, he and JJ would need the better resolution provided by the tablet.

The pilot set down in a clearing.

"We're going to stage near the port of entry to look as incon-spicuous as possible, but we'll pick you up again as soon as you make contact. Let me grab you some supplies." The copilot jumped out and retrieved several bottles of water from the cargo area and thrust it into their hands along with some MREs.

"Thanks. Let's hope we find these bastards before the sun comes up." He and Hersh removed their headphones, climbed out, nodded to the pilot and copilot, and hit the cold desert once more.

The machine rose up into the air and quickly disappeared.

His sat phone buzzed with the attachment McKenzie sent him. The image was taken at a wedding or some other kind of formal occasion, but he still recognized the petite blonde.

It was a kick in the gut.

He showed the photo to Hersh.

Hersh's lips tightened. "Shit."

"Yeah, shit." Seth tried not to think about what these guys might be doing to a woman like her in a deserted location.

"Think they took her friends too?"

Seth shrugged. "Guess we're gonna find out."

"Roger that."

Seth pulled down his night vision goggles and the two of them started jogging through the wilderness, praying they reached her in time.

———

Karina was starting to hyperventilate.

Zoe grabbed her friend's hand and held tight. Her own throat was raw with a fear so all-consuming she could barely breathe. This man was a killer. She could see it in his eyes. As far as he was concerned, she and her friends were already dead and he wanted her to behave so as not to inconvenience him more than necessary.

She frowned thinking about her abductor's words.

"Whose orders?" she asked.

He turned and looked at her, black eyes shining with amusement that was terrifying for the lack of empathy they contained.

"*Who* told you to kidnap us?" she repeated.

"They must know who you are," Karina whispered.

Zoe shot her friend a warning look.

"Who are you?" the man asked with lazy interest. He seemed

genuinely curious and Zoe was suddenly certain this had absolutely *nothing* to do with her mother.

"My dad's a Hollywood producer. He has money. He can pay a ransom for all of us." It wasn't a lie, although he'd recused himself from any position of direct authority in his company so his wife's reputation wasn't compromised. Zoe knew she needed to stall their abductors, and maybe tempting them with the promise of cash would be enough to keep them alive long enough to be rescued.

Karina stiffened and sent her a look.

Her captor appeared to sneer, although he still wore the bandana so it was difficult to tell. "Hollywood is pretend, *chica*. This is reality."

Fucking *chica*? What an asshole.

Something in his tone though was absolutely terrifying. He dealt in death and destruction with the same ease most people picked up a latte. He was one of the reasons this desert was such a dangerous place and she knew he would kill her without conscience.

"*Who* gave the orders to kidnap us?" she pressed.

He said nothing, just stared at her. She and her friends were another day at the office for this guy. Another fucked-up entry in his weekly planner.

They bumped over the road and then onto the same dirt track the four of them had traveled earlier that day.

Zoe glanced around. "Where are we going? Why are we here?"

Again, the hidden smirk that creased the skin at the edge of his dark eyes. "Maybe you and your friends should learn to keep your noses out of our business and then you wouldn't be in this situation."

She and Karina shared a surprised look. This wasn't about Zoe or her mother, it was about their work.

"We don't investigate crimes. We help families reunite with their loved ones. Wouldn't you want your loved ones to have your remains to bury if something happened to you?"

He shrugged and looked away, but not before she caught a subtle shift in his eyes.

As familiar as he was at handing out death, she didn't think he was as comfortable with his own mortality as he wanted to pretend. Maybe he should have chosen a safer profession. And perhaps he didn't have a choice.

She wasn't about to feel sorry for him. The majority of people south of the border were good, honest, hard-working members of society. Everyone made choices. But some choices could not be unmade.

Zoe watched out the window and realized they were headed to the *exact* spot where they parked earlier today at the Brady's trailhead. A shiver crawled over her flesh.

They pulled to a stop and two of the men got out and checked the surrounding area. They were both carrying assault rifles. They nodded and the driver turned off the engine and the vehicle sat cooling in the cold desert night.

Zoe wanted to look around but the leader of this group was staring at her again, almost daring her to disobey his earlier instructions. She gritted her teeth and wondered what the hell they were waiting for, what they were doing here, and what these men wanted from her and her friends.

She had never been so scared in her entire life, but she didn't think showing her fear would gain her any mercy—probably the opposite and they'd see it as weakness and attack. She had no idea if her SOS signal had reached her parents or the authorities. She had no idea if it even mattered. She and her friends would probably be dead long before help ever reached them.

Her door was opened and she was dragged outside. She would have fallen if not for the bruising grip on her arm.

She glanced up to see James and Fred stumbling out of James's truck, their hands still bound behind their backs and fresh blood smeared across their faces. Both men looked as if they'd been pistol whipped.

The guys stared at her and Karina who'd been pulled out of the other side of the SUV, despair written on their features.

The kidnappers dragged them across the parking lot and made them kneel in a row. The rush of fear almost melted Zoe's spine as the hard earth pressed into her kneecaps.

"We haven't done anything to hurt or threaten your organization," she argued.

"You're making a big mistake," said James. "Zoe's—"

"I already told him," Zoe cut in.

"That her dad was a Hollywood producer." Karina shot her a frown.

Did they really think that if these thugs found out that her mom was the Vice President of the United States of America, they would *spare* them? It would more likely earn them a bullet that much quicker and possibly a deeper grave.

Suddenly another man walked out of the darkness leading a pack mule. Zoe gasped in surprise. He wore all black and was tall and lean and even wore a black bandana over his mouth and nose. The other kidnappers immediately snapped into a state of heightened readiness.

Clearly this was the man who gave the orders. The man who'd had Zoe and her friends kidnapped.

He spoke to her original captor and then strolled toward where the four of them sat on their haunches in the dirt. In his hand he held a small, yellow marker, the sort they used to indicate evidence. The sort she'd left on the trail earlier that evening to mark the position of the body of the woman she'd found.

Zoe's teeth chattered.

The man in black paused when he reached her and stood staring down at her. She lifted her chin and shot him a glare. She was pretty sure they were going to kill them anyway. She wasn't about to make it easier for him or bow her head in submission.

Not while her nerve held.

He pivoted away and stopped at James's truck and indicated someone open the tailgate for him. He tossed the yellow marker inside, then pulled one of the boxes toward him, lifted the lid. Zoe couldn't see his expression, but he leaned back as though repulsed. A mean smile touched her mouth.

Despite his obvious distaste, he shook the contents and seemed to be searching for something amongst the bones.

He did the same with the other box, ferreted around like he'd lost something, picking up the crucifix before dropping it back inside. Then he cursed.

"Where are their phones?" The newcomer held out his hand and her captor handed all four of their cell phones over to the man.

Zoe wasn't sure if her cell would register some sort of emergency signal on the screen from her watch if he turned it on. She held her hands behind her back and blindly pressed the button on the side of her watch and then slid her finger across the top of the screen in the hopes of turning the signal off without any of their captors seeing.

But the man in black didn't turn on the phones, instead he tossed them into the bed of the truck.

"You have all their belongings? Their clothes? Everything? You're sure?" The newcomer barked at his second in command.

Zoe's abductor opened the trunk of the car they'd traveled down here in and pulled out her canvas bag. The man in black pointed to James's truck and her bag was tossed inside with everything else.

Dammit.

"Douse it in gasoline," the man in black ordered.

She and her friends stiffened.

Then the man in black went over to his mule and removed something from the animal's pack. Zoe was torn between the desire to run and the need to curl into a fetal ball and weep. If she ran, he'd still shoot the others.

She caught Fred's gaze in the light of the moon. He was obviously thinking the same thing.

Their only chance of survival might be if they *all* ran.

The man in black came back to them and tossed the two shovels at James's and Fred's feet. Then he pointed into the desert behind them and uttered one terrifying word.

"Dig."

———

Seth and Hersh moved stealthily while still covering the ground at a rapid pace. One thing was for damn sure, Seth no longer felt cold.

They weren't far away from the vehicles used in the abduction. He and Hersh crouched together for a moment and took a quick look at the drone's thermal image on the tablet. Seven bad guys and what appeared to be four hostages. They had not peeled away into the desert in different directions to confuse pursuers—which was good and suggested they didn't know the authorities were onto them. Instead, they were congregated near the cars in a small parking lot. One man had joined them on foot from the desert along with what looked like a mule.

Did they plan to sneak the VP's daughter over the border on foot?

Seth zoomed out on the drone's camera and didn't see any other people lurking in this immediate area.

Were the three other victims the same people he'd seen Ms. Miller eating with at the motel earlier? It seemed likely. They were spaced out as if being interrogated.

He and Hersh had originally planned to find a vantage point and observe until backup arrived, but this setup looked more like an execution than a kidnapping. Maybe the hostage takers planned to kill the three friends and keep Miller?

Seth didn't intend to let that happen.

He and Hersh crept closer, close enough to hear voices floating across the empty landscape.

They both froze at the word "dig," and looked at one another.

There was only one reason to dig out here and it wasn't to search for buried treasure.

Seth pointed to the map. Kept his voice to a low whisper. "You head around this area. Cut back to this point and take out this guy here. I'll go here." He indicated another man hanging out near the vehicles as the other five tangos followed the hostages as they staggered into the desert. "We'll meet up here," he indicated another spot, "and reassess."

The opportunity to better the odds was one he'd willingly take. Seth shoved the tablet into a pocket in the front of his equipment vest as Hersh faded into the night. They'd be blind to one another's movements and to what was happening with the bad guys for a few minutes, but they needed to keep their situational awareness up anyway, and not rely completely on technology.

They each knew how the other worked. Hersh might be a sniper but he also trained as an assaulter, the same way Seth was an assaulter but regularly practiced his marksmanship with long guns.

Seth headed west and narrowly avoided getting spiked by a massive saguaro that had probably stood sentinel in the desert for more than a hundred years. He wound his way through the vegetation aware of movement twenty yards to his right where the unfortunate captives were being marched at gunpoint. It was the order to dig that had given him and Hersh this chance, although there was always the concern the bad guys would get bored of waiting for the hole to be deep enough and simply end this thing sooner rather than later. Or decide to take turns raping the women while they made the men dig the graves.

That idea filled Seth with rage but he pushed it aside to access the zone he needed to do his job.

Did they know who Zoe Miller was related to? If they hadn't taken Ms. Miller because she was the USVP's daughter, then why had they taken the group and brought them out here?

Seth pulled his KA-BAR knife and stopped thinking about

anything except the moment. All that mattered was rescuing the hostages, with Miller being the number one priority.

He crept to the edge of the parking area that was lit by the headlamps of a rusted out old sedan. He'd already lifted his NVGs so he wasn't blinded by the additional light. The half-moon was bright enough to see by.

The scent of gasoline hung thick in the air which made sense when Seth realized one man was siphoning gas out of a red truck —a red truck he'd seen parked outside the motel earlier that evening. The man stood, spitting out what had obviously been a mistimed suck on the rubber tubing, before pouring the contents of the jerry can over the roof and hood of the old automobile.

It took Seth a moment to locate the other guy. As soon as he did, he moved stealthily through the shadows, up behind the man who was taking a piss into a thicket of mesquite at the edge of the clearing. Seth covered the kidnapper's mouth with one hand and slit his throat with the other. He eased the dead man silently to the ground.

When he looked over his shoulder Hersh was dragging the second man into the darkness. The mule flicked his tail, clearly bored.

Seth and Hersh faded back into the night and flipped down their NVGs as they moved together toward the rest of the group in the desert. Finally, they came in sight of the captives.

What Seth saw didn't look good.

5

Zoe was shaking from fear as she stumbled after Karina through the night. The icy cold penetrated her thin cotton clothes and raised gooseflesh all over her skin but the temperature was the least of her concerns.

Five captors accompanied them. Two men stayed behind with the vehicles. Better odds than earlier but unfortunately their abductors all had weapons, NVGs, and hearts of stone.

She and her friends were unarmed, plus Fred and James had their hands bound behind their backs. Still, the kidnappers would have to untie them if they wanted them to dig what had to be their own graves. The only hope of survival she and her friends had was to scatter into the desert and run.

"Don't think about doing anything stupid, *chica*." The words were soft as owls' wings on the night air.

She stiffened.

Her initial captor seemed determined to stick close and she didn't think it was because he was going to offer her any protection.

"Why not?" Bitterness ripped through her. "Are you going to *hurt* me if I don't do as I'm told?" She didn't bother to hide her derision.

She felt the hard poke of a gun barrel in her ribs.

"There are worse things than death, *chica*."

Her lip curled. "You think I don't know that?" She glared at the guy over her shoulder. "I am intimately familiar with death, and she doesn't scare me one bit. People like you, however..."

He gave a soft laugh. "Then you are smarter than I gave you credit for."

She narrowed her eyes at his patronizing tone.

"Why are you doing this?" She was desperate to find this man's humanity, to make him see them as individuals, not part of the daily to-do list. "My friends and I help people unfortunate enough to die out here. We send their bodies home to their loved ones for burial. We don't have anything to do with law enforcement." And if she personally detested drug traffickers that was her own damn business.

He huffed out an annoyed breath. "You think there are many choices for men like me in my country?"

My heart bleeds.

"No one made you kidnap us out of our beds."

Her reaction clearly wasn't what he expected from someone he'd obviously already labeled a do-gooder.

He gave her another jab with the end of his gun barrel. "Move."

"Tell them," Karina whispered when Zoe drew close again.

"It won't make any difference," Zoe muttered. "They'll worry about law enforcement coming after us and kill us that much faster."

Or they'd kill her friends and take her as leverage.

Zoe heard the hissing slice of a shovel through dry earth as their kidnappers set Fred and James to work.

Zoe stared into the night. A rattlesnake shook his tail in warning somewhere in the desolate nightscape. When her captor moved away to speak to his boss she whispered to Karina, "We need to run."

Karina shook her head slightly. "I can't leave, James."

"If we escape and split up in the desert it will give the guys the opportunity to do the same or fight back without worrying about us."

Karina swallowed thickly. "I don't know if I can do it."

"You *have* to. The more we divide them the better odds we each have. Scatter, run, hide. It's only a few hours until dawn. The authorities will be looking for us."

Fred and her captor both glanced in her direction and she stopped talking. She held her breath and stared meekly at the ground. One of the men shouted at Fred in Spanish to keep digging.

The four of them didn't have much time.

Slowly, when no one was paying her any attention, she edged back a step. Then another. Hoping Karina would follow. The man in black said something to his minions who all laughed, and Zoe used the moment of distraction to ease into the shadow between two large cacti. Then she turned around and took off, ignoring the vicious scratch of needle-sharp spines on her bare skin.

She'd barely gone a dozen yards when she heard someone shout out in anger and pursuit began. Someone started firing a weapon and yelling in Spanish. The next thing she knew she was tackled to the ground from the side. Tears of frustration sprang to her eyes.

The large form clamped a hand over her mouth before she could scream in frustration.

"Stay quiet and stay down, I'm here to rescue you," a voice whispered warmly near her ear. Then the weight was gone and she rolled onto her side and craned her neck to see the dark silhouette of a man in combat gear kneeling above her in the darkness.

He fired and she heard the grunt of pain as the bullet connected with flesh.

"My friends are back there," she said desperately.

Several loud explosions went off nearby and the air was

suddenly filled with noxious smoke and the sound of automatic gunfire.

Fear for her friends gripped her. The soldier shifted closer and continued to fire. A bullet flew so close she heard the whistle through the air. He didn't flinch. Simply pressed her head to the ground as he continued shooting.

"Please don't kill my friends."

"Two of them took off and the other hit the deck when we started firing. The tangos are retreating."

He dug around in his protective vest and handed her something hard and flat. A tablet. "Cover the light from the screen and see if you can figure out where everyone went. The last thing we want is someone creeping up on us from behind."

Zoe did as she was asked, using her arms and hands to shield the dim light. The soldier backed up a little, still on one knee and scanning the area through his NVGs. He moved her hand aside so he could glance at the screen.

Two figures were running back toward the vehicles. Four figures lay prone nearby. Another two people were running into the desert to the east of them. And yet another figure was creeping toward where she and her rescuer hunkered down in the dirt. Zoe's hand gripped the man's pant leg as she gasped and pointed.

He laid his warm hand flat on her back. "He's with me."

A moment later a second soldier hunkered beside them.

The first guy pulled out a satellite phone. "We have the asset. The asset is safe. Five kidnappers dead. Two on the run."

Five dead? She tugged urgently on his arm. "What about my friends?"

Suddenly the night was lit up with a giant whoosh of noise and light as flames leapt into the sky fifty yards west of them.

Her rescuer ignored her. "Tell backup to head toward the giant bonfire that just lit up the desert. A Ford truck." He gave their location. "Looks like the two remaining kidnappers split up and took off in the sedan and SUV." He reeled off two plate numbers seemingly from memory.

Zoe sat up and tried to climb to her feet. "I need to go to my friends."

The soldier pressed down onto her shoulder, holding her in place. "Not until we know it's safe."

"They could be hurt." She rolled her shoulder away from his hold and tried again to stand. This time he helped her, then took the tablet and stuffed it down the front of his vest. The massive bonfire made it easy to see despite the lack of sunlight.

"Fine, but we do this my way. If you don't behave, I will cuff you and leave you here until I am sure the situation is safe."

Zoe glared at the guy and repeated, "We need to hurry. They could be hurt."

"You are my priority."

"And *they* are mine." Her teeth locked.

"Ma'am." The words were both an acknowledgment and a warning, but the voice made her freeze.

She gaped at him. "It's you, from the motel."

A half-smile touched his lips, and her heart gave a little bump.

"FBI Special Agent Seth Hopper, ma'am. This is Agent JJ Hersh. We're on secondment from HRT."

"*FBI?*"

The other man nodded as she brushed the dirt off her clothes.

"Where is the rest of your team?" Earlier there had been at least ten at the motel, maybe more.

"I'm afraid it's only the two of us until the cavalry arrives."

Zoe didn't understand but she knew asking more questions would only slow them down and she desperately wanted to reach her friends.

The three of them eased with frustrating slowness toward the clearing. They paused in the shadows. The agent behind her slipped past her to check the bodies of the prone figures lying on the ground. He zip-tied the hands of each man there even though they all appeared to be dead.

She spotted a dark mound near the shallow pit. "Fred. Fred!"

The mound moved, causing a wave of relief to rush over her. Her new bodyguard grabbed her arm before she could reach her friend.

"Wait." Seth Hopper's tone brooked no argument and he pushed her behind him again. Fred uncurled from the ball in which he lay and slowly sat up in the dirt. He held his hands up in the air and then, to her fury, Agent Hopper went over, hauled Fred to his feet and patted him down for weapons.

Fred held her gaze the entire time. "You okay?"

Seth Hopper stood back and let Fred go.

Slowly Zoe drew in a relieved breath so huge it pressed painfully against her ribs. She nodded before stepping forward to wrap her arms around her friend.

"I'm so glad you're alive."

Fred hugged her back and pressed a kiss to her hair. Zoe held him tightly.

She couldn't believe they'd all almost died tonight.

———

Zoe Miller's boyfriend sent Seth a glare as he gathered the woman to him and kissed her mussed blonde head.

Seth looked away because it wasn't any of his business. It was one thing being attracted to an anonymous stranger. Another entirely to have the hots for the daughter of the Vice President of the United States, Madeleine Florentine.

Zoe Miller was now firmly in the "work" category of his life and he never mixed business with pleasure no matter how tempting.

Not that it had ever been a problem in the past.

And not that she was offering.

He pulled up the drone footage on the tablet. "Any idea how to communicate with your friends before they end up in Texas?"

His voice was a little sharper than usual but he had just killed three men rescuing these people.

Zoe stepped away from her boyfriend and put two fingers in her mouth and produced a piercing whistle that echoed for miles around the desert.

Seth grinned despite himself. "Impressive."

He switched his gaze back to the screen and the two figures had stopped running.

"Come back, Karina. It's safe now," Zoe yelled, and Seth had to admit he was surprised by such a large volume of sound coming from such a pint-sized person.

On screen the two runaways slowly turned, hanging on to one another before starting to make their way cautiously back in their direction, guided, no doubt, by the fiery beacon of the burning truck.

In silent agreement, he, Hersh, Zoe, and the boyfriend moved toward the flames.

"How come you guys arrived here so fast? You have a tag on her or something?" Fred's tone was a tad aggressive for someone who'd so recently had his ass saved.

Zoe frowned up at the guy.

Seth didn't let it ruffle him. This wasn't high school. "We received word while conducting other duties in the area of an emergency alert sent by Ms. Miller."

"You called for help?" Fred looked down at the woman in question.

"Yeah. I used the SOS button on my smartwatch back at the motel when the kidnappers weren't looking." Zoe tugged her watch strap until it was face up. She laughed a little breathlessly as she pressed the button on the side and the watch lit up. "I can't believe it actually worked."

"*I* can't believe you don't have a Secret Service detail," Seth muttered irritably under his breath, although evidently not quietly enough.

"I don't need a Secret Service detail," Zoe shot back sharply.

Seth tucked in his chin as he negotiated his way past another cactus. "Five dead bad guys and a midnight walk in the desert at gunpoint suggest otherwise."

She flinched and maybe that had been a tad harsh. But it was true.

Fred jumped in—because of course he did. "Are you seriously blaming Zoe for this fiasco?"

"Not what I said." *Jackass.* Seth's teeth clenched over the silent insult. "Ms. Miller's quick thinking tonight saved your life." Seth faced the other man who was slightly taller than he was, but height did not reflect the size of a man's balls, nor the fighting zeal in his heart. "But if the Secret Service *had* had a team on your girl-friend, then perhaps the cartel wouldn't have jumped you at the motel and dragged you all out here for summary execution."

Seth scanned the parking area before he stepped out of cover. He shielded his face from the heat coming off the old truck which still burned fiercely. He hoped the blaze didn't set the desert alight because that would be the last thing they needed.

"He's *not* my boyfriend," Zoe muttered irritably.

Seth looked over his shoulder, keeping his expression neutral despite the fact he wanted to grin. Fred's expression darkened.

It didn't change the circumstances. Not really. She was VPOTUS's daughter and he, for all his elite FBI HRT status and former Navy SEAL glory days, was a poor boy from the wrong side of the tracks. He didn't even know who his real parents were for god's sake.

He kept his eyes on drone footage, watching the other two kidnap victims and wanting advance warning should the escaped tangos return with a fresh army. The cars had disappeared off screen while the drone remained overhead. Hopefully, the FBI had more eyes in the sky and agents ready to track down those bastards.

"Can you fill me in on what happened earlier tonight?" Seth asked.

"Those thugs turned up at the motel after we'd all gone to bed and ordered us at gunpoint to get in their vehicles. No one at the motel tried to help us," Fred said, a little less belligerent now. Blood was smeared across his upper lip and chin. He'd clearly taken a bit of a beating.

Sounded as if the locals knew to keep their heads down. The motel might have security footage that could prove useful in helping to identify the culprits though.

"And they insisted on us bringing all our stuff with us so they could set fire to it in the desert." Zoe's expression was troubled as she stared at the flames. She clasped her hands together and then vigorously rubbed her arms.

She was cold, he realized.

He quickly removed his equipment vest and then his top layer of tactical gear. Underneath was a high-grade woolen base layer which he stripped off as both civilians watched him wide-eyed. Hersh scanned the surroundings from the other side of the clearing.

The last thing he needed was Zoe Miller succumbing to hypothermia. And if Seth flexed his muscles a little, so what? Fred had pissed him off and Zoe Miller had liked his body just fine earlier. He handed the warm wool to Zoe and hoped it didn't stink too much of sweat.

"Put that on under your t-shirt." Which was baggy and about as useful for conserving body heat as a sail. He turned his back and Hersh did the same. He had no idea what the "not boyfriend" did.

Seth grinned.

Didn't mean she was single or even interested in him, but it did mean that smug jerk had been rejected because he obviously had the hots for Ms. Zoe Miller.

Too.

Dammit.

Not going to happen.

"Thank you," she said gratefully.

"You're welcome." He put his own clothes and vest back on and turned around as she was pulling her t-shirt over his.

"What was in the boxes in the truck?" He'd noticed them through the dirty windows of the canopy when he'd walked past the vehicle earlier that evening.

Zoe pressed her lips together, her expression growing suddenly grim. "Human remains."

Seth blinked hard.

Of all the things he'd expected to come out of her mouth, that was not even on the list.

She spotted his obvious surprise and a reluctant laugh escaped. "We're forensic anthropologists of one variety or another. We met during a long hot summer internship with the Pima County Medical Examiner's Office and have affiliate status there. They are amenable to us collecting fully skeletonized remains with appropriate data recordings." Her expression tensed as she looked at the dying flames of the burned-out truck. "The chance of the people we found today being identified has now dropped dramatically."

"We might still be able to get usable DNA," Fred argued, taking a few steps toward the truck before the intensity of the fire drove him back again.

The fact the truck was a funeral pyre of sorts made Seth pause in a moment of regret, but there was no time for sentiment.

"How did the cartel know who you were?" he asked Zoe Miller.

"I don't think they did." She took the bottle of water he offered, so did Fred. Hopefully, whichever agency barged into the desert on a rescue mission remembered to bring a few basic supplies. Although, he suspected they'd send a chopper for Zoe Miller and get her out of the area ASAP.

"The man who kidnapped me said we'd brought this on ourselves or something along those lines. And we should have kept our noses out of his desert."

Anger stole through Seth's veins. "This isn't cartel land."

"You tell them that," Fred said bitterly.

Seth watched as the guy went over to a large plastic jug of water placed on a rough wooden bench and refilled his bottle.

Zoe followed his skeptical gaze. "It's safe. We left it here earlier. At the end of a day in the field it's become a habit to leave behind any water we have to spare."

Their gazes locked and he spotted defiance in hers. Did she think he'd object to giving a fellow human being water under any circumstances? That wasn't who he was.

"This is where you were today? This exact spot?" he asked.

Zoe nodded. "We parked here. Searched about a mile west." She dragged a hand through her short blonde hair. Everything about her screamed cute, except for her job and the stubborn set of her jaw.

He checked the screen again and saw the two figures were close now. They were creeping around to the north of their position. He didn't blame them for being cautious or checking things out first.

He shifted so he was between the newcomers and his principal. Habit and training. Like it or not, she was his mission.

Finally, the two stumbled into the clearing. The tall red-headed guy stared slack-mouthed at them and the burning truck. The woman's face was haggard and gray even in the orange glow of the flames.

Seth exchanged a look with Hersh and the other guy stepped forward. Seth tossed another bottle of water to his teammate and the guy caught it one-handed and then offered it to the two victims before drawing them forward to where they all stood in the southeast corner of the parking lot. Farthest from the flames and the two dead kidnappers, but close enough to take cover if they needed. Unlikely, but training was training. Never make yourself an easy target. Never let your guard down.

"Where are you hurt?" Hersh eased the woman to a sitting position on the ground.

"You're hurt?" her boyfriend exclaimed in surprise.

She obviously hadn't told him.

Zoe went to step forward but Seth held up his arm across her path. "Let's give Operator Hersh a little space to work." He turned his head and they locked gazes. "Unless you have medical training?"

She blinked and shook her head. His gaze dropped to her full lower lip before he snapped his attention back to the others.

Hersh lifted the second woman's shirt up at the back and it was easy to spot the blood that had been invisible against her dark jeans. Hersh pulled his medical pack off his vest and began cleaning her up.

"Why didn't you tell me you were hurt?" The boyfriend sounded anguished as he knelt before her.

"I didn't realize until we'd already run for about a quarter of a mile."

Terror was a great painkiller.

"I felt something hit when the bullets started flying but didn't want to hang around to find out what it was. I figured if I ignored it, it would go away." Her voice was breathy.

Unfortunately, bullet wounds didn't work that way.

"Any idea who shot you?" Fred asked with a look in Seth's direction.

Seth and Hersh exchanged a glance that silently labeled the guy a douche.

"We only shoot at things we can identify," Seth returned evenly, giving the guy a hard stare. "And we knew who the threats were from the assault rifles they held in their hands."

Basic training. Watch the hands not the face. People couldn't shoot you with their face.

Although he was sorry this woman had caught a round, the fact there weren't more injuries amongst the hostages was a goddamn miracle. It had a lot to do with Zoe Miller taking off the way she had even though it had been a risk. Considering she hadn't known the cavalry was coming and a grave was already being dug, it had been the smartest and bravest thing to do.

Hersh made the injured woman lie down on a thermal blanket he pulled from his kit. He eased her pants lower over her hip, poured QuikClot on the entrance and exit wounds. The emphasis on trauma wounds was always stop the bleeding and get the person to a hospital as quickly as possible. Seth wasn't happy to be using battlefield tactics on civilians on home soil.

Hersh pressed gauze pads to the wounds and taped them firmly into place. He eased the jeans back up. Then he began setting up a field IV.

Seth pulled out the sat phone to update McKenzie who he'd worked with a few times now.

"What's happening?" McKenzie asked without preamble.

"One of the hostages was shot and injured. The others are unhurt."

Zoe Miller's brows raised then. At the term hostages? Maybe it wasn't completely accurate, but victims didn't sound great either.

"Which one?" McKenzie asked quickly.

Seth leaned closer to Zoe Miller. "Can I get everyone's names?"

Zoe nodded. "Karina Järvi. The person who was shot is Karina Järvi. That's her fiancé, James McAllen, and our friend, Fred Pengelli."

Fred shot Seth a glower. He did not like being in the friend zone and definitely considered Seth a threat. Seth wasn't, of course. He couldn't afford to be, but he had no intention of letting the other man know that.

"We're sending a helicopter to pick up you, Hersh, and Ms. Miller. Backup is thirty minutes out. I'll order a medivac for immediate extraction of the injured party. The vehicles that fled the area split up north and south. We have agents in pursuit."

Zoe's eyes shot to his, proving she could hear both sides of this conversation.

Seth wanted to ask if they'd caught Roger yet but that was a classified mission and Ms. Nosey didn't have clearance.

"Tell your boss that the first helicopter can airlift Karina out of here. There's something I need to check before I leave," said Zoe. "I'll be fine alone but I'd appreciate some sort of flashlight and a ride out of here in a couple of hours. I assume you have to call the medical examiner to pick up these men's bodies regardless?"

She thought he would leave her in the desert unprotected?

The set of her jaw reminded him of the mule who was grazing on a straggly patch of grass nearby. He needed to secure the animal because it was entirely possible there was forensic evidence on his tack.

"I heard what she said," McKenzie said wearily. "Remind Ms. Miller that I am following my own orders and perhaps she should call her mother to tell her she is safe so maybe then the FBI director will, in turn, get off my ass?"

"Roger that," Seth said with amusement as Zoe narrowed her gaze.

A gentle hum on the night air told him the helicopter was approaching.

"Whatever happens, you and Hersh stay with Miller." McKenzie's tone firmed. "That is a direct order regardless of Ms. Miller's wishes. If she balks, take her into protective custody."

"Roger that," Seth hung up. Sent the woman in question a sidelong glance. "I take it you heard that?"

She gave him a resigned grimace and then reached out to grab the phone.

He held on to it, conscious of their hands so close together but not touching.

"If you genuinely want to avoid getting on that bird you should maybe wait to speak to your mother until after it takes off. Because if the VP gives me a direct order to put you on that flight, I will follow it. I value my job too much not to."

Zoe Miller flashed him a look that was both pissed off and grateful.

"Where's the best place for the pilot to land around here?" he asked, packing the sat phone away. This whole area was a massive crime scene that the Phoenix and Tucson FBI field offices would have to process—along with the area of the ambush on the BORTAC team earlier tonight. This desert would be crawling with Feds and MEs and Evidence Recovery Techs in the not-too-distant future.

Were the night's two events related? It seemed unlikely and yet nothing criminal happened around here without the cartels knowing about it.

What he did know was that he and Hersh would have some major paperwork associated with tonight's goings-on, but at least the drone footage would verify what had gone down in the firefight that had left five men dead and one woman injured.

Zoe Miller pointed north. "The road rises about fifty yards away. Tell the pilot to avoid any old cacti he sees."

Seth nodded but he knew the pilot would do his best regardless, more for the sake of his machine than the plants, but the result was the same. Seth pulled out a flashlight, changed the settings from red to white and handed it to Zoe. He exchanged a look with Hersh.

The wounded woman changed things. The fact Zoe Miller wasn't doing what she was told also altered the situation.

Hersh shrugged, clearly understanding Seth's silent acknowledgment that they were stuck here until Zoe Miller or the Vice President of the United States decided otherwise.

"Let's carry Karina closer to where the pilot is likely to land," Hersh said to James who looked as if he was in danger of passing out. "You guys wait at the hospital until an FBI agent arrives to interview you, understood? We'll catch you up."

Seth messaged McKenzie with a reminder to send agents to wherever they took Karina Järvi for treatment.

The two men lifted the woman between them. Zoe and Fred followed closely behind. Seth brought up the rear. The noise of the chopper became louder and louder until he could feel the wash of the rotors on his face. Using flashlights and arm signals they directed the pilot north of the bonfire in the parking area.

It would be nice to conserve some evidence.

The helicopter touched down and the copilot jumped out and helped Hersh load the patient and her boyfriend. Karina was obviously in a great deal of pain and who knew what the bullet had hit internally. She needed to be treated immediately.

Hersh waved Fred toward them. Fred shook his head and backed away. Seth put his hand on the guy's shoulder and said loudly to be heard above the roar of the blades, "The chopper can only take three passengers. It can come back for us. Our orders are to stay with Ms. Miller."

"I'll stay too," Fred yelled. "I can help."

Seth shook his head and widened his stance. "We need to clear the area for law enforcement activities."

"Now law enforcement is interested?" Fred gave a bitter laugh and then stared at Zoe who was looking at them both anxiously. "Do you want me to stay?" he yelled at her.

"I don't care. I just want Karina to get to the hospital ASAP."

Seth did care but he figured it would sound better coming from her.

The copilot waved Fred forward again and Seth took a few steps back. With a last longing look at Zoe, Fred Pengelli climbed into the machine and the copilot shut the door before quickly jumping into the front seat. The pilot waited only for safety harnesses to be snapped into place before rising rapidly into the air.

———

Zoe watched the helicopter lift off, Fred staring out the window with a look in his eyes that tore her apart. It was part grief, part trauma, and part something that looked suspiciously like heartbreak. Until tonight, she hadn't realized he'd harbored the hope they might get back together after so many years of being only friends.

If it had been anyone except a person she considered one of her best friends, she'd have been annoyed, as she'd never led him on or suggested her feelings had changed. But she loved him, and he loved her, and sometimes emotions got messy and lines blurred.

After the night they'd endured, the last thing she wanted was to cause more hurt. She didn't want to lose him from her life, but she wouldn't pretend emotions she didn't feel. He wouldn't want her to.

The helicopter veered northeast, lights fading to pinpricks as it gained speed and height. Part of her wished she was on it. The other part felt compelled to check on something. On someone.

"Will Karina be okay, do you think?" she asked the FBI agent, Hersh, who'd treated her friend.

"I hope so, ma'am."

"Please call me Zoe."

"Yes, ma'am," Hersh replied, straight faced before a grin broke over his boyish features.

Seth pulled out the sat phone and handed it to her. "Now might be a good time to call your mother. Then you can tell us what we're still doing here."

"Besides letting someone with a gunshot wound get to the hospital?"

One side of his mouth quirked. "Besides that."

She was reminded how incredibly attractive he was and how the last thing she wanted now was to think about him as anything except a federal agent doing her mother's bidding. Zoe looked at the phone and then took it even though there was no way she was talking to her mother just yet. She didn't want the argument about her immediately leaving the area or risk these two getting orders they couldn't refuse. Nor did she want the guilt trip her mom would take her on. Instead, she called Joaquin.

He answered with a groan.

"Hey, sorry to bother you at home in the middle of the night." He grunted.

"We were abducted from the motel, but we're safe now."

"What?" Joaquin exclaimed.

The FBI agent, Seth, touched her arm to get her attention, clearly concerned about what she was saying and to whom. The contact sent heat suffusing her skin and made her hyperaware of the space between them. His stern expression—visible in the waning firelight—told her to be circumspect with details. But he didn't know who she was talking to. "And now you'll need several medical examiner's rigs down here. In fact," she blew out a deep breath, "you might save some time and drive a refrigerated container."

"Are you okay? Fred, James, Karina?" Joaquin sounded like he was getting out of bed, probably so he didn't disturb his beautiful and long-suffering wife.

"Karina was shot and is on her way to the hospital. I think she's going to be okay but..." She choked in a sob because her friend had been shot and they'd all almost died tonight. "I'm obviously not an MD."

This time Seth cupped his hand gently over hers that held the sat phone and shook his head. She realized he didn't want her telling anyone she was out here in the desert with only two, albeit heavily armed, bodyguards.

Her ex would have yelled at her for not doing as she was told and angrily ripped the phone out of her hands.

Her mouth went dry at the memory, but she pushed it aside.

She nodded in understanding. These men had saved her and her friends' lives tonight. It was hard to put into words how grateful she was for that act even though it had meant the death of five men. Five extremely dangerous men.

"Anyway," she cleared her throat. "I suspect by the time you get to the trailhead at Brady's the FBI will be able to show you where the bodies are."

"The FBI?"

"My mother called in the troops."

"Thank goodness for your mother."

"Yeah, thank goodness for my mother." Zoe owed her mom big time. It was disconcerting to think what would have happened if she hadn't been wearing her smartwatch and her mom hadn't been in a position of power. In all likelihood she'd be running through the desert like a fugitive or decomposing beneath a thin layer of dirt while being devoured from the inside out by her own microbiome and an array of opportunistic insects.

"I have to go. I'm getting another call—probably the FBI or Chief Ranger. Let me know how Karina is doing as soon as you hear, okay?" Joaquin requested.

"I will," Zoe said softly.

"I'll see you later?"

She was supposed to be driving to Richmond today, but she couldn't leave until she was sure Karina was going to make it. And she was pretty sure the FBI would have questions. "I'll make a point of it. Talk to you later."

She hung up and handed Seth his sat phone back.

"What about your mother?" he asked with a cocked brow.

"She knows I'm okay, right? The FBI told her I'm alive and unhurt?" She held his unflinching gaze.

A muscle flexed in his jaw before he nodded.

"Let me finish here and then I'll call her. 'Kay?"

The two operators exchanged an uneasy glance.

"It won't take long and it's vitally important."

They exchanged another look and then Seth's lips firmed and he nodded. "Fine. Let's be quick."

6

She refilled her plastic water bottle from the jug James had left earlier—they hadn't expected to need it themselves, but she was grateful for it now.

The two agents took the opportunity to do the same. Zoe took another drink of the warm liquid as she waited for them. The flames had died down and, thankfully, no vegetation had ignited. The last thing they needed was a wildfire.

James's truck was completely toast.

More important was the damage to the remains they'd spent the whole day retrieving. The families might never know peace. Her heart felt heavy at the thought of their continued sorrow.

The mule pulled on the lead rope and Hersh went over to make sure the animal was tied securely before giving it a long drink.

The flames were dwindling now to a subtle orange glow, leaving a vast echoing midnight void that seemed to electrify every nerve. A coyote barked in the distance and the warning rattle of an angry snake reminded her of the natural hazards to be encountered in this part of the world on top of the human predators.

She flicked on the flashlight Seth had given her earlier. That one guy—the man in black—had been looking for something in those boxes. She didn't think he'd found it. She headed in the direction she and the others had searched yesterday.

Both agents scrambled after her.

"Where are we going?" Seth asked like a man preparing for battle. And maybe he was.

"I found a body late this afternoon." The cold air chilled her flesh but Agent Hopper's borrowed undershirt stopped her from shivering uncontrollably.

"The one in the box?" he asked.

She shook her head. "Another one. The ME was going to retrieve her first thing this morning. I think the men who grabbed us might have been looking for her. I want to confirm her location for Joaquin and the others. They won't have much time to spend searching for her." Zoe didn't want the dead woman to be forgotten.

"Can you tell us our general direction so one of us can scout ahead?" Seth asked, obviously striving for patience.

She glanced at him sharply.

His stance and tone were confident and commanding but he seemed willing to work with her rather than bully her into doing what he wanted.

She shone her flashlight over the ground looking for the right path. "The desert looks different at night and I'm not really sure of the way, but I'll know it when I see it. I think it'll be easiest if I go first."

"Not sure *easiest* is part of my job description," he said wryly.

His humor caught her off guard. She laughed and then all the violence and terror of the day slammed into her and she drew in a ragged breath.

"Hey." He touched her shoulder, the squeeze of his fingers warm and reassuring. "You're okay. I've got you." He cleared his throat. "*We've* got you."

"I didn't say thank you earlier. For saving us. Without you we'd all be dead, so thank you."

"Oh, I don't know about that." He let her go and adjusted his rifle. "You were on your way out of there when we turned up."

She shook her head and kept walking. She would have probably been shot in the back if it weren't for these two men. It beat meekly going to her death but...*damn.* She didn't want to think about it.

"What are two lone HRT operators doing out here in the desert anyway? Where are the rest of the team I saw at the motel?" She looked over her shoulder.

He gave an exaggerated shrug.

"Can't say or won't say?"

"It's complicated," he deadpanned.

She laughed again, unexpectedly.

He reached out and caught her arm before she walked into the branch of an organ pipe cactus.

She jumped. "Thanks."

Seth cut ahead of her. "You concentrate on finding the right direction, I'll scout ahead. Tell me if I go the wrong way."

The fact he was still worried about the potential threat from the cartel made a frisson of fear race over her flesh, but she thrust it aside. Not everyone was lucky enough to be rescued by HRT. She was safe.

She shone her beam of light over the dirt. There were hoof prints intermingled with human shoeprints that she didn't think had been here yesterday. The outline of the silhouette of the low mountains against the western sky told her she was going the right direction.

"She was about a mile west of the trailhead and then we cut into a small canyon." But which canyon? "It looked as if she'd been assaulted and died about a week ago." Zoe's mouth parched as she realized she might have faced the same fate if not for the dramatic rescue these two men had staged. "I took photographs and recorded GPS data but the bad guys tossed our cells into the fire." They hadn't taken everything though and there was a good chance the day's cell photos had uploaded to the cloud.

"Good thing they didn't spot your watch."

"Seriously." She smoothed her fingers over the device. "I'm never gonna take it off again."

"What makes you think the bad guys were interested in this vic you found?"

"I left a yellow marker on the trail. The man who came out of the desert with the mule was carrying it and threw it into the truck. Then he went through the boxes as if looking for something. Hey." She jerked on his vest to get him to stop. "Can you call your boss? Ask him to make sure the rooms at the motel are kept as crime scenes until I get there?"

"I have no doubt they are being processed as crime scenes as we speak. Why the urgency? I thought you said they made you bring all your belongings with you."

"Yeah. They did. But I left my field jacket and hat on the back of the bathroom door after I showered. The guy who grabbed me found my wash bag, but he didn't notice the clothes on the back of the door."

"What's so special about your green vest?"

She cocked her head. The fact he remembered the color of her clothes from earlier probably had more to do with his training than anything else, but it warmed her in a strange way. Reminded her of the spark that had flared between them at the motel. "I picked up some evidence at the scene and left it in my pockets. It might give us some clues as to who this victim is."

"And maybe who killed her?" Seth said quietly.

"Exactly." Although it was a long shot. If the tooth contained enough viable DNA in the pulp, they still needed a known sample to compare it to in order to get a match.

"Explain to me again why we are going back to the body now as opposed to letting the Feds deal with it—her—when they arrive?" he pushed.

"Because something about this whole thing doesn't make

sense. The fact the man in black had the yellow marker, the fact they kidnapped us at all? It seemed to be related to our search yesterday afternoon." An owl hooted and her heart raced. "I mean, we've been working in this region for years and usually we only get hassled by Border Patrol."

The FBI agent didn't defend his sister agency, which she appreciated, but that might say more about his tact than his politics.

"Weren't you with Border Patrol earlier?" she pushed.

"Did you hear something, Hersh?" Seth projected his voice slightly.

The guy behind them snorted. "I didn't hear a thing, Hop."

"Ha, ha," she muttered grumpily. "Funny."

Their mission was obviously classified.

Seth stopped abruptly and held up a clenched fist. They all halted. Then she saw what he'd spotted in the dirt. Blood. And drag marks. He sent the other agent into the area while he tugged her down to take a knee beside him.

Hersh was back moments later. He hunkered beside them. "Two dead men. Looks like they were both shot."

"Were they kidnapped the same way we were?" Zoe asked, unable to hide her horror.

"Hard to say, but I doubt it," Hersh said quietly. "These two look Hispanic. In their fifties or sixties. Worn, dusty clothing. Poor quality. They look like the kind of men the cartels often use as packers in this area."

"Can you record their location and send it to your FBI contacts and the local ME's office?" Zoe asked.

"Of course. Believe it or not, that's part of our job." Seth laughed softly as he took a GPS reading on his sat phone and sent it in.

"Let's go." Zoe didn't miss the look the two men exchanged. They didn't like the increased sense of danger.

"I'm not sure it's a good idea to go any farther," Seth stated.

"You *saw* the bad guys run away." Zoe clenched her hands into fists and then decided a little begging might be in order. "Please. Another five minutes and if we don't find what I'm looking for we can head back to the trailhead."

Dawn was starting to lighten the eastern edge of the world.

From the expression on his face, Seth Hopper wasn't happy about the idea of going deeper into the desert. Hersh looked impassive, as if he was content to let Seth make the decisions.

Zoe was not. She didn't want to give up now.

"You know there's no one around here from your drone footage, correct?"

He pulled out the tablet and sure enough a camera showed three figures huddled close together. He zoomed out as much as he was able and not another living soul appeared on the screen.

He slid the tablet into his vest. "Five minutes and then we head back."

Zoe quickly cut ahead again and concentrated on the landscape. She paused by a fork but ignored it and carried on. A few seconds later there was another split in the path. Based on the shape of the rocks above her head and the mule tracks, she was pretty sure this was the right way. She veered left, heading deeper into the canyon. Finally, she spotted the massive saguaro in whose shadow she'd spent several hours yesterday afternoon.

"Time's up," Seth said.

"She's just along here," she insisted. And took a few more steps.

Seth caught her arm. "You said five minutes."

"A woman died here." She jerked away from him, furious. "Don't you care?"

"I care about my principal's safety."

"I am not your *principal*." She pushed past him another few feet and found the other big cacti and the prickly pear where she'd retrieved the medallion.

"Here." She pointed. "She's right here."

Zoe shone the flashlight through the bushes to where she'd

found the dead woman earlier. The two men stood behind her, staring silently at the dirt and scrub.

She swallowed with difficulty. "What the hell?"

The desert was empty. The woman was gone.

———

Rage consumed Bruno as he abandoned the SUV and climbed into the car of a woman he'd instructed to wait here for him on the side of the road.

"Do you want some water?" she asked quickly.

"Shut up and drive."

Her knuckles gleamed white as her hands tightened around the steering wheel. Cautiously she pulled onto the asphalt and headed for the main highway. She was usually paid to pick up packers at assigned places along 85. She was expected to provide food and drink for those who'd spent days crossing the desert from Mexico carrying the cartel's precious product.

She obviously recognized he wasn't a packer. He was something completely different.

His cell rang. *Luis.*

"You got away okay?" his little brother and second-in-command asked breathlessly.

Bruno growled. "I'm fine."

They spoke in Spanish. He glanced at the woman. She was white but around here many people spoke Spanish. He didn't trust her, but she was paid to keep her mouth shut. More importantly, she knew he'd kill her for even the hint of failure or betrayal—and her debt, if incarcerated or killed, would transfer to her son or daughter or the next person foolish enough to cross the cartel.

Even so, Bruno was careful with what he said. "Where the fuck did they come from? Why weren't we warned?"

"I don't know. No one followed us, I swear. I posted lookouts on the highways and no one came after us, but cops are heading there now. In force."

Why?

How had the cops known what was going on?

Bruno stared out at the passing landscape still bathed in shadows. Everything had gone to shit tonight. At least Gabriella was no longer a problem. But his boss would be angry at the loss of so many men and the increased presence of the *federales* in the area.

"Find out where our little friends go next...and figure out exactly who attacked us in the desert."

"On it."

No one got away with shooting at him and killing his people. No one.

"And, Luis," he kept his voice low and calm. "No talking to anyone else about what happened tonight, understand? Report to me alone. I need to figure out what the hell happened out there."

And why they'd all almost died.

———

Seth marked the coordinates where this dead woman was supposed to be and sent them to headquarters. He didn't know what was going on, but if Zoe Miller was right about a missing corpse, it could be important to the investigation.

"Look, more mule tracks..." Zoe pointed the beam of light along the trail and took a step toward them.

"No," Seth stated firmly. "The FBI will send a team to search for the body."

"But we're here now," Zoe insisted, glancing up at the sky that was now a deep transparent indigo with soft pinks and golds kissing the horizon. "What if it rains?"

A smile wanted to tug at his mouth because she was nothing if not persistent. "It's not gonna rain."

She went to take a step anyway but Seth planted himself in front of her.

"Look, Zoe, in thirty minutes the sun is going to be up. We don't have any supplies, no tools, little water, and we have no idea where this body of yours may have disappeared to."

She bristled and opened her mouth to argue but he was done being accommodating.

"It's a *massive* area to search and we don't know if someone removed the body entirely or buried it. Operator Hersh and I have multiple crime scenes to deal with and co-ordinate with local Field Offices and other agencies. Agents will want to question us all in detail about what happened last night. We also have direct orders from high up to get you to safety and we're already pushing those boundaries more than I'm comfortable with." He raised his voice when she once again opened her mouth to argue. "What we do *not* have is permission to traipse all over the Arizona desert with the daughter of the Vice President of the United States while she searches for a missing corpse."

Through the NVGs he could see her pretty eyes cool with resentment. "You don't get to tell me what to do."

"No, but I do have the authority to detain you if need be. Look," he said patiently. "I don't want to do that." The fire in her eyes faded a little. "I know your job is important to you but understand something here, our jobs are important to us too. More importantly"—although really nothing was more important than his job or his colleagues—"your safety is our priority because neither myself nor HRT Operator Hersh want to see you get hurt."

Apparently, he had a lot to say on the subject.

He caught Hersh's gaze and nodded to the guy to start leading them back the way they'd come. Hersh began walking along the track but Zoe remained stationary, glaring at Seth defiantly with her chin lifted. He gave her his best stare-down—one that made terrorists and criminals quake in their boots.

She didn't budge.

"I'm happy to carry you if you require assistance," he said quietly.

She narrowed her eyes. "You wouldn't dare."

"Is that a challenge?"

"I'm heavier than I look."

He couldn't restrain a smile. "And yet, I think I can manage."

Hersh stopped and stood waiting for them to catch up, his gaze constantly scanning the surrounding scrub.

Zoe's expression crumpled and her suddenly defeated demeanor twisted something inside Seth's chest.

Her left hand cupped the side of her face. "I hate that of all the people out here, out of all the victims, she's the one most likely to be ignored and forgotten."

Zoe Miller seemed to genuinely care for the dead. He respected that. But it didn't change a goddamned thing about his responsibilities for the living.

Seth stepped closer. For a moment it looked as if she flinched in fear, but it was gone in an instant and he must have imagined it.

"I'm sorry, Zoe. I really am. But I can't save her. You can't save her. She's already dead. Let's head back to the rendezvous point and then you can make tsunami-sized waves with your mother—who you still haven't called by the way—and she can get the FBI and Border Patrol and the president himself involved in finding this dead woman and getting her the justice she deserves." That reminded him. He pulled out the sat phone. "Call your mother."

The crushed look on her face tugged at his heartstrings, but that didn't change the fact the three of them were out here alone in this vast wilderness. He didn't like it. Nothing but rattlesnakes and corpses lined the whole fucking place.

Dawn was breaking in earnest across the desert bringing with it a symphony of light and color, blinding in its intense natural beauty. With the dawn came a switch in advantage from the criminals back to the legal authorities which made Seth relax marginally, but only marginally. Zoe took the phone from him and started to turn away just as Hersh bit out a curse and the telltale warning of a pit viper rattled through the air.

Fucking fuckity fuck.

They both shot forward and found Hersh hopping backward on one leg.

Seth reached his friend and steadied him. "Stop moving."

He kept one eye on the pissed off diamondback undulating angrily off into the desert.

"Did it break the skin?" Seth asked, fearing he already knew the answer.

"Yep." Hersh blew out an irritated breath. "I didn't even see it. Stepped on the poor thing."

Seth shuddered. He really hated snakes. He crouched and jerked Hersh's pant leg up as far as it would go, exposing a sheathed knife and, beside that, two small angry holes punched into the guy's shin.

Fucking fuck.

The bad luck that had dogged the team lately was starting to feel like a curse. Seth was damned if he was losing another friend. Not today.

"Zoe, call the second to last number dialed on that phone and tell the guy we need an immediate medivac for a venomous snakebite."

"Best place to land around here is where we were earlier," she said anxiously as he grabbed supplies out of his medical kit. "Do you know what you're doing?"

Irritation hit him.

"Yes, I know what I'm doing. Make the call. We'll meet the chopper at the parking lot." The long days spent learning first aid had been mind-numbingly boring at the time, but he was glad of it now. He removed Hersh's knife, cut away at the pants to expose Hersh's leg from the knee down. He passed the knife to his friend who slid it into a pocket.

Zoe dialed looking anxious. "He shouldn't walk—"

"He won't be walking. Make the damn call."

Seth felt the skin above and below the wound. Hersh's flesh

was already hot and was starting to swell. "I've got you, JJ. I'm getting you out of here and back to Liv."

"Shit man, I feel like such a freaking idiot," Hersh said hoarsely.

"The main thing is to keep calm. You'll be in the hospital in less than thirty minutes and the calmer you are, the slower your heart will beat, the less this venom will spread through your veins and the less your wife will smack me around. Use your cold-ass sniper brain and give me some of that icy Zen you're so famous for."

Seth looked up as he pulled a bandage from his kit.

Hersh grinned which slightly reassured him.

"I have to admit I like seeing you bow before me, brah. Feel free to kiss my feet while you are down there."

"Do me a favor and don't die on me. Then you can kiss my ass when this is all over."

Hersh chuckled but his breathing wasn't as even as it should be, and Seth did not like this situation one fucking bit. He bandaged from the ankle, all the way up to Hersh's knee. Once Seth was sure the bandage was secure, but not tight, he tied it off and stood.

"I'm gonna need you to take off your equipment vest." It was an extra sixty pounds that would slow Seth down. He took his off too but removed some essentials, including ammo and placed it about his person. "Don't worry. I'll come back to retrieve it later."

The fact Hersh didn't bait Seth as to his physical fitness suggested the guy was in worse shape than he let on.

Zoe hung up the call and stood there holding the phone.

Seth took Hersh's safetied Remington and handed it to her. Without a word she slung the weapon across her back. Then he gave her the tablet, which she clutched anxiously in the other hand. Hopefully the threat was gone, but he wasn't about to leave behind something that could give the enemy a tactical advantage should the unexpected happen.

He adjusted his H&K 416 carbine so he could still use it, if need be.

"Stay right behind me," Seth told her. "No veering off the trail for any reason. Got it?"

Zoe looked pale and anxious. She nodded. "Of course."

He lifted Hersh over one shoulder. It was important to keep the heart above the wound in snake bite situations, so Seth clamped the back of Hersh's knees to his chest as the guy made himself relax. It wasn't comfortable but it was probably the easiest way to carry another person any distance.

He shifted the guy's weight and Hersh grunted.

Seth started moving at a fast walk. He would have run but he didn't want to joggle the venom in the man's limb and, from the conversation he'd overheard Zoe having with the pilot, it would take ten minutes for the chopper to arrive. He'd run when he heard the rotors, if necessary.

"Try not to vomit down my back."

"As long as I don't shit my pants." Hersh laughed and then added, "Sorry, ma'am."

"If you don't start calling me Zoe, I'm going to get mad."

"Wouldn't want that," Hersh mumbled on a laugh.

Zoe offered, "Do you want me to call your wife and tell her—"

"No." The word was sharp. "I'll call her from the hospital. I don't want her to worry."

"I'm so sorry." Zoe's voice was full of regret.

"Not your fault."

"I'm the one who dragged us into the desert."

"We were already in the desert," Seth said dryly.

His friend's weight was not insubstantial and Seth was starting to sweat. He was thankful he wasn't wearing that extra base layer as he scanned the ground so he didn't trip over any other pissed-off serpents.

He heard the helicopter when they were still half a mile from the LZ. He started jogging despite Hersh's grunts of complaint. The trailhead was now, thankfully, full of park rangers and FBI agents. Vehicles stretched along the dirt road, exactly where the chopper needed to land.

The agents glanced up warily as the three of them popped up out of the bush.

Seth pointed with his free hand. "Move those cars. We have a medical emergency and the chopper needs to land on the higher ground." The helicopter was close now. Hovering high above, looking for a safe place to put down.

Lawmen and women scrambled to clear that section of road, reversing down the long line of vehicles that now edged the rudimentary track. Seth waited impatiently as the machine landed and the copilot jumped out with a worried expression on his face. He opened the rear door and then indicated Seth approach.

Seth took the tablet from Zoe before striding over and gently easing Hersh to his feet next to the machine. The guy wobbled a little. His cheeks were flushed but that could have been from the uncomfortable ride.

The copilot assisted Hersh awkwardly into the back seat. Seth looked over his shoulder. Zoe was talking to a man in a suit who was likely the ranking agent on scene. As much as Seth wanted to go with Hersh and make sure his buddy was okay, he knew he needed to get the people on the ground up to speed ASAP so they knew where the bodies were and what had gone down.

Hopefully then they could catch the bastards who'd escaped.

He stood on the step, gripped Hersh's arm and met his gaze. "If you die on me, I will fucking kill you."

"Love you too, Hop. Look after our girl," Hersh yelled, looking pale and feverish.

Seth gave him a tightlipped smile and stepped away. He handed the copilot the tablet he'd borrowed earlier. The man nodded gratefully and jumped into the front seat as Seth backed out of range of the lethal tail rotor.

The pilot wasted no time and immediately took off, once more heading east to Tucson.

Seth dragged a hand over his sweaty face and wished to hell this day was already over.

Someone caught his elbow and gave his arm a gentle hug.

"He'll be okay." Zoe Miller's voice was soft as the dawn's light.

Seth found himself choking up a little, unable to speak. He nodded brusquely. Then he forced back the emotions and braced himself to do his job and keep his promises.

"Call your mother, Zoe. No more stalling."

7

"No, Mom, I swear I'm unhurt," Zoe assured her mother on Seth's sat phone. She'd been given paper booties to don and told not to go anywhere or touch anything by a harassed-looking field agent who'd taken her statement. Now Zoe stood obediently on the sidelines, trying to find shade beside a truck while the mercury steadily climbed. "I'm worried about Karina though. Our cell phones were destroyed so I can't check on her and they can't call me."

"Your father was in touch with James earlier and he said they'd taken Karina into surgery but that she was stable." Her parents knew her friends well as Zoe invited them almost yearly to a Fourth of July long weekend getaway at her parents' California home. The house was enormous with two pools and multiple tennis courts and access to the beach, plus two small cottages. It was like a fancy hotel but with no other guests. Her parents also owned a home in DC and, these days, the California mansion was empty most of the time as Zoe's brother lived in a studio apartment in LA pretending not to be related to one of the most influential men in Hollywood and, arguably, the most powerful woman in the US.

"I'll have someone check on Karina's status again. When are

you flying back? I want to come visit you. Reassure myself you're really okay."

"Don't you have a tour of Southeast Asia coming up?" Zoe glared at the latest news helicopter that was hovering at the edge of the no-fly zone the Feds had set up. Too far away to get decent images of her thankfully. The sun was bright, but the telltale signs of a possible storm were forming to the north. The cold front currently pummeling the Midwest might be about to bring some much-needed rain to Arizona. Great for the parched earth. Not so great for evidence collection.

"I can cancel it or delay it by a day or so."

Zoe laughed. "Not sure the leaders of whichever country you bump will be particularly understanding."

Her mother snorted. "The amount of aid the US provides, none of them are going to say a word if we have to rearrange a few meetings."

Except they'd call her mother soft because she was a woman, easily manipulated by emotion. Or they'd label her harsh and uncaring if she didn't stay. Whatever actions Madeleine Florentine took, her mother wouldn't win with the media. Zoe was used to the wrangling of politics, but she wasn't about to become part of the circus. She was hoping to keep her identity and involvement here out of the papers.

"Mom, I get that you're worried. Without your help I don't know what would have happened last night and I am beyond grateful you were able to call in the troops." Emotion hit her all over again and she fought to steady her voice. "But I'm fine now, I promise. Please don't delay your trip for me. I'll see you when you get back. I'm going to head to the hospital as soon as I am released by the FBI to check on Karina."

"Not alone, you're not."

Zoe glanced around, exasperated. "I'm nearly thirty years old, Mom. I'm literally surrounded by legions of Federal law enforcement officers all bristling with weapons. I'm sure that one of them will give me a ride to the hospital."

She watched the calmly competent Seth Hopper direct other agents with a cool, unflappable demeanor even though she knew he was as anxious about his friend as she was about hers. He was still ridiculously handsome but thankfully she wasn't thinking of him like *that* anymore. Nor was she remembering the way water had dripped down the defined muscles of his torso…

"You could have been killed."

Zoe's attention snapped back to her mother. She knew she was blushing from the direction of her thoughts but no one could read her mind, which meant it was okay. She fanned her face. She was simply hot, that was all. "Thankfully, I wasn't killed. The people who kidnapped us are either dead or on the run so that danger is over."

She couldn't believe so many people had died tonight, and for what?

"They won't get far, I promise you that. And I will be talking to the Mexican President later today to make my views crystal clear on the matter."

"Please don't mention me by name. I don't want to be singled out any more than Karina, James, or Fred. And see if you two can figure out a more humane immigration policy while you're at it."

Her mother sucked in a breath and Zoe felt a twinge of conscience that she'd ambushed her while she was off-balance with worry about her child.

"We are working to stabilize the governments and economies in South and Central America. If other countries could get a handle on their criminal gangs, we wouldn't be in this situation—"

"This crime definitely happened on US soil, Mom."

"And that's what worries me, Zoe. That criminals will be emboldened and try to hurt you again before law enforcement can apprehend them."

"Do you really think the cartel are so stupid as to come after me again?"

Her mother released a pent-up sigh. "Not stupid, no, but they are far more powerful than I want to admit and the idea you might be a target because of my position..."

"Mom, I honestly don't think this was about you."

The short silence felt strangely taut. "It was about the work you do in the desert, wasn't it?" Her mother's voice held a familiar disapproving edge.

"Yeah, I think it was. And as I'm finished with my work here for the foreseeable future, you have nothing to worry about. But people like James and Karina and Fred and all the others who look for missing migrants? They need to feel protected by their government. This is not just about me."

Her parents had been thrilled when she'd taken the job in Richmond. And resigned when she'd told them that she was driving her things across the country. Alone. Her father had offered to come with her, but as that would involve a Secret Service detail, Zoe had firmly rejected the offer.

"I have to go. There's an FBI agent heading my way with his notebook at the ready." She winced at the lie but needed to get off the phone.

"Zoe..."

"Yeah?"

"Remember, whatever happens, I love you."

The words were surprisingly sentimental for a woman who wasn't prone to outward displays of emotion.

"I know. I love you too."

Zoe sipped warm water out of a plastic bottle and eyed the heat haze beginning to shimmer from the desert floor to the south. She had a suspicion two weather systems were going to collide overhead in the next few hours, and it wasn't going to be pretty. She should have caught a ride out of here on that helicopter with Agent Hersh.

Unfortunately, she was stuck for the time being. She'd been asked to "stay available" for follow-up questions—as if she could leave without assistance anyway?

She couldn't even walk out to the main highway and hitchhike because the press was crowded like vultures at the end of the dirt road, and she definitely smelled like carrion. Not that she hitch-hiked anywhere. As much as she wanted to believe in the kindness of strangers, she was too familiar with the victims of crime to take that kind of risk.

She crossed her arms over her chest, feeling increasingly frustrated by the boredom of standing here doing nothing. She could have been helping, but the FBI didn't want her contaminating the scene. She rolled her eyes. As if she hadn't been traipsing over the damn scene all last night and yesterday.

The agent she'd offered her help to hadn't taken her seriously when Zoe had insisted she was a trained forensic anthropologist. Maybe because of the way Zoe was dressed—a borrowed long-sleeved base layer under her own sleep shirt, and yoga pants. Dusty boots. No socks or underwear. Face dirty, hair a mess, teeth unbrushed, morning breath probably full throttle.

The lack of autonomy and control over her life undermined her usual feeling of self-confidence.

She didn't like it. Didn't like it at all.

She was reminded of a class she'd taken in college on the importance of identity. She had no money or ID with her. Her cell phone, credit cards and even her driver's license had been destroyed in the fire. At least she knew her own name and could speak the language. And, with a mother in politics, Zoe would never truly be in danger of being sucked up by the system. She was privileged. She knew that. And it was still scary and unsettling to be so dependent on the whims of the federal system.

A newly arrived man, tall, thin, wearing a blue, short-sleeved shirt, suit pants and shiny black leather shoes looked up from where he was talking to a now stone-faced Seth Hopper. The stranger narrowed his eyes and then headed in her direction.

"Miss Miller?" The newcomer's tone was curt.

"Actually it's Dr. Miller," she corrected and was rewarded by a telltale tightening of his lips.

If he hadn't been so obviously disapproving, she would have

told him to call her Zoe.

A lot of guys couldn't handle an intelligent, assertive woman and she was honestly done with pandering to their fragile egos. Maybe her ex had done her a favor by reducing her bullshit tolerance to zero.

"*Doctor* Miller. My name is Jeremy Patterson, Assistant Special Agent in Charge of the Violent Street Gang Task Force working out of the Phoenix Field Office. On the request of the National Park Service, I'm taking the lead on this case." He planted his hands on his waist in a combative stance.

Zoe's brows rose. She wasn't sure how to respond. *Excellent? Bravo?* "Great?"

She knew enough about the FBI to realize this wasn't normal. The Assistant Special Agent in Charge wasn't usually the case agent.

Is this because of who my mother is or because of who the bad guys are?

"Can you tell me exactly what you were doing in the desert yesterday?" asked Patterson.

Zoe blew out a long, frustrated breath. "I've been over this in detail with several other agents already—"

"If you don't mind humoring me..." His smile was flinty. He was mid-fifties. His face rugged rather than handsome with brown hair, liberally sprinkled with silver and cut short enough that his scalp was going to burn under the intense sun. The coolness in his dark blue eyes told her she wasn't going anywhere until he was good and ready.

She quickly recounted what they'd been doing yesterday, finishing with, "The second dead body I found had been moved when we went to check this morning."

"Ah, yes, HRT Operator Hopper informed me about your unsanctioned trip into the desert. He shouldn't have allowed you to leave the area."

She hiked an unimpressed brow at Patterson. "I didn't give him much choice."

The upper lip curled a little as he planted his hands on his hips. "Seth Hopper's a big boy, Miss—sorry, *Doctor* Miller—not to mention supposedly an *elite* HRT operator. Now he has to live with the fact that his, and your, actions resulted in another operator being airlifted to the hospital with a life-threatening injury."

"Operator Hopper applied first aid and carried his colleague to the helicopter, probably saving his life."

Patterson's face remained impassive.

Zoe tried to push her hair out of her eyes, but it wasn't quite long enough to hook behind her ears and kept flopping forward. She glanced at Seth who was talking to a pretty agent who must have said something to make him smile. Zoe ignored the irrational spurt of envy that spiked inside her. She had no right to be jealous. "None of this was Operator Hopper's fault. Agent Hersh could have as easily been bitten in the parking lot—"

"But he wasn't, was he? He was bitten more than a mile from here. I will be making a report to the Office of Professional Responsibility over Operator Hopper's conduct." His gaze dared her to raise her mother's position in the conversation but she had no intention of doing so.

"Well, that seems kind of harsh." Zoe held his gaze and spoke through a forced smile. "Considering the body I found yesterday had been moved, I think—"

"Isn't it likely you failed to locate the exact same spot because it was dark and you were upset from what had happened earlier?"

Zoe frowned. "No. It's not. I'm a trained—"

"Look," the man's expression was so dismissive as to be almost bored. "I know you're on a mission to recover missing migrants which is commendable"—he made it sound like she spent all her time as a volunteer or working for charity, rather than being a professional with a doctorate doing humanitarian work in her spare time—"but we don't have time to search the entire park for unconfirmed bodies that may or may not be here. We have a serious crime to investigate and seven dead men."

Was he calling her a liar?

Zoe strove for patience. "Don't you think the two men shot over there," she pointed west, "could have been involved in moving the dead woman before—"

"We have only your word a body was even there, let alone moved. The chances of it being connected to your abduction are small at best."

"Her," Zoe corrected, clenching her teeth together so tightly her jaw ached.

She thought of the mystery of the destroyed evidence in the burnt-out truck and the man in black's strange behavior. Then there was the evidence she'd collected yesterday. The tooth, the medallion, the cell phone photos that were hopefully in her cloud. If she gave them to this guy, she was afraid they wouldn't be processed any time soon.

If Patterson knew she had them though, he would definitely want them, regardless of his dismissive words.

It was his case.

She stared at him mutely, weighing her options. Weighing how much she trusted him to get the job done...

Patterson stretched out his neck to one side as if he'd slept poorly the night before. "Ever heard of a man named Lorenzo Santiago?"

"No." Zoe lifted her hand to shade her eyes. "Who is he?"

"Only one of the most ruthless cartel bosses in Mexico."

"These were his people?" she asked.

Patterson frowned. "I didn't say that."

Zoe huffed out a soft laugh. "You didn't have to."

He stared at her in a way that made her uneasy. He was pissed she'd leapt to an obvious conclusion. She bet he was a terrible leader and horrible mentor.

"Do you have a photo of this Lorenzo guy?" she asked. "Maybe he was the man in black who came out of the desert with a mule and a couple of handy-dandy grave digging shovels?"

"I thought you said they all wore masks?"

"They did, but I'm an expert on the human body, remember? There's a chance I might recognize him anyway."

Patterson looked skeptical and glanced around as if to make sure everyone was working. "Check out the FBI's Most Wanted list for a photograph, but we know he wasn't here last night."

"You have someone inside his organization? Someone watching him?"

He took what felt like a threatening step toward her. Zoe flinched and then stood her ground and raised her chin.

"I didn't say that either and you'd do well to keep your baseless speculations to yourself if you care about the safety of others."

Zoe ground her teeth. Of course she cared about the safety of others. All her worries about concealing evidence from him evaporated. She'd hand deliver it to one of her friends who worked at the FBI Laboratory in Quantico. It was probably useless as evidence for a trial now anyway as it had been out of her possession for the last ten hours.

"Am I free to leave now, ASAC Patterson? Or would you like me to talk you through the abduction one more time?" she asked with sugary sweetness.

Patterson glanced around and took a step away. "You're free to go. I'll have the first agent who leaves give you a ride to the airport."

"Thank you. I appreciate that." She smiled widely without an ounce of sincerity. She wasn't going to the airport, but she wasn't about to fight with this guy about that in front of his team. He'd double down and probably put her in protective custody. She'd pick her battles and timing and go where she damn well pleased without permission from this jerk.

Patterson walked away and she looked around for Seth Hopper.

A shot of disappointment raced through her when she realized he was gone.

8

Seth jogged down the path to fetch his and Hersh's equipment vests before someone decided they were part of the investigation and they were declared evidence or, worse, fell into the wrong hands and disappeared. He did not want to have to explain to Gold team leader Payne Novak that he'd lost their expensive, specialized gear.

He spotted agents from the local field offices setting up search grids and looking for evidence around the bodies of the two dead men dragged off the trail he and Hersh had discovered earlier that morning. The area was vast and the temperature already becoming uncomfortably hot. It was going to be a shit day for all involved.

He'd reminded one agent at the staging area to have cases of bottled water delivered and some sort of temporary shelter erected as a command post so no one came down with heatstroke. She'd got on it straight away.

That asshole Patterson had tried to pull the senior-agent bull-shit on him earlier but didn't even know how to look after his own people. Seth had let it roll off his back. He didn't answer to Patterson. He'd been following orders and had dealt with tougher men every day in the Teams and at HRT. Patterson was one of those guys who could talk-the-talk but not walk-the-walk and he knew it. Easiest thing in the world was to let the guy give himself a hard-on jabbering on about all the power he thought he wielded while internally ignoring the prick.

Seth had been busy thinking about other things. Like how Hersh was doing, and about the serial killer HRT had chased to ground, and whether or not Red team had found any evidence as to why his former boss and mentor, Kurt Montana's, plane had crashed.

Thankfully, Hersh was fine. Anti-venom had been administered and the guy was resting comfortably. Payne Novak hadn't been happy Zoe Miller had put them in that position, but they all knew the risks when working in the field. Seth had found himself defending her, which had felt a little weird.

Seth was grateful Gold team were on a sixty-day support phase as team members were spread over half the country, but if they needed to mobilize, they could do it. That's why they trained constantly—for the surprises and complications no one ever expected.

He hadn't liked the sight of Patterson belligerently questioning Zoe Miller, but it wasn't his business. She was a grown-up who could take care of herself. Seth had forced himself not to go all overprotective on her excellent ass. She wasn't his business. Not any longer.

No matter that fierce blast of attraction when they'd first seen each other and the slowly growing admiration for her as a person, he couldn't afford to get involved with a politician's daughter. She was so far out of his league as to be playing an entirely different ball game. His career was too important to him to jeopardize for what would likely be a slam, bam, thank you ma'am.

No matter how tempting...

He reached his and Hersh's gear laying where he'd left it in the dirt. He stopped to shake out his kit for any errant creepy crawlies, and then slipped his vest over his head despite the stifling heat. His gaze ran ahead along the path as he fastened the Velcro.

Had someone really moved a woman's body last night?

Why, for fuck's sake?

Why move one body and leave so many others behind?

Unable to ignore the nagging questions he headed down the path for another look. He scanned the ground for any tracking sign.

"Top sign" was anything above the ankle. Unfortunately, he wasn't as experienced as some in determining the age of a broken twig, especially when that broken twig happened to be a cactus. "Ground sign" was anything below the ankle and included everything from disturbed leaves to animal droppings. More commonly, it was any impression or mark left by the feet. He made out hoof-prints and several different sets of human shoe impressions going in both directions.

A lot of traffic for a remote region of the park.

He found the spot where he, Zoe, and Hersh had stopped and peered into the bushes, where Zoe had said the body should be.

He skirted a big cactus, casting his gaze across the dry earth as he squatted nearby, staring at the scene. He recognized the tracks left by Zoe's hiking boots easily enough and saw where she'd stood, and the patterns in the dirt that might have indicated a person had lain there, might have struggled there. Other fresh prints were visible too, overlaying Zoe's and, not far away, more hoof prints.

Faint traces of older spoor were discernible in the dirt—but it was degraded to the point of almost uselessness.

His brows rose.

Dammit, Zoe's right.

A fist-sized rock with a rusty discoloration caught his eye on the ground nearby. Seth took out his cell and photographed the item. He stared grimly up at the gathering storm clouds brewing in the north. Zoe had been spot-on about the possibility of rain too.

He glanced around the endless, silent stretch of desert between here and the parking lot. There was no way this particular patch of earth was getting searched any time soon. Patterson had dismissed their nighttime trek through the desert in search of a corpse as part of some sort of secret agenda Zoe had—and had threatened to report him.

He stared at the rock and twisted his lips.

Zoe had his satellite phone and there was no cell service out here. He made an executive decision to preserve potential evidence and took another series of images of the footprints and the rock in place, using his knife for scale. Then he slid the rock into a paper bag he'd taken from one of the evidence techs earlier and placed it carefully into a pocket in his pants.

A bird called, and Seth stared at the surrounding canyon walls. Did the cartel have men out here, even now, watching them? Or had they all skittered away like roaches?

He didn't know but didn't like the sensation of unseen eyes on him. He went back to the trail and gathered Hersh's gear and headed back to the circus.

———

A noise caught Zoe's attention. A large, refrigerated truck was trundling ponderously along the dirt track. As it came closer, she saw it was being driven by Joaquin Rodriguez, with two assistants from the medical examiner's office riding shotgun. She crossed to the other side of the wide trail and Joaquin halted beside her, lowered the window, and looked over his sunglasses with dark eyes full of concern.

"Are you okay?"

She forced a smile. "I'm fine. A little shaken."

"I spoke to Fred. He told me some of what happened—they burned all your belongings along with the human remains you collected yesterday?"

She nodded somberly. "Yeah. I'm not sure if there will be any recoverable DNA left. I'm so sorry." Those people might never be identified. They might be lost to their families forever.

"This isn't your fault, Zoe. And anyway, techniques are getting better all the time. We'll try with the remains we have left and if that fails, we'll hold on to the bones until a time in the future when we *are* able to extract viable DNA. It's coming." He held her gaze solemnly. "You know it's coming."

Zoe swallowed the knot of guilt that had been eating her up all morning. Nodded.

Joaquin pushed his dark glasses back up his nose. "Fred was pretty freaked out and worried about you." Joaquin glanced toward the FBI agent who was waving him forward to an area in the parking lot they had allocated to the ME's portable morgue. Joaquin raised his hand in acknowledgment and then carried on talking to Zoe.

"It was pretty scary." Understatement of the century. Her eyes traveled over the large truck. "Glad you took my advice."

"I always pay attention to your suggestions, Zoe. You know that."

After being treated like a moron all morning that was nice to hear from someone she respected. He went to pull away but she put her hand on the edge of the window.

"Joaquin…"

He lifted his cleanly shaven chin in question.

"The body I told you about yesterday. I went back this morning to find her again but she was gone, along with the yellow marker I'd left on the trail." She rubbed her arms as a shiver wracked her body. "The yellow marker ended up in the back of James's burnt-out truck. Can you make sure they search for her? I think she's related to what happened here last night."

Joaquin frowned. "Why would anyone move a corpse? Unless you're us?" He barked out a laugh.

"Or a killer?" Zoe pressed her lips together and stared over the dusty landscape.

"I'm relieved you weren't badly hurt." Worry dug deep

grooves beside Joaquin's eyes and Zoe would give anything to have not stayed in Gila Bend last night.

To lighten the mood, she shifted the topic of conversation. "I can't believe Rosy's already four. Wish her happy birthday from me and send the family my love and apologies." Zoe had babysat for Joaquin's kids upon occasion and they were all adorable.

She glanced around and saw ASAC Patterson staring at them like a high school principal looking for truants.

"Do you have the GPS coordinates where the woman was located yesterday?" she asked Joaquin.

He shook his head.

Zoe reeled them off from memory and one of the assistants made a quick note. "I don't think the FBI actually believe me about her. They think she's a figment of my imagination."

"Why would you invent a corpse?"

"Because I'm so flighty and unreliable?"

"Heh, it's probably your lack of business attire and badge." His eyes took in her outfit with an amused gleam.

"Actually," she leaned closer and stage whispered, "I think it's my lack of a penis."

Joaquin whispered back, "How does he know you don't have a penis?"

Zoe grinned. "He made an assumption."

"Tut tut." Joaquin was clearly enjoying himself. "We never make assumptions. Never, never make assumptions," he spoke to his assistants, "not in our line of work."

"In this case he was right but I have no intention of providing empirical data." She pulled her lips to one side. "Please don't forget about the dead woman...and, yes, she definitely presented as a biological female." Zoe folded her arms not wanting to think about what had been done to the victim and yet unable not to, considering she was pretty sure the kidnappers had planned the same fate for her and Karina last night.

Joaquin smiled sadly. "I'll do my best."

"Thanks." She smiled back. It was what he did.

His expression grew serious. He murmured so quietly she had to lean close to hear the words. "Be careful, okay? You don't piss off the cartels around here and get away with it, *entiendo*?"

"I understand." She nodded. There was no one in the world whose opinions she respected more out here than this man—more than the FBI, more than Border Patrol, more than her own parents.

"Call me when you hear any news on Karina." He nodded and nosed the truck forward, past all the other vehicles. The wheelbase straddled the gravel road and soft shoulder, a terrible scratching sound emanating when he got too close to the unforgiving spines of a large cactus.

The sat phone in her hand suddenly vibrated and she stared at it, startled.

She looked around, relieved to see Seth Hopper back in the parking lot with the equipment vests he'd left in the desert after Hersh had been bitten earlier. He raised his head and stared straight at her. Then he excused himself as she answered the call.

"Hello?" she said.

A slight hesitation. "Is this Zoe Miller?"

"Yeah. Who is this, please?" she asked cautiously.

"ASAC Steve McKenzie from FBI HQ. I was looking for Seth Hopper. Is he around?"

"He's heading in this direction right now."

"How are you feeling?"

"Tired. Dirty. Cranky."

"Sounds like me on a good day."

She could hear the smile in the man's voice.

"Yeah, I was going to say I've felt worse but I'm not sure when." A headache was beginning to brew. She didn't remember the last time she'd been in the desert without supplies or her trusty hat. She needed to get out of here, away from the memories of last night and the authoritarian rule of ASAC Patterson—and before the impending storm turned the roads into a rutted quagmire.

"Getting kidnapped at gunpoint out of your bed will do that to a person," said McKenzie.

Zoe wiped her brow, feeling the heat of the desert suddenly pressing down on her. "Definitely not something I care to repeat."

"Amen to that."

Seth reached her side.

"Thanks for everything you did for us last night." Gratitude surged through Zoe once more. "Without the FBI's assistance I can't help thinking the outcome would have been vastly different."

"We were lucky to be in a position to act quickly. Extremely lucky."

Zoe handed the phone over to Seth.

He moved away, obviously not wanting her to overhear the conversation this time around. He watched her out of the corner of his eye.

She leaned against the hot truck and stared out into the desert.

She didn't realize she was beginning to nod off until Seth took her gently by the shoulders and inched her deeper into shade.

He placed a large palm over her forehead and she squinted up at him from under her lashes.

He had the most perfect symmetrical features—strong jawline, high cheek bones, a full lower lip. And those eyes…which veered in color from a pale olive-green to light brown and were probably technically hazel. They looked way prettier than any other hazel eyes she'd ever seen.

An unwanted quiver of awareness shot down her spine at the reminder of how attractive she'd thought he was when she'd first seen him at the motel about a thousand years ago. But, right now, he was examining her more like he thought she was a recalcitrant little kid with a fever.

"You okay? You feel hot. Did you drink enough water?"

"Probably not. I'll grab some." Zoe pulled away from him. "It's been a long night."

She felt overheated all of a sudden. She worked her way out of the arms of her clothing and then fed the material of Seth's borrowed shirt through the neck hole of her t-shirt, dragged it up over her head, all without taking off her own top. She folded the garment and handed it back to him. "Thank you for the loan of your shirt, Agent Hopper. Sorry about the sweat."

He blinked. "I have no idea how you just did that. It was a little like watching a slo-mo magic trick."

His expression warmed and she was once again reminded of her own current inadequacies in the sexy department. It irritated her that she even cared about her looks when so many people had died out here. She took a gulp of water from her bottle.

He checked his wristwatch.

"I'm going to borrow a vehicle from one of the Phoenix agents, pick up the rest of my and Hersh's gear and then head to the hospital to check on him. I can give you a ride if you want. The Secret Service wants to send a detail there to pick you up."

"Yes, to the ride. No, to the Secret Service."

He narrowed those pretty eyes at her. "What do you mean, *no to the Secret Service*?"

"I mean, no. I am not having a Secret Service detail." She crossed her arms over her chest not wanting to fight about this. She wasn't going to change her mind.

"Why don't you want a Secret Service detail?"

"Because I've had one before and I didn't like it."

"I know it can be confining—"

"Try *suffocating*." Emotion burst out of her and she hid it behind a plastic smile. "I'm not wasting taxpayers' dollars. Anyway, what are they gonna do, take turns driving the U-Haul?" She snorted and waved to indicate all the law enforcement people scattered across the desert. "Surely the cartel isn't going to be interested in me any longer. The FBI is looking for them now."

Sweat glistened on Seth's temple and she resisted, barely, from laying her palm against his brow to check his temperature the way he'd done to her earlier. It was probably better if she didn't touch him.

Seth stretched his neck to one side. "You say that like it's a statement of fact even though you have no idea why those men abducted you in the first place. And what do you mean about a U-Haul?"

"I already told you I think they abducted us because of the dead woman I found yesterday afternoon."

"The one whose body disappeared," Seth stated blandly. "What U-Haul?"

"The one whose body someone deliberately moved last night probably because they realized I'd found it." Which meant they'd been watching her in the desert yesterday.

Not a relaxing thought.

"Those two dead guys you found off the trail probably did the manual labor." She pointed west toward the foothills. "I bet their DNA is all over the shovels the man in black gave to Fred and James. I bet Johnny Cash made the dead guys move the woman's body and bury her. Then he killed them because he didn't want anyone to know the location of her new grave. He abducted us to get rid of any evidence we collected." She chewed her lip and squinted against the glare of the sun. It made perfect sense in a horrific sort of way. "That's my theory. That first missing victim is key to your investigation but no one in the FBI wants to believe me."

Seth blew out a tired breath. "Firstly, it's not *my* investigation. I don't work cases anymore. Secondly, the body may have been put on the back of another mule and carted off somewhere where we will never find it. Thirdly, I do believe you. There was a body and for some reason it was relocated."

She blinked at him in surprise.

"Fourthly," he looked around when he appeared to realize he'd raised his voice. He lowered it, leaned closer and, despite a mild expression, seemed to be speaking through gritted teeth. "What U-Haul?"

"*My* U-Haul. The one with all my stuff in it, sitting outside Karina and James's house in Phoenix." She fought off a yawn that was pure exhaustion. Her legs felt like noodles, and it wasn't only because of Seth Hopper's masculine charm. "I need to be in Virginia by next Monday for my new job."

"And you're driving this moving truck?" Two lines cut between his brows as some of his forty-two facial muscles produced a frown.

"Yes, I'm driving." *What else did you do with a moving truck?* She quelled the *duh* that rang through her head. He was probably tired too. "I originally planned to leave today but I need to make sure Karina is okay before I go anywhere."

"Alone?"

He was so close she could smell his skin. He should have been sweaty and gross, but...he wasn't.

"You are driving more than two thousand miles, alone?"

She hunched her shoulders and crossed her arms, aware that the t-shirt she wore was a little on the thin side, especially when perspiration was becoming an issue. She really needed to get out of here.

"I know it's a long trip. That's why I gave myself a whole week to do it. Should be fine if I take it in stages."

The guy was staring at her like she'd sprouted horns.

"What?"

"The cartel sent a hit squad to kill you last night."

Ice traveled along her nerves at that reality check, but she wasn't convinced. "I think they sent a group of people to destroy any evidence we might have found in the desert yesterday."

Seth's pupils flared at her words, and she remembered she'd told him about the evidence she hoped was tucked inside her vest pocket back at the motel. Did he remember? She wasn't about to remind him.

"They got what they wanted. And once they figure out who my mother is I doubt they'll risk starting a war by continuing to attack me. The drug cartels aren't stupid."

He shifted his stance. "Your theory is pure conjecture."

"It's the only thing that makes sense as they obviously didn't know who I was related to and my personal life is too boring for words." Annoyance surged. "That dead woman did not up and walk away on her own. I doubt anyone—other than an ME—would see her and think, oh, I know, I'll take this rotting corpse with me. The people who killed her didn't expect her to be discovered, but I did find her and suddenly the cartel was forced to react…"

Seth Hopper continued to stare at her.

She couldn't read him.

"What?" She finally blew out a tired breath. "Am I supposed to spend the rest of my life hiding? If the FBI does its job and finds that woman's body and identifies her, then I'm pretty sure the cartel won't care about me anymore."

His eyes flicked over her even as his expression remained bland. "How exactly are you going to drive when you don't have your license?"

She shrugged. "The rental company has a photocopy of my license. I don't plan on breaking any laws so hopefully I don't get stopped along the way." She batted her eyelashes. "Maybe the FBI could write me a note?"

He shook his head, staring at the ground as he rubbed the back of his neck.

"Could we take a quick detour to Gila Bend so I can pick up what's left of my clothes from the motel?" Not to mention the evidence. "And if you're going to Tucson, I'd definitely appreciate a ride to see Karina. As soon as I know she's okay I'll catch a ride back to Phoenix with Fred."

"Fred who has the hots for you Fred?"

She rolled her eyes. "Fred who has been one of my best friends for the last six years Fred."

"That guy does not want to be your friend." Seth tilted his chin and raised his brows as if she was being naïve.

She felt the need to defend herself and her friend. Maybe explain the complex feelings swirling around them right now.

"We dated briefly years ago. I think last night he was hoping to rekindle something before I left town." She pushed away from the hot metal of the truck. "It doesn't matter." Her skin was starting to burn, and it wasn't even 10 a.m. "Just drop me at the first town and I'll call a cab."

His eyes grew hard and she couldn't read him. He considered her for so long she became uncomfortable.

Finally, he spoke. "I don't mind giving you a ride. We're going the same direction anyway."

She heard his sat phone vibrating again and watched as he fished for it. He checked the screen before putting it to his ear.

"They catch him yet?" Seth's jaw flexed and his knuckles shone white against his skin. "He's dead?"

Zoe stiffened beside him. Was he talking about one of the two men who'd escaped from the desert last night?

Seth sent her a sideways glance as if aware of her potential for eavesdropping. She did have excellent hearing.

"I want all the details as soon as I get back to Quantico." He grunted and then said, "I can't talk right now. I'll call you back later."

He hung up.

Was that about this case?

Zoe narrowed her eyes at him thoughtfully. "What can't you say to whoever that was that you didn't want me to hear?"

An unexpected grin curved his lips. "I guess you'll never know."

He was extremely annoying. And extraordinarily sexy.

Zoe felt an unwanted surge of lust shoot through her. Then she was struck by a horrible thought. What if he had a wife or girl-friend back home?

Her gaze flicked to his left hand. He didn't wear a ring but then neither had Hersh and she knew he was married.

Seth spotted the look—because of course he did. Amusement flickered in his gaze and part of Zoe wanted to die from embarrassment. The rest of her was too tired to care.

"Come on. Let's track down our gear and I'll give you a ride to the motel and the hospital. After that I'll let you battle it out with your mother and the Secret Service, but I'm not getting involved."

———

Seth wasn't quite sure how he and Zoe Miller found themselves alone in a car traveling back to Gila Bend. The last twelve hours had taken on a surreal aspect to the point he half expected to wake up and have to start last night's op over from scratch.

He'd pulled on a hat and sunglasses to drive through the media scrum. Zoe had bent forward into the footwell, hiding her face. He didn't think anyone even noticed she was in the vehicle.

"How is Agent Hersh?" she asked.

He glanced at her. Her face was flushed from the sun and her bangs were sticking up in some places. From the lack of focus in her gaze he could tell she was exhausted. But there was still something compelling about her that he was doing his utmost to ignore. Not simply the outer package which had attracted him from the instant he'd seen her climb out of that old Ford truck. But her spirit and that sharp intellect which made him wish he could get to know her better even though she was not the sort of woman he usually got involved with.

Not that anything could happen now, despite the fact he was positive she was as attracted to him as he was to her.

Somewhere in the last twelve hours Zoe Miller had gone from being an attractive stranger in a cheap motel, to becoming his not exactly official and yet he knew he'd lose his job if he let anything happen to her, mission. Not to mention someone with direct access to the top tier of US politicians who could seriously fuck up his career if they wished. Those were not his people. His people were the enlisted men and women of the military, law enforcement, teachers, and nurses. They were the poor working class barely managing to scrape by but still managing to have a good time while doing it.

"Seth? Do you mind if I call you Seth?"

He realized she was still waiting for an answer.

"Or would you prefer Agent Hopper? Or Operator Hopper?"

He cleared his throat. "Seth is fine. Hersh is doing okay. The doctors administered anti-venom and now he's being monitored, although all indicators are he's going to fully recover. He's expected to be held overnight and released tomorrow morning as long as there are no complications. I spoke to his wife, and she's decided not to travel down here yet—mainly because JJ, Operator Hersh, persuaded her not to."

Zoe yawned widely. "I'm really sorry he was bitten."

"So is he, but he'll have a cool story to tell the guys when he gets back and a nice set of scars from some nasty fangs."

Zoe stared out of the window and let out a gusty laugh. "It was a hell of a night."

Seth grinned. "It was. I haven't had that much excitement since Washington State last month."

Her pupils widened. They were ringed by irises that were almost turquoise in the morning light. "What happened in Washington State?"

He shot her a look, but he wasn't allowed to talk to strangers about operations. Not even those whose mothers could read the reports.

She shifted in her seat and turned toward him looking intrigued. "You were at that standoff on Eagle Mountain?"

Seth kept his mouth shut and kept his eyes on the road.

"Blink once for yes and twice for no."

He fluttered his lashes at her.

"You're no fun." She laughed.

His fingers tightened on the steering wheel. He could be a lot of fun under the right circumstances. Probably best not to think about those circumstances considering the shift in their dynamic and current close quarters.

She yawned again.

"Get some sleep. I'll wake you when we get to the motel."

"If I fall asleep I'll probably snore and drool."

"Your secrets are safe with me."

She yawned again then seemed to give up the fight. "I don't think I have any choice." She adjusted her seat and closed her eyes. "Don't say I didn't warn you."

"I think I can deal." Seth kept his gaze on the highway, passing a dead roadrunner on the side of the road being feasted upon by turkey vultures.

He was also bone tired. First the ambush and shootout with the cartel followed by the race across the desert to rescue Zoe and her friends, followed by juggling a thousand requests and orders at the crime scene. He wondered again if the events of last night were connected. Was it the same group of criminals or competing ones? It was certainly a lot of activity this side of the border—more than anyone in the FBI or Homeland Security wanted to see on American soil.

Another glance across to the passenger seat told him Zoe Miller was already fast asleep.

He smiled and yawned, then shook it off. He didn't have time to rest. McKenzie wanted him on a flight out tonight so he could go over everything in person at HQ first thing tomorrow morning in a full debrief with other sections within the Bureau as they planned a strategic response.

HRT trained to operate on little or no rest. Selection involved fourteen days of crushing physical and mental challenges served up with an excess of sleep deprivation on a starvation diet. It was based on the same principles originally developed by the British SAS and then adopted and adapted by Delta Force, the Navy SEALs, and many other top tier military units around the world. Pushing a candidate beyond exhaustion, beyond pain, to see how someone functioned under extreme duress. To test their stamina and mental acuity under pressure. To see how individuals operated as a team when they were stripped to their absolute core.

Less than twenty percent of candidates finished the FBI's two-week Selection course. Even fewer were chosen to attend the challenge of NOTS. He was proud to have been one of them. He'd graduated and been picked by Gold team a little over three years ago. It had been his Navy SEAL training that had enabled him to keep going through that general suckfest. The instructors pushed everyone to breaking point, no matter their prior experience. As last night proved, real life operations were sometimes even more arduous and challenging than the fake ones developed for training.

Zoe made a small whimper and Seth glanced at her.

In sleep, her features held a residual tension he hadn't expected. A small "v" had formed between her brows. But considering what had happened last night he wouldn't be surprised if she suffered nightmares for a while.

His fingers tightened on the steering wheel. The fact those assholes had planned to hurt and kill this woman and her friends reinforced exactly how dangerous the cartels were. These groups needed to be controlled, contained.

Memories of his little sister flooded his mind. Seth blew out a long, tortured breath and forced the old memories away.

Anything that damaged the drug trade was a good thing.

He opened the window for some fresh air to help keep him awake.

The hour's drive was straight and boring. He pulled into the parking lot of the familiar motel feeling like it was a year ago rather than only last night since he'd left. The place looked deserted. Nothing like news of the cartel hijacking a group of civilians out of their rooms at gunpoint to put off the customers. The crime scene van and tape probably didn't help either.

Seth pulled up beside the vehicle and was grateful when Zoe didn't stir.

He got out, left the engine running for the AC and quietly closed the door. He showed his creds to the Evidence Response Team technicians. The two of them were almost done processing the three adjacent rooms. Seth explained that he needed any belongings left behind from Dr. Miller's room—or any of the others for that matter—and waited while the guy called his boss for permission.

No reason to believe the items held any physical clues as to the identity of the men who'd taken them last night. If the kidnappers had seen the belongings, they'd have taken them, along with everything else, to burn in the desert.

Seth couldn't help thinking that Zoe's theory about the missing body might be legit...and the fact they'd both collected some physical evidence might give them some answers but might also put them in jeopardy. He didn't intend to mention the bloody rock to anyone except Novak until after it was submitted for testing.

The tech came back to him. "I spoke to my boss and he said it was okay to hand them over as the victims are alive and well and nothing appears to have been touched. I'd bagged the items but didn't examine them yet."

"Victim says the kidnapper didn't see them hanging on the back of the door."

"Sounds right." The guy handed over the paper sack somewhat reluctantly.

Seth took it. "Thanks."

The tech peered at Zoe's sleeping form. "Is that one of the vics?"

Seth nodded. "All four were safely recovered. One suffered a gunshot wound and is in the hospital."

Those facts were all over the news. Thankfully, Zoe's relationship to Madeleine Florentine hadn't been revealed outside the FBI or Secret Service. Yet.

"You secured the surveillance footage from last night?" asked Seth.

The guy nodded. "Owners reluctantly handed it over. I don't think they expected us to turn up so fast to be honest."

Because abductions were so common around here? Or because the cops couldn't keep up with policing cartel crimes and everyone knew it? It made Seth wonder what would have happened to the four anthropologists had one of them not had connections. Seth and Hersh had only been mobilized because of Zoe's relationship with the Vice President. Although Zoe had had a large hand in saving herself with the SOS she'd sent and the fact she'd run when she'd had the opportunity.

She was more than book smart. She had good instincts.

Seth searched for and found one of his business cards wedged into a pocket in his creds and didn't miss the surprised hike in brows when the guy read the HRT designation.

"Can you send me a copy of all the footage you have from yesterday and the three days before? There was a group of law enforcement personnel staying here and I want to check if anyone was watching us or went into our rooms when they shouldn't have."

The man twisted the edge of his mustache. "Will do."

Seth nodded his thanks. Then he placed the paper bag on the floor behind his seat. He had his fingers on the handle of the driver's door when a large black Suburban swerved erratically into the parking lot. Seth's hand went to his handgun.

Then he recognized the driver. Arthur O'Neill. The BORTAC team leader.

The guy looked pissed.

9

Arthur climbed out and stalked toward him. Seth met him halfway.

Arthur shoved him. "You fucking asshole."

The second time Arthur tried to lay hands on Seth, Arthur found his face pressed up against the glass of one of the motel windows, his arm bent high enough behind his back to get his full attention. If he moved, he'd dislocate his own shoulder.

"You're making a scene," Seth said.

"I had a right to know what the hell you were investigating." Arthur was a big man, but he didn't have Seth's training. Seth held the man immobile, wishing he didn't have to.

Seth eased his grip a little. Gave the guy space to breathe. "I was following orders. You need to take it up with your superiors."

"Fuck your orders. Your orders got one of my men killed."

"Bullshit." Seth stepped back and cautiously let the other man go. "All I did was observe while carrying out my duties on your team as required. I didn't let anyone down, in fact, we saved your skin out there." Seth planted his feet and lowered his voice so no one could overhear their argument. "I'm certainly not the Federal agent who ignored a warning about possibly hostile movement on our six before giving the call to go anyway."

Arthur's brows lowered. "I assumed they'd be more smugglers. I expected them to turn and run and consider themselves lucky. I did not expect them to open fire on us."

"And yet they did." Seth pressed his lips together in a closed mouth smile and didn't take his eyes off the other man. "I'm sorry about Ike. I really am. He seemed like a good guy. Shit went down fast. We were lucky to get away without more injuries."

Arthur swallowed and looked away. "Do you know how long Roger was dirty?"

Seth shook his head. "I only know that your bosses noted a marked decrease in success rate over the last year or so and began to suspect the cartel had turned one of the BORTAC agents—and I'm not even supposed to tell you that much."

Arthur's face settled into disgruntled folds. "If I ever get my hands on that little fucker—"

"Did they catch him yet?"

Arthur shook his head. "Not as far as I am aware, but apparently, I don't deserve to know everything. His wife is denying she knew Roger was dirty."

"Of course, she is." Seth rolled his eyes.

Arthur scowled. "She could be telling the truth."

"She'd be a damned fool to admit anything at this point and she presumably knows it. Her husband works for the cartel. You don't enjoy the spoils without getting your hands bloody." If she wasn't involved, the best thing she could do was change her name and disappear forever.

Arthur placed his hands on his hips. "Why do you think they attacked us last night? You think Roger suspected you were onto him or was it supposed to be some sort of diversion from whatever event had you scrambling afterward?"

That was a damn good question. Seth didn't have any answers. "Where did the tip-off about the cocaine shipment come from?"

Arthur pulled a face. "You think they told me?" He snorted then stared through the windshield of the Bucar Seth was driving. "Hey, that's the girl from the motel last night." Arthur nodded to where Zoe slept in the front seat. "She was one of the people kidnapped? One of the ones you and Hersh raced off to rescue?"

It wasn't that surprising this guy had put it together. The abduction had been splashed across the news, but even if it hadn't been, law enforcement personnel talked.

Seth watched Zoe sleep and felt a swell of gratitude that nothing truly bad had happened to her. "Yeah. The other woman who was with her last night was hit by a bullet during the rescue and is in surgery. Two of the attackers escaped. Five suspected cartel members died at the scene." Add that to the number of people who'd died during the attempted ambush on the BORTAC team, and the cartel had racked up a hefty casualty bill for one night of violence.

"How'd you find her so fast?"

"She sent an SOS from her watch."

Arthur grinned. "Good for her. What happens now?"

Seth wasn't sure if the guy was asking about Zoe, Roger, or his own job. "I honestly don't know."

"And wouldn't say if you did." Arthur rested his fists on his thick waist. "Hopefully, we can start making some big busts again now we've got rid of the rat—that fucking Judas. You want your stuff?"

Seth looked at the big guy in surprise. "You brought it with you?"

"Sure. Spoke to a guy name of McKenzie and he said if I was quick, I'd catch you here." Arthur sent Seth a stern glare that had lost most of its heat. "So I was quick."

Seth walked over to the Suburban with him, grateful he didn't have to race all over Arizona tracking down his and Hersh's belongings.

Arthur opened the rear door and handed them over. Seth slung both enormous bags over his shoulder. Arthur held out his hand to shake.

"Don't take this the wrong way, but..." He squeezed Seth's hand firmly.

Seth raised a brow.

"I hope I never see you again."

Seth grinned and took a step back as he watched the other man drive away.

———

Bruno jerked awake and picked up the cell that had started to buzz on the coffee table. This was not the phone he'd taken with him into the desert. This one he kept safe in one of his luxurious homes, this particular residence located on the outskirts of Phoenix. Only one person knew the number.

"Do you know who you kidnapped last night, you stupid fucking imbecile?"

Bruno bristled at his boss's tone but knew better than to express it. Lorenzo was the only person who dared speak to him this way. As head of one of the biggest narco-trafficking organizations in the world, Lorenzo Santiago shouted at whoever the hell he wanted.

But he didn't usually yell at Bruno whose heart rate kicked up a notch. "Some do-gooders sticking their noses too closely into our sandbox." He swung his legs to the floor and scrubbed his hand over his face. He hadn't gotten a lot of sleep lately. And when he did drift off, his dreams had started to haunt him.

Lorenzo made a low sound some might assume was amusement unless you knew him better. Cold fear stole over Bruno's skin.

"Is that so? Is that so. Well, one of the *do-gooders* you snatched out of that flea-bitten motel in Gila Bend happens to be the daughter of Madeleine Florentine the Vice President of the United States of America. Ever heard of *her*, motherfucker?"

Bruno sucked in a sharp breath.

The bitch who'd run.

"You almost murdered the daughter of the Vice President because she was playing in our sandbox? *Ours*? Because, trust me on this, *amigo*, the Americans are under the illusion it is still their sandbox and I would have preferred to keep it that way." A crash accompanied the words suggesting Lorenzo was smashing something.

Not a good sign.

"Boss, I swear I didn't know." Bruno had told Luis to track down the four escapees. He was going to have to fob it all off as a fact-finding mission, rather than a desire to finish the job.

What, if anything, had the blonde woman seen yesterday? Could she somehow identify the rotting corpse?

He doubted it.

"What are the chances of the Feds tracing this kidnapping back to us?"

"There's no proof except for the bodies, boss. Nothing. They may suspect a cartel is involved but they can't prove which one. We could blame it on a faction who went rogue…"

"And make me look weak? Ah, no, my friend. I'd rather face a group of their American Special Forces than look like I can't control my own men."

Because the appearance of weakness led other cartel leaders to think they could take over without a blood war that would cost them everything and everyone they loved. Lorenzo would never allow that. Worse than death was the threat of losing face, and Lorenzo's pride was a beast all its own.

How had Lorenzo discovered the names of the victims unless they were splashed all over the news? Bruno flicked on the TV and saw local coverage of the desert where they'd been last night but as he watched the ticker tape at the bottom of the screen there was no mention of the American Vice President's daughter being involved.

Interesting.

He knew Lorenzo had sources inside the Federal Government.

Bruno would dearly love to know which one had given him this information.

"What about the ambush on the CBP agents last night? Why did we lose so many of our people?"

Because the men Lorenzo had sent had been sloppy? Because the plan to attack a crack team of BORTAC agents wasn't the wisest choice to make? Bruno had made his concerns plain but then he'd used the distraction to his own advantage. It had been Lorenzo's plan and the strategy had succeeded to a point. It had just been extremely bloody.

"They must have been expecting us."

"You think someone betrayed us?" Lorenzo asked quickly.

"Our informant believed the FBI had been embedded with his unit for the express purpose of exposing him. They were not unsuspecting."

Had Lorenzo expected the Americans to lie down and die? They were heavily armed and well trained. Of course, they'd fight back.

"Did you speak to Roger yet? I assume he made it across the border safely."

A small non-committal *hmmph* told him Lorenzo was calming down. "He's safe enough for now…"

What did that mean?

"Don't kill him," Bruno warned. "We'll never get more Federal agents to work for us if you murder those who are compromised."

"We can always persuade people to work for us, unless you've lost your touch, Bruno?" His boss gave a sharp little laugh that crawled up his spine. "Maybe that's what you were doing last night—*persuading* Zoe Miller to come work for the cartel? Spy on her mother. Weaken the border so we can cross more easily?"

Bruno ignored the jibe. "If you kill the CBP agent, people will stop trusting our word. The promise of money is always more effective than threats."

"Then you really are losing your touch, Bruno."

Bruno gripped the cell so tight it was a wonder the thing didn't shatter. One day he would blow Lorenzo's head off, but not today. He couldn't simply kill him and take over. He needed to give people a reason to believe it was necessary first. Show them that Lorenzo was unstable and bad for business. That he was deranged and psychotic.

"Will they come after us?" asked Lorenzo.

Us? Bruno rolled his eyes.

They were both on the FBI's Most Wanted List, although, naturally, Lorenzo occupied a much higher position. But Lorenzo was safe inside his beautiful, highly protected compound in Mexico. Bruno glanced around his home with the massive glass windows and spectacular view of the desert. His only permanent member of staff here was an old woman called Agnes who cooked and cleaned for him.

Maybe that was his own prideful nature showing through? His own inherent arrogance?

"I'm sure they'll be watching for us, boss, as always. It might be a good time to lay low for a little while." Bruno stared at the fingernails of his one hand. Still rimmed with grime from the desert. Lorenzo kept his hands strictly clean nowadays unless it was to make a statement. "It was a risk we took. I think it was worth a few dead men."

Lorenzo grunted like a little pig. "No more fuck ups, Bruno. No more hurting daughters of politicians who can start a war." Lorenzo's voice grew soft. "No one is indispensable. Understand?"

Was the fucker really threatening him?

"Of course, boss. I understand. I would never have touched her if I'd known who she was." Bruno let the other man hang up first and slowly unclenched his jaw. He used another cell to call Luis to make sure these anthropologists were followed but not harmed.

While his boss might sound lethal right now, he would go apoplectic once he realized his little sister wasn't where he thought she was. Bruno needed to erase every speck, every trace of Gabriella Santiago before the man began to even suspect she was missing.

And although last night had been costly, Bruno was pretty sure he and his men had succeeded.

———

Zoe woke as they were speeding down I-10, entering the outskirts of Tucson. The charcoal clouds above them were boiling and angry. She yawned and stretched her arms over her head.

"Oh boy, I was completely out of it." She glanced at the man beside her. "Are *you* okay? You want me to drive?"

He hadn't gotten any sleep last night either.

"I'm fine." He nodded. "It was good you got some rest."

"No kidding." She covered a fresh yawn with her hand. "But I'm in desperate need of a shower and a fresh set of clothes. Maybe even some underwear." She ran her tongue over her teeth and grimaced. "Not to mention a toothbrush." She sat up in her seat. "You know, if you take the exit coming up there's a mall. I could run in and grab a few things... I'll be quick, I promise."

She thought he was going to refuse but instead he glanced in the rearview and peeled off the highway.

Two minutes later they were outside a big box store. Thankfully, it wasn't raining yet. Zoe put her hand on the door latch, then stopped. "Oh crap. I don't have any money."

Seth's mouth curved into a smile that once again turned his rugged good looks into Mr. Blindingly Handsome. Her pulse fluttered even though she told it not to. Darn autonomic nervous system.

"I'll spot you some cash." He lowered a dark brow. "I know where your family lives if you don't pay me back."

She grinned. "I pay my own debts."

He reached into the seat behind them, into a large, black gym bag that hadn't been there when she'd fallen asleep. A plain brown paper bag sat in the footwell behind his seat.

She reached over and grabbed the evidence bag. Opened it up and saw her grubby clothes from yesterday including the hat and vest she liked to wear in the field. A surge of relief hit her and she wanted to hug it to her. Not just because her favorite field clothes were a sort of good luck charm, but also in the knowledge that she might still have the evidence she'd collected yesterday. She might still have a way to identify the missing dead woman.

"How long was I out for?"

"A couple of hours." He bumped up a shoulder. "I made good time."

"With your lead foot and FBI number plate?"

"Something like that," he admitted.

She pulled out the vest, surreptitiously felt the pockets. The envelopes crinkled beneath her hand and she felt the outline of what was likely the tooth and medallion against her fingertips.

Seth stared at her. She'd told him about the evidence out in the desert before dawn. Had he forgotten with everything going on? If she reminded him now, he might insist she hand it in to ASAC Patterson.

"Did I snore? Or drool?" She joked, hoping to distract him. She wiped her hand quickly over her chin just in case. "Or embarrass myself in any other way?"

"No." He looked away, scanning their surroundings. "You did make a lot of squirming noises though."

She could tell from his tone that he was teasing her.

"Oh." She lowered her voice and wiggled her brows. "Well, that's...awkward."

"Not that kind of squirming noise." He shot her an unreadable look and the air was suddenly electrically charged between them. His cheeks reddened and she was shocked to realize he was blushing.

Years spent studying human anatomy and physiology had rendered her almost immune to embarrassment when it came to bodily functions. She was still more than capable of humiliating herself in a myriad of other ways though.

But this man, this elite operator, still blushed when she obliquely referenced orgasms and he was pretty darn cute when he did it. Who was she kidding. He was beyond cute.

She quashed her amusement. "Sorry. I didn't mean to make you uncomfortable."

He turned his head to hold her gaze. "You didn't embarrass me. It was that double whammy of dream sex and the fact I now know you aren't wearing any underwear." He shook his head. "There aren't a lot of men who could survive that combo."

Her pulse sped up.

He sent her a grin that was pure rueful humor. "Forget it. Let's go get you one of those things."

Which one?

Thankfully, she kept that thought locked behind her teeth.

Seth got out and transferred the two kit bags into the trunk—presumably they contained the rifles from last night—along with the two equipment vests. Then he grabbed his wallet and stuffed it into one of his many pant pockets.

She checked the time before she got out of the car. It was a little after one. She pulled on her green field jacket, grateful for its familiar comfort.

She patted her pocket again. The fact she had some physical evidence proved the woman had not been a figment of her imagination. These criminals had probably assumed that if she, Karina, James, and Fred were dead, the cops would take a while to find their bodies—assuming they ever did—and a lot longer to figure out what the hell had happened. And the bad guys would assume no one would think to search for the woman Zoe had found in the desert—especially if she wasn't where Zoe had said she would be.

It struck Zoe again that, if not for the fact her mother was a high-ranking politician, she and her friends may not have lived to see today.

Zoe was incredibly grateful to have survived. But who was the mysterious woman who'd been murdered in the desert and why did someone want her to remain lost?

Seth locked the car.

"Let's go." He urged her to walk slightly in front of him but within arm's reach. His head constantly swiveled from side to side, up and down, as he scanned the area. Looking for threats. She was familiar with the routine from the few times she'd accompanied her mom to campaign rallies where Zoe had stayed firmly in the shadows.

And from the way her ex had acted in their short time together.

Acid churned in her stomach at the reminder of things she would prefer to be erased from her memory.

"Do you need anything?" she asked, pushing aside the feelings of fear and betrayal.

Seth shook his head. "I have my go-bag. After I deliver Hersh's stuff, I'll head back to Phoenix to drop this vehicle at the FBI field office before catching a flight back to DC tonight. I'm good as long as people don't get too close." He pretended to sniff his t-shirt and pull a face.

Was that a warning? Or just a self-conscious declaration? Hard to tell.

She nodded, trying not to feel disappointed their time together would soon end. She concentrated on not holding him up any longer than necessary. He was doing her a massive favor by allowing her to make this pitstop and lending her some money. She grabbed deodorant, toothbrush, and toothpaste. Picked up a charger for her watch. Then she speed-walked over to the sporting section and selected a sports bra, cheap t-shirt, and plain black leggings. Some panties and socks to finish the job. She had a small case of clothes back at Karina and James's house which she'd pick up before she hit the road later.

Seth shadowed her every step.

She checked behind him. "Are you expecting trouble?"

Security guards were watching them but Seth had hung a gold shield on a cord around his neck and no one approached them. Not that open carry was an issue in this state.

He took all her purchases off her as they arrived at the register. "Considering what happened last night and how embedded the cartel is in some of these cities along the border, I'm not taking any chances."

Fear pinpricked her skin.

"We don't know for sure why they grabbed you."

She started to open her mouth.

"I realize you believe their motivation is linked to the identity of the mysterious missing dead woman," he murmured as he quickly scanned the items through a self-checkout machine. "But maybe they wanted you as leverage or for some kind of revenge?"

She guffawed as he paid and they started walking again. It didn't seem likely that they'd target her on this side of the border as opposed to any CBP or ICE official's home or their families.

Unless they really did want to start a war with the US which seemed contrary to good business sense.

She spotted the restroom and put on the brakes. "I'm going to run in here to change."

Seth nodded and then mortified her by accompanying her and standing near the door. He placed a yellow closed-for-cleaning sign across the entrance.

"You can't do that," she exclaimed. "What if someone else needs to—"

"Sure, I can. Hurry it up, Miller."

She gave up arguing and slipped into a stall and quickly stripped off everything and draped it over the top of the enclosure. She used the toilet, aware of the man who'd volunteered himself as her bodyguard listening to every sound. Great. Then she quickly began pulling tags and stickers off her new purchases before dragging on the clean panties, socks, and leggings. Then she pulled the sports bra over her head and generously applied deodorant. She tugged on the t-shirt, toed on her boots after emptying the dirt down the toilet. She gathered all the other things into the plastic bag.

Quickly, she washed her hands and face and brushed her teeth.

In less than five minutes she felt a zillion times cleaner. She waved the double toothbrush pack at Seth. "Want one?"

He eyed her narrowly for a moment. His glance shot to the side, checking the door, and then he strode over to her and she squirted paste on the second brush and handed it over.

He scrubbed and spat in record time and then stuffed the brush into her plastic bag. "Let's go."

Outside he suddenly slammed to a halt. "Let's grab something to eat. I'm starving." He went back the way they'd come. Ducked into an attached fast-food joint.

He went to the counter and ordered food but he seemed spooked and kept scanning the area.

"What is it?" she asked as she picked up their food.

He frowned and shook his head. At first, she didn't think he was going to answer but then he said, "I thought I saw someone watching us, but he's gone now. Let's go."

She glanced around as she followed Seth out the door. Fat drops of rain were starting to splat on the asphalt. "I suspect you might be a little paranoid."

"Let's move it." His eyes never stopped raking the parking lot and when they reached the car, he popped the lock for her to get in, then did a quick check beneath it and inspected all the wheel arches even though the rain was starting to come down more strongly now.

She quickly attached her watch to the charger while she had the opportunity.

"Were you looking for tracking devices?" she asked when he climbed inside, wiping the rain from his face.

"Just checking the tires." His hazel-green eyes held hers, but his blank expression didn't fool her for a moment.

"Sure." She rolled her eyes.

As she opened the big bag of takeout food, she couldn't quite shake the feeling someone was watching her—just like yesterday in the desert. She glanced around. Were they both being irrationally anxious? Was she being naïve to assume she was no longer in danger?

They ate as he drove, inhaling the food as if neither of them had eaten in a week.

Twenty minutes later, having driven a circuitous route, they arrived at the hospital and parked underground. She wiped her mouth on a napkin and stuffed all the garbage into the original sack. She unplugged the charger and slipped her watch back on. Then she grabbed her small plastic bag of belongings along with her hat from the now empty evidence sack.

She climbed out and put the garbage in the trashcan and stood beside Seth as he paid for parking. She was hit by the sudden realization that they'd soon be parting company.

She cleared her throat. "Do you have a card or something so I know where to send the money I owe you?"

His countenance was one of studied disinterest. Whatever had arced between them when they'd first met was definitely dead for his part.

It shouldn't sting. It wasn't as if she wanted a relationship with some big, hotshot HRT operator. She was perfectly happy being single, but...

"Send it to Seth Hopper, HRT at Quantico. It'll find me."

She sucked in a breath that felt a lot like hurt. If nothing else, she'd thought they were becoming friends. "Gotcha. I'll do that."

Ironically, she was pretty sure he'd have given her his number last night at the motel, before he'd discovered who she was related to.

What had felt natural earlier now seemed awkward and stiff. She wrapped her arms around her body in a loose hug. "I was hoping to find out how Agent Hersh is doing. If I can discover which unit he's in I'd like to pay him a visit later, if that's permissible."

"Sure. I'll escort you to the ICU."

His tone was that of a professional stranger and she had to

wonder if she'd imagined the earlier heat and easy camaraderie. Had she been so taken in by his looks that she'd misread him? It was possible. Maybe he'd simply been amused by her ogling him last night, and then used her obvious attraction to manipulate her. Perhaps the supposed *heat* between them was a figment of her overactive imagination.

Humiliation surged through her bloodstream.

"Let's go." He caught her elbow but she jerked away and shot him a look.

He lifted his hand in surprise. "Apologies."

Her throat went dry with embarrassment. They climbed into an elevator and Zoe forced herself to say something. To make things less uncomfortable than it suddenly felt.

"I appreciate everything you did for me and my friends last night, Agent Hopper. I don't know what we would have done without you or Agent Hersh."

Seth frowned as if genuinely confused by her sudden distance. "Glad everything worked out."

The silence that followed was excruciating but she didn't know how to break it.

Thankfully, they arrived at the nurses' desk.

He touched her shoulder to get her attention and she forced herself not to react. He checked his watch.

"Agent Hersh is also on this floor but down that way." He pointed down another corridor. "You're not planning on going anywhere else except to see Karina, right?"

She shook her head. Not yet anyway.

"I'll check with JJ to see if he's up for a short visit."

"I'd appreciate that. Thanks."

"Okay." He looked unsure about leaving her.

"Go, Seth. Check on Hersh while I do the same for Karina. No one's going to attack me in a public place like this."

He opened his mouth to say something then obviously thought better of it. "Don't go anywhere else. We'll figure out the next move as soon as we're done here."

Hah. He meant the fact the Secret Service were supposed to be taking over her security, which simply wasn't going to happen.

"Sure."

Seth walked away with a backward glance and she was suddenly alone.

She genuinely doubted she needed protection. She couldn't imagine a valid reason for the cartel to come after her—at least, not one anyone else could possibly know about. As soon as she was sure Karina was going to be okay, she'd get on the road and head to Virginia. She'd be fine.

Hopefully.

She found James sitting in the waiting room, hands sunk deep into his red curly hair.

As they hugged one another she had to fight tears. "How's she doing?"

James wiped tracks of moisture off his face. His nose was swollen, bottom lip split. "She's out of surgery and she's going to be fine. Surgeon said the bullet only hit fat tissue which will piss her off." He drew in a gasp of air. "They won't let me see her yet..." He hugged Zoe hard to him. "What the fuck *happened* last night? Do you know?"

Zoe shook her head and squeezed him back. "My guess is that certain people weren't happy about the fact I found that dead woman yesterday."

"When you say 'certain people' you mean a drug cartel," James murmured making sure no one could overhear their conversation.

"I honestly don't know but I guess from the looks and actions of those men last night, it has to be."

She thought about mentioning the tooth and necklace sitting in her pocket but decided the fewer people who realized she still possessed physical evidence the better.

Zoe's mood darkened. "I went back to try to find the body after you guys left, but it was gone. Joaquin promised to look for her."

"What the *fuck*?" James exclaimed. He slumped back into the uncomfortable-looking plastic chair, looking wiped out. "It sounds to me as if it might be safer if he doesn't find her."

Zoe sat next to him. "We can't just let them get away with this."

"Why not?" His blue eyes were vivid against his pale freckled features. "They kidnapped us from a busy motel, Zo. In front of witnesses who were all too fucking scared to interfere. We all know these guys don't fuck around and if it wasn't for your mother, we'd all be dead."

"So now we let killers get away with everything because they threaten us with violence?"

He shook his head and then looked away. "Don't be naïve."

"I'm not being naïve—"

"You don't have to live around here anymore, do you?" Bitterness crackled through his tone. "You don't have a wife and little kids the way Joaquin does."

She scrubbed her face with her hands. The thought of anyone hurting Tonya or Rosy or little Isiah made her gut churn. "The FBI are in charge now."

James crossed his arms and barked out a bitter laugh. "Are they? And what happens when they leave?"

She slumped in her chair. The thought of the cartel winning was gut-wrenching. That they could terrify them all to the point of silent obsequiousness was beyond demoralizing. And yet, the idea of anyone she loved being hurt simply because she needed to find justice for the dead... It was unbearable.

Tiredly she asked, "Where's Fred?"

"He went to grab a coffee." James gave her a long, hard look and then relented. He heaved out a deep breath. "Zoe..."

"Don't." She hunched her shoulders knowing what he was going to say but not wanting to hear it.

"He's still in love with you. I don't think he ever stopped."

She closed her eyes as emotion punched her throat. The last twenty-four hours had been a rollercoaster. "I don't feel that way about him. I mean, I love him, but I'm not *in* love with him. It would be like me suddenly desiring my brother. Or you."

James wrapped an arm around her shoulders. "There's a horrifying thought."

She squeezed out a sad laugh. "I know."

Voices warned them that someone was coming their way. The double doors swung wide and a nurse in blue scrubs walked through, his eyes searching for and finding James.

They stood. Zoe gripped his hand.

"She's awake," the nurse said. Relief bloomed. "You can see her for a few minutes."

10

Seth pushed open the door to the private room and saw his idiot friend lying against the snowy white sheets. JJ Hersh looked like an angel when he was sleeping but Seth wasn't fooled on either count.

"I can smell you from here." Hersh cracked one eyelid. "You bring my stuff?"

Seth grinned and raised the guy's vest and go-bag. "Your rifle is in your kit bag." Which was why it weighed a fucking ton. "I haven't had time to clean it."

"What the hell have you been doing all day?"

Seth laughed. "Not sleeping like some people."

"I almost died."

"Sure you did." It felt good to rib the guy now the danger had passed. "I had to deal with an asshole ASAC who wants to report me to the Office of Professional Responsibility for getting you bitten. Probably report you too, for endangering a snake."

Hersh's lip curled. "You have got to be kidding me."

"Nope. Tried to ream me a new one." Seth glanced out the window and the city's downtown. It was gray and overcast. The storm clouds busy unleashing a little fury. "I ignored him. He can deal with McKenzie and Novak. They get paid to deal with the clowns."

"You hear about Livingstone?" Hersh asked with a hard gleam in his eye.

"Damn right I heard."

"I mean, it doesn't change what happened…"

Seth thought about his dead teammates and a wave of emotion crashed over him. "I'm glad you're all right. Not sure the team would forgive me if we lost anyone else this month."

Hersh grinned. "You saved my life, brah. But you also crushed my fucking balls against your shoulder. I told Liv to blame you if we can't have kids."

Seth rolled the shoulder in question. "If you need a sperm donor—"

Hersh laughed. "Ew. Your sperm is not going anywhere near my wife's eggs."

Seth snorted.

"What happened to Zoe Miller by the way?" asked Hersh innocently.

Nice segue. Seth knew what the guy was trying to imply. Hersh knew him too well and had seen how the two of them hadn't been able to keep their eyes off each other in the restaurant last night. So much for that.

When she'd sat in the front seat of the car after telling him she was *sans* underwear and then joked about being sexually aroused in her sleep… He'd gotten hard so fast he'd worried he was going to embarrass himself. He was not used to losing control that way. He wasn't used to losing control, period.

He scraped a hand through his short hair. "She's fine. Held her own with the asshole ASAC who tried to blame her for me getting you bitten by a snake. The guy didn't get very far, I'm happy to say." Seth shifted so he was fully inside the room, put the bags on the other side of the bed near the window and took a seat. "She's here actually. Asked to see you. I think she's feeling guilty about the whole thing."

He'd hated leaving her.

When he'd spotted a guy maybe watching them in that store it had reminded Seth that Zoe Miller was a job, not a potential date. Not to mention way out of his league. He'd decided a little distance would be wise as he was starting to like her a little too much and that was taking his focus off keeping her safe. He knew he'd hurt her feelings. He would have felt flattered if he hadn't felt so damn miserable.

Hersh shrugged. "Wasn't her fault either. I'm the one who stood on the poor thing."

"Maybe the ASAC will find the snake in question and give him an official warning." Seth shuddered. Maybe he'd have to do aversion therapy one of these days. Get over himself and his fear of the serpents.

He clasped his hands together and leaned forward, bracing his elbows on his knees. "I spoke to Arthur. He was pissed he hadn't been informed about our mission."

Hersh gave a wry grimace. "Can't say I blame him."

"Nah. I'm glad he wasn't the rat though."

"Yeah, me too. He's a good guy. Unlike that fucker Roger."

Seth stared at his thumbs. "Why do you think those four anthropologists were abducted?"

Hersh turned his head on the pillow, obviously still exhausted from fighting the potent toxins in his bloodstream.

"I don't know. Maybe as an extra special 'fuck you' to CBP? Roger Bertrand tells the cartel where the BORTAC team is staying. Cartel is watching the place. Someone decides it's a good idea to lift four tourists just after we leave to prove no one is safe from them and to remind people what happens to anyone who opposes them, as soon as law enforcement leaves the area?" Hersh shrugged. "Or maybe Roger noticed you looking at Zoe last night and decided to fuck with your head."

That was a distinct possibility. "Yeah, well, that was before I knew who she was."

"What difference does that make?" Hersh's confusion seemed

genuine. "I mean, I get keeping your distance while she's under our protection, but afterwards?"

"She's the daughter of VPOTUS."

"You're saying she's not good enough for you?" Hersh frowned in contemplation. "You might be right but don't tell anyone else I said that."

Seth didn't want to discuss his love life, or lack thereof. He'd sworn off women for a while.

"It was a bold move by the cartel," Seth said. "And why take the anthropologists back to the exact same place as where they were working earlier?"

"Coincidence?"

"Hell of a coincidence." The fatigue of the day scratched at the back of Seth's eyeballs but he still had a lot to do before he could rest.

"Coincidences happen. Maybe the cartel wanted to muddy the waters with what was happening at the CBP ambush or divide Federal responses?" Hersh didn't look convinced even as he suggested it.

"Seems at odds with sending a 'fuck you' message."

"Could be part of a turf war or internal fighting within the organization. Or one group trying to set up a competitor."

True.

"What about this dead woman of Zoe's?" Seth asked.

"We never found a body. Maybe Zoe got turned around in the dark and went back to the wrong spot."

Seth shook his head. "That's what I thought at first. But when I grabbed our kit, I went back to check out the area again."

"And?" Hersh leaned closer, sensing a story.

"The footprints and sign match what she told us."

Hersh's eyes widened. "You really think the cartel moved a corpse out of the wilderness?"

"I honestly don't know what to think." Seth rubbed his jaw, thinking about the rock in his pocket.

"She still have that evidence she told us about? That might

identify the corpse?" Hersh was obviously thinking along the same lines.

Seth nodded. "Yep."

She'd been coy about her reasons for wanting her jacket. She seemed to believe he wouldn't remember she'd already told him about the evidence. He tried not to be insulted.

"Any idea what she's planning to do with it?"

Seth shook his head. "Presumably pass it to someone who can run DNA analysis or fingerprints or something."

"Maybe she can run DNA?"

Seth looked up. He hadn't thought about that. He didn't know her skillset. He didn't know much about her at all. The realization depressed the hell out of him.

His cell rang. It was McKenzie. Seth answered and grimaced as he hung up. "Secret Service are on their way to pick her up."

Hersh tilted his head. "And how do we think Zoe is going to react to that?"

Seth exchanged a look with his buddy. "Not well, but it's for the best. They can get her safely back to DC and protect her."

"She's going to hate it."

Seth closed his eyes and gently rubbed his eyelids. She was going to hate it but it was for her own good. No point being stubborn just because the Secret Service got in the way of her private life. At least she'd be safe.

"Don't let on if you speak to her before they turn up," Seth warned.

"I hope I get to see the show."

Zoe had made her views on the USSS more than clear. Not that there was anything Seth could do about it. Orders were orders and he had a job to do. The fact something in his chest had started to hurt was irrelevant. Time to make a clean break.

———

Zoe came out of the recovery room feeling slightly nauseous. Karina had been groggy, listless, and obviously in a lot of pain.

A few inches higher, the surgeon had explained almost gleefully, and the bullet could have hit something vital and Karina could have bled out in the desert. As it was, she hadn't lost any vital organs or reproductive capabilities—so her value as a woman was apparently intact.

At the implication, James had crushed Zoe's hand with his own in an effort to hold them both back from saying something that might get them thrown out of the room as neither of them were legally "related" to the patient.

Zoe had a feeling the wedding plans had just moved up to as soon as Karina felt up to it, even if that meant a quick private service before the planned ceremony in a few months.

Zoe came to an abrupt halt when she saw Fred standing in the middle of the waiting room.

"Hey." Fred's expression fell, tiredness letting his emotions show clearly on his face. His lip was puffy and he had an ugly cut on his left cheekbone.

They embraced awkwardly.

"How is she?" he asked.

"She's awake if you want to go in. Surgeon said she should make a full recovery, but she'll be sore for a few weeks. Surgeon is also an asshole, so we assume that means he's good at his job and knows what he's talking about."

She rubbed her bare arms. She'd met a lot of assholes in the last six months. She'd also met a lot of surgeons over the years, and few had endeared themselves to her. She preferred those who used their blades on dead people rather than the living.

"Thank god she's okay." Fred sat down and then looked up at Zoe. "I've never been more scared in my life than I was last night." He shook his head, his hands still visibly shaking. "I thought we were all going to die, Zo. I thought they were going to make me watch them do terrible things to you and Karina while forcing us to dig our own graves like a couple of cowards."

Zoe sat beside him. "You are not a coward. They would have killed you if you'd tried anything."

"Who behaves that way?" His voice was hoarse.

"Monsters."

"I've never felt so helpless or so frightened."

"I know. I'm sorry."

"Why are you sorry? You're the one who saved us."

"I think I'm also the one who put us in danger in the first place." She told him about the missing corpse.

"Fuck." His gaze held hers. "Did you tell the FBI?"

She nodded. "The agent in charge didn't share my views as to the importance of the missing body. I asked Joaquin to look for her."

"Might be better if he doesn't bother."

"That's what James said." Emotion swelled inside her. That poor woman.

Fred cleared his throat. "Zoe, I need to say something. Something about last night."

She looked away, ill at ease. "Fred—"

"Please, let me finish." He grabbed her hands and held them steady on her knee. "I know what you think I'm going to say. Please allow me the dignity of saying this instead." He paused and stared at their joined hands. "We've been friends for a long time. I know you don't love me the same way I love you. I respect that. I promise you I will never cross that boundary or make you feel uncomfortable ever again. Ever. I mean it. You've already dealt with one asshole, and I will not do that to you."

The lump in Zoe's throat grew thicker.

"We're going to pretend I didn't act like a jealous fool when the stud muffin turned up"—she elbowed him in the ribs—"and I'm going to start seriously looking for a girlfriend who isn't you."

She blinked at him. "You've had plenty of girlfriends."

His soft smile caught her off guard. "But at the back of my mind I think I've always subconsciously hoped that you and I might get back together and, without meaning to, sabotaged those relationships..." He shook his head. "I've been a fool and the women I've dated deserved better. It's time to move on and stop mooning over my best friend."

Zoe couldn't speak, instead she gripped his hand tighter and closed her eyes, blinking back tears. Finally, she managed, "I couldn't bear to lose you."

He kissed her cheek. "I will always be here for you as a friend. Always."

She drew in a full breath and slowly released it. "What are your plans now?"

"I'm going to head in and see Karina. Insult the surgeon and see if James needs anything. What are your plans?"

"I was hoping to catch a ride to Phoenix and pick up the U-Haul and start driving to Virginia tonight. I'll fly back the weekend after next to see Karina."

Fred's lips tightened. "Did the FBI finish interviewing you?"

Zoe shrugged. "I think so? What about you?"

Fred nodded. "Earlier but they warned us they might have follow-up questions."

Zoe pulled a face. "It's not like they can't track me down if they want to."

Fred laughed. "Thank god for your mom, Zo, seriously. And the FBI. Otherwise, I don't know if any of us would have made it out of there alive last night." He checked his watch, clearly pretending he wasn't on the edge of tears. "I can give you a ride as soon as I see Karina, if you want. James has a key to my place and can let himself in if he wants to crash. You still okay driving all the way to Virginia alone?"

"Yeah. Should be." She'd been looking forward to it. To the road trip. To the adventure. Now she was a little nervous but fuck those guys.

Seth Hopper appeared at the entrance of the waiting room. He looked wary.

Fred let go of her hand, stood. To Zoe's surprise, he held out his hand to the other man. "Thanks for coming to our rescue last night."

Seth took the handshake and gave the other man a nod. "Glad we could help."

Fred nodded, turned back to Zoe. "Catch me in thirty minutes if you still need a ride." He headed through the double doors that led to the ICU.

Zoe stood and lifted her chin. She hadn't forgotten the earlier brush off Seth had given her. She knew when to take a hint. She smiled brightly. "Can I see Operator Hersh now? I promise I won't tire him."

Seth's eyes were hooded as he watched her. He gave her a curt nod and let her lead the way.

She was almost at the door of Hersh's room—she could see him lying propped up in bed—when she spotted two men in suits stepping out from around the corner.

"Hello, Zoe."

Fear slammed into her heart and she froze as her biggest ever dating mistake sent her a malicious smile.

11

"Ms. Miller," said another man. "You're coming with us."

She found herself forcibly grabbed. Her ex, US Secret Service Agent Colm Jacobs' fingers squeezing her arm so painfully she knew she'd have bruises tomorrow. Not that he'd care.

She was not doing this. She was not putting herself at his mercy or under his so-called "protection."

She fought. Catching her fist on his jaw in an uppercut that would make her kickboxing instructor proud. Colm retaliated by shoving her up against the wall hard enough that her head connected with the plaster with a sharp bang.

He was right in her face and the scent of him made her gag.

"You want us to cuff you, Zoe? Drag you out of here like a prisoner? Is that what you want?" Anger blazed in his dark blue eyes.

The next thing she knew both men were down on the ground.

"Get the hell away from her," Seth said, pointing his gun at them while simultaneously shielding her with his body.

"Secret Service, asshole!" One of the guys on the ground shouted.

"FBI, *asshole*. Show me some ID." Seth flashed his shield.

The older guy on the floor who Zoe didn't recognize eased his sport coat aside and revealed his shiny golden shield. "She's coming with us, son. Those are our orders, so step aside."

"My name is not 'son.' My name is FBI HRT Operator Seth Hopper and there seems to be some confusion about what is going on here. You're supposed to be a protective detail, not the violent criminal apprehension squad."

Zoe slid away from the men on the floor keeping her back pressed against the wall. "I am not going anywhere with you two. I declined your services and you have no right to detain me."

People were running around. Nurses and doctors, calling security in case this armed confrontation turned nasty. Tension knotted in her stomach. Zoe hated this.

Colm climbed to his feet, a dangerous glitter in his eyes. "Your mother wants you secured until the danger is passed."

Secured?

What the hell did that mean?

Rage rose up inside her but fear too. Her mouth tasted like sawdust. "Last I heard my mother wasn't in charge of the Secret Service."

Colm Jacobs made his expression warm and caring but he was a chameleon, and she knew all his personas by now. Most of them were as fake as his blindingly white smile. "Your mom's worried about you. The Director of the Secret Service is also worried about you. Worried the agency failed to identify an ongoing threat to your life. We want you to feel safe. *I* want you to be safe."

A shiver of revulsion raised gooseflesh on her arms. She leaned forward, although Seth Hopper was still blocking her from his fellow Feds.

"*You* want me to feel safe?" Her lip curled and his expression hardened. "So you grab me in a hospital corridor and start dragging me off like a criminal? That, despite the fact I was kidnapped at gunpoint last night. How dare you attempt to snatch me like this." She didn't raise her voice. When she raised her voice, he accused her of being hysterical. But her vehemence was loud and clear. "*How. Fucking. Dare. You.*"

Colm's expression darkened further and she felt Seth tense as if he knew the man would react poorly to being challenged by a mere woman.

An armed man.

A trained armed man with a shiny gold shield.

Her mother's last words to her on the phone came back to her in a rush.

"*Remember, whatever happens, I love you.*"

Her mother hadn't been acting sentimental. She'd been begging for forgiveness in advance. Madeleine Florentine had always liked Colm Jacobs. Zoe had first met the agent when he'd been part of the VP's protection detail. Zoe hadn't wanted to make an even bigger enemy of him by telling her mother the truth, which would effectively destroy his career.

And maybe Zoe had been a chicken.

She'd been scared and hurt, never expecting a woman as supposedly intelligent and independent as herself to end up in an abusive relationship. As if her doctorate should somehow have been protection against the behind-closed-doors behavior of an egotistical jerk.

But she was done with being cowed by violent men. She was done shutting her mouth because some asshole thought he had a say in what she did and what she said.

"I'm giving you fair warning, *Agent* Jacobs. If I see your face again, or if you cause trouble for this FBI agent here, who I think we can all agree is doing a *fine* job of protecting me, I will tell everyone the truth about what you did to me. Everyone. Everything."

His blue eyes flashed with rage.

"And you will deserve all the consequences you reap. You're gonna want to think long and hard about that before you ever come near me again. Understand?"

What the actual fuck?

Seth exchanged a glance with Hersh who was now standing in the doorway of his hospital room holding his custom-made SIG pointed at the Secret Service. He should have looked ridiculous in his hospital gown but the cool mask of the sniper had slid over the man's features and only a fool would doubt the intent of either of them.

"The FBI will remain in charge of Dr. Miller's protection," Seth announced. He could tell she was about to argue so he shot her a quick glance, trusting Hersh to watch the suits and his back. "Unless you've changed your mind about going with the Secret Service?"

Her chin jutted out and her eyes narrowed. She shook her head.

"Let's go then."

The blond agent, Colm Jacobs, with his shiny hair, tanned skin, and expensive-looking sunglasses tucked into his jacket pocket, didn't look so arrogant now. His upper lip curled and he put his hands on his hips in a belligerent stance. Seth recognized the seething resentment boiling inside the man. The anger of being bested by a woman. The wrath that his prey had gotten away.

Despite all his training Seth was shocked by what had just happened. Shocked and enraged on Zoe's behalf. Ashamed that he'd played a small if unwitting part.

He herded her to the stairs rather than the elevator and they headed quickly down to the parking garage. She was shaking and breathing heavily.

The fury that had overcome him when the asshole had slammed Zoe into the wall had overwhelmed him with the need to step in and protect her. He knew Hersh felt the same way although possibly with a little less savagery.

"You actually know that motherfucker?" Seth asked as he

moved them quickly toward the Bucar, sweeping his gaze backwards and forwards looking for threats.

"Worse." Zoe gave a throaty laugh. "I dated that motherfucker."

Everything started to make a little more sense. The stubborn refusal to accept a Secret Service detail. The way she flinched sometimes and then tried to hide her reaction. That motherfucker had abused her.

This wasn't about Dr. Zoe Miller being difficult or a princess. This wasn't her pulling rank or being oblivious to danger. This was highly personal and wholly survival oriented and he could no more abandon this woman to Colm Jacobs than he could to the cartel.

———

Seth called Gold team leader Payne Novak as he gassed up the tank of the Bucar on the highway back to Phoenix. The rain was pounding on the gas station canopy so loudly he had to raise his voice to be heard. Zoe was using the restroom. He could see the exit corridor from here and kept his eyes on it.

"We've got a situation."

"Hersh already told me. Drawing your weapon on two Secret Service operatives isn't exactly being on your best behavior, Hop. What happened?"

"I did what anyone on the team would have done. Zoe Miller is going to have bruises from her brief encounter with USSS. The Secret Service were going to have to use even more force to control her and I couldn't stand by and watch them physically subdue the innocent victim of a recent kidnapping just because they were a couple of arrogant pricks."

The silence simmered. "Have you had any trouble with her?"

"Trouble?" She was trouble all right but not in the way Novak meant. "She's smart, resourceful, and professional. She's a little stubborn but she's not reckless or stupid. She isn't demanding or annoying. She knows what she wants." And what she didn't want, which included two really pissed off Secret Service agents.

Novak grunted. "I remember Kurt Montana going head-to-head with Colm Jacobs a few years back when they were supposed to be coordinating Super Bowl security together. Jacobs was a self-important asshole back then. I doubt he's improved with age."

"He's definitely still a self-important asshole." Seth cleared his throat. "They find Montana's body yet?"

His former boss and friend had been killed in a plane crash earlier this month and everyone at HRT was still reeling from the loss.

"No." Novak released a heavy sigh. "The crash site was a fireball apparently. We have a DVI team out there assisting."

Disaster Victim Identification.

That was the sort of work people like Zoe did. His respect for her grew even more.

"We know why Montana was there yet?" Seth asked.

"Nope. But interestingly we have someone from *Sayeret Matkal* joining the team tomorrow on an exchange."

Israeli Special Forces.

"Working for the Mossad?"

"Probably."

"You think it's somehow related to Montana's death?"

"I dunno but I've grown a little more cynical in my old age and the timing is…well, it's something."

"Colm Jacobs and Zoe Miller used to date and I am not kidding when I say she flipped out when he touched her. Something was seriously off about the whole encounter." Something that had made him want to put his fist through Jacobs' teeth.

"Director of US Secret Service made a call to Ackers demanding an apology and insisting you get kicked off the team after, of course, you deliver Zoe Miller into their care."

A feeling of cold dread stole through Seth and he clenched his teeth. Daniel Ackers was the director of HRT and basically God when it came to Seth's career on the Hostage Rescue Team.

"I told Ackers there was no way you'd have stepped in unless you felt like you had no other choice."

A wave of gratitude flowed over Seth that Novak trusted him that much.

Seth genuinely hadn't felt as if he had a choice. He also experienced another wave of guilt for not warning Zoe the Secret Service were coming. He hadn't wanted her to run and possibly put herself in more danger. But she was a mature adult, and he should have trusted she had good reason when she repeatedly stated she wouldn't accept a Secret Service detail.

Novak continued. "And I spoke to McKenzie at HQ who is now in charge of a task force investigating the BORTAC ambush and the Miller abduction under one umbrella." Patterson wasn't going to like that. "Luckily, McKenzie seems to like you. Said the higher ups in DC don't care who protects Zoe Miller as long as someone does. Ackers agreed."

Seth pressed his lips together. Zoe wouldn't see it quite the same way. "She's still insisting on driving her U-Haul to Virginia. She believes the cartel threat is over."

"She might be right. We've found no obvious reason she might have been a target. No unexplained cash infusions or suspicious cell phone or email activity. No underground chatter and nothing from any informants to suggest anyone in the cartels intentionally put a hit on her."

Seth watched Zoe come out of the gas station restroom and head to the refrigerator section of the store to grab some supplies he'd given her cash to buy. There was a long line to pay.

He scratched his stubbled jaw. She was going to be pissed when she realized the FBI had gone through all her private information, but she'd probably prefer them to the USSS.

"Did anyone find this corpse Dr. Miller reported seeing yesterday? The one that disappeared?" The drumbeat on the gas station roof made it difficult for Seth to hear.

TONI ANDERSON

"Not that I am aware of. Seven dead men in the Sonoyta Valley incident and another eight dead men from the CBP ambush who were all retrieved for autopsy, including the CBP agent. No mention of any females."

Yesterday had been a bloodbath by anyone's standards.

If Zoe was correct, and Seth had a feeling she was, it was going to be more difficult than ever to locate the missing woman, especially with the rain washing away any remaining evidence.

"Look, boss, I checked out the site in daylight when I had to go back and retrieve our equipment vests. I had a quick look around and took some photos of ground sign. There was activity there, but the storm will have washed it all away by now and I don't know if the Evidence Response Team got out there or not." He cleared his throat. "I did recover a rock that appears to have dried blood on it and gathered it as potential evidence."

Should he tell Novak about Zoe's evidence?

"Send me the photos of the tracks, I'll send them for analysis. Hold onto the rock until you get here, and we'll have it processed. Maybe we can figure out why the cartel might have been interested in this mystery corpse. The suits at headquarters are determining our next response. There's a task force meeting in the morning which I was hoping you could attend but I doubt that can happen now."

Seth still had time to catch the last flight out of Phoenix, but he had an impending sense of doom that he was shit out of luck when it came to flying home.

"As you personally volunteered HRT for Dr. Miller's security detail, you're now officially in charge of getting her back here safely."

"Just me?" Part of him was annoyed but, if he was honest, another part of him was excited at the prospect of spending more time alone with her even though it was a totally bad idea.

"We're a little short on personnel otherwise I'd send down a team. The new recruits could use a little close protection training." Seth could hear gunfire in the background. Novak was either near the range or the Shooting House. "All indications are the cartels are scrambling to lay the blame on each other. No one wants to claim responsibility for Miller's abduction, which makes the experts in the BAU think she wasn't targeted for political reasons. Now the cartels know who she is, it makes another attack less likely."

Seth thought about his little sister. "I wish we could shut those motherfuckers down once and for all."

"Someone else would rise up and take their place. They always do," Novak muttered bitterly.

Fatalistic but true.

"The evidence tech at the motel sent me the surveillance footage from the abduction." Seth eyed the black clouds overhead. "I had planned to take a look at it but now—"

"Send it to me. I'll have someone take a look at it here."

Seth was all out of excuses.

"You have two days to make the 33-hour drive, Seth. The task force wants to question you both on Wednesday morning in DC." Novak lowered his voice. "I'm thinking you might be more successful at avoiding detection while posing as a couple as opposed to a group of highly visible operators squashed into a truck."

That was true. At the first sign of any visible security these days, out came the cell cameras, and covert operations were splashed all over the internet. They might have more chance of staying under the radar if it was only the two of them.

"As this is a last-minute op, feel free to improvise—within reason."

Seth grinned. Permission to bend the rules. "Roger that."

Zoe came out of the store, dashing through the rain until she was back under cover, holding a couple cans of soda, two packs of sandwiches, and two packets of chips.

She smiled at him, looking a little anxious before climbing into the passenger seat. He knew she was still unnerved by what had happened at the hospital and was desperately trying to pretend everything was all right. It was ironic she seemed more scared by her protection detail than by the freaking cartel.

"Seth?" Novak said.

"Yeah?"

"Be careful, yeah? If we're wrong and the cartel is still after Dr. Miller, then they won't care about going through you to get to her. These fuckers believe they're above the law."

Seth had no illusions about this particular brand of criminal.

"I'm not going to let them get to her, boss. I'll call you later after we hit the road." Seth put the nozzle back in the pump. He'd already paid with a credit card. He climbed in. Glanced at his passenger who was biting her lower lip with worry.

"Buckle up." *Ready or not, we're going for a ride.*

———

Zoe directed Seth Hopper to Karina and James's new home in the 'burbs. They'd saved it from soullessness with incredible metal sculptures that Karina's mom had made. Combined with a knack for desert gardening that had skipped Zoe despite all her best efforts, the property looked slightly avant-garde in the boring neighborhood.

Zoe's distinctive orange and white rental truck sat in the driveway.

She and Seth hadn't spoken since they'd left the gas station. They'd eaten in companionable silence as the rain had pounded all around them, the windshield wipers going at full pelt, the much-needed deluge brightening the landscape and clearing away the usual haze of dust.

She wasn't sure what was going to happen now, and half expected more Secret Service agents to be waiting at Karina and James's home to arrest her or something, but there was no sign of them from the outside.

She'd ignored a series of frantic texts from her mother. Instead, she'd contacted her father to tell her mom to back off. Zoe was still furious, but that was a step up from overwhelming terror and incandescent rage.

Seth drove past the property and around the block.

"You missed it." She twisted in her seat with a frown.

Seth took a few different turns and then ended up on a street that backed onto her friends' place.

"What are we doing here?" she asked as Seth stared at the house.

Black clouds obliterated the sun and it looked more like nighttime than early evening. Seth hadn't slept but you'd never know by looking at him. His black t-shirt was a little dusty. The first hint of scruff was appearing on his jaw. But his gaze was sharp as a tack.

"Can I fit this vehicle into their garage?" he asked.

The loss of James's truck hit her all over again. Maybe a small thing in the scheme of things, but important and impactful for James. She wondered what he'd get from the insurance company. Probably not enough to replace it. She'd talk to Fred, and they'd see what they could pool together.

Seth was staring at her expectantly.

"If I move Karina's car onto the drive, sure, but why? I thought you were heading straight to the field office."

A deep frown marred his dark brows. "Did you really think the powers-that-be were going to let the daughter of the sitting Vice President wander around without any security after there was a direct attempt on her life from a foreign entity?"

"Well, when you put it that way." She shivered. Looked away. "I figured the sooner I got on the road the less likely anyone was going to care about me one way or another."

"Zoe." His tone was chiding.

"What?" she protested.

"Denial is not a strategy." Seth shook his head and she found her heart beating a little faster.

What was he planning to do? "It works for me."

"Not today. We have two choices."

"We?" she asked warily.

"Yeah, since I stepped in and assaulted two Secret Service agents on your behalf, you and I are now a 'we.'"

"Oh." She ignored the warm, fuzzy feeling that thought gave her. She'd been so grateful he'd supported her decision at the hospital that she hadn't really thought about how the incident might impact him professionally. "I didn't mean to get you into trouble."

His grin was sharp. "I got myself into trouble."

"I definitely contributed." Her mouth went dry at the thought of the repercussions Colm Jacobs might attempt to inflict and the lies he'd tell... "I will make a full report and tell people exactly what happened—"

"Did he hit you?" Seth's question was direct as a punch and demanded a no-bullshit answer.

Zoe turned away from him and wanted to deny the ugly reality of that disastrous relationship. She let out a shuddering breath. "Once. He hit me once. And I immediately ended things, much to his annoyance."

Seth swore and looked away.

"Before that it was subtle things like discounting my opinion, berating me in public, twisting my arm or pushing me just a little harder than necessary."

"I hadn't appreciated there was an acceptable way of pushing a woman unless it was to save her life," Seth said with an edge.

"Oh, he made out it was all done to protect me, even though he was never my bodyguard. I think that's part of his spiel or self-delusion." The memory of the look on his face still haunted her. "At first, he didn't believe it was over—I mean, I was his meal ticket to the big leagues. Then when he figured out I was serious, he threatened that if I said anything, if I *lied* about him he'd take me down." He hadn't defined exactly what that meant but Zoe knew. He'd hurt her if he had the opportunity. She hugged herself. She worried he might kill her if he thought he could get away with it. "He said he'd tell everyone I was lying and have his fellow Secret Service agents corroborate his account of my *personality disorders.*"

Acid crawled up her throat and she swallowed repeatedly to get rid of the sour taste in her mouth. She didn't trust anyone in that agency. Not anymore.

She hadn't appreciated her fingers were all tangled up in a tense knot until Seth put a warm hand over both of hers.

"If you make a statement about what happened at the hospital are you willing to say why you were genuinely afraid? I mean, I'm happy if the fucker is exposed to the world, but you have to be prepared for that sort of scrutiny and a degree of blowback. We all know this country doesn't deal well with women who accuse men of being abusive, not unless there are ten other victims to back them up, and sometimes not even then."

She shook her head and fought off a wave of nausea. "I'll do whatever it takes to make sure you aren't unfairly treated. You were protecting me, and I appreciate that more than you will ever know."

"I'll be fine." He removed his hand and put it back on the steering wheel. His knuckles gleamed white beneath the skin proving he wasn't as relaxed as he pretended to be. "But I do wish I'd hit the motherfucker."

"Me too." She shook her hand. That uppercut had been worth it, but her fingers were still sore. A shudder ran up her spine at the memory of the look in Colm's eyes that had promised retribution. "He did not like the fact that I hit him, not at all."

Seth's pupil's flared and his jaw tightened in anger.

Zoe drew in a long, deep, steadying breath. "I appreciate you stepping in the way you did. I wish it hadn't been necessary. I can't believe my mother set me up like that."

Seth stared out at the sheets of rain. "Well, as a consequence, I have been instructed to get you to DC for an interview with a joint task force by Wednesday morning at the latest. Until then, you and I are definitely a 'we.'"

This had not been her intent. She didn't know what to say.

He turned to her. "Now the easy option would be for you and I to drive to the airport and catch a flight to Virginia or DC tonight—"

"But what about all my belongings? I'm moving into a new place. I'd only have to come back in a couple of weeks and drive it back anyway and I don't have time. The rental truck is packed and already cost a fortune. I don't see how the danger from the cartel will be any different then as it is now?"

"You could pay someone to drive it out to you."

"Ha. One, believe it or not, I can't afford it. Two, what's to stop the driver being someone from the cartel who then knows where I live and has access to my stuff?"

Seth's expression seemed resigned. "The other option is I accompany you on the drive. We should be able to do it within that timeframe easily enough."

Zoe stared at him. "Isn't that taking you away from other important duties?"

Seth sighed. "Not really. I do have a gigantic stack of paperwork regarding last night to fill out but I can do that in the truck as easily as at my desk."

"Wait." Zoe put her hand on his forearm and quickly withdrew her fingers from his shockingly hot skin. "What about the others?"

"What do you mean?"

"I mean, if you think I might be in danger then my friends might be in danger too. If I require protection, then they need to have it also."

He assessed her with those distinctive hazel-green eyes and seemed to realize he either had to concede she wasn't actually in danger or treat the four kidnap victims equally. With a sigh he made a phone call and arranged for the local FBI field office to put agents on each of her friends, including Karina in the hospital.

Zoe wished she had her own cell phone so she could call them. She needed to get on that.

He hung up. "I take it we're going with Option B?"

"I'm definitely doing Option B but I still don't see why—"

"Zoe."

She blinked. "What?"

"Give it up and let's get this show on the road."

"Tonight? I was going to grab a few hours' sleep—"

"You can sleep in the cab." He nodded toward the house. "Listen up. This is the plan. I go inside and make sure the place is empty. Then, when I give you the signal, you come inside and grab your belongings. I'll check the truck for explosives or tracking devices—just to be on the safe side," he said in response to her startled gaze. "We leave this vehicle in the garage after I remove the plates. The FBI can pick it up." He tapped the steering wheel to indicate the car they were in. "A few miles out of town I'll switch them with the plates on the truck so the cops don't stop us. We'll find a motel when we're a couple of hours away and then we'll both get some sleep."

Zoe felt tired to her bones but if she wanted her belongings, and she really did, then Seth Hopper appeared to be her best option of getting to Virginia without her mother calling out the National Guard. On top of everything else, she didn't want her colleagues in Richmond to figure out who her parents were. It was a small thing but she wanted to build a career on her own merits, not be judged by her successful parents.

"One more thing." Seth eyed her like she might balk at whatever this last thing might be. "We'll pose as a married couple to throw off suspicion and share a room. Think you can handle that?"

She held his intent stare for what felt like forever. The plan made sense even if the idea of spending more time with this man filled her with a jumble of unwanted nerves.

"Zoe?"

She nodded. "I can handle that."

———

Luis stood on the mat in the mudroom looking like a drowned rat.

Bruno walked up to his brother and gave him a quick hug. "What did you discover?"

The rain was good luck for Bruno as it would wash away lingering signs of their activity in the desert. Another sign of approval from up high.

Luis eyed the scab on Bruno's cheek but didn't ask how the injury had occurred. No one in the cartel liked questions.

"The dark-haired woman suffered a minor gunshot wound and is in the hospital in Tucson. The two men are both with her. They expect to release her the day after tomorrow. The blonde had an altercation with two government agents at the hospital and then left with another Federal agent, possibly one of the ones who ambushed us in the desert last night. According to my source, there's an FBI agent in the hospital receiving treatment for a snake bite."

Bruno smiled as he paced back to the kitchen and into his living room. His housekeeper had left hours ago so they were alone.

He didn't believe in having an entourage. He didn't believe in that many people knowing where he lived. Lorenzo, however, lived behind compound walls and only left home with an army of armed guards.

Bruno pressed his lips together. Many of his most trusted soldiers had died last night. Because that bitch Gabriella had baited him like he was a little boy she could order around. She'd begged him to help her cross the border without her brother knowing. Then she'd complained every step of the way.

The little princess had expected a carriage or something.

Bruno stood in front of the huge windows and watched the rain streak the glass and blur his reflection with the lights beyond.

Luis said his men had destroyed everything the four do-gooders had brought out of the desert that day including the old truck. The only thing Bruno couldn't erase was the memory of whatever the blonde woman had seen. But could those memories be enough to identify a victim? No. They couldn't.

Bruno had gotten a brief glimpse of Gabriella's face last night and if he hadn't already known who she was, he wouldn't have been able to identify her.

No, the danger was over. Best to beat a retreat and let the four lucky survivors enjoy their miracle escape. The less interaction now the better. But there were things he still wanted to know.

"How did Santiago discover the identity of Zoe Miller before I did, do you think?" He watched Luis's reflection in the glass. They were brothers but Lorenzo Santiago demanded fealty in the way of ancient kings and mobsters. You could only pledge allegiance to one person in the organization and that person had to be Lorenzo Santiago.

Confusion crossed his brother's features. "I don't understand."

"The press never released the identities of the four kidnap victims, but Lorenzo was able to tell me her identity. Did you know it?"

Luis shook his head. "I didn't know it until you told me. I don't know how he knew. I guess he must have a source inside the police department or the FBI."

Bruno nodded thoughtfully. He knew his boss had connections the same way Bruno had connections, but this was a contact Lorenzo hadn't shared with him and Bruno did not like the implications of that. He did not like to be outside the loop, not when the loop could turn into a noose at any moment.

"Do you know where she went? This Zoe Miller?"

Luis pulled out a phone and showed him the screen which showed two indistinct figures getting into a vehicle in an underground parking lot. "When she left the hospital, she and the man got into a Buick with government plates and headed back to Phoenix. I lost them shortly after we arrived in the city as the guy started doubling back and looking for a tail and you told me not to get made."

At Bruno's silence Luis continued, "I assume they were headed to the FBI offices or the airport."

Bruno nodded thoughtfully. "Do we know where she lives?"

"She just started a new job. Not sure where she is living yet." Luis gave him the name of the university where she worked.

Virginia. Bruno pulled a face. He had no desire to visit Virginia.

Bruno scrolled back through the images Luis had taken today.

He paused, his finger hovering over one of the pair outside a big box store. He stretched the image wider and zoomed in on the girl.

"What is this?" he demanded.

Luis looked over his arm and shrugged. "They stopped for some supplies before going to the hospital. The FBI agent seemed to sense someone was watching them so I had to hang back."

Bruno flipped back another couple of images and stared at one where Zoe Miller climbed out of the car. White-hot rage smoldered inside him. He thrust the cell back at his brother. "Do you notice anything about this photograph, Luis?" .

His brother looked puzzled. "No. I mean, I considered breaking into the trunk to search it, but you told me to keep a low profile—"

"What is she wearing, Luis?" Bruno's hands shook with the force of emotion that was coursing through his bloodstream.

Luis frowned clearly perplexed. "A t-shirt and an ugly green vest."

Bruno pulled out his own cell. Pulled up the photograph that one of his spotters in the desert had sent him yesterday, the image that had catalyzed everything that had happened since.

It was a long-distance shot, taken from the foothills, of a woman in a hat and olive-green utility vest who stood in the desert taking photographs of something on the ground. In another image she was placing something in her pocket, in another she carried a box.

Cold Deceit

Sweat beaded on Luis's temple. "I see she is wearing the same vest."

Bruno grabbed his brother by the throat. "You told me you destroyed everything they took from the desert."

Luis scrambled as Bruno twirled him and slammed him against the glass which reverberated from the impact. Luis pulled at Bruno's hands. "We did, I swear. I checked her room myself."

Bruno dug his nails into his brother's throat.

"I must have missed something. I realize that now." Luis fought for air. "I'm sorry, Bruno. I'm sorry. I can fix this."

Fury wanted to consume Bruno. He wanted to lash out and kill. Destroy everyone and everything that stood in his way. Luis's black eyes were bulging and he was turning deep red.

Bruno thrust the young man away from him. He would never kill his little brother. He loved him too much. But he couldn't afford any loose ends.

He pressed the tips of his fingers to his forehead.

It might mean nothing.

It might mean everything.

He couldn't take the chance.

"I'll fix it, Bruno. I'll hunt her down and find the jacket and destroy it."

It wasn't the jacket so much as what might be in the pockets. Bruno stared at the shiny marble floor of his beautiful home. It was too big a risk.

He shook his head. "I want her dead."

Luis froze. "Santiago said not to touch them…"

Bruno wanted to scream that he didn't care what Santiago wanted, but he couldn't. Those words would be a death sentence.

Instead, he said softly, "That is why we are going to have to make sure it looks like an accident." He held Luis's black eyes, so like his own. "So no one ever finds out how badly you fucked up."

159

12

Seth had headed away from the border and, therefore, cartel influence, driving northeast rather than back to Tucson and taking I-10. Unfortunately, they'd run into the storm that had settled over the Midwest twenty-four hours ago and showed no signs of abating.

Under normal circumstances he might have pushed on, but both he and Zoe were exhausted, and it wouldn't be prudent to travel any farther in the dark in these conditions.

Apparently, everyone in New Mexico had forgotten how to drive in the white stuff.

It was almost midnight as he reversed the U-Haul a few doors away from the motel room he'd just checked into, on the outskirts of the small city of Gallup, New Mexico. He took it slowly, wary of the icy surface, conscious that tires in these conditions were about as grippy as lube.

Zoe looked around and a small smile danced over her features, breaking out the dimples he'd first noticed last night. "At least it's pretty."

He grunted noncommittally.

The combo of the fairy lights strung up around the motel and the virgin snow was picturesque, some might even say romantic, but he was a California boy at heart, and the snow didn't really do it for him. On the plus side, at least he wasn't freezing his nuts off in the desert tonight.

Steam rose up as snow melted on the hood of the truck. Zoe went to get out but he stopped her. "Wait."

Her eyes widened as he checked his pistol and then pulled his carbine from behind the seat where he'd placed it for easy access.

"Are we expecting trouble?" she asked, glancing around nervously.

"Not really but that's exactly when I need to take extra precautions." He held her gaze as he slipped his rifle into the heavy kit bag he'd hauled over into the front seat. "And anyway, I can't leave the weapons in the vehicle and risk them falling into the wrong hands, now, can I?"

The crime rate in this city was well above the national average.

"I guess not." Dark shadows had formed under her eyes revealing a bone-deep exhaustion.

He thrust a ballistic vest at her.

"You cannot be serious." She glanced over her shoulder at the motel building. "It's fifteen feet away."

"It's unlikely anyone knows we're here," he conceded, "but it's possible someone followed us."

"Doubtful."

He'd been looking for tails the whole way.

"But not impossible. We'll need the vests when we leave as someone could identity the truck and catch up to us while we sleep. May as well put them to good use and keep me happy." He shot her what he hoped was a winning smile.

She rolled her eyes as she pulled it over her head, muttering obscenities under her breath the whole time. He did love a woman who knew how to curse. Reminded him of his great uncle who served in Burma during World War II. The guy had the vocabulary of a sailor with the disposition of a stoner. Seth had loved the guy. He'd been blessed with his adopted family. It didn't lessen the questions about his birth parents, but he knew how fortunate he'd been to land in a good place.

He checked for footprints on the sidewalk, but it didn't look like anyone had visited their designated room since the snow had started to fall. As he'd only chosen where they were going to stay ten minutes ago, he figured they were as safe as could be expected.

He stuck his ball cap on Zoe's head and she chuckled reluctantly. She had her overnight bag ready to go now and touched the handle again.

"Wait. Give me thirty seconds to sweep the room. Stay here. Do not go anywhere."

He jumped out and quickly cleared the motel room two down from where he'd parked the truck. Once he was satisfied the location was safe, he strode back to the vehicle and opened her door, keeping Zoe between him and the truck as he shadowed her into the motel.

"I'll be right back," he said.

He made another trip to the truck and quickly made sure there was nothing worth stealing in the cab and that the vehicle and cargo area were locked up tight. It was the best he could do.

He tromped up and down the path so that tracks would be harder to read. Then he headed inside the motel room and locked the door, wedging a stout chair under the knob. Finally satisfied, he turned around and stopped short.

There was only one bed.

———

Zoe came out of the bathroom to grab her wash bag and saw Seth standing there, mouth open, staring in horror at the king-size bed that occupied most of the space. When she'd come inside, she'd wondered if he'd done it deliberately to maintain their cover as a couple but from the stricken expression on his face it was obvious that was not the case.

His eyes met hers. "I swear I asked for two doubles."

Her lips twitched. "And the receptionist lied?"

"She barely glanced up. She looked about seventeen and was busy watching cat videos online. I'll go back—"

"How suspicious will that look for a married couple to be that desperate not to sleep together?" She'd dumped the ballistics vest on the chair as soon as she'd entered the room. Now, she picked up her wash bag and a clean sleep shirt.

"I guess it wouldn't exactly be blending in or keeping below the radar to insist on changing rooms," Seth admitted. He glanced at the bed again, resignation written on every line of his face. "I'll sleep on the floor."

"Oh my god, no." She shuddered with revulsion at the icky brown carpet. "I'm exhausted. You're exhausted. I'm perfectly capable of not ravishing your incredible body in your sleep."

"It's not that." His eyes held hers. "You aren't worried... You know. About me..." He trailed off. Clearly unable to say the words.

She didn't get it. Until she did.

"That you might attack me? Jesus, Seth. You've spent most of the last day showing me how brave and honorable you are." The lightbulb inside her head flared to life. "Colm Jacobs never sexually assaulted me if that's what you are worried about. I won't freak out in my sleep. I am sure it would have been a possibility if we'd carried on dating for more than a couple of months or if I'd stuck around after that first hit."

Seth's gaze narrowed.

"I appreciate your concern for my physical and mental well-being but it's a big enough bed for both of us."

Zoe was hoping for some easing of tension but his shoulders remained rigid and he was clearly uncomfortable.

"Look, sorry, I shouldn't focus on my experience." Maybe he'd been a victim of abuse. "If it bothers you this much, we can absolutely go ask for another room."

"No." He shook his head and took another reluctant step

inside, tossing his ballistics vest onto the sideboard. "It doesn't bother me. I needed to be sure it was okay with you. Go shower. I'll jump in next." He sniffed his t-shirt. "I still stink from last night's truck fire. We'll get a good night's rest and hopefully the snow will stop soon, and the plows will clear the roads by morning."

Her heart gave a little flutter.

She was starting to like Seth Hopper.

Really like him.

And not just the fact that he was hot, but his considerate nature and calmness in the face of chaos. Several times today she'd thought she was going to lose it completely and he'd been there to save the day. How did you repay someone for that?

This whole scenario was probably not what he'd had in mind when he'd stepped in with the Secret Service. She owed it to him to be professional and not cross any lines. No matter how much she was tempted.

She watched him retrieve the lethal looking rifle from his massive bag which reminded her exactly why he was here— because last night someone had tried to kill her, and it was his job to protect her. He wasn't here because he liked her. The heat that had burned when they'd first seen one another had clearly been pushed aside so he could do his job professionally. The fact she didn't think there was any danger now was irrelevant.

She shook herself out of her stupor and went into the bathroom and quickly stripped. She turned on the shower and washed the dirt and grime of the last twenty-four hours off her skin and out of her hair. Despite a couple of exhausted catnaps, she was so tired there was nothing on her mind except sleep.

They had an early start in the morning and a long drive ahead.

She quickly toweled off and dried her hair with the hairdryer attached to the wall. Finally, she dragged on her nightshirt and clean panties feeling a little underdressed to confront Seth, even though she'd worn similar clothing for much of the day. She opened the bathroom door to find him sitting in a chair facing the main entrance. His automatic rifle rested across his lap.

"Bathroom's all yours," she piped brightly. Too brightly.

He stood and pressed his handgun into her palm. He grabbed a toiletry bag and small handful of clothes off the dresser, taking his rifle for company as he took his turn in the shower.

Zoe stared at the heavy gun in her hand and felt a cold wave of dismay roll over her flesh.

She'd almost died last night.

Her mouth went dry.

She'd almost ceased to exist.

It was a sobering thought. As much as the processes after death didn't scare her, she wasn't ready to give up living yet. She carefully placed Seth's gun on the nightstand and turned out the bedside lamp.

Bright reflective snow shone through the drapes and lit the room with pale gray shadows. Zoe slid her toes between the cool sheets and laid her head on the pillow. The moment she closed her eyes she fell fast asleep.

———

Seth wasn't sure what woke him, but his eyes opened, and he was instantly alert. He was in a motel room—yet another in a seemingly endless supply.

For a moment he couldn't remember where he was or what he was doing here. Then he felt the warmth of another body in bed with him and he knew.

Zoe Miller.

He was sharing a bed with Zoe Miller.

Daughter of the Vice President of the United States of America.

The woman he hadn't been able to take his eyes off when he'd first seen her. A woman so far out of his league he was surprised someone didn't break down the door and arrest him just for breathing the same air as her.

And he knew that was his own bullshit talking, the prejudice he was carrying around in his brain, the byproduct of being abandoned as a baby and growing up without any idea of where his genes fit into this world. Still, his feelings stemming from an anchor-less biological heritage were very real.

His adoptive father had told him years ago that you made your own family. After a few rocky years, Seth had found his place with them. Later, he'd made bonds of brotherhood that would last until death in both the SEALs and, more recently, with the FBIs' Hostage Rescue Team. But that genetic uncertainty remained.

It was enough to keep him wary of certain people and certain situations. The worry that he wasn't good enough persisted even though he knew better. He hated that about himself. Hated that lingering insecurity when he did things every day that most other people in the world couldn't even contemplate.

Zoe turned over in her sleep and her arm went across his chest and then she snuggled up close to his side.

He froze in surprise, half terrified and half hopeful she was making a pass at him. The fact he wanted her, desperately wanted her with an intensity he'd never experienced before shocked him. His gravity-defying cock was living proof he wasn't as in control as he'd like to believe.

She was a job.

He couldn't afford to get involved or let his guard down, and yet...maybe he should take what he could get from a smart willing woman he couldn't stop fantasizing about.

When she didn't make another move, he realized the temperature of the room was chilly and she was simply cold.

Idiot.

She's a *job*.

He glanced at the clock. Three a.m. If the weather hadn't been so treacherous, he might have gotten on the road, but the snow meant he needed to wait until the roads were cleared and sanded.

He wrapped his arm awkwardly around Zoe and hugged her

to his chest to help keep her warm. Her scent enveloped him. Some sort of elusive sweetness, like lemongrass or honey. He inhaled deeply and let it wash over him. Slowly, his heart rate calmed and he found himself drifting off again, with his arms full of a soft warm woman that he would dearly like to know better, already realizing the idea was a non-starter.

Keeping her safe was his mission.

Nothing in the handbook said he couldn't enjoy the small perks when it was okay to do so though. Not that he planned to share this particular perk with anyone.

Ever.

He drifted off to sleep inhaling her scent like it was the most powerful elixir in the world.

———

Zoe cuddled deeper against the warmth at her side. Bad dreams plagued her sleep and made her feel unsettled and groggy. Tiredness clogged her brain but she knew she was safe in this moment. She lifted her thigh and snuggled even closer and encountered something firm.

She opened her eyes to find herself staring into the shadowy depths of Seth Hopper's smoldering gaze.

A voice inside her head whispered she should back away. Give this guy a little space as she had promised not to jump him.

But what if his arousal wasn't simply a byproduct of his parasympathetic nervous system…

She kept her gaze locked on his as she deliberately pressed her thigh gently against his erection and immediately backed off.

His nostrils flared and his arm tightened around her waist.

He didn't look like a man who wasn't interested. He looked like the same guy who'd eaten her up with his eyes when they'd first seen one another outside the Gila Bend motel.

And here they were in a similar establishment, although the situation was completely different this time. He wasn't a stranger anymore. And they were already wrapped up in one another's arms, sharing a bed, and he was obviously aroused.

Her pulse raced at the reckless direction of her thoughts, but she hadn't felt this level of attraction since she'd watched *Magic Mike* five times in a row. Yesterday's abduction had reminded her that life was short and you never knew when yours might be over. The short-lived abusive relationship with Colm Jacobs had robbed her of a libido for months and made her feel like a sexless shell of the woman she'd used to be. Right now, every erogenous zone in her body was zinging back to life after months of torpor.

She wanted her sex life back and Seth Hopper was exactly the man to help her get it.

"Are you awake?" she asked.

He didn't speak. He blinked though. Once.

It was not even five a.m. but the room was bright enough that she could clearly see his expression.

She swallowed the fear of rejection and grabbed hold of her nerve. She had a suspicion that if she didn't go for it now, she might never get another chance with this man. Since the moment he'd discovered her identity, he'd kept those fires in his eyes banked, but they weren't banked right now.

"Seth," she whispered.

He raised his brows in silent question.

"How would you feel about having sex with me?"

A quick expulsion of air told her he'd been holding his breath. "Fuck. Zoe."

"Well," she swallowed nervously, "That's kind of what I had in mind."

13

She leaned across him, then slowly straddled his hips. "Please."

He groaned as his palms slid up her bare thighs. "I want you so bad."

She sat back and felt a shudder move from his body to hers. She could come just from this, but she wanted more.

She reached out to stroke the muscle that formed one side of his pectoralis major. Seth Hopper might be the most anatomically perfect specimen of a man she'd ever encountered—and he wasn't even dead.

His skin was hot and silky smooth. She spread her fingers wide, her palm picking up the strong thrum of his heart.

Just so there was no doubt exactly where this was headed if he wanted, she said, "I have condoms."

His gaze sharpened and focused on her face as if he finally realized he wasn't dreaming. He started to say something but it was lost as she pulled her shirt over her head and was left wearing only a pair of panties.

His pupils went wide and whatever he'd been about to say seemed to evaporate on his tongue. He raised a large hand and cupped one of her breasts. Her nipples contracted, from the coldness of the room and the arousal that pulsed through her. He rubbed a thumb over one tip and a thousand nerve endings did a little dance. She quivered and pressed down against him.

His nostrils flared with every exhale, and the expression on his face was fierce with desire. It was his eyes that told her he wanted her as much as she wanted him. They burned.

She smiled, determined not to let the bad things that had happened over the last couple of days intrude on this moment. Seth Hopper was the best thing to come out of this horror show and now she had him exactly where she wanted him. Almost.

She stroked his abs and then the perfect curve of his clavicle before dipping into the tender triangle of skin above. His muscles were well-defined, but he wasn't bulky. He was a well-honed fighting machine. There was something almost vulnerable about his expression as he looked at her. Something unexpectedly sweet.

She noticed a tattoo with the name "Ellie" in a small discreet ribbon on his inner elbow. She touched it and he glanced down and met her gaze, almost daring her to ask about it. But she didn't want to break the spell.

Zoe didn't feel like she had the right to interrogate him about his relationship history at this stage. He didn't seem like the kind of man to cheat.

This is just sex, Zo. Don't go all crazy-possessive jealous psycho on him when you are seducing him, for heaven's sake.

She leaned down to kiss his jawline, loving the feel of his stubble dragging against her lips. She nibbled behind his ear and the tender line of his neck and felt him clench his fingers around her thighs.

She shook from arousal and nerves. This was the first time she'd ever seduced a man, unless you counted asking out a boy in high school band class. She'd been just as nervous then, although less naked.

She tasted her way across Seth's eyelids and slid her tongue lightly across his full lower lip. His hands cupped her breasts as he curled up off the bed to take one aching areola into his mouth.

She gasped and leaned her head back. Her toes curled as sensation shot straight to her core. She held him to her as his hands began exploring her body. Her waist. Her hips. Her ass. Then the wet heat between her legs as he pushed the panties aside and slowly inserted one blunt fingertip inside, gently slicking moisture across the folds of her labia and clitoris.

She moaned in arousal.

"Fuck." He groaned. "I really shouldn't be doing this."

She sank her hands into his short hair and gripped hard as she stared into his eyes. "If you stop now, I'm going to cry."

She saw some of his doubts kick in.

"Seth, we're attracted to one another. We're alone."

"My job is to get you safely to DC."

She reared back. "How is having sex any more dangerous than sleeping?" Except to her heart maybe. "I want to feel alive again." A wave of sadness crashed over her and she suddenly felt overwhelmed by everything that had happened yesterday. She closed her eyes and tried to hold herself together because she couldn't afford to fall apart now. "I want to feel something good, Seth. Something uncomplicated and real and joyful."

She opened her eyes and held his gaze, wanting to convince him but not wanting to force him.

He kissed her then, and his doubts seemed to disappear as he explored her body with his competent hands and hungry mouth. All she could think about was how good it felt, and how desperately she wanted him inside her.

She reached over for her wash bag on the bedside table and pulled out a strip of condoms. She was also on birth control, but between the dangers of ripped latex and STDs she never had sex without protection. She had no intention of getting pregnant until if and when she was ready. No one owned her body except her.

Seth's mouth was now doing something magical to her navel which she hadn't even imagined could feel so good.

He picked her up and she squeaked as he laid her gently back on the bed before moving down her body.

"I *really* shouldn't be doing this but you taste so damn good, I can't resist."

She lay there and took all the pleasure he was dishing out. It felt incredible. Like good sex. Like lovemaking should.

Just when she was nearing her climax he stopped, and she shook so hard she couldn't speak. Had he changed his mind? She peeked and was relieved to hear the tearing of a packet. She watched him roll the condom over his thick length.

She swallowed audibly.

"Ready?" he asked, his gaze meeting hers.

"If I was any more ready this would already be over," she quipped.

"Over?"

"Over." She'd been so close. She couldn't believe they were having this conversation now with him poised above her and her wanting him deep inside. He didn't seem to be in any rush as he waited for further explanation.

"I only ever orgasm once. Not that I don't enjoy the sex afterward," she assured him.

"Is that a challenge?" His gaze held hers and a smile curved that pretty mouth of his.

She laughed and some of the tension she hadn't even realized she carried eased. He was competitive. Of course, he was. So was she.

"If you think you're up to the job. But I read somewhere pleasure is a journey, not a destination." Her heart hammered at the thought they might do this more than once. She was still terrified he might change his mind this time.

"I like that idea. A journey and not a destination. We are on a road trip." He laughed as he crawled up her body and she tasted herself on his lips as he kissed her mouth and she found herself swept up in everything about this big, sexy man whose life she had somehow collided with.

He nuzzled her ear. "Ready for more?"

She couldn't believe he was checking in with her again. Most men thought a kiss was the green light for sex. Cunnilingus...? That was generally accepted as a gold-plated key into a woman's vagina. But this guy? This guy wanted her to be sure. And she wanted him to know this wasn't some impulsive decision she was going to regret as soon as they were finished.

"I want you inside me, Seth Hopper. I want you so badly I can't think about anything else."

He pushed inside her. He was thick and hard and it took a second to catch her breath. Her fingernails bit into his shoulders as her legs wrapped around his ass and pulled him even deeper.

They held each other's gaze.

"Still okay?" He kept most of his weight on his elbows.

She grinned as her inner muscles rippled around him and made his pupils flare. "Better than okay. How about you?"

There was a glint in his eye. "This is what I wanted from the first moment I saw you. So I'm feeling pretty, goddamn incredible right about now."

So was she. Then he started moving.

She'd thought he'd be rough because of what he was—a soldier, a warrior. But he was slow and gentle, and very, very thorough.

Arousal climbed inside her again and tightened like a coil. He hooked her leg high over his hip and went even deeper, pushing into her, over and over.

She tried to hold onto him but her fingers slipped off his damp skin. Suddenly a wave of sensation burst over her as her inner muscles spasmed around him and she cried out.

He never stopped moving and she rode the wave of her orgasm like a champ.

Seth braced his elbow on the bed and cradled her head as his own needs took over and he started pounding harder into her body, striving for his own release. She reached a hand between their bodies and stroked the tender sensitive skin behind his testicles. He stiffened and jerked against her, the ligaments in his neck straining against the skin as he thrust out his jaw.

He held himself still for a few frozen moments. Then collapsed on top of her, before carefully rolling them so she was once again on top.

And, as incredible as that orgasm had been, her body wanted more.

———

Seth knew he was making a terrible mistake but when Zoe slipped from his body and caught his hand and dragged his ass off the bed he didn't resist.

He did lift his SIG off the bedside table, proving he hadn't totally lost his mind but that was almost worse. He couldn't blame this less-than-professional conduct on temporary insanity.

He'd already broken the golden rule of close protection. Never get personally involved with a client. And even though Zoe was correct in that there wasn't much difference between his ability to react when asleep versus when having sex there were other issues. Like getting distracted on the job thinking about all the ways he could make her come. Like forgetting she and her family could destroy him without mercy if they so chose. Like knowing his boss would be bitterly disappointed that Seth had abandoned all his training at the first chance of a quick fuck.

Didn't seem to change his immediate need for this woman. Or hers for him, apparently.

Seth dumped the condom in the bathroom trash and saw Zoe had another foil wrapper in her hand which she tossed on the counter.

His pulse gave a little skip. "Optimistic."

She laughed her throaty laugh that was so freaking sexy.

He'd thought his dick was sated but looking at her standing naked in the ugly bathroom had him growing hard all over again. Her body was soft in all the right places. Her curves made his knees go weak. The taste of her had settled onto his tongue like a memory.

She reached into the tub to turn on the shower, checking the temperature with the back of her hand.

"I thought we could save water by showering together." She turned to face him, laughter lighting up those captivating turquoise eyes of hers.

"I am all about the environment."

She climbed beneath the spray of water and he was toast.

He put the SIG and the condom within easy reach. Then he locked the door behind him. It wasn't much protection but on the off chance someone burst into the room with a gun it might give him the split second he needed to get the drop on them first.

He climbed in behind her and reached over to squirt soap into his hands then smoothed it over her arms and over her shoulders. His fingers dug into the tight muscles of her neck and she tilted her head to one side as he massaged her shoulders. She moaned softly. She felt ridiculously good, but also tense.

He ran his unshaven jaw over her neck, gently scraping the delicate skin. He knew she liked what he was doing from her shortened breath and soft moan of arousal.

He slid his hands under her arms and came up to cup her breasts. She leaned her head back against his chest. She was so responsive that it was intoxicating.

He pinched her nipples and she arched her back.

"You like that?"

"I love that." She practically purred.

He grabbed more soap and slicked it down her body, sliding between her legs with teasing strokes.

His erection nudged her backside and she reached around to touch him. He was wise to her wily ways now though. He took both her hands and pressed them to the wall. "Don't move."

She tried to turn around but he held her too tightly. Her laughing eyes met his. "But I want to touch you."

"We're trying to prove *you* can experience two orgasms during a certain time frame, not me."

She laughed. "Fine. For now."

He squirted more soap into his palm then stroked between her legs, teasing her over and over by not touching her where she so clearly wanted to be touched. She moaned as his other hand rolled her tightly bunched nipple.

"Oh god. You're good at this. I knew you would be."

He huffed out a quiet laugh not sure whether or not that was a compliment.

He pressed more soap into his hand and slicked it down her thighs and over her vulva and through her folds and finally inside her. He ignored his own growing hunger for release. Her body was slippery and wet and his was hard and aching. Her mouth opened on a groan as he worked her slowly and firmly in a rhythm that made her breath hitch and her inner muscles start to tighten around his fingers. It took time and dedicated effort to find the exact right tempo. Finally, she cried out loudly and he felt a surge of satisfaction shoot through him as her whole body shook from release.

He held her until she came back to the present. She quickly twisted in his arms and her eyes were huge and a little bit stunned.

"You win." She grabbed him and kissed him on the lips but when he went to wrap his arms around her so he could put that condom to good use, she'd disappeared.

She urged him gently backward until he was pressed against the cold tile wall.

Part of him wanted to object but the other part of him...

She grinned up at him from under her lashes, water raining down on her face. She traced a line up his penis with the tip of her tongue.

She reached out to grip him and guide him, and then she took him into her mouth and made his world shift into technicolor. He fisted his hands in her hair to regain a little control that was rapidly slipping from him.

The vision of this woman all wet and naked on her knees swallowing him made his legs start to shake.

Her other hand moved to caress his balls, and this was going to be all over for him in seconds and he didn't want it to be because he knew that once they climbed out of this shower and back into reality, this couldn't happen again. Not ever.

Gritting his teeth, he eyed that condom and eased her gently back.

She slowly climbed to her feet as he reached for the package and ripped it open. She surprised him by taking the condom and rolling the sheath over his hot flesh. Apparently, she was into torture.

He picked her up and she made a noise that made him smile.

"You're a squeaker." He braced her against the wall, holding her up with his thigh.

"I have never *squeaked* in my life."

"It's okay. I like it. It's cute."

"I'm not cute."

"You are so cute."

"I hate cute."

"I fucking love it."

Her legs went around his waist and he positioned himself against her. He held her gaze as he slid deep inside and watched the way her pupils dilated and she bit her lip as she gripped tight to his neck and tried hard not to make a sound.

"Still okay?" He grinned.

She nodded and wriggled a little but she had zero traction and he was in complete control of this next adventure.

His tanned skin was a sharp contrast to the paleness of her thighs and stomach. He shifted his feet so she was pinned there and sank into her over and over again until she was gasping. Sweat bloomed on his skin, washed away by the hot spray. She felt so incredible. So perfect. Wrapped around him tight and wet and amazing.

He wanted her to come again but he needed his hands to hold her securely because he didn't want to drop her.

"Touch yourself."

After a slight hesitation she obediently rolled her nipple between her thumb and forefinger until it was a perfect raspberry peak. Then, aware of his hypnotized gaze following the path of her fingers, she slid her hand lower and stroked them over her clit.

Her mouth opened and her eyes closed and it only took a few moments for her to climax again, hard. He felt her squeezing around him and knew he was done.

He closed his eyes.

Holy fuck.

His body shuddered fiercely as he came in an avalanche of sensation that exploded into shocked bliss. When it was over and the bells stopped ringing in his head, he rested his forehead on the tile beside hers, inhaling deeply as he tried to collect himself. They stayed that way for a few seconds until he reluctantly withdrew.

He ditched the condom and tossed it into the garbage. Grabbed some shampoo and quickly washed himself as she leaned seemingly stunned against the wall.

That orgasm had rocked his world and Zoe looked similarly affected.

He scrubbed the short hair on his head. Tilted his head toward her. "You okay?"

"You just blew every lover I've ever had out of the water." She smiled but he could see deeper emotions hovering beneath the surface.

Was she already regretting this?

Shit. "I didn't hurt you, did I?"

She shook her head and slicked back her wet hair, once again showcasing her incredible breasts.

"You didn't hurt me at all. It was perfect. Thank you. This was exactly what I needed. You were exactly what the doctor ordered."

She made him sound like a frigging gigolo. He frowned at that. "Glad to be of service."

He stepped out of the shower and grabbed a towel, scrubbing

it over his body, quickly and efficiently. He slung it around his hips and moved his weapon to beside the sink before brushing his teeth.

Zoe turned off the shower and climbed out of the tub. She wrapped a towel around herself.

Her fingers touched the tattoo on his back. "This is nice. And anatomically accurate. Why a frog skeleton?"

His throat went dry at the memory of a long-lost friend. "Bone frog." He shrugged. "It's a SEAL thing."

"You were a Navy SEAL?"

He nodded. The silence felt awkward now and he didn't want to talk about his time on the Teams. A lot of women in his past had dug that tattoo. He didn't want to think about them now.

He held up the one on his arm. "My late baby sister. In case you were wondering."

"Late?" Her eyes found his in the mirror. "I'm so sorry for your loss."

He nodded. He didn't want to talk about Ellie either even though he'd stupidly brought her up.

"I wasn't though." She picked up her toothbrush. "Wondering about the tattoo."

He watched his brows lock together in the mirror. "You weren't wondering why I had another woman's name tattooed on my body a few moments before I came inside you?"

She pulled a face. "I was curious but I didn't feel like it was the right time to start an interrogation."

"You mean like are you single, are you married?" He spat out the toothpaste and rinsed. Seemed kind of important to him.

"You don't seem like the sort of person to cheat but if you were, you'd probably be the sort of person to lie about it too." Zoe was clearly flustered by his response now. "I didn't think it was really any of my business. I mean, it was just sex, right?"

He was shocked by the jab to his heart but made sure his reaction didn't show on his face. "Well, I'm definitely single, although apparently, it wouldn't be an issue if I wasn't." He tossed the towel into the tub. Forced a laugh. "But, lady, *that* wasn't *just sex.*"

She'd caught on to the coolness in his tone and the change in his expression. She frowned and her lips pinched.

"*That* was a grade-A perfect fuck," he said. "Worthy of the record books."

And maybe Zoe Miller wasn't the person he'd thought she was because he hated how disappointed he felt. How freaking naïve. He picked up his gun and his toothbrush and unlocked the bathroom door and told himself not to be a damn fool. He'd been used for his body plenty of times. He hadn't expected it to sting quite so much this time.

"Experiment is over. Time to get back to work."

14

Ryan Sullivan leaned against the wall of the briefing room and yawned. It was 8:00 a.m. which wasn't early by his standards, but it had been one hell of a weekend—the work kind, not the fun kind. Although, he loved his job so it was all the same to him.

Novak was giving them a rundown on the various team members' Saturday night/Sunday morning adventures.

Meghan Donnelly shot him a death glare, her jaws clamped so tight together she looked like her teeth might crack. She clearly hadn't forgiven him for teasing her about her driving last week. She didn't appreciate his sense of humor which he could admit was a little juvenile.

Ryan had already heard and seen all the details from his team-mates, including photographic evidence that JJ Hersh now sported a snake bite that would heal into cool scars.

Ryan had plenty of scars of his own. He was grateful Hersh was okay.

He yawned again and Novak caught him with one of his "don't fuck with me" expressions.

Ryan covered his mouth and winced. He'd been on the phone with his brother for half the night. His favorite mare had suffered a twisted gut and the local vet had only just managed to save her. She'd been fine when he'd visited the ranch at Christmas, but these things happened fast. Ryan was grateful his brother had spotted the problem in time.

"Cowboy," Novak commanded as the others started filing out of the room. Donnelly jostled him trying to escape the meeting as fast as possible.

Ryan had the feeling he'd missed an important piece of information.

"Donnelly," Novak shouted.

The operator froze at the threshold of the room.

Ryan waited for the crowd of bodies to clear and went over to see his team leader.

He yawned again. "Sorry, boss. Had a late night."

Donnelly sneered and Ryan sent her a look.

"Is there a problem between you two?" Novak glanced from one to the other of them.

They both shook their heads.

"Good." Novak pulled open a laptop that sat on the desk at the front of the classroom. "Seth Hopper sent me this surveillance tape from the scene of the abduction on Saturday night. It was the same motel where he and Hersh stayed with the BORTAC team. I want you two to go through all the footage from when they arrived to when the ERT show up."

Shit, that was four days' worth of footage. "Isn't this what analysts usually do?" Ryan rubbed his eyes.

Novak shot him a look that would make most men quake. "Yes, they have a copy. But I want this done yesterday. I want a note of every license plate on every vehicle that parks in that lot. I want the clearest photograph of anyone who comes on camera. Do a screen capture and we'll run them through facial recognition programs."

"The quality is usually terrible from these things." Donnelly shifted her feet.

Novak nodded. "Do it anyway. Start on Saturday night and then work backwards."

Novak strode away and left him and Donnelly staring at one another warily.

Ryan rolled his shoulders. "Which one of us is fetching coffee?"

Donnelly shot him a look that if it had been a blade would have pierced his heart straight through.

"I vote I get the coffee and a notepad." Ryan grinned. "You set up the workstation. See if you can hook up the laptop to the screen on the whiteboard." Her brows rose as if she was surprised he'd had a good idea.

He turned to walk away.

"Don't you want to know how I take my coffee?" she called after him.

"Black, two sugars." He glanced over his shoulder. "We stopped for coffee when we did that prisoner pickup last week."

Her brow creased. "Oh. Yeah."

He headed outside to the break room and stole a notepad and paper from HRT's receptionist and gatekeeper, wondering how the hell he and Donnelly were going to get through this without killing one another.

———

Zoe was approaching the outskirts of Albuquerque. She had been a little surprised that Seth had accepted her offer to take the wheel but they had another twenty-six hours of driving to do and it was sensible for them to share the load if they wanted to make that Wednesday morning meeting.

She glanced at him. He was in full-on professional-bodyguard mode even though he was dressed in old jeans, a black, long-sleeved t-shirt, and a leather jacket—presumably his attempt to look like a civilian.

He still looked like a man on a mission to her. Or paranoid. She wasn't sure which.

But surely the cartel would assume all the evidence from her and her friends' trip into the desert had been destroyed along with James's poor truck? They must have enough resources to figure out Zoe wasn't some random forensic anthropologist who'd been in a place they thought she shouldn't be. Whether Zoe liked it or not—and most of the time she was proud of her mother's achievements and dedication to public service—she was the daughter of the current Vice President and the DOJ tended to view any attack on someone like her as an attack on the government itself. Going after her or her friends would lead to the sort of attention criminal organizations usually preferred to avoid.

The mystery surrounding the missing dead woman remained. Who was she? Who'd killed her? Why had someone moved her body? And where was she now?

Without a body there was only one way to find out. Zoe needed to get the gold medallion and tooth to her friend at the FBI Laboratory as soon as possible.

She gripped the steering wheel tightly as a car ahead braked and skidded a little.

The snow had been cleared off I-40 and the highway had been sanded, so conditions weren't terrible. She was taking it steadily, keeping her foot off the brake pedal as much as possible. The truck was heavy enough to have decent traction even on the hilly sections.

Seth watched her and the road with eagle eyes, but he hadn't taken over or given her any more instruction than had been necessary. She didn't kid herself that he wouldn't grab the wheel if the occasion demanded, or that she wouldn't welcome his help in an emergency.

Apparently, the snowstorm had hit most of the Midwest from Wyoming to Oklahoma City and it hadn't blown itself out yet. This was going to be a long trip.

She shot her reluctant bodyguard another glance. No one

would guess from looking at the two of them what had happened in the motel earlier.

He was typing reports onto a laptop. She caught him checking the side mirror before glancing at her. He seemed surprised to find her watching him. His expression went bland as he lifted his brows in silent question before returning his attention back to his laptop.

He was annoyed with her.

When had things gone from being the most incredible sex of her life, to feeling chilled to the bone by the coldness in Seth Hopper's eyes?

Not that she had felt physically threatened by him in any way. The man had gone out of his way to make her feel safe and protected, before, during, and after sex. But the fire of attraction had burned out so fast she felt almost foolish for being hurt by his rapid withdrawal. It wasn't as if she'd expected flowers and chocolates. She was the one who'd said it was *just sex*.

A "grade-A perfect fuck," apparently.

That still stung the way he'd intended it to sting.

Was it simply a case of a guy being nice to get what he wanted and then shutting the woman down afterward? There were plenty of guys like that in the world—except she'd been the one doing all the coaxing and with another night on the road why would he shut her down now when they could do everything all over again later?

Something had flipped like a switch in Seth Hopper and she was pretty sure she was the cause. She'd upset him in some way, hurt him enough for him to be nursing the wound while acting all unaffected and stoic.

It had started when she'd complimented him on the sex, she realized. She hadn't known what to say and some garbage had come out of her mouth before her brain had caught up. She'd been knocked off balance by the intensity of their coming together. It had been physically incredible and, more than that, she'd felt special, cherished, right up until the moment she hadn't.

The incident with the tattoos had cemented the frost into a thick layer of ice.

She'd said she hadn't wanted to interrogate him about his relationship status…but in not wanting to come across as clingy or possessive she'd instead obviously insulted him. Insulted his sense of right and wrong. Insulted his honor.

She pressed her lips together in annoyance at herself. Her *just sex* comment had probably made him feel like she was only interested in him for one thing.

A grade-A fucking.

Dammit.

She'd messed up because she'd been concerned with her own emotions, her own shields, and fears. But what about him?

It wasn't that she didn't care about Seth's feelings, she did. But trying to find the balance between keen interest and fierce independence was tricky, especially for someone who'd gotten it so wrong the last time she'd been involved with a guy.

The engine changed up a gear and the sound drew her full attention back to the road, which was where it should be, considering.

She gave him another sideways glance and caught him watching her again. He immediately looked away, avoiding eye contact, engrossed, or at least pretending to be, in whatever he was reading on his screen. Her gaze flicked to his cell before going back to the road.

Her fingers itched to get on some sort of device to check her cloud for photos. Maybe call the others and ask for updates on Karina's health. She had her smartwatch, but it wasn't the same. The fact she was going to have to replace her phone and laptop was a major pain in the ass. She wasn't certain her insurance policy covered getting kidnapped at gunpoint.

She passed a sign for I-25. "You ever been to Santa Fe?"

"No." He shook his head.

If she wanted to get to know him better maybe she should

have tried conversation before she'd gone straight in at the deep end of seduction.

"It's beautiful—the oldest capital city in the US. This whole area is fascinating as well as geographically stunning." He didn't look up, but she could tell he was listening intently. She decided to bore him to death with history. Defrost the ice with a nerd offensive. She wanted to apologize for upsetting him but figured she needed to go slowly and ease into it, so he knew she was sincere.

"The Spanish arrived to colonize this region in the late 1600s— well before the English crown granted a royal charter to the Virginia Company of London to settle the east coast. Before that, this area was inhabited by the Tewa people who'd lived here from at least the 10th Century. In typical European style, the Spanish conquistadors crushed the indigenous people—but luckily an impressive series of historic pueblo settlements remain."

She could see her attempt at conversation had sparked an interest, but he was holding on to his mood.

Classic male pique.

"Not far up the road from Santa Fe is Los Alamos. The birthplace of the atomic bomb." She pulled her lips to one side. While she understood the importance of weapons and military might— plenty of despots were out there who viewed war as an opportunity and were ready to take advantage of the weak—she struggled to find joy in any weapon of mass destruction.

He turned to look at her then. "You sound like a tour guide."

She laughed. "A lot of cultural anthropologists do become tour guides but I was always more interested in biological anthropology and bones."

"What's your expertise, exactly?"

She blew out a long breath and he seemed to tense. "I'm interested in the intersection between climate change and biological anthropology."

He frowned. "Climate change and biological anthropology?"

"Sound like strange bedfellows I know, but they make sense when you think about it." She used the term "bedfellows" deliberately. She wanted him to remember how good they'd been together before everything had gotten muddled up. "Biological anthropologists are being called into more and more situations influenced by climate change. Everything from finding prehistoric remains in the melting tundra, dropping lake levels revealing decades-old murder victims stuffed into barrels, sea levels rising in some areas and threatening traditional burial sites of indigenous peoples." She swallowed. "Not to mention identifying mass fatalities from wildfires that now proliferate thanks to a drying climate."

"You've been involved in wildfire DVI situations?"

She nodded and her fingers clenched on the steering wheel before she forced herself to relax. "I assisted in a couple of California fires during my PhD. My main task was identifying bones from other debris. Nothing else quite feels like bone but it can be hard for untrained responders to positively ID. Then we separated possible human remains from non-human. The areas were still smoldering when we went in, but people needed answers about their loved ones ASAP for obvious reasons."

"That can't have been much fun."

"It wasn't fun, but..." How did she express the satisfaction of returning the remains of loved ones to their families. Of bringing people home? "People would generally rather know that their family member is dead than to forever worry about them. Rapid DNA has proven very effective for quickly identifying remains to give relatives closure within a much shorter timeframe than was previously possible."

"You can't always tell family by DNA." His voice was gruff, and he'd turned his attention to the wing mirror again.

Was someone following them or was he avoiding her gaze?

"True. DNA analysis isn't perfect but considering sometimes all we have to work with is a charred humeral head it's a miracle of modern science that we have a chance of actually identifying who that person was in life."

He was silent for so long she thought he was going to clam up in broody contemplation but he surprised her.

"I'm adopted." He scratched the back of his neck and a vulnerable expression settled on his features. "My DNA doesn't connect me to anyone I love."

A tiny fissure started in her heart. It seemed to mirror the small crack that had appeared in Seth's armor.

"You're right. DNA doesn't define family. It can be used to connect biologically related individuals though. It's a tool. We have others." She took a breath and decided to jump all-in in the hopes of repairing where she'd gone so wrong earlier. By maybe not being interested enough in him as a person rather than as a guy she was attracted to. She hadn't wanted to reveal how much she thought she could like him given half a chance. She hadn't wanted to be that exposed or vulnerable.

"You said your sister, Ellie, died… Was she your biological sister?"

She saw his lips tighten out of the corner of her eye but concentrated on the road ahead as traffic slowed due to congestion.

"No, but we were close. My parents adopted her a couple of years after they adopted me which proved they really are saints."

She found herself smiling because his tone was happy. "I take it you were an energetic kid?"

He blew out a quick breath. "I was what the social workers like to call 'troubled.' However, I was not troubled. I was hell on wheels."

"How old were you when they adopted you?"

"Two."

Zoe tried to contain the emotions his words evoked. By the time a kid was that age sometimes it was hard to repair the damage done by abusive or neglectful guardians. "Do you remember anything about your early years?"

She watched emotions race over his features as if it was a trick question. She decided to talk about her own childhood which she was often reluctant to do because unscrupulous people could use the information against her parents.

Seth Hopper wasn't the only paranoid person in the vehicle.

"My first memory is from around that age, two. I was playing on the beach in Monterey. My brother was supposed to be watching me when my mom ran back to the house for something but he turned his back, probably digging a hole in the sand which seemed to be his main purpose in life back then. I disappeared. My mom came back and suddenly I was missing. Ben hadn't even noticed."

She could still hear the gulls screeching overhead and feel the salt-laden breeze blowing her hair. "She thought I'd gone into the ocean. She ran into the waves in her dress searching for me. A guy who was surfing paddled in and pointed into the dunes. I was sitting hidden by the tall grasses. I'm sure I thought I was playing the best game of hide-and-seek ever, but I also remember how much it hurt when she grabbed me and held me. She was sobbing so loud I can still hear it."

She felt Seth's gaze intent on her face. "How did she cope with living on the beach after that?"

"Hah. She enrolled me and my brother in every swimming lesson available and instilled the ever-loving fear of God into us both that if we so much as thought of dipping our toes in the water, we cleared it with her first."

"So," he asked, picking up the olive branch she'd offered. "You have a brother?"

"Yeah. Ben. He's a screenwriter in Hollywood trying to make it on his own. Trouble is, everyone who's anyone knows he's the son of Hollywood royalty."

Seth laughed. "You're both trying to make your own way in the world without help from your parents."

Zoe pulled a face. "I'm not doing a great job either considering I'd probably be dead without my mom's ability to mobilize the troops."

"That's not completely accurate," he argued. "We would have

attempted to rescue you regardless of political connections. But the mission might not have been classified as urgent or had quite so many resources thrown at it so fast if you weren't related. You were extremely fortunate we were in the area."

"I'm sorry if we took you away from something important. I never thought about that before."

"We'd finished. Had a shootout trying to arrest some drug traffickers."

Zoe knew her eyes went wide. He didn't seem fazed by the constant danger. "You had a busy night."

The memories of them in bed together instantly rose up and Zoe felt a blush heat her cheeks as she stared fixedly at the road.

"Yeah, I haven't been getting a lot of sleep lately," he said wryly, driving the point home.

"I apologize for that too." She squeezed her thighs together determined not to remember how ridiculously good at sex Seth was.

His tone grew serious. "It was a mistake for me to let down my guard. It shouldn't have happened."

The unexpected shot to her heart made her blink in an effort to conceal her emotions. The fact he could so easily ignore what had occurred between them suggested it had meant something different to him than it had to her.

"I get the feeling a lot of women throw themselves at you, Agent Hopper." She forced humor into her tone.

The silence grew thick and thorny.

"Must be difficult to be so darn attractive." She didn't know why she pushed him but apparently, she couldn't stop herself.

He huffed a quiet laugh. "You tell me."

It was a nice thing to say but she was not anywhere close to his level of physical beauty. "I don't generally have men lining up to date me."

"Date?" he queried.

"Sorry." She stared hard at the road ahead. "I didn't mean to imply you wanted to *date* me."

He shook his head. "I didn't mean that—"

"I know what you meant. Look, Seth." She was steadily strangling the steering wheel with both hands. "What I am struggling so terribly to say, is that while I was attempting to appear cool about what happened between us this morning, the words that came out of my mouth were idiotic. Believe it or not, I was making an effort to not appear more deranged than I generally am by saying how much I enjoyed being in bed with you, and how much I like *being* with you. But it all came out wrong. It's been a while since I was in a healthy relationship, and I don't generally hook up with guys I barely know."

He shifted in his seat.

"Not that you have to believe me about that, I mean, I was pretty pushy this morning with the whole climbing on top and fucking you, thing..." She drew in a deep breath as the words poured out of her mouth. "The thing is, I do like you. Not only your body, which is *ridiculous* by the way. I like you even though we barely know each other, and you are probably horrified by me saying these things when we are going to be trapped in a vehicle together for the next two days and you can't escape, but—"

"Zoe—"

"I took advantage of the position we found ourselves in this morning by practically begging you to have sex."

"Zoe—"

"And I am so sorry about that because I obviously made you uncomfortable in the aftermath." She swallowed. "But I think somehow I gave you the impression that I do that all the time and that it didn't mean anything to me."

"Zoe—"

"Except, it *did* mean something. And I'm not suggesting you're going to be interested in anything except, well, fucking, ever again, but I needed you to know you weren't just convenient, and I didn't jump you simply because I had a sexual itch to scratch—"

"*Zoe—*"

"Although, I am not sure how else to describe the need I felt at the time. It was pretty all-consuming..."

He took the wheel and jolted her attention to the here and now. "Take the next exit."

Her heart pounded. *Dammit.* Her mouth went dry as she indicated and drove the truck off the highway. She'd obviously completely overstepped. *Again.* Maybe rather than trying to relate she should keep her mouth shut.

"Take this left."

She turned. Twice more as he watched the mirrors.

"Pull over here."

Her teeth were almost chattering in reaction as she brought the rig to a halt on the side of the road.

He'd put his laptop on the floor, unsnapped his seat belt and then hers. She thought he was going to give her a stern lecture on her being a job and how she was making it impossible to work without him feeling sexually violated.

Instead, he dragged her across the seat until she straddled his lap and she realized he was hard as rock with arousal at exactly the same moment as he crushed his lips to hers.

15

—————

S eth didn't ask permission this time.

He kissed her deeply and thoroughly. He ground her against the thick ridge of his jeans and burrowed one hand beneath her layers to find her breast and squeeze her nipple with enough pressure to have her crying out in less than thirty seconds.

She shuddered in his arms and he held her tight against him with a fistful of her fine blonde hair in one hand, her head tucked beneath his chin. He kept his eye on the mirrors searching their surroundings for possible tangos, all the while throbbing with the need to bury himself inside this woman when his only concern should have been protecting her.

"I like you too, Zoe Miller. Now please stop saying the word 'fuck' because you are driving me insane with lust every time it comes out of your mouth." He kissed her brow and slid into the driver's seat.

He pulled her seat belt across her body and buckled her in as she sat there looking stunned. Then he put the truck in gear and got back on the highway.

—————

Zoe was still mute by the time Seth got back on I-40.

It was almost certainly a mistake to get more involved with a woman like Zoe considering her connections, but it was already too late to reverse course. It might have been too late the moment he'd stepped in with the asshole Secret Service agent. Or maybe from the moment he'd helped rescue her in the desert.

Hell, he'd known at the Gila Bend motel that they were attracted to one another and had bitterly resented himself for not getting her number. And while he still might not have her number, he currently had something much better. He had time. Time to get to know her. Time to charm her with his incredible wit and dashing good looks.

As long as he didn't get distracted from keeping her safe.

That was the priority.

Always.

He'd seen no sign of a tail. Heard no chatter from the higher ups that the cartel was still actively hunting Zoe Miller or her friends.

She was staring at him with huge eyes and a flush in her cheeks. He liked knowing he'd done that to her.

He knew women liked the outer package. False modesty was not his problem. But he wanted a woman interested enough in who he was beneath the surface. And maybe he owed her a little more of himself. Harsh to accuse someone of only wanting you for sex when you refused to give them any insight into who you were under the uniform.

You might pick up a book based on its cover, but you kept reading because of what was written inside.

"I like to say that my earliest memory is the day my adoptive parents came to the foster home and met me for the first time. My mom has a photo of it hanging in her bedroom so that might be why I do remember it so clearly." The snow and ice were melting on the asphalt as the sun struggled to burn off the gray clouds. "They'd tried to get pregnant for years but after several miscarriages and rounds of IVF they settled on adoption instead."

The dazed expression left Zoe's face. He kind of loved the way she blissed out after an orgasm. Her earlier confession had made him feel like a prick for reacting so poorly that morning. No matter how confident he was in his job or appeared on the outside, relationships—especially romantic ones—were his Achilles heel.

"You were in the foster system?" she asked.

"Yeah. Someone left me on the steps of the hospital like out of some Victorian novel." He tried to force all the bitterness out of his voice but knew he failed.

She shifted in her seat. Watching him. Paying attention. "You said that you 'like to say' your first memory is meeting your parents." Light reflected in her pale blue eyes. "What is it really?"

She'd caught something that most people missed.

He grunted. "It's a feeling, not a specific moment." He concentrated on the pretty scenery and warm blast of air coming through the heater vents. "That oppressive sense of abandonment. That feeling of loneliness, and of not being wanted." Not being loved.

He knew she was looking at him closely, but he didn't want to see her pity. He was telling her this out of a sense of honesty. His last ex had dismissed his feelings because he'd been adopted when he was so young, but those experiences were etched onto his DNA regardless. And maybe this wasn't the way to impress a woman like Zoe, but he'd rather she knew what she was getting involved with upfront. He wasn't some perfect guy. He wanted to smash that whole hero illusion into a million different pieces. He was fucked up when it came to relationships, and he wanted her to know it, now, before either of them got in any deeper.

"The truly sad thing is Mom and Dad were on the application list the whole time I was waiting for a family. We missed out on the early bonding because of the bureaucracy and red tape involved in adoptions."

"I'm so sorry." She drew her knee up onto the seat. "We retain so much from those formative years and from our biological parents that we can't consciously recall. The science of epigenetics suggests we can inherit stress and trauma in ways we are only beginning to appreciate."

He glanced at her.

Her hair was mussed from his earlier attentions, but she didn't seem to realize. He tried not to be turned on by the memory when they were discussing something with so much gravitas. He liked her mind and her obvious smarts.

"Hungry?" he asked.

"Starving."

They were about to leave Albuquerque so he pulled into a drive-through to stock up on caffeine. The trip was going to take longer than he'd hoped because of the weather but he didn't intend to be late for that meeting. Who knew what would happen after that.

The fact he was hoping something *would* happen between them came as a shock.

"Were you part of the process when they adopted your sister?"

The question was like a paper cut against his skin and the flash of pain caught him unexpectedly. He'd opened this door. It wasn't a surprise Zoe had decided to walk through it.

"Yeah. At first, I wasn't keen on the idea of a sibling. Jealous, I 'spose, and worried I was going to get pushed aside." His cheeks heated because a lot of that needy little boy still existed.

He grabbed the takeaway cups of coffee, and bacon and egg sandwiches that would keep them going until lunch, from the server. He drove away from the window with a "thanks."

"My mom told me that love was never divided between children. There was always enough to go around for everyone. She convinced me that her and dad would never run out of love for me, and that Ellie needed us the way I'd needed them."

Zoe reached over and squeezed his thigh before picking up her cup and cautiously taking a sip. "Your mother sounds like an amazing woman."

Seth grinned. "She is. She really is." His mood dimmed as he thought about his sister's death.

Zoe seemed to read his mind. "What happened to Ellie?"

"Drug overdose." He passed an SUV that was crawling along.

"I'm sorry," Zoe said simply. "That must have been terrible."

He nodded. "My parents noticed a change in her—she was moody and resentful—but they put it down to the usual acting-out phase."

"I'm acquainted with that phase." Zoe smiled but her eyes held a depth of sadness.

"When they figured out what was really going on, Ellie promised she'd quit, but it wasn't that easy apparently." His voice went gruff, fighting that familiar knot of grief and anger. "She'd secretly started dating an old high school buddy of mine and he gave her a few pills—probably to get her to sleep with him." Seth was glad he hadn't killed the motherfucker because it would have taken his life in a totally different direction. He had permanently rearranged his former friend's features. "They'd only been together a couple of months when she took something that was laced with fentanyl and it killed her."

Seth concentrated on the road and not those dark memories. "This was a decade ago now. Drugs and gangs were a big problem in my old town. It's better nowadays but still a constant battle, you know?"

Zoe nodded. "Going up against the cartel is personal to you?"

He thought about it. "There are all sorts of bad guys in the world and they all get my undivided attention on an op, but when I take down a drug trafficker," he nodded, "I do experience a little extra job satisfaction."

Zoe's aqua eyes remained sad. "I wish you hadn't lost her."

Emotion hit him hard in the throat and he swallowed repeatedly. "Yeah. Me too."

"So, about that orgasm..." Her eyes sparkled suddenly and her brows hiked sky-high in question.

His lips quirked at her attempt to use humor to lighten the mood. "I kind of liked it. There was no squeaking, but some definite gasps."

"I do not *squeak*." She laughed in mock outrage.

"And it was fast. Four in one day. I did tell you you were wrong about the whole multiple-orgasm thing."

"I am happy to be proven wrong." She yawned. The sun was up now but they hadn't gotten as much sleep last night as they should have.

"Get some rest. It'll be your turn to drive again in a couple of hours." He had work to do, but he also recognized the need to keep things switched up to maintain focus.

She covered another yawn with her hand. "Part of me wants to call everyone and see how they're doing but I don't have a cell phone."

"Get an hour's sleep and I'll let you use mine."

"Are you bribing me with minutes and data?"

"Is it working?" He overtook another vehicle crawling along while he ate his sandwich one handed. He'd taken enough advanced driving courses to be confident now the road had some traction.

"It's totally working." She found a blanket and stacked it behind her then took off her boots and turned sideways, placing her stockinged feet against his thigh.

A weird shockwave went through his body at the contact. He squeezed her foot and felt an almost overwhelming surge of possessiveness and rightness in the moment.

He forced his mind back to checking vehicles and drivers. For any sign of something out of the ordinary. He'd seen no indication anyone was following them and was beginning to think the danger really was over. He hoped so. For Zoe's sake.

For his sake.

Zoe snuggled against the back rest and closed her eyes.

He kept his eyes firmly on the road.

———

An hour and a half later, Zoe was awake. Seth had lent her his personal cell phone to use as a hotspot and she was working on his laptop which was probably against the rules, but she wasn't about to tell anyone. She tried to access her cloud, but it had a one-time access security code that was sent to her cell and, as her cell was a melted mess of components, that wasn't going to get her very far. She didn't want to risk getting permanently locked out of her account, so she gave up after one attempt.

She'd called Joaquin. He and his team had failed to locate the woman's body or find anything that looked like a new grave. He'd told her he'd had his hands full with all the other dead bodies and investigators, not to mention the torrential rainstorm that, however welcome to the parched region, had washed away any tracks and trace evidence they hadn't already collected. Unless the authorities struck lucky, the woman was going to remain a mystery forever. Maybe Zoe could persuade the ME's office to conduct an aerial LIDAR survey of the area? Or perhaps talk to other researchers at the university to see if anyone had the equipment and time to conduct a survey?

She dug into the side pocket of her small suitcase and retrieved the evidence bag containing the medallion.

"What's that?" Seth didn't look away from the road.

Zoe paused. It wasn't as if she hadn't already told both Seth and Agent Hersh about the evidence she'd found. She doubted he'd forgotten. If this was a test of trust she wasn't about to fail. Not now.

"Remember I told you in the desert that I found some items near that dead woman?"

He nodded.

She knew it.

"One thing was a gold medallion depicting *Santa Muerte*."

"The narco-saint." Seth's lips thinned.

"Yes, but she's much more than that. *Nuestra Señora de la Santa Muerte* is a folk hero whose origins are linked to indigenous spirituality and the Aztec goddess of death. The Protestant and Catholic Churches naturally disapprove." She pulled a face.

Her mother was raised as a Christian but was non-practicing. Her father was Jewish and their family had spent more time at the synagogue than at church. Zoe considered herself spiritual rather than religious, but recognized religion played an important role in most cultures. She wasn't about to tell anyone practicing any of them that they were wrong, unless they impinged on other's freedom, or started performing human sacrifices—which people had done for *Santa Muerte*. She wasn't a fan of that.

"People pray to her to cleanse negative influences and for protection amongst other things. She appeals to everyone that traditional religious institutions have left behind—LBGTQ+ people for instance, and the poor whose faith has failed to raise them out of poverty, as well as those outside the law. Her cult is the fastest growing new religious movement in the Americas."

Seth's expression narrowed further.

Maybe his antipathy wasn't surprising under the circumstances. *Santa Muerte* was a narco-saint and his sister had died of an overdose.

"Anyway, I took photos at the crime scene, but I'm locked out of my cloud account and don't know if they uploaded or not. Mind if I take a photo of the medallion with your cell and upload it to a missing migrant database? Someone might have entered a description of it for someone who is presumed missing and we might find a match."

It was a long shot.

"Sure. Do you want to use my work cell so the FBI has a record?"

She pulled a face. "I don't know. I didn't mention it to asshole —I mean ASAC—Patterson when we were chatting yesterday." It felt like a thousand years ago now. "I could claim I forgot but I honestly didn't trust him to take my concerns seriously and didn't think he'd prioritize the evidence."

"Patterson is a classic blue-flamer."

"A what?"

"Someone so eager to impress they have blue-flames coming out of their ass. The trouble is he doesn't care who he burns on his way to the top."

"Sounds painful."

He laughed.

"If, for some reason you were investigated, which phone would be better for you?" She watched his strong, capable hands on the steering wheel and tried not to think about what else they'd handled so expertly.

"If it's on the work cell then the FBI will have access to it immediately." He gave her the side-eye. "They wouldn't want me allowing you to load it onto any outside database, not without the case agent's permission."

"I vote for your personal cell then and you can say you lent it to me to make a few calls and deny all knowledge of any nefarious deeds I decided to commit."

"I am not afraid to take responsibility for my actions, Zoe."

"I know that." She stretched out her legs, stiff from the cramped environment. "I just had the impression that Patterson would enjoy nothing better than roasting your balls over an open fire."

Seth barked out a laugh. "Yeah. He didn't exactly take a shine to you, either."

"Right? What is wrong with that guy?" She chuckled and it struck her that, despite all the terrible things that had happened lately, she felt happier than she had in ages. "What do you bet he tried out for HRT as a younger man and was rejected. Now he has it in for men like you—"

"We have a female operator, I'll have you know."

"Oh my god, I want to meet her." Zoe couldn't imagine how physically fit and mentally determined the woman must be to get through a course designed to make the strongest men fail. "Patterson would immediately detest her and make her get him coffee every morning."

"Or report her to the Office of Professional Responsibility for not having all her pencils sharpened, just so."

"Is there truly such a thing as the Office of Professional Responsibility?"

He nodded.

"It sounds faintly ridiculous."

"It is faintly ridiculous, but they take their jobs seriously. I'll probably get both a Commendation and a Letter of Censure in my file for taking you for that unsanctioned hike in the desert and for Hersh treading on that damn snake."

"But I made you—"

He snorted.

"I did. I think you need to remember exactly what happened. You'd have had to physically restrain me to stop me going out there—"

"Which is why I carry zip ties."

It was her turn to snort. "No way you were gonna zip tie the daughter of the Vice President."

"And that's exactly what ASAC Patterson wants me to say." He glanced sideways and overtook another U-Haul. "I think he wants to suggest our actions were somehow politically motivated but there's no way Hersh and I are going down that worm hole. We basically had time so why the hell not search for a dead body, as opposed to stand around doing nothing?"

She reached out and touched his arm. "If we hadn't gone, we wouldn't have realized the corpse had been moved—even if the case agent doesn't believe me. And we might not have found the two other dead men."

Operator Hersh had flown back to Quantico that morning, thankfully with no lingering ill effects from his snakebite.

"How usual is it for the ASAC to be the case agent?" she asked.

Seth pulled a face. "Pretty unusual. But Lorenzo Santiago and his second in command are both on the FBI's Most Wanted List so if this investigation leads to the arrest of one or the other, the case agent is going to look pretty damn good on paper. Headquarters is gonna fast-track their career advancement."

Zoe hated that Patterson's motivation might be entirely selfish.

"Patterson might simply be a good guy who doesn't like your mother's politics." Seth cocked a brow.

"Which is no excuse to take it out on me."

"He shouldn't let his own politics affect how he runs a case," Seth agreed.

"Now I want to bitch about the guy," she grumbled.

"Bitch away." He grinned and her heart slammed up against her chest wall at the reminder of how breathtakingly handsome this man was.

She breathed deep to force the reaction away, and inhaled the clean, fresh scent of his soap which reminded her of his smooth warm skin, and how soft it had felt beneath her lips.

Dammit.

She cleared her throat. Got back to business. "Do you have any clear plastic evidence bags with you?"

Seth nodded. "Side pocket of the go-bag. Before I joined HRT, I was a case agent in the Ozarks and got into the habit of being prepared for everything."

"Like a regular Eagle Scout."

"Just so happens..."

She grinned. "Of course, you were. I was thrown out of the brownies for being a disruptive influence."

"I'm sensing a theme."

"Ha. I wanted to do something exciting like go camping but all we ever did was make crafts using a lot of glitter. I staged a rebellion—"

"Knew it."

"They tossed me out." She pouted. "My mother wasn't pleased."

"With you or with them?"

"Both."

"I can't imagine she's the easiest person to live with," he said carefully. "I mean, I'd say that about anyone crazy enough to go into politics."

Zoe grimaced. "She's not, but no worse than most parents in Monterey in my experience. After she entered politics, everything shifted a little. Ben and I were warned in no uncertain terms that we better not do anything to drag the family reputation into disrepute else we'd be sent off to boarding school. Before that, Dad had always been the one who got all the attention, and no one really cared if one of us acted out."

"Then getting thrown out of brownies was a big deal."

"Oh my god. You'd have thought they'd caught me turning tricks or snorting coke." She froze. "Not that I'm being judgmental."

"I'm pretty damn judgmental when it comes to kids turning tricks or people snorting coke."

She watched him roll his shoulder and change lanes. He'd taken off his jacket as the cab was warm now, and he'd pushed up his sleeves. She recalled her explosive orgasm sitting in this seat a few hours ago. The cab had been downright hot ever since. It had been an extremely effective way of shutting her up and she'd take that punishment again if she had to.

"My parents were pretty cool about everything but not about making bad choices or committing crime," Seth said after a long moment.

Zoe wanted to know more about them. "What do they do?"

Seth seemed oblivious to the effect the tensed muscles of his forearms had on her libido.

"Mom is a teacher. Dad works for the city doing landscaping and stuff. He did not pass on his green thumb to me."

"Something we share." She grinned as she found a small clear evidence bag and dragged it out. She carefully tipped the medallion from one bag to the other with as little transfer as possible. She examined it carefully and saw some sort of initials were engraved on the back although they were hard to distinguish.

"You know any trace evidence isn't admissible in court?" Seth told her.

"Yeah. I know. But I'm hoping we can find a latent print or some contact DNA that might give us a starting point. I have a friend at the FBI lab who will process this and the tooth I picked up."

"You found a tooth?" he asked in surprise.

"Right next to the body. I didn't examine the victim's mouth to see if it might belong to her. I figured Joaquin would do that on the autopsy table."

And they both knew how that had worked out.

"If we get DNA and if I strikeout on the missing person DNA databases, I might fudge an account with one of those family tree places. See if I can get a hit." Threatening-looking clouds were gathering on the horizon again. More bad weather ahead. "You ever thought of putting yourself on one of those?" she asked casually.

His jaw flexed, and his nostrils flared.

She didn't think he was going to answer.

He gave a sharp exhale. "I thought about it. More than once. But I can't get over the fear that I might be related to some monster like the Golden State killer."

"It wouldn't change who you are, Seth."

"Maybe. Maybe not." He swallowed and she could tell this was hard for him to talk about. "The other thing is even if I find my birth mother, I'm not sure I can forgive her for leaving me that way. Anonymously. On the hospital steps? Who does that?"

Zoe couldn't imagine how badly that would mess with your head. "I suspect she was very young or very scared. The fact she left you somewhere you'd be found quickly and where you'd be properly looked after, suggests that she probably did care."

He grimaced. "Maybe. Then there's the other fear, that she was raped and that's why she didn't want me..."

Zoe's heart broke. It explained a lot about how careful he was with the issue of consent this morning. "If it's any consolation, and I know it isn't, I think you turned out pretty amazing. Someone any parent would be proud of."

One side of his mouth quirked. "You're just saying that because I made you come four times today."

"Ha." She'd actually lost count. "I bet I could make *you* come four times today."

The moving truck swerved slightly before he brought it back under control. So much for being unaffected.

She huffed out a laugh and then turned her attention back to the website, entering as much information as she could from memory and from the notes she'd written on the envelopes. It would take time to upload and be made available in the database, but they had plenty of that. The road signs said Amarillo was approaching and it was her turn to drive.

16

Five hours in and, so far, Ryan and Donnelly had managed not to kill one another. They had a list of nineteen vehicles and a bunch of badly pixilated images they'd started running through facial recognition programs.

His stomach growled from hunger, but he'd be damned if he'd be the first one to break.

The Gila Bend locals had scattered as soon as the cartel boys had showed up, but not before pointing them in the right direction of the forensic anthropologists' rooms. Ryan wished they had footage from inside the office but apparently *that* camera wasn't working.

It was probably a miracle they had any footage at all.

Ryan hadn't missed the two encounters between Seth Hopper and Zoe Miller, nor had he failed to notice the obvious instant attraction between the two of them. It was a body language he was intimately familiar with. He would love to be a fly on the wall on this road trip because he had no doubt that sizzle was creating a lot of problems for the usually hyper-focused Hop.

Ryan didn't bring it to Donnelly's attention though. He wasn't sure how she'd react. Was she the type to tell tales? Or was she the type to protect her teammates?

"Donnelly." Daniel Ackers, the director of HRT stuck his head in the classroom. "I need to speak to you in my office immediately."

Ackers caught Ryan's gaze and Ryan didn't like what he saw there.

Donnelly scraped back her chair.

"I'll grab us some lunch," Ryan offered.

Donnelly nodded absently. She looked worried about what Ackers wanted and Ryan couldn't blame her.

Ryan followed her out.

"Hey," Ryan went over and leaned over Maddie Goodwin's desk. "How's the baby?"

"Great." Maddie smiled but her expression remained distracted, and she didn't pull out her phone the way she usually did when someone asked about her kids. Something was going on.

"What's up with Donnelly?"

Maddie pressed her lips together and shot a look at the closed door to Ackers' office. "I can't say."

Ryan frowned. "Why not?"

Meghan Donnelly burst out of Daniel Ackers' office. She glanced at him and immediately looked away, but not before he spotted that her eyes were bloodshot and her face was splotchy with tears.

Ryan's gaze shot back to Maddie. *What the hell?* "If this is about the fact Donnelly and I weren't getting on—"

"It's not about that," Maddie murmured in a barely audible whisper.

Ryan leaned closer, fighting the urge to chase after Donnelly. "What then?"

Maddie sent another swift glance at Ackers' office.

"She lost someone," she said in a hushed whisper. "The boss had to break the news. Don't tell her you know or else I'll lose my job."

Ryan gave Maddie a nod. He'd never betray a friend.

Ryan decided to track his fellow operator down. Her SUV was still in the parking lot, so he knew she hadn't left yet. He asked around, but no one knew where she was. Everyone assumed he'd pissed her off and she'd gone somewhere to cool her heels. He didn't correct them.

He finally tried the women's locker room a second time. As Meghan was the first woman to pass Selection and NOTS, the area wasn't exactly heaving. It had been waiting for Meghan to crash though that barrier and she'd smashed the hell out of it. The whole team felt a weird sense of pride in having the first female operator—pride that they hadn't earned.

It probably put a lot of pressure on her—other people's expectations. Pressure she didn't need.

He knocked on the door again but no one answered, so he stepped inside. Listened intently.

There was something about the quality of the silence that told him he wasn't alone. Someone else was in here. Someone was hiding.

"Meghan?"

No answer.

He let the door close behind him. It took a full minute before the soft sound of sobs reached him.

He found her in the showers, fully dressed, slumped against the wall with her face hidden against her knees.

He recognized that deep agonizing sorrow and could no more walk away without trying to help than he could stop himself breathing.

"Go away." Her voice was full of tears.

As a man who dealt with his own grief with all the grace of a prize fighter brawling with a grizzly bear it was probably wrong to ignore her wishes. He understood the need for privacy, for space. But there had been a time when the words of a friend had been the only thing that had gotten him through the first few days, possibly that entire first year, without the love of his life.

He slid down the wall next to Meghan and wrapped his arm

around her shoulder. She was as stiff as a poker at first but he pulled her into his arms anyway and cradled her to his chest until she finally let go. She didn't like him much but that didn't matter. Sometimes it was easier to be real with people you didn't need to impress.

Huge sobs wracked her body. Tears soaked his t-shirt. Her fingers gripped so hard she pulled out the few hairs he had on his chest. He ignored the discomfort and felt the familiar dull blade of his own grief gouging around in his heart, searching for a bottle of whiskey or a warm willing woman to blot out the feeling that his life was done.

Over.

Finished.

But it wasn't.

And the guilt of that realization had almost killed him all over again.

Meghan finally stopped crying and started to pull away. He kept his arm around her even though he loosened his grip. If she genuinely wanted her space, Meghan Donnelly was more than capable of getting it.

"Want to tell me what's going on?" he asked quietly.

She wiped her face and blew her nose on a tissue she had clenched in her fist. Released a huge rush of breath that managed to somehow not turn into a sob.

"My dad died."

Oh, shit.

There was a fresh round of tears.

Ryan's fingers squeezed her shoulder as he hugged her. "I'm sorry."

For another few minutes the silence was filled with nothing louder than the beat of their own hearts.

Eventually, Meghan sniffed. "We weren't always close, but over the last few years he'd mellowed."

Ryan closed his eyes at the heartbreak in her tone.

"We were finally becoming close and I think he was proud of

me for getting into HRT even though I failed Ranger School." She rolled her eyes before wiping them. "He was a Ranger and proud of it."

He gave a wry laugh. "Half of the people here are former Special Forces. They're no better than you are."

"What about you?" she asked, clearly curious.

He scoffed. "Never in the military. Never in the police either." Which was the most common route to becoming an agent.

She frowned. "What's your degree in?"

He winced. "Agriculture."

She laughed and caught herself. Her expression darkened.

"You get used to it."

"What?"

"The guilt at feeling happy or smiling or even forgetting sometimes for a little while that someone you love is dead."

Her lower lip wobbled and for the first time ever, Ryan noticed the lush mouth of one of his teammates. He thrust the thought back in the box where he kept all the things he didn't let himself think about.

He met her dark brown gaze, making sure none of that showed. It didn't mean anything. Ryan loved women. All women. But if there was one woman on the planet he could not touch, it would be this one.

"We were finally at a place where we were starting to connect as grown-ups. And now he's gone and I'm so angry and devastated and lost." She started crying again, cries that broke his own shattered heart. This woman who was tougher than most men he knew. But grief could sideswipe you. It had sideswiped the entire team at the start of the year, and they hadn't really begun to work through that yet.

Ryan inhaled deeply, grateful his teammates were safe and not letting himself think about the ones who were gone. He held Meghan against his chest and let her bawl it out.

When she quieted again, he gently rubbed her back.

"I lost my wife eight years ago." His voice cracked. "Her name was Becky and I loved her with every fiber of my being."

He held himself still at the rusty taste of his dead wife's name on his tongue. His throat was so tight the words came out like a growl. "Cancer." He swallowed, not allowing himself to cry. Not even now, in front of Meghan whose vulnerability was so raw. "I almost went mad with grief—and I mean that quite literally."

Tears shimmered in Meghan's dark eyes.

"The only thing that got me through that first year were the words of a good buddy of mine. He told me that sometimes all you can do is keep breathing." Ryan pressed his lips together. "I know it's not much but sometimes when everything else is going to shit, concentrating on inhaling and exhaling actually works. You come out the other end, if not intact, then at least more or less in working order."

Her chest hitched. "Like yoga?"

He guffawed. "I was thinking more like tactical breathing—"

"Concentrating on the breath is the basis of every yoga practice, and it's a lot older than the concept of 'tactical breathing.'" She deepened her voice mockingly.

"Okay, yoga breathing. One breath at a time."

Meghan swallowed noisily and wiped her eyes. She seemed steadier now and released his hand and they both stood. He found himself looking down at her.

"I'm sorry I'm such an ass generally." He looked up at the roof tiles that could do with re-grouting. "It's my coping mechanism. Well, one of them." He met her brown eyes again. "I don't recommend any of the others except for the breathing thing."

Her lips quirked. "Novak told me I'd get used to you but I wasn't sure I believed him."

"I'm positive I can still annoy the hell out of you within thirty-seconds flat and it wouldn't even be a challenge."

"If you ever tell anyone I cried on you I will kill you dead on the spot," she warned.

He grinned as they started to get back on familiar ground. "This never happened."

"What if someone sees you coming out of the women's locker room?"

"I'll say you dragged me in here to screw my brains out but I turned you down."

Her eyes were brighter now. Clearer. "*You* turned me down?"

"Fine." He rolled a shoulder. "You turned me down."

"Better." She nodded. She looked down at the ground and swallowed a gusty breath.

"We all have our ghosts, Meghan. Go home. Get some rest." Ryan took a step away from the other operator. "I'll finish up with the tapes. Something tells me we're going to have a busy week."

Unless he missed his mark, Ryan figured this thwarted abduction of VPOTUS's daughter was bound to have consequences both inside the United States and across the border in Mexico. "Unless you're taking leave?"

She shook her head, pulling her hair back into a no-nonsense ponytail.

"Funeral is next week. I'll take some time then. My sister is handling the details."

He headed toward the door.

"Ryan."

He stopped and slowly turned around.

"Thank you." She nodded, eyes bright and earnest and dazzling.

"Get the hell out of here, Donnelly." He forced a laugh, but he didn't like the shift he'd just felt in his chest. He didn't like that one fucking bit.

———

It was approaching ten p.m. and as much as Seth wanted to keep going, he was tired, and the roads were slick with yet another storm that couldn't quite make up its mind between sleet or snow.

They'd made it to Memphis which was more than halfway. Less than he'd hoped for today but probably better than expected given the atrocious driving conditions.

Zoe yawned. "Want me to take over for a while?"

He glanced in the mirror and spotted the same dark Suburban he'd noticed a couple of other times already today. "No. Let's stop for the night."

"Okay. Cheap motel or nice hotel? I vote for the latter but it's up to you. I'll pay you back I promise."

He glanced in the mirror again. "I think we have a tail."

Zoe immediately stiffened and peered into the side mirror.

"I'm almost certain it's the Secret Service. I don't know if it is your ex following you of his own volition." A dull rage rose inside him at the thought. "Or USSS wanting to act as backup should the cartel attack someone they consider theirs to protect."

Zoe's eyes went huge and haunted. "It's the sort of thing he'd do, but it's also possible my mother would have asked USSS to follow us for additional protection whether I like it or not."

"I won't let him get to you, Zoe, I promise you that. If you'd rather I lose them, I can do that, but it wouldn't take them long to track us down in this city considering we can't change vehicles and our van is rather...orange."

She smiled at that.

"Or we can get a good night's sleep and let the USSS keep an eye on the truck all night."

Her lips pinched and her eyes darted nervously to the mirror. This was so different from the woman who usually gave him such sass. He wanted to take Colm Jacobs into a dark alley and give him a sound beating. But Zoe's safety was his priority.

"Let them follow us. As long as I don't have to see him or speak to him..."

"I won't let him get anywhere near you."

She nodded again and pointed to a sign downtown. "Let's stay at The Peabody. We stayed there once when Mom was traveling for some convention." She checked her watch. "We'll miss the ducks but they have great room service."

He shook his head. "As intriguing as that sounds I want to stay as close to the highway as possible. And from what I know of heritage hotels, the parking garage probably won't be able to accommodate your lovely truck."

Zoe patted the dash. "It is a lovely truck, and good point. I wasn't driving back then and don't recall the garage."

"How old were you?" He was trying to keep her mind off their tail. He'd rather it be the Secret Service than the cartel, but Zoe seemed equally upset by either. He took the next exit off the highway and curved around back on himself toward where he'd spotted a couple of hotels near the Federal Reserve Bank.

"Eleven, probably?" She was checking the passenger mirror and, sure enough, the dark Suburban took the turn with them. Whoever was following wasn't trying to hide anymore. Or they were terrible at their job. He sincerely hoped it was the former.

He drove around both hotels and picked the one with decent underground parking. He would rather have a cheap motel with parking out front but it was never a bad idea to switch things up and change routine to mess up people's plans. "When did you decide to become a forensic anthropologist?"

She swung to face him as if surprised by the question. "Not until I started college. I took Anthropology on a whim. I thought I wanted to be an environmental engineer before then, but it turns out *math is hard*."

She grinned at him and he laughed. He bet *Dr.* Miller had done fine at math. She'd simply found her passion the way he'd found his.

He headed off the dark road into the well-lit parking garage. The Secret Service vehicle did not follow them underground. He found a certain grim satisfaction at the idea of the agents freezing their asses off in the car all night long or imagining the mad debate they were having right now about whether or not to get a room and risk losing Seth and Zoe in the interim.

But the USSS knew where they were headed.

Seth didn't mind the additional eyes as long as they concentrated on the job of protection and not some half-assed personal vendetta.

In his experience, Secret Service agents did not like to slum it. Most of them were good enough at their jobs, but they weren't the type to crawl around in the mud and get themselves dirty looking for the perfect shot. And to him that was dangerous. USSS should hire HRT or DEVGRU to test how close they could get to a target the USSS were protecting. Maybe modernize a few old-fashioned practices and ideas.

It wasn't that long since terrorists had made a direct attempt on President Joshua Hague's life. It had been thwarted, not by the President's bodyguards but by another FBI agent, Jed Brennan, who worked for the Behavioral Analysis Unit and had thrown himself between the shooter and POTUS.

Seth quickly reversed into a tight space that was covered by a security camera as Zoe looked on with big eyes. He liked that he could impress her with simple stuff like maneuvering a truck. Imagine if she could see him doing a HALO jump or a hostage rescue assault.

He winced. Hopefully she never had to see the latter.

"I'm going to call and book a room," he said. "Collect everything you need into your bag and put on the ballistic vest."

She passed him his cell phones. "Don't you think we might be a little conspicuous walking through the lobby in body armor?"

"We'll skip the desk and use a phone key if we can. You have a sweater or coat you can wear over it?"

She nodded and dragged out a hoodie.

"Okay then. Problem solved."

Fear had a habit of paralyzing people's thought processes—even smart people—and there was no doubt Zoe was super smart. But she genuinely feared her ex and that made her fumble. Seth clamped down hard on the anger that wanted to take hold. Now wasn't the time.

He made the call and got a room on the second floor close to the fire exit. As he made the reservation, he wondered if anyone had identified the individuals who'd kidnapped Zoe and her friends yet? Or the cartel casualties from the desert?

Last he'd heard, the FBI suspected Lorenzo Santiago's cartel which had broken away from the *Mano de Dios* Colombian organization. They were deadly and ruthless, and Santiago had a reputation for being slightly unhinged.

Seth pulled on a light ballistics vest that was barely discernible under his leather jacket. He and Zoe each hauled their own gear as they made their way quickly to their room.

"Is room service still available?" Zoe asked.

"Until eleven." He noted her tired eyes. It was the second time she'd mentioned food so she must be hungry.

They arrived at the room and Seth was disappointed to note there were, as requested, two queen-size beds. He checked the bathroom but it was empty. He closed the blinds and drapes. He took his backup Glock and pressed it into her hand.

"Order enough room service for both of us, but don't let anyone inside. If I'm not back tell them to place it outside the door. Wedge that chair under the handle after I leave and don't be afraid to shoot anyone who tries to force their way inside, understand? Password is 'duck.'"

Zoe's face was pale. The shadows under her eyes like bruises. "Duck as in 'quack' or duck as in 'crouch down and hide'?"

"Which would you prefer?"

"Duck as in quack."

A smile tugged his mouth. "If I say anything else except 'duck as in quack' or if I'm not back in twenty minutes, call McKenzie and then 911." He handed her his personal cell again. She already knew the access code. "I have my work cell on me. Number is in the contacts."

Her lips pulled into a worried line as she nodded. "Where are you going?"

He brushed his thumb over her cheek. "I want to do a quick

check around the outside. Make sure no one else followed us here and see exactly where our USSS friends are." He had to force himself not to kiss her, but when she rose up on tiptoes to press her lips to his, he couldn't resist pulling her closer for one short moment.

He stepped away. "Don't forget the chair."

"Seth," she said quietly. "Be careful."

———

Seth slipped out the room and listened as Zoe jammed the chair under the handle. Again, it wasn't foolproof, but it would give her enough warning to grab the gun, aim, and fire should the cartel send an attacker.

Not that he was expecting trouble.

And Seth hated the fact he'd become complacent.

He called his boss to give him a quick update as he headed to the lobby and exited through one of the side entrances. Then he stood in the shadows, looking for anyone sitting inside their cars.

He spotted the Suburban parked with a view of both the main lobby and the parking garage. Plate was government issue. One man was in the front seat. He wore a suit and tie. Not Colm Jacobs. Seth suspected the other man was either using the restroom or crashed out in the backseat.

Or creeping up behind him…

Seth didn't indicate he'd heard anyone approaching from his six. He waited until he sensed the man within touching distance and whirled around, catching the guy's arm and slamming him up against the brick wall of the hotel.

17

He removed Jacobs' SIG from his hand while wrenching the man's arm a little harder than was strictly necessary.

"Agent Jacobs. Good to see you again."

"You better let go of me, you little prick, before I—"

"While I'd enjoy whatever playtime you had in mind I must get back to my principal. I just came outside to see if you guys wanted me to send you out some room service."

"You are assaulting a Federal agent."

"Well, as another Federal agent, I'm doing my job which is to check out any tails and potential danger. And it is certainly my job to make sure no one sneaks up on me in the shadows with their gun drawn."

"I'll have your badge, you fucking little prick."

Seth wasn't sure why the guy kept calling him little considering Seth was several inches taller and broader than the guy. Some sort of transference maybe? Napoleon complex?

"Are you officially authorized to follow us or are you using your initiative? Because if it's the latter I'm going to have to ask you to turn around and crawl back under your rock."

"It's authorized." Jacobs' voice was high and thin. "My boss was pissed when you interfered with us taking over Zoe's protection."

"You should have thought of that before you assaulted Dr. Miller last year, you cowardly motherfucker."

"Whatever she told you, she's lying."

Rage bubbled up inside, but Seth's training kept it squashed into a tight ball. He wouldn't risk jeopardizing his position as Zoe's bodyguard for the short-term satisfaction of smacking this guy around.

"She doesn't seem like the lying type to me and you don't seem like a credit to your agency." He shoved the man away from him. Removed the bullets from Jacobs' gun and tossed them in a nearby planter.

He held out the empty weapon to the other man. "I appreciate the extra eyes on our vehicle, but we're not planning to hit the road until six at the earliest, so if you want to get a room? Better yet, give me your cell number and I'll call you when we head out."

"What room are you in?" Jacobs snatched back his weapon.

Seth gave him a sharp smile. "I'd rather not say. I promised Zoe she wouldn't have to see your face ever again."

The other man grew visibly enraged at Seth's words. "You touch her and I will end you."

Seth slowly shook his head and took a step forward. "What you don't seem to understand is that it's up to Zoe who touches her. But let's get one thing straight. *You* will never touch her. *You* will never touch, assault, or hit her ever again. You won't email, call, or stalk the woman. And if you think she won't tell her mother about you, you're mistaken. She is done with you, asshole."

Seth kept his eyes on the man as he backed away, and then he headed into the hotel. He made sure he wasn't followed and took an indirect route to the room, avoiding the elevators.

He knocked on their door. "Duck. Like in quack."

The sounds of movement inside were followed by Zoe unlocking the door.

"Everything okay?" she asked anxiously.

He stepped into the room and closed the door. Locked it.

"Yeah." Then he turned and she stepped into his embrace. He held her tightly and rubbed his chin over the top of her head. He knew he should make some effort to put them back on a professional footing but damned if he could find the willpower tonight.

Zoe Miller was going to be his downfall, and fuck if he could find the energy to care.

———

They were running out of time before the blonde reached her destination and Bruno couldn't take the chance she had removed something from the scene that had either his or Gabriella's DNA on it. Nor could he risk going directly against his boss's orders. Not if he liked his head attached to his neck.

Luis had arranged spotters along the highways, and they'd tracked their target to Interstate 40 which was the route he and Luis had also taken. The fact this woman was traveling with only one bodyguard on the most direct route to Virginia suggested the authorities believed the danger was over.

Officially it was. Unofficially, he needed the woman neutralized.

"According to my source she checked into a hotel for the night. U-Haul is parked underground."

Bruno mulled it over. He wanted it to look like an accident and unrelated to the cartel, but options were limited. Mowing her down with a vehicle created its own problems. A bomb hardly screamed accidental. A random robbery at the hotel? Probably hard to do effectively with the FBI bodyguard.

A drive-by shooting while on the road? Again, tricky, and no guarantee the Federal agent wouldn't get lucky and take them out first.

Bruno was sick of being on the road. He and Luis had been driving all day through horrendous conditions. He wanted to go home. If his face wasn't all over the FBI's Most Wanted list he'd have gotten dropped off at the nearest airport and let Luis drive back alone. But his biometrics were flagged and it was late anyway.

His cell rang. The one that only Lorenzo had the number for.

"Boss?" The word curdled in Bruno's stomach.

"Where the hell are you?" Lorenzo sounded manic.

"Keeping my head down until some of the excitement dies off," Bruno said evenly. "Is everything okay?"

"Gabriella is missing. She's not answering her cell and when I searched for it with the tracking app, I couldn't find it. She's turned it off even though I told her never to do that."

Fear cut across the strings of Bruno's heart.

"She's with that asshole. The one I warned if he ever went near her again, I'd cut off his balls and feed them to a lizard."

"You sent someone to Mexico City?" Bruno asked.

Had Gabriella told anyone of her plans? He'd warned her not to. Told her to turn off her cell and destroy it or leave it in her freezer. Told her to buy a new one when she got to the States. Had she revealed her plan to cross the border illegally to any of her friends? His heartbeat sped up. Bruno had promised to help her disappear from her brother for a little while so she could visit the boyfriend in California. He hadn't meant to make her disappear forever.

She'd pushed him and teased him like he was some boy. And she'd known he wanted her. Had wanted her for years... What had happened had been as much her fault as his but there was no way he could let her live afterwards.

No matter how much he regretted his actions, what was done was done. No bringing her back. He needed to stay alive long enough to get rid of Lorenzo and take over the cartel himself— maybe repair the bonds that Lorenzo had severed with Manuel Gómez who'd escaped from a US prison a year ago.

"Of course, I've sent people to Mexico City. They spoke to her friends and professors, but she hasn't turned up for classes. I know she's with that sonofabitch and I will kill him for disobeying me."

No mention of punishing her. That had been her downfall. Gabriella had been spoiled by an overindulgent older brother who had never made her pay the consequences for her actions. When she'd pushed Bruno, she'd expected him to react the same way. But that wasn't how he was raised. Real men didn't cater to girls, no matter how pretty.

"Maybe you should let her be with him for a few months. She'll tire of him soon enough and want to come home." And her trail would go well and truly cold. "If you kill him, she'll never forgive you."

"I don't care if she forgives me," Lorenzo spat out each word. "That *hijo de la chingada* needs to know I keep my promises."

Bruno rolled his eyes. This was all about Lorenzo's obsession with keeping Gabriella to himself. The fact he'd let her go away to the university had been a major victory for the young woman. Bruno felt the guilt swell again. If only she hadn't taunted him, she'd be exactly where Lorenzo thought she was, and he would have enjoyed dragging her back to Mexico and teaching her a lesson.

"That *puto* needs to be made an example of."

"I'll arrange it."

"No. Bring him to me. I'll deal with him. Personally."

A million questions burst through Bruno's mind. Had Gabriella told the boyfriend the name of the person helping her across the border? Could Bruno kill the man without Lorenzo lashing out in a rage? Probably not. Unless he didn't have any alternative.

"I'll pick him up and be there tomorrow. Can you send a jet to California or shall I hire one?"

"I'll send a jet. Call me immediately if you find her or when you have him."

Lorenzo hung up and Bruno hid the unease running through him so Luis didn't see it on his face and suspect something was amiss.

"Change of plans. Looks like you and I need to find a private airfield and a trustworthy pilot."

"What's happened?"

Bruno stared at his younger brother. Luis was a handsome man but at times looked so much like their late domineering father it unnerved him. This was one of those times.

"Gabriella is missing. Lorenzo wants us to help find her."

Luis blinked. "What about the woman, Zoe Miller?"

Bruno turned to stare thoughtfully out into the darkness. Then he had an idea.

———

The next morning, Seth was driving and Zoe was once again riding shotgun. She glanced in the side mirror and saw the black Suburban not even trying to be subtle about following them today. She spotted Colm Jacobs in the front seat wearing the requisite dark shades and dark suit. Looking at him now, she wondered how she'd ever thought the man was attractive. Sure, he was handsome but there was an edge to his looks. A jadedness and sour curl to his lips when he wasn't forcing his mouth into a smile.

Seth glanced at her but didn't say anything. He'd promised her that Colm wouldn't approach or talk to her, and she had to wonder if he'd confronted the man when he'd left her alone in the room last night.

It felt decidedly unsettling, letting one man protect her from another when she was usually quite capable of looking after herself. But when a man wore a badge, things got decidedly more complicated. And when they worked for the Secret Service…

She'd decided to tell her mother everything as soon as she'd forgiven her for interfering in such a heavy-handed manner in the first place. She'd wait for her to return from her overseas trip.

Her mom would never have sent Jacobs to protect her if she'd known what he was really like, so that was on Zoe. She'd correct the record and hopefully her mother would respect her wishes in the future.

Her new cell rang and she felt a surge of excitement. Zoe had persuaded Seth to stop at a store in Nashville and pick up a burner. She now owed the guy serious money but she would pay him back.

She was ridiculously happy with her new device. You'd think she'd never had a phone before. She'd already reached her brother, and James, and left a message for Fred. Karina was still in the ICU but recovering and expected to be moved to a regular room tomorrow morning.

She answered the call.

"Zo." It was Fred. "You okay?"

"Yes. Still driving the U-Haul. Should arrive home late tonight."

He lowered his voice. "I take it from the FBI agent shadowing my every move that you are not alone?"

Zoe looked at Seth, aware that the man who'd held her in his arms all through the night even though they hadn't had sex, was listening attentively to the conversation. It had felt like a soft reset after the passion and misunderstandings of the night before. It wasn't that she hadn't wanted to make love with Seth, it was that she accepted he wanted to keep things professional between them despite the fact they'd already crossed that line. And maybe they needed to get to know one another better before they jumped each other's bones again.

It was possible they had a chance of an actual relationship, but she was nervous. She didn't want to make another mistake by talking about it too early and she didn't want Seth to feel obligated to get involved in anything deeper than a quick fling.

"Operator Hopper kindly offered to share the driving of the moving truck."

Seth snorted.

Fred grunted.

Zoe rolled her eyes.

"My bodyguard is driving me crazy," Fred said gruffly.

"It won't be for long. I think the cartel who abducted us are a high priority for the Feds, so they'll be busy keeping their heads down," Zoe stated firmly.

"I hope so. That is one experience I never want to repeat. I'm not gonna lie, it's going to take a while until I'm comfortable going back out into the desert again."

"I know. I'm sorry."

"This isn't on you. It's on corrupt powerful people who'll do anything to keep control...and the cartel."

She laughed the way she was supposed to. It was ironic how antiestablishment her friends were, considering how much they enjoyed spending time with her parents.

"You getting on okay with Agent Beefcake?"

Zoe choked. "Don't call him that."

Seth scowled. She'd never met a man with so many hang-ups about his good looks.

Beautiful people struggle too.

It was a joke the four of them shared whenever Karina was stereotyped because of her incredible natural beauty.

Apparently, it was true. Who knew.

"We're getting on fine." Better than fine.

Seth shot her a look from under his brows which she studiously ignored.

"Operator Hopper rescued me from the Secret Service."

"That fucker Jacobs?"

"Yeah." Zoe's mouth went dry. "He tried to snatch me at the hospital yesterday—that's why I disappeared without saying goodbye. My mom somehow thought that might be a good idea."

"You still haven't told her?"

"I thought I'd never have to see him again, so I took the easy way out. I never imagined she'd specifically request he form part of my protection detail."

She banded an arm around her stomach. There was a long pause on the other end as Fred seemed to absorb the fact she'd obviously told Seth the truth about her troubles with the Secret Service agent. She was not someone who easily confided in others.

"Any sign of trouble?" Fred asked.

She eyed the Suburban in the wing mirror. "No, just terrible weather."

Zoe was suddenly distracted by the white-knuckled look of concentration on Seth's features. They'd been climbing for a while. The heavy van sometimes struggled on the inclines, but they'd just crested the brow of a hill and were racing down along a narrow gorge.

Seth generally drove faster than she did, but he always seemed in total control even when the conditions were hazardous. Now they were quickly approaching the back of one of two large trucks that were side by side on the highway and he wasn't slowing down.

They got closer and closer to the rear bumper and Zoe looked at Seth in alarm.

"You might want to hold on," Seth told her grimly. "The brakes aren't working."

18

"Fred, I have to go." She hung up and stuffed the phone into her jeans back pocket.

She braced her hand against the dash.

Instead of moving into the fast lane, flashing his lights, or honking his horn, Seth stayed in the inside lane and rammed the milk tanker in front of him.

Zoe grabbed the handle over the door. "What are you doing?"

"Using the rig to slow us down."

The U-Haul shuddered a little but Seth held it steady.

Zoe's mouth went dry as her heart galloped.

The trucker didn't know what was going on and sped up to avoid the lunatic seemingly set on self-destruction behind him. They were heading down a steep hill. Without the physical barrier of the truck, the U-Haul once again careened forward.

"What about the parking brake?" Zoe suggested, torn between closing her eyes and not missing a thing that might help.

"I'll use that when we've slowed down or get to an uphill section." His voice was as calm as always while she felt as if she was screaming on the inside. "Hopefully, it will be enough to slow us down then. If I apply the emergency brake here with this much speed, we might spin out or it will burn out without doing a damn thing."

She glanced around while holding on for grim life. There was too much traffic to risk spinning out. She didn't want to die but neither did she want to kill some oblivious person happily driving down the highway.

"Where's the next uphill section?" she asked, craning her neck around the trucks to see the terrain ahead.

"I'm not sure," he said grimly. "But I know there's a town at the bottom of this valley."

Oh hell.

The implications were not lost on her. Careening through a populated area with no brakes was a catastrophe in the making. The incline became steeper rather than shallower and Zoe couldn't breathe. Seth bumped into the tanker again and the trucker once more put his foot on the accelerator.

Zoe gritted her teeth and tightened her grip on the grab handle.

"Doesn't he realize I'm in trouble here?" Seth shook his head with the first sign of frustration.

"He probably thinks you're some crazy road rager." Zoe's voice came out unnaturally high-pitched.

"If he thinks I'm trying to force his eighteen-wheeler off the road with your truck then he's the crazy one."

They touched bumpers again and the van shuddered and lurched. Seth's attention was intent on keeping them on the road behind, but not under, the vehicle in front.

"Do you know Jacobs' cell number?" he asked suddenly.

"I blocked him but I remember it."

"Use my cell, call him quick. I'll speak to him."

Even now, with their lives speeding toward an ugly end, he was protecting her. She forced herself to let go of the handle. Her hands shook as she picked up Seth's cell and turned it on. She dialed Jacobs' number from memory and put the call on speaker.

"What the fuck is going on, Hopper? You having a coronary?" Colm's familiar grating voice came over the line.

"Our brakes have failed. I'm using the truck in front of me to control our speed, but I need you to get in front and make him slow down and pull over, gradually, if possible."

"Now you want our help?"

"Do your fucking job, Jacobs, unless you want to explain two dead people under your so-called watch."

Colm swore but Zoe saw the Suburban put on its cherry lights and roar into the outside lane. The car raced ahead, overtaking the tanker. One of the Secret Service agents stuck his hand out of the window and moved it up and down repeatedly, to indicate the truck pull over.

The screech of airbrakes rang out as the milk tanker slowed and indicated to pull off the road.

Relief flooded her, although it wasn't over yet. Her fingers once more seized the grab handle and her teeth fused together.

Seth shadowed the truck as the two vehicles reduced speed. He worked the parking brake to help slow them and reduce the force of the impact with the rear of the tanker. Their bumpers scraped loudly against one another before both came to a shuddering halt.

Zoe and Seth sat in silence for a long, taut moment. She felt numb and terrified all at the same time. She couldn't seem to let go of the handle even though her arm screamed with tension. She looked at Seth, spotted the whiteness of his lips and the sweat that had beaded his temple.

"We survived." She couldn't believe what had just happened.

They'd almost died.

Seth took her free hand and kissed the back of her fingers. "Would have been trickier if that truck hadn't been there." He grinned and she realized this sort of thing didn't terrify him the way it did her. This was what he did—he overcame obstacles and took on challenges that would boggle most people's minds. Tracking her down in the desolate Sonoran Desert. Taking on the cartel. Hunting killers. He did it all with the same calm competence with which she examined the dead.

"Everyone okay back there?" Jacobs voice on the speaker jolted her back into the present.

"We're good. Thanks for the assist." Seth ended the call.

Then he cupped her chin before kissing her quickly on the mouth.

———

He kept the kiss short and sweet and out of sight of the Secret Service agents who were bound to appear any moment.

"Wait here. Lock the door and keep the ballistic vest between you and the traffic."

Zoe looked shaken but she paid attention to the quick-fire set of instructions he gave her. She'd held up well under the circumstances, although she thankfully hadn't realized the seriousness of the situation until he'd collided with the rear bumper of the milk tanker. Without that truck in front of them there had been nothing to slow them down before they'd reached the next town and that would have been carnage.

What the hell had happened?

Was it an accident, sabotage, or was this an ambush?

The Secret Service agents must have spoken to the truck driver. Now he could see them reversing the Suburban rapidly back along the highway when the lane was clear of traffic. They parked behind the U-Haul which was good.

Seth put in a quick call to Novak with a request for local assistance and promised an update as soon as he had one, then he called Highway Patrol requesting support.

The two Secret Service agents positioned themselves at each end of the moving van in a protective stance. Jacobs thankfully stood at the rear of the vehicle and out of Zoe's line of sight.

Seth got out and jogged up to the truck driver who'd climbed out of his cab and was walking back to inspect the damage. The man was large and grizzled with a gut that overrode his belted jeans and a too-big plaid shirt. His beard looked like a home for wildlife and his eyes sparked with more humor than Seth would have felt if he'd been deliberately rear-ended on the highway.

"Sorry, pal. Brakes failed. It was using you to slow us down or risk losing control of my vehicle. I'm afraid you lost that coin toss." Seth handed the guy his card with the official metallic raised seal of the FBI.

The man's eyebrows rose.

It wasn't every day an HRT operator drove a U-Haul across country, but it happened more than people might think. Considering how an operator and his—or her—family had to pack up and move to Quantico on acceptance into the elite unit.

"Glad no one was hurt," the trucker said, shaking his head and staring at the card. "Also relieved I'm not getting a ticket."

Seth laughed with the guy. They checked for damage and both took photographs of the tailgate of the tanker for insurance purposes, but the chrome of the heavy 18-wheeler was barely scraped, whereas the moving van's front bumper and grill were badly crumpled.

They took each other's details and Seth waved the guy on his way.

Seth jogged back to the U-Haul and opened the passenger side door. "You okay?"

She nodded. She looked calmer now, but still uneasy—probably because that asshole Jacobs was so close by.

"I won't be long. Stay here." Seth had a plan, which he hoped didn't get him fired. Or shot.

He shimmied under the vehicle on the wet asphalt, the damp chill soaking through his t-shirt and jeans.

"What are you doing?" Jacobs crouched to stare at him from the rear of the truck.

"Looking for evidence."

"Evidence of what?" The guy sounded slyly amused.

Seth glanced at him sharply. "What the fuck do you think?"

The man's expression soured. Would Colm Jacobs have gone to the extremes of sabotaging this vehicle? Of trying to kill Zoe and him? Or were these two Secret Service agents so incompetent that someone had damaged the vehicle under their watch?

Seth honestly wasn't sure which, but neither was a good look for the USSS.

It could be an accident but what were the chances?

Ignoring the cold discomfort, he shuffled until he was near the passenger-side front wheel and easily found what he was looking for.

Sonofabitch.

There was a ragged tear in the brake hose. All the brake fluid was gone. He took a photograph.

Then he checked the other side. Another small tear, as if someone had drawn a hacksaw blade across it a few times to give the appearance of it being frayed rather than sliced cleanly with a knife. He took more photos but didn't touch anything.

No way was this an accident—both brake hoses at the same time? No way.

And maybe he shouldn't exclude himself from censure. He was the one in charge of getting Zoe safely to DC. Although he couldn't be in two places at once, he hadn't noticed any fluid under the moving van that morning. The parking garage was dimly lit, but he'd overly relied on the deterrent of the surveillance camera and presence of the other federal agents, which had led to a false sense of security.

Rookie error.

He'd fucked up.

He didn't bother looking at the rear wheels. He shimmied out just as the State Troopers drew up and began diverting traffic safely around them. Then, in record time, field agents from the FBI's Knoxville satellite office arrived.

Seth introduced himself and they exchanged IDs. He explained what had happened.

"I need this rental truck transported to Quantico ASAP for

evidence of potential brake tampering." He lowered his voice and leaned closer. "At a certain point I also need you to distract those Secret Service agents long enough for me to get away with their Suburban—I'll return it to their offices in the morning, promise."

"How come the Secret Service is involved?" Agent Grant asked, checking out the suits standing at stiff attention.

"The person in the U-Haul is the daughter of the Vice President who's repeatedly refused their protection. The thing is," Seth lowered his voice, wishing he didn't have to divulge any of Zoe's secrets but knowing that the truth would work best when dealing with a fellow agent being asked to run interference with another Federal agency. "The blond guy used to be in a relationship with my principal, a relationship he didn't want to end. He's still angry about being dumped. And those two jackasses were supposedly watching this truck last night, a truck which now has at least two damaged brake hoses."

He let the female agent absorb his suspicions.

"Doctor Miller and I have to be at JEH for a task force briefing at 8:00 a.m. tomorrow morning and I'd really like to have the opportunity to change before I'm grilled by the suits. I don't have time to waste arranging fresh transportation and I do not trust those two clowns to have our backs if they give us a ride. Nor do I trust them with this truck which contains Dr. Miller's personal belongings and could possibly contain evidence that someone tampered with the brakes in a fit of revenge. Well," he pulled a face, "it's either them or the cartel."

Agent Grant jerked her chin as she processed what he told her. He suspected she'd heard about what had happened in Arizona. She looked at the USSS agents in an assessing manner. Nodded. "Let me talk to Dr. Miller while you grab the belongings you need out of the cab."

It was good she was verifying things with Zoe because for all she knew Seth was the crazy stalker and weird-hair guy was the knight in shining armor.

"You know USSS can track that vehicle, right?" Grant pointed out.

"Of course." It wasn't ideal but it had a few plus points over alternate strategies, and he could disconnect the signal easily enough if he wanted to, not that he planned to tell Agent Grant that. He shrugged. "USSS knows where I'm headed, their Suburban is bulletproof and with that license plate I won't get pulled over if I go a little over the speed limit." Or a lot. "More importantly it will slow these two clowns long enough I don't have to worry about them even if they aren't actively trying to kill us." He softened his expression. "I know it sounds farfetched but..."

The agent's expression told him she didn't believe it was that implausible. "What about the higher ups? Who's going to deal with them?"

"I take full responsibility. I'll call my boss at HRT, and he can call the person in charge of the task force and the director of USSS." Seth straightened. "I was ordered to get Zoe Miller to DC safe and sound by tomorrow morning. I was told I could bend a few FBI rules as it was last minute and I'm on my own."

Agent Grant chuckled. "Stealing the USSS car tailing you is definitely bending a few rules but that's DHS's problem." Her lips quirked. "Way above my pay grade."

Seth smiled and nodded, then walked over to the driver-side door and opened it. Zoe hadn't moved and was hunched down in the front seat, actively avoiding Jacobs.

"Do you trust me?" he asked, staring intently into her robin's egg blue eyes, and waiting for her answer.

He wasn't sure why it mattered so much, but it did.

19

Did she trust him?

Zoe opened her mouth in surprise at the question. Adrenaline was pumping through her body from their near-death experience and the close proximity of someone who'd physically and mentally abused her.

How could she *not* trust a man who'd saved her life multiple times, made her heart race with desire, and held her gently in his arms as she slept all last night?

He'd made her feel safe after months of insecurity. He bolstered her confidence after incessant self-doubt.

She had the terrible feeling she was falling for this man and she had no idea whether that was wise or not. She'd sworn off alpha males after Colm Jacobs, but Seth Hopper was making her forget Colm existed even though the guy was less than twenty feet away. Seth Hopper was an alpha with a soft heart.

Except she'd watched this soft-hearted alpha kill multiple times to protect her so maybe that was the wrong description. Dedicated, honorable, patient, highly skilled, quick, intelligent, sexy.

She swallowed tightly and nodded. "I trust you."

He grinned then, his handsome features lighting up at her words.

"Talk to Agent Grant here while I grab our stuff and put it in the Suburban."

Her eyes widened in alarm and she saw Seth regarding her patiently.

Was trust enough?

Enough for her to get into a vehicle with her abusive ex?

Those calm hazel eyes of his told her he knew her inner battle. He wasn't angry that even though she'd said she trusted him, and she really did, she still hesitated. Her instinct was to get as far away from the source of her anxiety as possible—and Seth was asking her to do the exact opposite.

Could she do it?

She straightened her spine and raised her chin. Yes, she could. She was done being scared of a man who was nothing more than a bully with a badge. She was done letting him dictate any aspect of her mood or life. Of course, that was a lot easier to do when she had another Federal agent backing her up.

It bothered her that she wasn't as brave as she wanted to be, but the world seemed to always favor the abuser. She needed to up her game. She wasn't going to let Colm Jacobs intimidate her even if she had to ride all the way to DC with him.

"Okay."

"I'm going to get this rig towed to the FBI Laboratory at Quantico." Seth patted the U-Haul. "And have the evidence techs look for possible brake tampering. I'll help get your belongings released and moved into your place by this weekend, if at all possible. Is that okay?"

"Brake tampering. That's what I was afraid of," she mumbled.

Seth's mouth twisted. "Looks like it."

Her gaze locked on his.

Damn. Was the cartel still after her? Or had Colm decided to get rid of the problem she now presented by sabotaging the van?

She glanced at the man via the mirror and he smirked at her.

She turned away. The fact Seth was now getting a ride with the USSS suggested he must have figured this was the cartel. Either way, she realized, the danger wasn't over. She couldn't afford to drop her guard. She and Seth needed to get to Quantico as soon as possible with her two small pieces of evidence. Maybe then the cartel—if it was the cartel—would stop chasing her.

"Don't worry," Seth said, reading her mind. "I've got you."

She blew out a long breath. It was embarrassing how much she wanted that to be true.

She grabbed her cell and the charging cords from the console and climbed out to talk to the FBI agent waiting nearby.

"Stay behind the engine for cover." Seth stood back, in full professional mode now. No hint of the affectionate lover.

"Dr. Miller? I'm Agent Grant." The woman wore a dark pant suit and heeled boots. She towered over Zoe as she steered her off to the side of the road.

An icy drip of water fell off the tip of a bare branch and hit Zoe's cheek. She wiped it away like an unwanted tear.

"First thing I want you to know, I am willing and able to provide you with a protection detail to take you to our Residence Agency if you feel uncomfortable with any of the people here."

Reluctantly Zoe's eyes found Colm Jacobs who'd switched positions with his partner and was now watching her over the hood of the moving truck, rather than watching the road.

Zoe turned her back on him as a shudder ran over her shoulders.

"I don't want to spend time with the Secret Service agents, but I'm happy with the protection Operator Hopper has been providing." She doubted anyone else would have prevented them from wrecking on the highway the way he had, let alone tracking her down in the desert. "Thanks for the offer though. I appreciate it."

Agent Grant's intelligent blue eyes watched her closely, possibly seeing more than Zoe wanted her to. Then the other woman nodded and took a step back. She handed Zoe a business card. "I wanted to verify what Operator Hopper told me. Call me if you change your mind. I love your mother by the way. Hoping she makes a run for president one day." Agent Grant walked away toward the USSS agents.

Zoe's biggest nightmare—aside from the cartel and her horrible ex—was her mother becoming the US President, but that was purely for selfish reasons. Zoe liked her anonymity even if that had been jeopardized over the last few days. At least the press appeared to have lost interest in the abduction and had moved on to other things.

Seth was finishing putting their belongings in the rear compartment of the large SUV.

He jerked his head slightly, urging her to come toward him and get in the vehicle.

She drew in a deep breath. Stupid to be disappointed that he couldn't keep her away from Colm Jacobs the way he'd said he would. But the disabled van put a serious crimp in their travel plans.

She checked the cab for anything they might have left behind but, true to form, Seth had been thorough. She closed the door and strode over to Seth with her chin held high. She was damned if Colm would see her cower again.

"Slide in the back and buckle up," Seth murmured as he moved past her.

Her eyes widened as she realized he'd removed all the Secret Service agents' belongings and stacked them just out of sight behind the vehicle.

He raised his hand to the agents as he climbed in beside Zoe.

The USSS men ignored him and turned back to Agent Grant who was questioning them both. Neither man looked happy with the interrogation.

"You strapped in?" Seth asked.

She clipped in the belt as she watched him slither into the driver's seat and start the engine with the key that sat in the console. He put the vehicle in drive and accelerated fast, merging into traffic before the men from the USSS could react with more than open-mouthed shock.

Zoe raised her middle finger at Jacobs although she doubted he could see her through the tinted windows.

Seth caught her gaze in the mirror. "Told you I wouldn't let him anywhere near you."

Tears unexpectedly stung her eyes but she blinked them away. Her throat was so thick she couldn't speak.

Instead, she unclipped her seat belt and climbed into the passenger seat beside Seth. She pressed a kiss against his cheek before putting her belt back on and adjusting the seat. "I can't believe you did that."

She watched his knuckles tighten slightly on the steering wheel.

"I promised he wouldn't get near you. And I'm not completely convinced Jacobs isn't the person who cut our brake hoses in the night. The last thing I want is to be at his mercy in a vehicle for any length of time." Seth checked the mirror and changed lanes. He was going a lot faster than they'd driven in the truck.

The fact he also suspected Jacobs of possibly trying to kill them was both strangely reassuring and absolutely chilling.

"I need to call Novak to get him to secure the hotel's surveillance footage from last night before any other agency decides to get their hands on it."

Damn.

"And now I'm gonna need you to do something you obviously have not wanted to do in the past. I'm going to need you to call your mother and explain that you haven't been kidnapped by some rogue FBI agent, which Jacobs is sure to claim. And maybe mention I've simply borrowed this vehicle for a few hours rather than stolen it."

Zoe stared at him, eyes widening, realizing he'd put the career he obviously adored on the line. And he'd done it largely so she wouldn't have to endure being subjected to Colm Jacobs' presence who her mother liked so much.

"I don't know how to thank you," Zoe said carefully.

"You don't need to thank me," Seth said sternly. "I'm simply doing my job."

Zoe flinched. "Of course."

God. She'd been half falling in love with the guy, and he was "doing his job." Despite the fact they'd had sex and grown closer, she realized she had no idea if Seth Hopper had any feelings for her beyond that of being his "principal" and a very willing lover.

He'd told her he liked her, and she knew he was physically attracted to her, but she had no clue as to whether they had any chance of a future together or if he was even looking for anything else in his life. He hadn't spoken about romantic relationships. As much as they'd gotten to know one another over the last few days, they hadn't talked about any possibility of a "them." And she'd already gone and become emotionally attached to the guy.

Very. Emotionally. Attached.

"Zoe."

She shook her head to clear away the unwelcome thoughts about this man who'd so unexpectedly fallen into her life. "What?"

"Call your mother."

———

Seth kept glancing at Zoe, but she'd been withdrawn for a few hours now, ever since she'd reached her mother in the middle of the night in Karachi.

Listening to Zoe explain the situation had been painful. The fact her mother hadn't believed her at first—probably because she hadn't wanted to acknowledge she'd put her daughter in physical and emotional danger by disregarding Zoe's express wishes regarding getting the Secret Service involved back in Tucson—had compounded that feeling.

Zoe had closed her eyes afterwards and pretended to sleep.

But maybe Zoe wasn't quiet because of her earlier upset.

Maybe it was because they were approaching the end of their road trip and she was almost home.

He clenched his jaw.

Perhaps Zoe was pulling back because she was getting ready to disentangle herself from him. She hadn't mentioned the two of them seeing one another once this trip was over. Hadn't expressed any interest in continuing this unexpected and unplanned relationship.

Was it just sex?

She certainly wouldn't be the first woman to want him on a temporary basis purely for his body. The fact he felt more than that, a lot more, to the point he'd broken every rule of conduct in the handbook, was his own stupid fault. He'd known all along getting personally involved with this woman could destroy his career—and he'd done it anyway. And he didn't feel as if he could press her for more because the absolute last thing he wanted to do was to come across as a pushy asshole after her last disastrous relationship.

It felt like more than just sex.

He didn't remember the last time sex have been that intense and uninhibited, but it wasn't just that…

He rolled his shoulders. He needed to not freak out like a high school teen. He could express a desire to continue this thing between them after the danger was over. Call her up and ask her on a proper date. Maybe help her unload the moving truck this weekend—if he could get enough time off to go to Richmond.

He didn't know if the Feds planned to continue her protection beyond the meeting tomorrow. Despite her resistance to the idea, it would be wiser to keep some security in place until they figured out exactly what the cartel's agenda was.

The idea of her being vulnerable didn't sit well. At least Jacobs would hopefully be too busy answering to his superiors to contemplate revenge, but maybe not. Seth doubted the guy would be fired unless his prints or DNA were found under that U-Haul —too much hinged on the classic "he said, she said" dynamic. But a desk job was probably in the man's future for the duration of this current administration—or something to persuade Jacobs to stay far away from Zoe. Seth couldn't always be there to protect her. And angry jilted men often took out their aggression on their perceived persecutors.

Seth wasn't sure exactly how much danger Zoe might be in. He needed to talk to a buddy of his, another former Navy SEAL, who now worked at the Behavioral Analysis Unit. Matt Lazlo would have a good idea how worried Zoe needed to be about Colm Jacobs and the likelihood of him escalating.

The cartel was another beast entirely...

Hopefully, once Zoe passed on her evidence for analysis the threat would diminish. He thought about the bloody rock he'd collected, the one he hadn't told Zoe about.

How did he bring it up now, all these hours later?

He didn't. It was evidence in a case, and he wasn't allowed to discuss an open investigation with a civilian—except he didn't know if there even *was* a case. Had the FBI opened a case number with regards to this missing woman?

He doubted it.

He had documented the information in his report but Patterson and the task force probably hadn't read that yet, or figured it was important.

He'd submit the rock for processing at the Laboratory Division, and between it and Zoe's items maybe they'd be able to identify the woman Zoe had seen in the desert—or her killer. And maybe that would explain why the cartel had abducted the four forensic anthropologists a few days ago.

They reached the turn to I-64. At Charlottesville the road forked south to Richmond and north to Quantico. It struck him that, although not a perfect scenario, Zoe was close enough for them to start seeing each other if she wanted...

He pushed the thought aside. It wasn't fair to put any additional pressure on her. It would either happen or it wouldn't, but he wasn't going to push it right now. Best to take it slow.

Tonight might be their last night together, and even if it was just sex, he wasn't ready to give her up yet. The intimacy they shared was addictive and he wanted to hang on to every last shred he could get.

After the brake-fail incident, he'd considered flying to Quantico, but Zoe had no ID, and the flight times hadn't been much faster than driving. And he'd be lying if he said he didn't enjoy this time alone with her.

Zoe yawned and finally gave him the smile he'd been missing. "Sorry. I know I've been quiet. I should have been entertaining you as you're doing all the driving."

"I don't need entertaining." He shot her a look. "You've had a traumatic experience. You need time to process it all."

Her eyes filled with uncertainty as they met his. "I guess."

Payne Novak had almost swallowed his tongue when Seth had told him what he'd done to the USSS detail. But after Zoe's conversation with her mother, and the official investigation that was now being conducted into the brake failure on the van and into Colm Jacobs' past conduct, Seth's decisions had been retroactively given the green light.

Thankfully.

Unfortunately, Zoe couldn't share the driving because it was a government-issue vehicle. Heaven forbid you broke those kind of rules while running for your life, else the Office of Professional Responsibility really would have your ass.

"Let's call ahead to your friend at the lab and then I need to check in briefly at the HRT compound and pick up my truck." Most of the guys were back from Colorado but would probably have gone home by the time they arrived. He wanted to catch up on the details of the team's recent adventures, although that might have to wait until he got back from the meeting at JEH tomorrow.

He cleared his throat. "I realize you'd probably prefer to stay in DC tonight, at the Naval Observatory or a nice hotel—"

"I don't want to stay at the Observatory if my parents aren't there and I can't afford a fancy hotel." She held his gaze. "Like I said, I prefer to pay my own way, but I am aware of the privilege I wield while being able to do so. I have a good education and the cushion of wealthy parents as a backup. Most people don't." She pulled a face. "I hope the vehicle rental company won't keep charging me if the van is impounded."

"Call them tomorrow and see what they say—I'm sure they'll want to send an investigator of their own. If they need some sort of warrant or paperwork, I'll talk to our admin and see what she can come up with."

Maddie Goodwin knew exactly what to say to companies in these situations.

He cleared his throat again, feeling like a kid asking the girl he was sweet on out on a first date. Give him a terrorist situation or a high threat alert and he was as cool as an ice cap. Confront him with a woman he really liked and he was a bumbling idiot.

"We could stay at a hotel, or we could use my place in Quantico and leave early for DC tomorrow morning. It's nothing fancy, but you'd be more than welcome, and it would give me the opportunity to dust off my suit for tomorrow."

He tried to remember the last time he'd changed the sheets on his bed. He wasn't a pig, but he'd been away for a while, and housekeeping was never as important as cleaning his weapons.

Those liquid turquoise eyes went wide, and he wondered if he'd overstepped. Then a smile curved her lips.

"I'd really like that."

Something warmed inside him.

He was going to add there were no-strings but decided that should go without saying. He'd be happy with a few strings but now wasn't the time to discuss it with a woman who'd recently been traumatized.

And now wasn't the time to drop his vigilance or guard either. He snapped his attention back to their surroundings. Someone had tried to kill them today. That someone was still out there.

Bruno had always liked California but he hated LA. Too many cars. Too many people. The stench of elitism and bullshit combined with exhaust fumes made him want to gag. But business was good here. Not as profitable as the East Coast maybe, but certainly booming.

He and Luis sat in a dark Escalade outside a large house situated halfway between the medical school and the Playboy Mansion. Bruno had paid someone to watch the young man on and off ever since Lorenzo had forbidden Gabriella to see him. Bruno had a good idea as to the young man's routine.

"Do we go in and grab him?" asked Luis who was growing impatient.

"Not yet." The last thing Bruno wanted was to alert the authorities. "Let him come to us."

Derek Belmont was a rich kid from an affluent neighborhood. The nearby mansions cost more than some Mexican towns.

Belmont was a second-year medical student who'd met Gabriella a little over a year ago on a beach in Cancun. The fact he was in medical school suggested he might be intelligent but would he have the instincts to realize he was being hunted?

Bruno doubted it. Young men tended to believe they were invincible. He certainly had. So had Lorenzo.

The silence between him and his brother hung thick and heavy like smoke. Where would Luis's loyalty lie if forced to choose between family and the boss?

"Has Lorenzo said anything about me, recently?" Bruno probed.

"Like what?" Luis frowned.

"Nothing." Bruno shrugged. "The boss has been sounding more and more paranoid these last six months, so I wondered..." Bruno tapped his fingers on the steering wheel.

"It wouldn't surprise me if Gabriella simply decided to run away," Luis said sullenly. "We all know how she can be."

"I agree." It was amazing. If the images of what had happened that night hadn't been quite so vivid in his mind, Bruno could have probably convinced himself she had simply fled. The only people who knew the truth were himself and Gabriella, and neither of them were talking.

Luis shifted uncomfortably in the seat. They'd been sitting here for hours.

"I wondered if you'd heard any rumblings from the others." He held his brother's dark gaze. "I've been dreaming a lot lately." His family set a lot of store in dreams. "That something will happen to me. Something bad."

He pulled his face into a twisted sneer as if it didn't bother him. No one in the cartel was openly scared of dying. Their chances of surviving to an old age were remote at best. Their chances of dying of natural causes? Infinitesimal.

But, inside, they all feared death.

Luis watched him attentively now. "Do you ever wish..." His brother spoke then trailed off.

"What?" Bruno asked, curious.

Luis's chest rose as he inhaled. "That you hadn't followed Lorenzo into this business?"

Bruno nodded reluctantly. "I often wish I'd stayed on the family farm but we needed money and Papa didn't give me a lot of choice."

Their father had been a violent pig who'd beaten their mother whenever he was drunk and no one else was home. Bruno was glad the man had died before he'd put a bullet in him. He would have enjoyed the moment and burned in Hell for eternity. But as he was going to burn anyway, perhaps he should have just killed the old bastard years ago.

He huffed out a dark chuckle. "This is the hand we've been dealt. We better not disappoint the boss, huh?"

At that moment a small door in the gate opened and a young man with cropped blond hair stepped out carrying a bicycle. He was hard to miss wearing full neon cycling gear.

Luis pulled a bandana up over his nose. Bruno rolled the car slowly forward until he was level with the young man. Luis jumped out, pulled a gun and held it to Derek Belmont's head while explaining he either get in the vehicle or die on the sidewalk.

Derek chose unwisely and climbed into the back seat.

Bruno had also pulled a bandana up over his lower features.

"Get rid of his cell and helmet." The helmet had a camera attached.

Luis tossed the items out of the window and they smashed on the sidewalk.

"What do you want?" The young man was pale beneath his tan now. Perspiration beaded his skin despite the coolness inside the Escalade.

"I think you know what we want, *puto*." Bruno made his voice low and threatening. "Santiago told you to stay away from his sister."

Derek's Adam's apple bobbed up and down his skinny white throat. "She contacted me but I never replied."

A cold smile touched Bruno's lips. "Where is she?"

Derek's eyes bugged. "I don't know. I haven't seen her in nearly a year."

"She's missing, *compadre*, and she told a friend she was coming here to be with you."

"What?" The man swayed in his seat. "I don't know what you're talking about. Her brother warned me away from her and I haven't gone near her since."

"But you spoke to her? Encouraged her?"

"I ended it! I swear. I loved her, but I can't put my family at risk." Derek's eyes darted to a woman jogging down the street as if she might be able to rescue him. Any attempt would end in her death. "Her brother threatened my parents, my grandmother." He shook his head and the coward had tears swimming in his eyes. "I gave her up for them. I swear, I haven't called her in months."

Bruno might have believed him except Gabriella had told him that Derek would pick her up in Phoenix.

But what if *she'd* been lying to Bruno? What if, in an act of callous disregard equal to her brother's, she'd decided to go to her boyfriend despite his best interests, ignoring the threats Lorenzo had made? Had she truly not believed what Lorenzo was capable of?

Bruno pursed his lips and met his brother's dark gaze in the mirror.

It didn't matter. None of it mattered. All that mattered was keeping Lorenzo happy until such a time as Bruno could justifiably kill the man.

He watched as his brother stabbed a needle into the young man's thigh and pressed down the plunger.

"Sorry, *compadre*. I might believe you, but Lorenzo Santiago is another thing entirely. Sleep. Sleep and this will all be over soon."

20

Zoe met her brilliant friend Dr. Coco Montserrat in the secure reception area of the state-of-the-art laboratory building in the heart of the FBI's campus on the Quantico Marine Corps base.

They hugged one another for a long moment and Coco squeezed her tight.

"I saw what happened on the news and heard via the grapevine who was involved. I am so glad you're okay."

The other woman was tall and slender with deep brown skin and curly black hair pulled into a no-nonsense bun. She wore red reading glasses that made her look like a sexy librarian and Zoe was once again reminded of her own physical shortcomings. Especially when Coco's eyes bugged at the mouth-watering sight of Seth in his t-shirt which showed off every jacked muscle in his chest and arms, and the soft blue jeans that hugged and cupped all the male anatomy the two of them had once giggled and snorted over in class.

Zoe introduced them.

"Agent Hopper." Coco kept an arm around Zoe's shoulders as she shook Seth's hand. "Thank you so much for *taking care* of my friend here." Coco thought she was being cute as her pitch changed and her expression became suggestive.

Zoe rolled her eyes. Coco had obviously been talking to Fred and probably recognized from the heat in her cheeks that Zoe's feelings for this man had veered way off platonic about seven states and two time zones ago.

"Thank you for agreeing to meet with us so late." Seth widened his stance and smiled the sort of smile that gave grown women the vapors.

"What was it that was so important?" Coco asked curiously.

Zoe held out the evidence bags. "I found a tooth and a medallion in the desert that I'd appreciate being checked for prints and DNA. Anything you can discover might help identify either a killer or a murder victim."

Coco's delicate brows arched as she took the items. "You found these in the desert?"

"Near a corpse that subsequently disappeared. This is all that's left." Along with maybe a few photographs.

Their most recent near-death experience had shaken Zoe more than she wanted to admit. But if it was the cartel trying to kill her then the danger had possibly passed on to her friend.

She hugged her arms tightly around herself. "I'm worried that the reason for the attempts on my life stem from the evidence in those bags. And if the cartel discovers you're working on them, you might be in danger too."

Coco's expression grew serious. "The idea that anyone outside the FBI could access lab records or even know who is working on what is extremely unlikely. Even people inside the FBI don't have direct access to our database."

"We're talking some of the wealthiest and most ruthless criminals in the world, ma'am," Seth added somberly. "The ones who'll kidnap and threaten your loved ones in order to get what they want."

Coco pursed her lips thoughtfully. "Well, we already know these items are not admissible in court." She chewed her bottom lip. "I'm going to stay late and see who I can persuade to examine these for me." She lowered her voice. "There is a very attractive latent print expert I'd love an excuse to talk to. And I can send a DNA swab along with a priority label and it will go to the front of the queue, but I'm not sure if we'll be successful getting a sample off the chain. It depends how long it was in the desert and if we find any epithelial cells."

Seth drew a sealed-evidence envelope out of a small pack he carried. "You might have better luck with this. And this *is* admissible in court as I collected it at the scene, and I've had it with me the entire time since. I don't know what the case number is though."

Zoe blinked in surprise. "What is that?"

"A rock. With what looks like blood on it." His expression was solemn. "From the same area you said you found the body. I told you I went back to the area in daylight while Patterson was lecturing you on your personal conduct."

Coco snorted. "I bet that went well."

Seth handed Coco the bag and she signed the chain of evidence log.

"You never mentioned it." Zoe frowned.

"I figured the less people who knew about it the better."

"Even me?"

"Even you," he said calmly.

Zoe was stunned. "So you really did believe me?"

His eyes were somber when they met hers. "I told you I did. I also took photos of the shoe prints out there. Sent them for analysis two days ago. Tracks looked to the naked eye as if they supported your story."

Emotions rushed her. He'd genuinely believed her.

"You need somewhere to stay tonight, hon?" Coco offered. "I mean, I'm going to be here working late on a rush job," she laughed, "but I can give you a key. You can both stay." She sent Zoe a wink which Seth would have had to be blind to miss.

Zoe pretended not to notice. Her friend was killing her.

"Thanks for the offer. I'm going to stay with Agent Hopper

tonight." She looked at him and found him staring at her with surprise.

Had she overstepped?

She knew not to reveal details for security reasons, but she didn't want him to think she was ashamed of their association or what her friends might think. But she also didn't want to get him into professional hot water. "We have a meeting in DC first thing tomorrow morning."

Coco nodded. "Raincheck."

"Be careful, Coco. Promise me. These people are ruthless."

"I'm not even going to leave the building until the results are in and uploaded." A sad smile curved her lips. "I wish I could give everyone this level of service but then I'd cease to function."

Zoe hugged her friend close. "Thank you. Stay safe."

"Next time I see you we're doing a night on the town. Hopefully Agent Hopper has some single friends he can introduce me to."

"No one I'd introduce to a lady."

"In which case they sound like my kind of people. I'll call your new cell, Zo, as soon as I have any results." Coco gave Zoe another hug and they said goodbye.

———

Seth drove the Secret Service's Suburban over to the Hostage Rescue Team compound and parked it next to his truck.

It was 8:00 p.m., the sky overcast, mist scraping the tops of the trees and shrouding the base in creepy darkness. The compound was lit up with security lights.

Many of the team's vehicles were parked in the lot but that didn't necessarily mean they were here. They might be on an op or training exercise. He didn't like being out of the loop.

"My truck keys are inside my locker. You can leave everything here if you want. It's safe." He shot Zoe's pensive face a smile.

She'd been fine at the lab, relieved even, but she seemed a little uneasy now.

His next words were not going to help. He cleared his throat. "Zoe, it's probably best not to mention the fact that we had sex or became personally involved on this trip."

Her eyes grew big.

"I mean, it's not like I expect you to blurt it out like a performance evaluation." She laughed like he'd hoped. "But if the brass finds out they will assume my ability to protect you has been compromised and they'll put another team in place." He frowned. "Maybe they *should* put another team on as your protection detail. Or more people at least."

"No."

"No?"

"Do you really believe the cartel would harm me now? The evidence has been handed over for analysis, there's no going back. There's no stealing it away from me. And my mother is not someone you want to anger on a whim no matter who you are."

He'd almost forgotten for a while there that her mother was the *Vice President of the United States*. What the hell was he doing even thinking about getting involved with her? And yet, here he was, waiting for those elusive dimples to appear.

She rubbed her hands together. It was cold and she only wore a light purple hoodie. "I can't imagine they'd chance another attack."

"I'm not expecting an attack but I wasn't expecting someone to cut our brake lines either." Seth ached to draw her into his embrace, but he couldn't risk someone seeing them. He desperately wanted to have these next few hours alone with her but not if it put her in jeopardy.

Zoe leaned toward him and he fought to keep his gaze on her eyes and not her lips.

"That brake-line thing didn't feel very cartelish to me. I mean, I've seen what they do to people who they think might have crossed them. They've massacred entire towns when they feel someone has betrayed them. Chopped victims into little pieces and fed them to the vultures. I've seen the knife marks on the bones. I've witnessed Colombian neckties and remains of victims so charred they may as well have been cremated. The cartel is not subtle when they kill people. They like to send a message. A cut brake line does not send the same kind of message." Zoe shook her head again and huddled into herself. "If I had to bet, I'd say that was on Jacobs in reaction to you telling him to back off last night."

Fuck.

"All the more reason to get more operators who can do a better job of protecting you—"

"Do you really think someone else can protect me better than you can?" She nailed him with those eyes of hers.

His throat squeezed and he shook his head. "Zoe, I would willingly take a bullet for you. I will not let anyone touch you. I made a promise to get you to that meeting tomorrow and I always keep my promises."

She took his hand. "I don't want you to take a bullet for me, Seth."

"I don't plan to." He smiled and squeezed her fingers before releasing her. If anyone suspected they were personally involved neither of them would get a say in who was assigned. "Come on. Let's go inside. I live in an apartment building that has decent security and where at least six other HRT guys stay. And you're right. Somehow this doesn't feel like a cartel hit, but let's talk to my boss and see if he has any intel. Ultimately, it will be his decision who protects you—"

"Actually, that's not true," Zoe stated. "It'll be mine."

Their gazes locked.

"Absolutely." No way was Seth leaving Zoe without backup even if he had to covertly shadow her. "But better not rock the boat until after we finish at JEH. We can figure out the next steps, if any, that are necessary after that," he added.

A frown pinched Zoe's brow. She'd clearly expected the situation to be magically resolved by the time she arrived back east. She climbed out and stretched her arms high over her head. He tried to keep his gaze on their surroundings rather than the scenery.

At that moment, Meghan Donnelly hurried out of the compound. It looked as if she'd been crying. Seth frowned. She gave him a terse nod and moved along purposely without speaking.

Ryan Sullivan, who everyone on the teams called Cowboy, followed her out about ten seconds later.

"Hey, Hop." Cowboy grinned when he spotted Seth. "Look at you sticking it to the Secret Service." He held up his hand to high-five him. Seth didn't miss the way Ryan's eyes took in Zoe from the ground up. The man was a notorious womanizer.

"And you must be Dr. Zoe Miller. Forensic anthropologist and daughter of VPOTUS." Ryan held out a hand to shake Zoe's.

Seth had to grit his teeth as his friend and teammate didn't let go quite as fast as he'd like.

"I must say the surveillance footage from the motel did not do you justice, Dr. Miller," Ryan said, shooting Seth a knowing look.

Zoe's lip quirked.

Seth frowned. "You went through it?"

Ryan nodded. "Me and Donnelly. We were able to ID one of the vehicles and someone in the Arizona Department of Public Safety found us a traffic cam image of the men who abducted you before they donned their masks." Cowboy pulled out his cell and opened a picture of two men sitting in a car at a light. "Novak said he'd sent it to your email. Recognize either of these guys?"

Zoe angled her head to peer at the screen. Then she pointed at the guy in the passenger seat. "Him. He's the one who came to my room."

Ryan nodded. "Luis Ramirez. Bruno Ramirez's little brother. He is indeed the fellow who entered your room and abducted you at gunpoint. He escaped the shootout in the desert."

So, it was Lorenzo Santiago's group of thugs who'd ordered the kidnapping.

"Good work," Seth said. "What's wrong with Donnelly?"

Ryan frowned. "What do you mean?"

"She headed out of here in tears."

Ryan's head snapped toward where the lights from the other operator's truck were fading into the distance. "She's crying?"

Seth huffed out a laugh. "You're saying you didn't upset her?"

Ryan's lips curled on one side. "Not this time." He lowered his voice to a murmur. "Her dad passed yesterday."

Seth winced. "That sucks."

"Yeah, well, nice to meet you, Dr. Miller." The other man covered a yawn. "Excuse me. I've had a long day flying to Colorado and back, entertaining the onboard medical staff." His brows bobbed and Seth shook his head wryly. Ryan pointed his finger at him as he took a step away. "Call Livingstone. He wants an update."

Ryan tipped an imaginary hat at Zoe and winked at Seth. "See you tomorrow at the debrief."

"I have a meeting at JEH at 08:00."

"Later then. See you around, Dr. Miller."

Seth froze.

Why did he think he'd see Zoe around? What else had Ryan noticed on those tapes?

Cowboy jumped in his truck and sped out of the parking lot like he was late for a date which was a distinct possibility.

"He's...interesting." Zoe sounded a little bemused.

"Ryan's not usually quite so full-on certifiable but we've all had a stressful month." Seth's voice roughened with the reminder.

Zoe glanced at him with a frown, but Seth looked away. He didn't want to talk about it.

They headed inside and up to the main office. He was surprised to see Daniel Ackers' door was open.

He figured he may as well confront Ackers head-on rather than avoid the guy, so he went over and knocked on the door.

Jordan Krychek straightened in surprise. The guy had dark circles under his eyes and grief shadowed his gaze. Ackers glanced up with an annoyed frown that shifted quickly to relief when he spotted Seth with Zoe in tow.

"Sir. Thought I'd introduce you to Dr. Miller. Dr. Miller, this is Director Ackers."

Zoe stepped forward to shake his boss's hand.

"Dr. Miller. Glad you arrived in one piece."

"Only because Operator Hopper saved my life on multiple occasions. Operator Hersh too. I hope he's recovering from the snake bite?"

Ackers nodded. "He's made a full recovery and will be at your meeting at JEH in the morning. He—"

"Director, I need you to know your men went into the desert at my insistence." Zoe spoke over Ackers in a way Seth wouldn't have dared. "The only way they could have stopped me was by handcuffing me which Operator Hopper did threaten at one point."

Seth remained expressionless and half wondered if she was trying to help him or get him fired.

"The trip yielded vital information that I believe will be pertinent to the task force's investigation, although the case agent didn't seem to agree. ASAC Patterson was condescending toward Operator Hopper and threatened to report him to the Office of Professional Responsibility simply for searching for more possible victims of cartel violence."

Ackers bushy eyebrows met in the middle. "Did he now?"

Seth wanted to high five Zoe but remained motionless. The only thing Ackers hated more than HRT personnel fucking up, was another Federal agent or agency criticizing their actions. Not that HRT was beyond reproach, but Ackers stood up for his people when the occasion warranted.

"And I appreciated Operator Hopper's assistance dealing with the distressing situation I found myself in with the Secret Service."

Ackers' expression darkened. His mustache twitched. "I heard. I'm sorry." The man's glance caught Seth's and told him he wanted to be filled in on all the details when Zoe wasn't around.

Seth inclined his head.

"Glad we could be of assistance," said Ackers. "I suspect the pair of you need a break from one another."

Seth's brows rose. Because he was so hard to put up with?

"I can assign someone else—"

"No," Zoe said firmly enough that the other man's bushy eyebrows flashed skyward.

Krychek was watching Seth closely and Seth had to work hard to keep his thoughts off his face.

Zoe's throat worked as if she struggled to swallow. "I-I've become comfortable with Operator Hopper and I'm sure you can appreciate why that isn't always the case for me with Federal agents."

Seth didn't flatter himself this was an act. Zoe's distrust was real.

Ackers bent his head because no one wanted to think about a woman being abused, especially by a man who was supposed to protect others.

"If it's okay with Operator Hopper, I'd like him to continue to shadow me until I get to DC tomorrow morning." Zoe's eyes were wide and earnest. "I know I can't impose on him or HRT after that but I'm hoping someone by now has figured out why the cartel grabbed me in Arizona and whether or not the danger is over."

"Operator Hopper will be happy to finish the job he started and we can reassess the situation in the morning. Right, Seth?"

Seth nodded. "Yes, sir. Happy to. I have to be in DC anyway."

Jordan Krychek's lip quirked just enough to tell Seth he'd guessed exactly what lines Seth had crossed with the woman at his side. Seth held his breath, wondering if Krychek planned to interfere. It didn't even need to be true for Ackers to pull him off Zoe's detail. It only had to be inferred and Seth would be sleeping alone. Zoe would probably end up in a shouting match with

Ackers and whichever poor bastards were assigned the duty. Seth was pretty sure they'd have to physically restrain her if they were to even hope to stop her walking out of here and he wasn't sure he'd be able to deal with any of that.

As was becoming a habit these days Krychek kept his mouth shut and his thoughts locked firmly behind his lips.

"Any intel as to who was behind the abduction or why?" asked Seth.

Ackers smiled. "Ryan Sullivan and Meghan Donnelly helped identify Luis Ramirez who is one of Lorenzo Santiago's men. The dead men in the desert are all believed to work for him also but were low-level soldiers."

"Any clues about the motivation?"

Ackers shook his head. "Nothing that's been shared with me. I'm sure the task force would have informed us if there had been an increased threat level to Dr. Miller or her friends."

Seth patted his kit bag. "I'm gonna drop off my gear and collect my truck. I'll make sure I get Dr. Miller to JEH in time for the meeting tomorrow."

"Novak will also be at HQ," said Ackers.

The Gold team leader would be attending in case a further HRT response was necessary. Seth hoped to hell this mess was sorted out soon and that Zoe was safe, even if that meant he would no longer have an excuse to spend so much time with her.

———

Ryan caught up with Meghan as she pulled into the driveway of the small ranch house she rented on the edge of town.

He parked behind her car and she watched him in the side mirror.

He got out and strolled up to the driver's door and opened it. She sat there and looked at him. Her eyes were bloodshot.

"You okay?" he asked.

She shrugged a shoulder, stepped out of the vehicle. "Sure."

She headed tiredly to her front porch and Ryan followed, keeping a few feet back.

"You making sure I get safely home?" She eyed him. "You know I carry two guns and two knives and can kick the asses of most people I meet?"

"It wasn't that."

"I'm not going to have sex with you," she said firmly.

His chin shot up. Christ. "I wasn't asking."

"Yeah, well, you do have a reputation."

Ryan's smile turned predatory. She'd pushed him firmly back into enemy territory and he was fine with that. "A well-earned reputation."

"Nothing to be proud of." She unlocked her door and left it open so he followed, looking around with interest.

"Nothing to be ashamed of either." He thought of the nurse he'd met on Alex Parker's private jet today. They'd had a little fun. Shared a little stress relief. Parted company with a happy smile and nice memory.

Meghan snorted. "Unless you're a woman."

"You're the one slut-shaming, Megs. Not me."

Her lips pursed as she shot him an angry look. Then she sagged and looked like she might cry again. "Sorry."

"I forgive you." He shrugged. "I told you I lost my wife. My coping strategies are sex and booze." He eyed the bottle of whiskey on the kitchen counter.

She noticed him looking and put it up in a cupboard. "You said your wife died eight years ago."

He watched her from under his lashes, wishing he'd never told her that and yet strangely relieved to finally be able to talk about it.

"Does it still hurt as bad as it did in the beginning?"

Emotion hit him in the throat and he hid it by going to close her drapes. "No, and I resent the hell out of that every fucking day."

She crossed her arms over her chest. "How long...?"

Ryan scratched his forehead. "I don't know. I don't think there's a handbook."

She grabbed a tea kettle off the stove and began filling it with water.

"I know that losing my parents was different. Grief, regret, and anger. But I didn't feel quite so scorched earth afterward. But everyone is different. There are no rules."

She licked her lips and then tears filled her eyes again. "I can't remember the last time I told Dad I loved him."

Ryan wanted to wrap his arms around her like he had yesterday, but the air was crackling with tension tonight and he didn't dare. "He knew."

"I have so many regrets." She blew her nose. Sniffed. "I keep being mean to you and you keep being nice. You're incredibly annoying but you are not who I thought you were, Ryan Sullivan."

He winced even though he'd created his alter ego with clarity and precision. "Don't tell anyone."

She smiled. "Maybe I'll go out and find myself some hunk to bring home."

His lips tightened. The fact he didn't like the idea was only because he was worried about her safety.

"Or shoot some whiskey to take the edge off. Want one?" She headed to the kitchen cupboard and pulled out the bottle and two glasses.

"I'll have one for the road. Don't want to have too much in case we get called out."

She laughed as she poured. "Is that a not-so-subtle warning not to get hammered?"

He smiled as she handed him the glass. Meghan was a smart cookie.

She took a sip, then took a step toward him and rested her hand flat against his chest.

"Maybe you could help me forget for a little while." She raised herself on tiptoes and pressed her lips to the side of his mouth. He closed his eyes as a wave of want rushed over him. "No one has to know."

Maybe she wasn't so smart after all. He took a step back. Threw the whiskey down in one swallow. "I'm flattered, but I don't want to be something you regret tomorrow, Meghan."

Tears filled her eyes, and he knew she wasn't thinking straight. "Seriously? I'm being rejected by the guy who sleeps with literally anyone?"

Being upset by the truth was stupid but hurt lashed him anyway.

"I don't sleep with people I work with." He was doing them both a favor. Ryan gave her a smile and a nod and backed away. It was one of his few rules. No FBI agents. No support staff. No HRT operators. "Tomorrow you'll be thanking me."

Her eyes shimmered, and he had to force himself to get the hell out of there before he did something they'd both regret in the morning.

———

The waxing gibbous moon was close to setting when Bruno and Luis arrived at the small private airstrip in the Western Sierra Madre. Derek Belmont was unconscious from the injection Luis had given him earlier and Bruno half wondered if the dose had been too high.

It would be better for Derek if it was, although Lorenzo was unpredictable enough to kill both Bruno and Luis for failing to deliver what he'd demanded.

They exited the small jet but left the unconscious Derek where he was. Unless he could pilot an aircraft there was no escape for him here. No one would help him. No one would rescue him. He belonged to the cartel now.

Lorenzo impatiently paced the tarmac.

"Where is the bastard?" he demanded when he saw them.

"He's still out of it." Bruno inclined his head to his boss and then scanned the faces of the other men here. They were his friends but no one smiled.

Tension crackled and danger seemed to hiss a warning through his ears. Bruno closed his eyes and inhaled the perfume of his homeland. The slight scent of gunpowder lingered as if someone had been setting off firecrackers at a nearby fiesta. The smell of fresh tortillas mingled with the elusive scent of gardenias. It smelled like Heaven.

"Take him," Lorenzo demanded.

Bruno tensed. Would this be his last moment as a free man? Someone brushed past him and pounded up the steps into the jet.

Bruno opened his eyes to see Lorenzo with his hand raised to his forehead. His skin was gray as if he hadn't seen the sun for weeks, the scar on his face bright white.

Lorenzo rarely left the house in daylight nowadays. Terrified of a drone attack as the Americans' technology became more and more advanced. He was also convinced the US had a spy in their midst but even the torture of several of their associates had failed to turn up any proof.

"I don't know where she is, Bruno." Lorenzo's voice was close to a sob and Bruno felt a sliver of regret for what he'd done.

He took a step forward. "She probably skipped school and headed to the beach."

Lorenzo grabbed him by both arms and stared deep into his eyes. "She wouldn't scare me this way."

She absolutely would scare him this way.

"Maybe she lost her phone? You know how she is." Spoiled. Selfish. Beautiful. The image of her corpse flashed through his brain and he fought hard to dispel the revulsion that filled him.

"My Gabriella. My baby sister. I will destroy anyone who has hurt her." The man's eyes bulged with rage.

"We'll find her." Bruno consoled the man.

He prayed to *la Santa Muerte* it wasn't true.

21

————

Zoe followed Seth into his apartment as he turned off the security system.

The immediate impression was one of nice clean lines and zero clutter. He closed the door and reset the alarm. He looked at her, but she couldn't read what was going on in his head.

Suddenly she was hit by a yawn which she quickly covered. "Sorry."

"You must be exhausted. Let me show you where you can wash-up and crash while I order something for us to eat. Then I'll gather everything we'll need for the morning."

She squashed her disappointment.

She wasn't sure what she'd expected. That they'd walk through the door and immediately fall into one another's arms? He seemed reluctant to get close to her now. Maybe his words outside the HRT compound had been a way of letting her down easy...

He led her to a bedroom with a king-size bed neatly made, the sheets carefully folded back. He crossed to the windows and closed the blinds.

"Did the Navy teach you how to make a bed?" she asked brightly, determined not to humiliate herself.

"My mom taught me the basics." His glance was hooded. "The Navy honed the details."

Zoe placed her bag against the sliding, mirrored closet door. She caught his reflection and found him staring at her with heat in his eyes. Their eyes locked and the air suddenly sizzled.

She turned.

"Seth?" Her voice wobbled with uncertainty.

He approached her slowly—and the way he moved, with such effortless grace, entranced her. He raised a hand to gently cup her jaw. He was always so careful of her. So considerate.

She captured his hand against her skin and turned her head to kiss his palm.

His hazel eyes had a rim of warm brown around the pupils. He stared at her intently but seemed reluctant to speak. She wasn't sure where they stood or what he might want, long term. She didn't even know what she wanted long term except the chance to get to know him better. She did know his job was important to him. She would never jeopardize that, but she didn't intend to publicly reveal what happened between them in private.

"Seth, I'd really like to make love with you tonight." She frowned suddenly. Maybe he was reluctant for reasons beside his job. "I hope you aren't worried I'm the sort of person to make false accusations—"

"No. No, I don't think that. I don't think any of that. I just..." A deep "v" formed between his brows as he captured her shoulders with his hands. "I'd never forgive myself if I let my guard down and something happened to you..."

She thought he was going to add something else but he changed his mind. It wasn't fair to push him when she wasn't ready to tell him how she felt. Her emotions were in turmoil and she had a feeling they would have been even without the cartel abducting her at gunpoint and threatening to kill her.

Seth Hopper had affected her from that first smile, and nothing had happened since to dim that attraction.

She stroked the roughness of his unshaven cheek and he closed his eyes.

"If it's okay with you, I'm heading to the shower. Feel free to join me, if you want, and equally free not to, if you don't. I don't want to prevent you from doing your job. I wouldn't like you trying to stop me from doing mine—" Which Colm Jacobs had regularly attempted.

Seth opened his eyes and stared down at her.

"But if you really thought I was in danger, you'd never have let me leave the HRT compound without a lot more armed guards."

She let go of him then and stepped away. Seth stood rigid as a drawn bow, staring down at the bedroom carpet.

Zoe headed into the bathroom and stripped off her grimy clothes. When Seth didn't immediately follow, she swallowed the ball of disappointment.

She refused to hold it against him. What she asked wasn't fair. It compromised him but had no professional consequences for her. Her repercussions were all personal and no one's business but her own.

Could she trust her growing feelings for the man? Or was it a case of sexual attraction and warped gratitude trying to convince her they had a chance of more than that?

She needed to find her balance again before she leapt into anything serious—even assuming Seth would be interested.

She quickly washed her hair and then applied conditioner.

When someone large and male stepped into the shower behind her, all the stress she'd been holding onto leached from her body and she released a sigh of relief.

She didn't turn as tanned arms came around her to grab the soap and began to slowly, thoroughly clean and massage her, muscle by tense muscle.

His hands were competent and relentless, but they skipped all the bits that begged for more focused attention. She tried to turn around but he stopped her with an arm banded across her stomach and a scrape of teeth where her neck met her shoulder.

She shuddered.

Her blood was reaching boiling point and her pulse raced. He cupped her breasts and dragged his thumb over her nipple. She leaned her head back against his shoulder and felt his erection nudge her butt.

He squirted more soap into his palm and lathered up her stomach, then lower between her thighs. She was trembling so hard she was worried she might collapse into a heap.

He held her up. "I've got you. Relax. Enjoy."

His finger slipped inside her, so slick the action felt like the glide of silk over her senses. In and out, over and over again, his fingers sinking deep before his palm glided back up over the sensitive nerves of her clit.

She could hear her own breath becoming fast and shallow, then the orgasm hit her like she was teetering on the edge of a cliff before diving headlong into space. Pleasure rippled, long and hard down her limbs and shook her to her core.

She felt him smile against her hair.

She turned and he surprised her when he turned off the faucet and picked her up in his arms. The fireman's carry was not what she'd expected.

It was possible she squeaked as her naked butt hit the cool air, but she'd deny it to her grave.

He dropped her gently on the bed where she laughed as she bounced, but there was nothing funny about the look in his eyes as he stared down at her.

———

Seth had been determined that he would follow the rules and be a professional even though the thought of not being with Zoe was driving him out of his mind. Then Zoe had asked if they could make love and it had destroyed all his good intentions like a lit match to a piece of cotton.

And he'd decided if he was going down, he was going down in flames.

She was naked and wet and on his bed. Her cheeks were flushed, her eyes intent on his, almost daring him to take her on the ride of her life.

He shook his head and grinned.

She went to sit up but he needed to taste her. He pushed her gently back down. Then knelt on the floor, dragging her to the edge of the bed and draping her legs over his shoulders.

He sank his tongue into her feminine folds and she made that sound that never failed to turn him on.

Her one hand gripped his short hair as her thighs relaxed and let him in. He closed his eyes and traced her with his mouth. He ignored the sharp bite of her fingertips against his scalp and sampled the delicate skin at the top of her thigh, the elusive nub of nerves all bundled up and hidden from view, then the searing heat of her vagina.

"Seth," she implored. "I want you inside me."

How could any man resist?

He opened the bedside table and pulled out a new box of condoms that he'd bought in a rare bout of optimism. He had to rip the plastic off with his teeth before tearing open the box.

Smooth. *Real smooth.*

She beat him to a packet and carefully opened it, rolling the condom over his swollen flesh as he lay on his back on the bed.

Zoe straddled his hips and he found himself mesmerized by her soft curves and understated beauty. She made his blood buzz and his heart ache.

He had to grit his teeth against the pleasure of her hot flesh gripping him as she took him inside her. As he lifted his head, he realized he could see the two of them in the mirror and the erotic sight almost undid him.

And then he stopped thinking altogether. He rose up to

capture her nipple in his mouth and found himself pushing into her as both of them tried to get ever closer. She moaned in pleasure.

He held her steady with one arm wrapped around her waist as need took over. He drove up into her over and over again, sweat blooming over his body.

She rolled to the side and they changed places as she wrapped her leg around his hips, drawing him in. The headboard knocked with the force of his thrusts and Zoe laughed as she grabbed tight to his neck.

Then he watched her whole face change, from laughter to wonder as another orgasm shook her. He rode her through it, so turned on and so desperate to come it was killing him. And then she touched his face and they were staring deep into one another's eyes. Seth felt that connection lock into place. All the things they'd been through together, all the complications, falling away and leaving only the two of them enclosed in this burning need for one another.

He grabbed her thigh and raised it, her mouth opening in shocked delight as he obviously hit the exact right place.

Only it wasn't just Zoe cascading over the edge this time. She took him with her as she made that noise again and it was all over for him. His brain exploded as every sensory receptor in his body shorted out as if he'd been struck by lightning.

He collapsed on top of her, barely having the awareness to take some of his weight on his elbows. His heart rate was somewhere in the thousands and his blood was liquid fire.

If this test—resisting Zoe Miller—had been included in Hell Week, he would never have made it into the SEALs. He'd have rung that bell and gone home happy.

When he reared back, he found Zoe smiling, those dimples flashing, her turquoise eyes twinkling with delight, her plump lower lip curving into a smile that made his cock begin to throb all over again.

His cell phone buzzed in the other room.

"Shit."

"Who's that?" she asked.

"Probably dinner."

"You stopped to order dinner before following me into the shower?"

He laughed as he pulled out, carefully removing the condom. "A man's gotta eat."

Zoe's smile suggested he'd already eaten but he wasn't going there. If he thought about how good she tasted he might never leave that spot between her thighs where he would be quite happy to worship her for the rest of his life.

The thought staggered him.

Shit.

No.

No matter the connection they shared in bed, getting too attached was a guaranteed route to ruin and heartbreak. She was the daughter of the Vice fucking President of the United States.

He frowned at his cell. It was Novak.

"Boss?"

"I'm hearing rumblings from higher up that Madeleine Florentine is seriously unhappy with the current security situation regarding her daughter. She wants a full team assigned for protective duty."

"Zoe isn't going to go for that." If Zoe realized her mother was once again attempting to interfere in her life it might permanently damage their relationship. Seth glanced toward the bedroom door and lowered his voice. "I know Zoe. She's not going to calmly accept being forced into anything against her wishes." The thought of it twisted his gut.

Novak cleared his throat. "Someone on the VP's team is also making noises that maybe you're personally involved and that's why you're 'flying solo.'" Novak didn't give Seth time to reply. "I told them you were a professional and highly-regarded member of HRT, and a decorated former Navy SEAL."

The lump in Seth's throat almost choked him. Novak had

staked his career on Seth's non-existent ethics. The idea of letting his boss down hurt almost as much as the thought of Zoe being endangered because he wasn't up to the job.

"I made an executive decision and asked Blue team to provide a four-man squad to watch your building tonight, and another squad to shadow you to FBI HQ tomorrow. I figured I better give you the heads up so you knew who was tailing you. Zoe Miller never has to know."

Seth closed his eyes. It was out of their hands now. "Understood."

"See you in the morning, Hop." With that, Novak hung up.

The door buzzer rang and Seth headed to the intercom.

"Yeah?"

"Delivery for Hopper."

Seth froze. It was one of his teammates who lived in the building. Damien Crow—known as Birdman by the team—part of the sniper unit and another of JJ Hersh's best friends.

"Figured I'd bring it up. You need to tell the delivery guy that I'm not going to steal your pizza."

Seth cleared his throat. "Sure, thanks, man. Don't forget the tip. You've saved me a trip down."

Seth realized he was stark naked and headed back into the bedroom. Zoe was in the bathroom. He dragged on some shorts and a t-shirt and straightened the bedcovers. He glanced at his reflection and saw the expression of a man who'd recently had the best sex of his life.

Fuck.

He wiped his forearm over his face and quickly ran a hand through his short hair, then he opened the window to get rid of the scent of sex. The cold air snaked inside and woke him up.

He contemplated knocking on the bathroom door and warning Zoe they had company but it sounded like she was in the shower again. He'd get rid of Birdman ASAP.

He grabbed his custom-made SIG, strode to the entranceway, checked the peephole. Then he opened it.

Birdman failed to notice Seth's "keep out" stance and elbowed his way inside, sliding the large pizza onto the counter.

"Hey, man. Glad to have you back. I heard you had some fun in the desert?"

"You could say that." Seth attempted to herd his friend back toward the door.

"Heard you're guarding a certain VIP. She back there?" Birdman nodded toward the main bedroom. There was a second bedroom that could theoretically fit a single bed. Seth had a futon in there for when his parents visited but generally used the space as an office.

Seth nodded. "Yeah." He knew Zoe would hate being called a VIP and could almost hear the argument she'd make against it. "She's taking a turn in the shower." Because last time it had gotten a little crowded.

"JJ said she was cute."

Seth shrugged one shoulder. "I guess."

Birdman gave him a raised-brow look. "You guess?"

"She's a smart and accomplished woman. She's a lecturer in Forensic Anthropology at the University of Richmond." Seth couldn't have made her sound less appealing to his friend if he'd tried. He didn't need anyone on the team speculating on his relationship—*fuck*—with Zoe Miller, especially now Payne Novak had staked his reputation on Seth's integrity.

"Blonde, right?" Birdman pulled a face. "Probably a good thing she isn't your type."

Seth paused in his effort to eject the guy. "What do you mean?"

"You tend to like them tall and dark and a little on the ditzy side."

"What the fuck does that mean?"

"You know what it means. What about Gemma?" Birdman pointed to an old photograph of him and his ex he'd left on the fridge next to the invitation to her wedding. They'd broken up about a year ago. Her rebound fling had caught Seth by surprise although some of the guys reckoned Gemma had been seeing the new guy before the two of them had split. She already had a new baby.

The photo served as a reminder of his failed relationships. A warning not to get involved.

"She was a classic Seth Hopper girlfriend."

Seth had no idea what the guy was trying to say. "Meaning?"

Birdman shrugged. "I'm telling you what I've observed, man. You tend to date women who are easy on the eyes but also easy to leave behind."

The observation slammed Seth between the eyeballs. He'd never thought about that before, but the guy was 100% correct. He dated women he would never quit his job for.

"So it's just as well this lecturer lady isn't your type, even if she is hot." Birdman lifted the lid of the box and stole a slice of pizza.

The bedroom door opened and Zoe wandered out wrapping a towel around her perfect naked body.

"Seth, do you know where I put my..." She looked up and all three of them froze in a shocked tableau. "Crap, I didn't know we had company."

It was the "we" that sealed it. That reference to the two of them being a team and not just a job.

Birdman didn't miss a thing. His mouth hung open, pizza forgotten in his hand.

Seth grabbed him by the shirt and dragged him to the door. "Thanks for delivering the food, man. We can take it from here."

Birdman's expression turned worried. "Seth—"

"Enough," Seth's tone held a warning. "Whatever you think you saw, you're mistaken. I'd appreciate you respecting the lady and keeping your damn mouth shut because I really don't wanna have to track you down and kill you."

"It's not the lady I'm worried about." Birdman dropped his voice. "Women like that don't give a shit about men like you and me."

"Zoe's not like that," Seth gritted out.

Birdman raised his hand and only then seemed to remember he was holding a slice of pizza. "You're one of the best operators on this team, Seth, and that's largely because of your absolute dedication to your job. Don't throw it all away for the sake of a quick fuck."

Fury rushed through Seth but the other man was gone. Birdman was also right. Seth's career did mean everything to him. No way would he jeopardize it—nor Payne Novak's—for a fling when he had no idea if Zoe wanted anything more than that.

He went back into his apartment and closed the door. Zoe stood there still clutching her towel. The smell of pizza filled the air but Seth had lost his appetite.

"Grab some food and feel free to take it into the bedroom," he forced himself to say calmly. "I'm going to camp out here on the couch tonight, just in case of any surprises."

"Seth—"

"*Please*, Zoe." He closed his eyes, holding on to his composure by a single thread. "For once, let me do my job without arguing." He pressed his lips together and looked away. This wasn't her fault. He was the idiot who'd allowed Birdman into the apartment. He was the man who'd sacrificed his principles. He desperately needed to think. "I need a little space."

———

Bruno watched Lorenzo drive his fist into Derek Belmont's face over and over again.

There was so much blood the young man's face was unrecognizable. His nose broken. His eyes swollen shut.

Lorenzo's men stood around watching.

"Wait," Derek begged. "Wait. I'll tell you anything, anything you want to know."

Bruno clenched his teeth, careful not to betray his surprise.

"She called me two weeks ago and told me she couldn't bear not seeing me. She told me she was going to cross the border and that she'd call me when she did, so I could pick her up. I told her not to come because I knew you wouldn't like it, but she insisted. I planned to pick her up and drive her straight back to the border, I swear. I wasn't going to see her again." Blood dripped off his chin. "But she never called me and I assumed she'd changed her mind."

Fuck.

Lorenzo hesitated. "How was she planning to get across the border?"

Bruno tried to relax his lower jaw and caught his brother watching him. He couldn't read Luis's expression. Was his brother putting it all together? What would he do if he figured it out? Bruno didn't know. They loved one another but this life tore families apart.

Sweat dripped down his spine.

"Boss." One of Lorenzo's men came running down the worn cellar steps. "One of our informants noted a description of a young woman that matched Gabriella was uploaded into the Missing Migrant database." The man looked up and hesitated. "The description was of a dead body—"

Lorenzo roared out his denial and Bruno winced at the pain in the man's voice. Everyone exchanged a nervous look.

Lorenzo pulled his gun.

Bruno touched the butt of the pistol he carried in a holster at the small of his back.

"She can't be dead. She can't be." Lorenzo yelled. He shot at the ground, the bullet ricocheted dangerously off the stone, pinging against a nearby wall.

They all looked at one another. The guy was clearly crazed.

For a moment Bruno considered shooting him right here, but Lorenzo still had too many friends in the room. If he killed Lorenzo, the others would kill Bruno and say they were justified. Then they'd take over the organization for themselves.

"No photographs were attached to the entry except the picture of a gold medallion... and no location was noted."

Bruno silently cursed.

"Show me." Lorenzo waved the messenger to him and then squinted at the screen. He reared back and seemed to shrink into himself.

"That's the medallion of *Nuestra Señora de la Santa Muerte* I gave Gabriella when our parents died. Her initials are engraved on the back. You recognize it, Bruno?" He thrust the screen at Bruno for confirmation.

Rage mixed with fear as Bruno nodded. It was Gabriella's necklace and must have come off during their struggle. He clenched his teeth. His men had all failed him that night when he'd sent them to eliminate the evidence the anthropologists might have found in the desert. Evidence that indicated Gabriella had been there—and that Bruno had killed her.

Even his own brother had failed him...

"Talk to everyone. Put out feelers. I want to know if they have a body matching Gabriella's description in any of the morgues. I want to know everything," Lorenzo grated out. "And I want that medallion."

The messenger's face was fearful.

Santiago in this mood could shoot anyone in a murderous rage. No one would blame Bruno for taking him out if that happened.

"Fetch me whoever entered that description. I want to talk to them." Lorenzo began striding out of the room.

"B-but..." The messenger stuttered. "It's going to be difficult, boss."

"I don't care if it's difficult, *pendejo*. Find them." The man screamed and the sound echoed painfully in the small, cramped cellar.

"The person who entered the data. It was that woman." The messenger blurted out quickly. "The daughter of the American politician."

Lorenzo stopped in his tracks and swung toward Bruno. "Why did you take her?" he demanded. "Why did you try to kill her last weekend?"

Bruno held Lorenzo's half-crazed gaze. "Because I saw her and her friends digging around in the desert and thought it was suspicious. I had no idea who she was. I just knew she didn't belong."

"Maybe she thinks she is above the law, immune from us and the Americans." Luis held Bruno's gaze as he spoke.

Did Luis suspect what had happened? Was he trying to deflect and suggest the anthropologists had been involved in Gabriella's death?

The others eyed one another nervously.

"You still want to pick her up? Madeleine Florentine's daughter?" the messenger asked.

"I don't care if it was the US President himself. I need to know what she knows. What she found. I want to know where she got that medallion. I want to see it so I can figure out if it belongs to my sister."

"If you touch the daughter, you will start a war," one of the others warned.

Lorenzo's face twisted and he tilted his head to one side. "Let me ask you a question, Pepe. Who are you more scared of? The Americans, or me?"

Pepe lifted his chin. "I will follow you wherever you go and do whatever you order me to do, *jefe*. I know you are worried about Gabriella. I only wanted you to remember who you are dealing with. You must be smart about this."

"You think I'm not being smart?" The last word hissed out of Lorenzo's mouth like a curse.

"It won't be easy to get to the woman." Bruno deflected Lorenzo's attention away from the other man. "The FBI are protecting her."

Lorenzo appeared to calm down. "Do whatever you have to do. Use every resource we have. Nothing else matters." He shot a long, considering look at Bruno. "The woman must have a weakness we can use."

Bruno nodded. Everyone had a weakness. Bruno's was buried in the desert a few feet underground.

"The Americans will come for her. Do you want to bring her here to your home?" Bruno asked cautiously.

Lorenzo looked thoughtful and then shook his head. "Ready the jet and helicopter. As soon as you have her, I want to know."

"What do we do with him?" Pepe pointed to the bloody, unconscious figure of Derek Belmont looking incongruous in bright yellow Lycra.

"Nothing. Leave him to rot. If—" Lorenzo swallowed repeatedly before he could speak again. "If Gabriella is dead, I will make him pay for not contacting me about her plans. If she is alive, and I believe she is alive," he stared down every man in the room, "then maybe I'll give him to her. Anything to keep her happy."

The man strode away.

Luis stood beside Bruno as they both stared at the battered figure they'd delivered into Lorenzo's hands. Neither said a word.

22

Zoe had spent last night alone, sleepless in Seth Hopper's bed. Now they were in his truck, headed toward Washington, DC.

They drove in silence. They'd picked up coffee from a drive-through and both assiduously concentrated on drinking it without spilling it or scalding their mouths. Zoe studied scenery like she was going to be quizzed on it later.

Seth wore a charcoal suit, white shirt and green tie and she almost didn't recognize him.

She had nothing more formal than jeans, boots, and a sweet flowery button-up shirt. Unfortunately, the blouse was hidden beneath her old University of Arizona hoodie.

Beyond the most basic of enquiries, they'd barely spoken since he'd requested some space last night. Seth was obviously worried that the man she'd flashed was going to reveal the fact they'd become sexually involved to his teammates.

Zoe understood Seth wanted to protect his reputation but they were both consenting adults and if they decided to have sex on their own time it was their business and no one else's. Not his boss's. Not her parents. Not his teammates. Except, she knew a bodyguard was strictly forbidden from getting involved with their client. Colm Jacobs had once said how happy he was that she'd refused USSS protection because it meant he could ask her out.

She instinctively knew Seth would despise himself for breaking that rule...and she had been very persuasive.

Another small kernel of doubt had taken hold. Maybe it wasn't just the fact he was her bodyguard that bothered him, so much as the fact she didn't look like the woman whose photograph she'd seen with her arms looped around Seth's neck, stuck to the refrigerator.

The woman looked almost as tall as he was, with long dark hair, skillfully made-up, brown eyes. She was the antithesis of Zoe in every way.

Now that their time together was coming to an end, perhaps Seth wanted to make sure Zoe didn't get the wrong idea about the two of them being anything more than a three-night stand.

The old Zoe would have asked him straight out if they could see one another again when this was all over, but Colm Jacobs had made her more cautious, less confident. Plus, there was the issue with the power dynamic between herself and Seth. Whether she liked it or not, her mom was a high-level politician and maybe Seth would feel unfairly pressured if she asked him if they could see one another again.

It was probably best to leave it up to him to do any asking. So that it came from him, not her, and that he didn't say yes because he was worried about his career.

And maybe he'd only ever been into the sex, and he'd never intended for what happened on the journey to continue past their arrival in DC. She had been the one to seduce him on each occasion.

Misery washed over her, dragging her mood lower. Not even incredible sex was worth this feeling of angst and insecurity. The sooner she got some space the sooner she could figure out how she really felt. Although maybe it didn't matter how she felt—not if Seth Hopper wasn't interested.

She blew on her coffee and tried to remember the last time she'd felt this wretched. It was different from the terror of the abduction or the fear that Jacobs invoked. This was bone-deep desolation that wanted to suck all the color out of the day.

They arrived downtown and Seth drove straight to Pennsylvania Avenue and headed to the underground parking lot beneath FBI headquarters.

"We don't usually get to park down here but I received a special concession because of you."

"Oh. Whippee."

Seth glanced at her sharply.

She tried not to act like a petulant child and forced a smile, not quite meeting his gaze. "I appreciate the FBI doing that for me."

It meant she could avoid any potential media and that was worth a lot. Not that the media had pursued the story of the abduction. There was always another crisis, another shooting, another scandal, and her name had been kept out of reports.

They went down the ramp and were immediately surrounded by armed security.

The officer tapped on the side window of Seth's truck. "Can you step out, ma'am?"

Nerves exploded as she undid her seat belt.

Everything about armed guards reminded her of the seriousness of the situation and she really didn't want to think about that. Zoe climbed out and stood to one side as the sentry ran a gadget over her body.

Seth showed his ID to another guard who checked it carefully before running a sensor under the truck.

"I'll need your electronics, ma'am." The security guard was polite but unyielding.

Her eyes flew to Seth who shrugged. "It's standard practice for civilian visitors."

She pulled out her new phone and handed it over.

"Take care of that," she added.

"Yes, ma'am."

They raised the barrier and Seth drove inside and parked near the glass-fronted security station.

He climbed out and then straightened his tie.

He was nervous, she realized. She hoped that wasn't because of her.

"You know where you're going?" the guard asked.

Seth nodded and raised his hand in thanks, then started walking toward a nearby bank of elevators.

"I don't really know what to expect today," she admitted nervously.

Seth held the elevator door for her and pressed a button. "They'll probably quiz you on anything you've been working on recently that might be relevant, and whether or not you've ever experienced anything like this before or had any previous run-ins with the cartel."

"Then it's going to be a short meeting," she quipped.

He glanced at her with a frown that suggested she wasn't taking this seriously enough.

"Then they'll want you to go over that night again in detail."

Zoe's mouth went dry at the thought of reliving it all over again. She'd successfully pushed all memories of the abduction aside over the last few days. She'd immersed herself in her road trip with Seth. With him.

She drew in a shuddering breath. "Seth, about last night. I should never have assumed we were alone—"

"That wasn't your fault." He frowned at her. "I should have warned you or thrown Birdman out on his ass. But I didn't want him to suspect anything was—" He cut himself off. "It doesn't matter."

"It feels like it matters." She stared at him, wide eyed and dejected.

"I can't talk about it here." He took a step away and glanced up at the surveillance camera. "I need to concentrate on this meeting. My job might be on the line if Patterson starts gunning for me, and my career is extremely important to me."

"I realize that. I don't intend to say anything that might jeopardize your job."

"I won't lie, Zoe." His voice was low and harsh. "But I am hoping it doesn't come up during questioning."

It.

Them.

She nodded. "I completely understand." She was suddenly overcome by cascading emotions that tumbled through her brain in a confusing mess. Even though they'd only known each other for a few days, it felt as if her entire life was falling apart.

After the camaraderie they'd enjoyed for the last two thousand miles, the last twelve hours felt awkward and stilted. This cleanly shaven, suited version of Seth Hopper seemed cold and remote and she hated that she felt immature and foolish and *emotional* in comparison.

She was a professional too.

She stiffened her spine.

They passed a couple of agents in the corridor. One of them pointed to a room and Seth led the way inside. He looked around and then seemed to balk when he saw the room was empty except for the two of them.

Her stomach pitched at the realization he didn't want to be anywhere near her right now. And this was the last place on earth she wanted to break down.

———

An FBI agent Seth didn't recognize shut the door on them and they were alone.

Shit.

Seth hated himself for the fact he'd upset Zoe, but today was all about work. He'd been aware of the Blue team shadows for the entire length of the journey from his apartment to DC but hadn't wanted to say anything and risk Zoe finding out her mother had interfered against her wishes.

He'd needed to concentrate. His job was on the line. If he even hinted at more than a bodyguard relationship with the woman who'd come to mean so much to him, he was fucked. All the years of training. All the sweat and pain and danger. All the grueling workouts, all the sacrifices—the family holidays he'd missed with his parents and a succession of girlfriends over the years. All wasted because he couldn't keep his dick in his pants while working with Zoe.

He had to detach himself and cool the feelings that arced between them.

The chance of a lasting relationship with Zoe would be worth the risk of what the VP could do to his career—*if* he knew Zoe felt the same way. But he didn't. And he had no right to push her after everything she'd been through. And he wasn't about to put Payne Novak's reputation in jeopardy when he had no idea how Zoe actually felt.

She liked him, sure.

She wanted him. Absofuckinglutely.

But she hadn't hinted at any time that he was anything more than a convenient fuck buddy the entire time they'd been together. He wasn't about to beg for scraps.

She sat down on one of the chairs, her spine straight, her clenched fists resting on her lap, the only thing betraying her nerves.

He wanted to hold her.

He needed to walk away.

Today.

Before she destroyed him with all the things he wanted but couldn't have. She was American royalty. He was an abandoned orphan from the wrong side of the tracks. It could never work between them.

He had to end things before either of them got too involved. Too invested. Too damaged.

She wasn't his type, and he certainly wasn't hers. Not really.

Not in their normal worlds. Birdman had reminded him of that fact loud and clear last night.

Seth had kept his promise. He'd gotten Zoe safely to the J. Edgar Hoover Building. His commitments had been met, responsibility upheld. He'd done his job.

He had to end things now, while he retained a shred of dignity.

He cleared his throat. "I'll speak to my boss about getting your furniture released from evidence."

"What?" She looked dismayed. "But... Why are you doing this?"

He kept his expression shut down and deliberately misunderstood her question. "You said your belongings were important to you. Isn't that why we drove thousands of miles rather than flying?"

If they'd flown, they wouldn't have screwed each other's brains out on the journey.

He hoped.

"I mean, why are you being so..." She trailed off and looked away.

"Professional?" He huffed out a bitter laugh. "Because that's what I'm supposed to be?"

She shot him a hard stare. "Cold."

He flinched.

"Seth." She swallowed. "I said I was sorry about last night. I didn't mean to get you into trouble."

"It's not about that. It's not about anything you've done or haven't done." Christ, that was a lie, but it wasn't her fault.

"Oh. The old 'it's not you it's me' chestnut." Her laughter was sharp, her eyes glittering. Her fingers twisted together in that way they did when she was nervous.

"Don't you *understand*?" The words ripped out of him. "I can't afford to get further involved with a woman like you."

Her eyes looked suspiciously bright and she raised her chin. "What do you mean 'a woman like me'?"

Dammit, those freaking eyes of hers.

"A woman whose mother is the Vice President of the United States. A woman I have been ordered to protect. A woman who will walk away from me without a backward glance the moment she no longer needs me."

Zoe looked stunned.

"You have all the power here, Zoe." And she could destroy not just his career but also his heart, and that terrified him. "You have all the power here and I do not like that. I don't like it one fucking bit." With that he left the room, careful not to slam the door and reveal to his fellow agents that he was completely one hundred percent, off-the-charts, fucked.

"Operator Hopper?" One of the agents said brightly. "Come right this way. The task force will see you now."

23

A woman like her?

Zoe felt as if she'd been tried and convicted without being given an opportunity to defend herself.

A woman like her?

Her smartwatch buzzed and she saw it was a call from Fred. She suspected she wasn't supposed to have the device in here, so she ignored it even though she wanted nothing more than to cry all over her friends.

An agent came to the door to say the task force might be awhile and offered her something to drink. The muscles in her throat constricted. Suddenly there wasn't enough oxygen in the room.

"No, thanks." She rose to her feet, struggling to pull in a decent breath. She couldn't stand facing Seth or the other FBI agents. Grilling her. Judging her. Not right now. She didn't think she could face Seth again. Ever.

I can't afford to get further involved with a woman like you.

Afford?

Afford?

What exactly did he think it would cost him?

She was such an idiot. But she didn't want him or anyone else to see her so shattered. Didn't want to admit she'd fallen so hard for a man who didn't think she was worth the price.

Panic started to inch through her veins. "I-I left something in Operator Hopper's truck and need to fetch it. Can someone escort me down to get it, please?"

"Sure. I'll take you." The agent eyed her curiously.

Zoe's pulse was racing and she had to fight the urge to cry.

She followed him out and back along the corridor and down in the elevator.

They reached the parking garage and she inhaled deeply but exhaust fumes tainted the air and hit the back of her throat and made her gag. She pretended she was fine as she strode over to the security guard she'd dealt with earlier.

"Can I get my phone back, please?" She forced out the words. "There's been an emergency."

She hated this feeling of weakness. After Colm Jacobs had nearly destroyed her with his behavior, she'd thought she was stronger than this. She hadn't expected to be wrecked by what she had the terrible feeling was heartbreak.

Why had she opened herself up to him? She'd gotten to know the man beneath the handsome exterior and all she'd accomplished was falling even harder in love.

Then he'd gone and rejected her.

She didn't know which version of Seth Hopper was real. The one who'd protected and held her tight, or the one who resented her for having a powerful mother—as if she had any choice in the matter.

She needed to call her friends. She needed to confess she'd had her heart crushed by a man she should never have been attracted to in the first place. She needed for them to console her and love her even though she was obviously an idiot.

Her hands shook when she took her cell from the security guard.

"You'll have to use that outside." He warned her sternly.

She turned to the FBI agent who was beginning to look a little anxious. "I'll just be a moment."

As much as she wanted to run away, she wouldn't. It wasn't her style. But she wanted to. She really wanted to.

She walked up the ramp and stood near a large concrete flower display currently full of ornamental grasses that no doubt doubled as a crash barrier.

She called James but he didn't pick up.

Then she tried Karina, but she was sleeping, according to the nurse.

Dammit.

She couldn't pour her heart out to Fred, that wasn't fair. She started to look for Coco's number even though she wouldn't badmouth Seth to her either. The two worked for the same government agency and it didn't seem fair to tarnish his reputation when he hadn't broken any promises, just her foolish heart.

She could ask if the lab had found any results yet.

Her cell rang. *Seth.*

She hated how an initial zip of excitement was quickly doused by a cold bucket of reality.

He was probably wondering where the hell she was.

She pressed accept and raised the phone to her ear as a man in a green uniform approached her on the sidewalk. She thought he was telling her to move farther away from the building and she looked around in confusion.

He was tall and bulky. He looked vaguely familiar, but she wasn't sure where she'd seen him before.

He held out a cell phone with an image on it and for a moment Zoe didn't understand what she was seeing.

Then a buzzing started between her ears as she registered the details of the photograph and Seth's voice asking if she was okay.

The man casually took her cell from her and tossed it in the planter. He took her hand and she thought he was going to put her in handcuffs but instead he slipped her smartwatch from her wrists and tossed it into the grass too.

Her heart hammered.

Oh my god.

He pushed her toward a black sedan that had pulled up to the curb.

This couldn't be happening.

Zoe's fugue state was broken as the reality of what was happening only yards from FBI headquarters crashed over her. She began to struggle but the man tightened his grip on her arm and forced it up high behind her back. She cried out in pain. He put his hand on the top of her head and propelled her forcefully inside the waiting vehicle.

She screamed and another man in the back seat clamped his hand over her face as the first man climbed in beside her.

Zoe bit the palm covering her mouth and the man swore and pulled her hair so hard it felt as if it were being ripped out by the roots.

"Bite me again, bitch, and I'll hit you so hard you won't be able to walk for a week. I don't care who your mother is."

Revulsion filled her but then the sharp pain of a needle had her lunging desperately for the syringe one of them had stabbed into her thigh.

She watched the small windows in the imposing concrete building above her disappear and had the terrible feeling she'd never see Seth Hopper or anyone else she loved, ever again.

———

Seth had handled everything with the smoothness and finesse of a rabid porcupine.

He'd come perilously close to confessing he was falling in love with Zoe—the only thing that had stopped him was the fact that when he'd said she'd walk away from him without a backward glance, she hadn't denied it.

Fuck.

That had hurt.

So much for being a tough guy. He was a pathetic piece of shit.

But he'd picked a terrible time to have his personal crisis. And the fact he'd been too cowardly to stick around to give her the chance to reply?

Because what if she'd confirmed all his fears?

That he was delusional to think they had a shot at anything real or long term? That, while a guy like him was fine for a booty call, he was not the sort of person one took home to Mommy and Daddy at their Hampton retreat?

His old demons had been whirling in his head ever since Birdman had shattered his fantasy romance with a box of pizza and a slice of brutal honesty.

Fuck.

It didn't change the fact he'd handled this poorly and hurt Zoe and now he needed to apologize while he had the chance.

Seth briefly addressed the task force and then went to fetch her. He'd been distracted in the meeting. She hadn't deserved his mood these past twelve hours. His surly broodiness. Even if she didn't feel anything for him except a kernel of friendship, she deserved an adult conversation no matter how chickenshit he was about getting dumped again.

He braced himself to open the door, determined to, if not put things right between them, at least make her realize this really wasn't her fault. It was all him. Cliches were cliches for a reason.

After a deep breath, he stepped inside but the room was empty.

He asked an agent in the corridor, a Black woman holding a file and a cell phone, if she'd seen Zoe.

"She wanted something from the garage. Agent Simpson walked her down."

Seth nodded. "Can I get his number? The task force is ready for her."

Or they thought they were.

His lips twisted. He didn't think anyone was ever truly ready for Dr. Zoe Miller.

The agent nodded and opened her cell and began searching her contacts.

Seth decided to try Zoe's cell on the off chance she'd gone downstairs to make a phone call, probably to tell one of her many friends about the fact he'd been an asshole.

He hung his head as he listened to it ringing. She had every right to be mad with him. She probably wouldn't even pick up…

The call connected.

"Zoe?" Seth could hear nothing except the faint hiss of traffic. "Are you okay?"

The sound of a scream being quickly muffled made him freeze, his attention sharpening.

Where was she?

The other agent showed him the number for Agent Simpson.

"Call him. Quickly," he ordered.

The woman did and he took the phone off her with a nod of thanks.

"Are you with Zoe Miller?"

Simpson sounded breathless. "I was. She got into a black car and drove away." Simpson swore.

What the hell? "Did she go willingly?"

"I don't know. I was talking to security when she made it clear she needed a personal moment to make a phone call. I'd gone up to check on her when I spotted her leaving in the vehicle."

Seth thought there was some weird feedback until he realized he could hear the agent talking on both phones.

His mouth parched with a growing feeling of dread. "Do you see her cell phone anywhere?"

There was a pause as presumably the guy looked around. "No, I don't see it."

"I can hear you on it. Keep looking," Seth said impatiently. He strode into the task force briefing room and over to Payne Novak who looked up in surprise.

"Where is she?" asked Novak.

Seth held up his finger to request a moment as he listened attentively.

"Shit. I see it in a planter."

"She's been abducted." Seth addressed the room in general. "Start searching for her smartwatch online."

"Don't bother," Simpson's voice came over the cell. "I see both a cell phone and a smartwatch here."

Seth's entire world crashed around him.

"Bag it and bring it up here ASAP," he said quickly. He hung up and handed the agent back her cell phone. "We need to check surveillance footage from outside the JEH building and we need roadblocks set up all around the city."

"What's going on?" McKenzie asked, joining them.

"Zoe Miller's been kidnapped." Seth spoke as if his heart hadn't been ripped out of his chest. "Her cell phone and smart-watch were found in a planter outside. The agent who accompanied her downstairs said he saw her get into the back of a black vehicle."

"How do we know she didn't leave of her own accord?" asked McKenzie.

"She wouldn't." Inside Seth was vibrating with fear and frustration, but he kept it locked down. Kept it concealed.

Novak eyed Seth as if he knew all Seth's intimate secrets, such as the fact he'd been sleeping with a woman he'd sworn to protect.

"How do you know she isn't in a cab to her mother's place?" McKenzie asked as others called security for that surveillance footage.

"Because she would never do that. She'd never run away from this meeting." No matter how much he upset her. She wouldn't throw him under a bus no matter how poorly he behaved. "I'm telling you she's been kidnapped," Seth said loudly. Forcibly. He wanted to scream it from the rooftops. The moment she was out of his sight, she'd been taken.

No one else appeared convinced.

"Look, she said she was never going to take her watch off again after it saved her life in the desert." And she hadn't, except when it had been charging. Not when they'd made love. Not in the shower.

Novak squeezed his shoulder.

Did he know?

Right now, Seth didn't care.

One of the agents on the phone with security confirmed. "Guards in the surveillance room say she was forced into a car by a man in uniform. By the time they alerted security on the ground the vehicle was gone."

"Get Capitol Police to put up roadblocks around the city and alert transport police to be on the lookout. I want airports notified, including all private airfields," McKenzie ordered. "Shit."

"We need to see that footage," Seth said.

"Come with me." McKenzie strode out of the room with Seth on his heels. Novak was right there with him. JJ Hersh appeared at his side. Hersh had been delayed by traffic but had received a pass because of the whole almost-dying-this-week thing.

"Zoe's been abducted?" Hersh asked, catching on fast.

"Looks like." Seth felt as if he was floating. All the training they did so they weren't ambushed and unable to function in the real world. Working this sort of thing should be automatic, but he couldn't get over that it was *Zoe* who'd been taken. Zoe with her turquoise eyes and impish smile and inherent sense of right and wrong.

If anything happened to her...

He might never get the chance to set things right between them. Might never get the chance to apologize. But none of that was as important as her being safe.

"We'll get her back." Hersh sent him a cool smile that somehow reminded Seth who he was, and what they did.

He held his friend's gaze and knew that Birdman had called Hersh and told him everything that had happened last night, which had likely confirmed what Hersh had suspected from the start.

They headed up to the Strategic Information and Operation Center.

"I need to see the security feeds, right now," McKenzie yelled as they stepped off the elevator.

The Unit Chief came out of his office and seemed to realize something big was going down. He grabbed his suit jacket and led them past the FBI's Top 10 Most Wanted posters, toward a room with twenty different large screens on one wall.

By the time they all arrived, including ASAC Patterson who thankfully wasn't in charge now that a task force had been created, the video was being patched through.

There were two different feeds playing. One angle was from too far away but the other was from directly above the bay that led to the garage.

Seth pressed his hands into the desk as he leaned forward and stared intently at the screen. Zoe's body language looked tense as she started making phone calls and he knew she'd been upset because of what he'd said to her.

"Who's she calling?" McKenzie demanded.

"We can check her cell history. I know her password," Seth said quickly.

"Fetch it," McKenzie told a bald guy Seth remembered from Washington State. The man immediately jogged away.

Everyone in the room tensed as they watched a uniformed figure appear on screen and walked toward Zoe from the south, holding something up to her.

"Is that a gun?" someone asked.

"No." Seth watched Zoe answer the phone—his call, he realized, and then she froze.

"He's showing her an image on his cell," Novak stated. "Presumably an image of someone they are threatening. Someone she cares about. We need to know who and where."

The kidnapper tossed her cell and then removed her watch

while Zoe was still processing the shock of whatever she'd seen on his screen. She started resisting then but it was already too late. Her abductor had her arm twisted behind her back and knew exactly the right pressure needed to ensure his captive had no choice but to cooperate.

That motherfucker.

"Get me the license plate. Put out a BOLO to all Capitol Police. Then get me a better image of the kidnapper."

"I know who it is." Seth watched the black car speed away, feeling like every inch the predator he was trained to be. "The leader of the BORTAC team Hersh and I were sent to investigate. Arthur O'Neill."

24

McKenzie narrowed his eyes at him. "You're sure?"

"Positive."

"The cartel burned Roger Bertrand to protect this sonofabitch," Hersh shook his head. "Why sacrifice him now?"

Seth's cell rang and he hoped against hope that it was Zoe, but it wasn't. It was her friend and his FBI colleague, Dr. Coco Monserrat.

"Hey, I tried to call my girl," Coco said, "but it went to voice-mail. We got DNA off the necklace and the rock. We are still processing the tooth because we wanted to make a mold of it before extracting the pulp."

"Did you find a DNA match?"

"Yes and no."

She sounded excited and he put her on speaker. "You're on speaker at JEH. Tell me what you found."

"The blood on the rock belongs to one Bruno Ramirez, a cartel guy who the FBI have been after for years. We also found someone else's DNA on the rock."

"Bruno Ramirez. Bring up what you have on him on the screen," Seth instructed the others.

"The DNA on the necklace didn't come back as a direct hit but probably belongs to a full sibling of someone who is in the database."

"Who?"

"I don't know who the sibling is obviously." Coco laughed because she had no idea Seth's entire world was now balanced on a crumbling precipice. "But she's closely related to Lorenzo Santiago, head of the cartel. Get this, traces of the woman's DNA were also found on the rock."

"Coco, thank you. I'll get Zoe to call you back as soon as I speak to her." His voice cracked. "One thing. Don't leave the campus today. Some things are going down and I don't want you to be in danger." Especially if they tortured Zoe until she revealed her friend's name. It was only a matter of time for anyone, but he didn't think Zoe would break easy. That thought made the lump in his throat grow big enough to choke him. "Find somewhere to sleep if you need to, maybe in the academy or even at the HRT compound, but don't leave, okay?"

Coco seemed to realize he was serious. "Okay," she said cautiously. "Is Zoe all right?"

Seth couldn't answer. "Talk soon."

He strode back to the Most Wanted posters and stared at the image of Bruno Ramirez.

The others followed him.

"Let's say he's the man who came out of the desert that night. The guy who brought the mule and the shovels." What did he want with Zoe? "A medallion Zoe picked up that day had the initials GS or CS engraved on the back. DNA found on it has been identified as belonging to the sister of this guy." He tapped Lorenzo Santiago's poster. The guy had a wicked scar down one side of his face.

"You're thinking Ramirez killed the boss's sister? Why?" asked McKenzie.

"Why do men ever kill women?" Seth asked darkly.

"Maybe Ramirez rescued the woman. Killed her assailant?" McKenzie suggested.

"Then why is his blood all over a rock found at a site where a dead body was discovered and subsequently disappeared? The sister's DNA was also on the rock," said Seth. "I'm guessing the sister hit Ramirez with the rock hard enough to make him bleed," and possibly dislodge a tooth, "and then he killed her."

Rage welled up inside Seth for this young woman.

"Otherwise, why hide the body?" Hersh added.

"No one except Zoe Miller ever saw a body," ASAC Patterson put in unhelpfully.

Seth ignored him and they all strode back to the operations room.

"Let's find an image of the sister, assuming Santiago even has a sister?"

"He does." This came from a man Seth didn't know but had seen in the task force briefing room.

He was blond with icy blue eyes and a hawklike gaze. "Gabriella Santiago. Currently studying in Mexico City." He held out his hand to shake Seth's. "Lincoln Frazer. BAU. From reports, Lorenzo Santiago is devoted to his sister, to the point of obsession and the US had considered using her as a lure for her brother at some point in the future."

Seth stared at the image of a beautiful young woman that appeared on one of the monitors.

"Interestingly enough, Gabriella's former boyfriend was abducted last evening from his LA home. Parents reported him missing but his expensive bicycle was left on the sidewalk," Frazer added.

"Any intel from our sources regarding Gabriella's movements?" Seth asked. "I mean, Zoe said the body she found had probably been there for about a week."

"I don't know," McKenzie said. "Let me call someone."

"But why do they want Zoe?" Hersh asked. "What does she have to do with any of it?"

Suddenly Patterson's words struck a chord inside him.

"ASAC Patterson is right. This all started after Zoe found that body and she was the only person to eyeball it. She tried to tell everyone but no one believed her." Except him. He'd believed her. And yet he hadn't trusted she wouldn't dump him the way Gemma had. He hadn't trusted she wasn't using him only for sex.

"She took photographs and gathered some physical evidence and someone on Ramirez's payroll saw her there and told the guy." That was the impetus for everything that had happened since. Seth thought about what she'd told him. "We need to get into her cloud. She couldn't access it because the security code went to her old cell phone which her abductors destroyed."

"On it," another of McKenzie's assistants volunteered.

Frazer sat down and stared thoughtfully at the screen. "This isn't the cartel waging war on the US government. It's Bruno Ramirez trying to save his own skin after he, for whatever reason, killed his boss's sister." He put his feet on the desk. "Lorenzo Santiago has the reputation of being a loose cannon but I'd categorize him more as a narcissistic sociopath who has—or possibly *had* —an unhealthy obsession with his sister."

"Any sign of Zoe from the Capitol Police?" Seth asked.

McKenzie shook his head.

Seth held everything he was feeling beneath a stoic layer of professionalism but inside he was freaking out.

"Where are they likely to take her?" Novak asked.

Seth tensed. HRT needed to prep for immediate action. But where...

Frazer pulled his lips to one side. "That's going to depend on whether it's Santiago or Ramirez who grabbed her."

Because Ramirez would likely have her killed immediately whereas Santiago, the unstable sociopath, wanted to interrogate her first.

Energy swirled inside Seth like a volcano about to blow.

"We need whatever intel we can gather from inside the cartel," Novak stated baldly. "And get DEVGRU involved and up to speed."

No one mentioned the elephant in the room. Zoe's mother

would need to be informed. She wouldn't be happy, and Seth couldn't blame her. He'd fucked up. He'd left Zoe alone when he'd promised he'd keep her safe.

"If it's Santiago, he's looking for his sister. We know where she was." Hersh put in. "I mean, how far could Ramirez realistically move her body that night?"

"Not far. No way Ramirez would risk taking her into a cartel tunnel should they have one in the area. They'd have cameras there." Seth stared at his buddy, his brain whirling. "Ramirez murdered the men who helped him move the body as soon as they'd done the job because he couldn't afford to leave any witnesses alive. Gabriella's remains are probably close to the initial dump site."

"Do you really think Santiago would risk coming into the US to find his sister?" asked McKenzie.

Frazer narrowed his eyes. "It's not likely. The guy is paranoid and spends most of his time holed up in a compound in central Mexico, but...it's not impossible. He has the ego to believe he can get away with anything, and his sister is his only living relative."

"Was," Seth corrected.

He could see some of the people in the room salivating over the possibility of capturing one if not two criminals on the FBI's Most Wanted List. And, as a man who took particular pleasure in bringing down drug lords, Seth understood that. But, right now, he didn't care about anything except getting Zoe safely out of these people's clutches.

"Let's mobilize Gold team to head to the border," Novak suggested. "If Capitol Police pick her up in the meantime we can redirect."

Seth nodded.

"Operators Hopper and Hersh have appointments with the Office of Professional Responsibility this afternoon," ASAC Patterson interrupted loudly.

Seth breathed in and held on to his temper. Novak and Hersh bristled.

McKenzie gave a dismissive swipe of his hand. "That can wait."

"But—"

"I require these men right now. OPR can deal with me about the matter later." McKenzie whipped off his tie and stuffed it in his pocket. "Your services on this task force are no longer required, ASAC Patterson. Have a nice flight back to Phoenix."

Patterson's eyes bugged. He'd tried to burn the wrong people this time. "I'll catch a ride back to Arizona with HRT."

"No." Novak shook his head emphatically, as if knowing one word from the arrogant fucker at altitude and Seth would toss his ass out of the plane without a parachute. "We're maxed out with operators and equipment. We don't have space." Novak gave the guy a forced smile.

Patterson stood there looking angry and vindictive.

Seth didn't care. "Let's go."

He turned and led the way.

———

Gold team was rolling. Ryan grabbed his and Seth Hopper's gear. Birdman was fetching Hersh's kit. Ryan hurried out of the cages, almost bumping into Meghan Donnelly in the hallway.

"Hey. Watch it." The words were sharp but her eyes were clear today. The expression on her face, grateful.

"Sorry," said Ryan.

They strode side-by-side down the hallway.

"About last night..." she said softly.

"What happened last night?" Aaron Nash was stealthy as a fox with the hearing of a bat. Ryan hadn't even noticed that he'd joined them.

"Last night?" Ford Cadell came out of a side room with his gear and the team's Belgian Malinois, Hugo, on a leash.

Out of the corner of his eye he saw Meghan stiffen.

"What about last night?" Hunt Kincaid and Will Griffin joined the group as they all hurried along.

She swore.

Well, shit.

"I asked Donnelly out on a date but she turned me down," Ryan said with an exaggerated drawl and despondent shake of his head.

"You don't date your teammates." Noam Levitt, a member of Echo squad like Meghan, sounded horrified.

"Shoot. I was gonna ask you next," Ryan shot back.

"Cowboy doesn't date anyone anyway. He just nails them, right Ry?" This from Grady Steel who was Donnelly's partner on the team.

It was Ryan's turn to flinch. "At least I can get a girl, Grady."

Grady glared at him. "Fuck you, man."

"Not tonight. I'm booked."

Grady scowled.

"Sorry, man, I didn't know getting a date was a sensitive subject." That was a lie. There wasn't much Ryan didn't know about what was happening with the people at HRT. "If you need any tips, let me know."

"Didn't work on Donnelly," Kincaid said wryly.

"Works 99% of the time. Obviously Donnelly is in the delusional 1%."

They turned the corner and a woman with long, ink-black hair stood on the stairs looking out of the window.

They all stopped and eyed her.

Dinah Cohen. On exchange from Israeli Special Forces, she glanced at them dismissively and then headed down the stairs toward the briefing room.

"Now that is one teammate I would love to—"

Ryan elbowed Grady in the diaphragm before continuing down the stairs. "We don't date teammates, remember? Or nail them either, for that matter." He didn't want anyone getting ideas.

"You're the one with the boundary issues." Grady rubbed his

chest. "If he ever bothers you again, Donnelly, let me know. We'll shoot him and dump his body in the lake."

"You can try." Ryan snorted which immediately got Grady's back up.

Meghan tried to come clean. "That's not—"

"Don't worry, Donnelly. I promise it was a one-off moment of drunken insanity." Ryan spoke over her. He knew she thought she was doing the right thing by trying to set the record straight but she was new on the team and he had armor plating as thick as a rhino hide.

"Jesus, that nurse on the flight yesterday wasn't enough for you?" Will Griffin shook his head.

"Nurse? What nurse?" Meghan glanced at him sharply and he pulled a face.

Fuck.

Life was getting complicated, and this was why he didn't even date.

"Her name was Deanna. She's an RN. She's thinking about going back to college to study medicine. Nice woman." Sexy, gorgeous, adventurous.

Meghan shook her head in apparent disgust and headed out the door.

Hadn't he told her he was doing her a favor?

He wished to hell he'd never followed Meghan home last night. Now his teammates hated him. She hated him and that damn little kiss on the side of his mouth haunted his flesh more than any connection had in a long time.

Nurse? What nurse?

———

Rather than drive, McKenzie ordered a helicopter. Seth, Novak, Hersh and a few others off the task force traveled with him to Andrews Air Force Base and arrived ahead of the rest of HRT.

The knowledge that Zoe was once again at the mercy of ruthless men who'd have no qualms hurting or killing her was driving Seth crazy. Fred Pengelli had been snatched on his way home from work, presumably to act as bait for Zoe. Fred's FBI shadow had been cut off by traffic and unable to intervene. No one had anticipated this latest act of violence.

Seth ripped off his tie and paced the tarmac.

"You okay?" Hersh asked quietly.

"This is all my fault, JJ." He stared up at the iron-gray sky and tried to hold it together. If he acted too emotional Novak would cut him from the team and Seth needed to be involved or he'd lose it. "After Birdman came over last night I freaked out and pushed her away."

Hersh's expression revealed frustration but not surprise.

"I know I have issues," Seth said, "but dammit a woman like her is never gonna stick around with a guy like me—"

"Why not?" asked Hersh.

"You know why not."

"I know what you tell yourself. That you basically aren't good enough for a woman like Zoe."

Seth bristled.

"Because you were abandoned when you were a baby. You're basically blaming that tiny infant for all the shit in your life. How reasonable is that?"

Seth closed his eyes. "It's not just that. I have no idea about my DNA—"

"Yeah, yeah, your daddy could have been a rapist or a serial killer." Hersh stood closer. "So what?"

Seth frowned. "What do you mean, so what?"

"Look at where you are, Seth. You were a frigging Navy SEAL. You are now an integral part of the best goddamn law enforcement unit in the United States, if not the world. You are not the sum of your biological parents no matter who they may be or what they may have done. You are the product of your own DNA plus your upbringing by damn fine people. You are a product of your training and years of dedicated public service. Zoe would be lucky to have you. What's more," Hersh leaned closer, "she knows it."

Seth wanted to yell out his frustration but he kept it locked down tight inside.

"I saw how she looked at you, not just the first night at the motel when the pair of you couldn't keep your eyes off one another. In the desert after the rescue. In the hospital when Dumb and Dumber turned up. She looks at you like you're her fucking hero."

"I am not her hero. I'm not anyone's hero." Seth rubbed his forehead. "Shit. I upset her before the meeting. I poured it all out and told her I couldn't get involved because I couldn't risk her walking away from me at some point in the future. I told her she held all the power and that I didn't like it."

"And you think from that she gleaned that you're completely head over heels for her?"

Seth hunched his shoulders. "Isn't that what I said?"

Hersh rolled his eyes. "You can't be subtle and guarded about this shit, Seth. It's not just your heart, brah, it's hers too."

Seth clenched his fists. "If I could go back, I'd tell her everything. That I want to help her move into her new home and paint the walls, maybe claim a part of the wardrobe for when I'm lucky enough to stay over. That I want to take her out for dinner that isn't from a fast-food chain. And that, at the end of a long mission, I want to end up in her bed, if only to hold her and listen to her breathe."

He swallowed and blinked away the mist of tears. HRT operators didn't cry. *Fuck*. "This is all my fault. I need to tell Novak we were involved."

Hersh grabbed his sleeve. "You are telling Novak jack shit. You really think he doesn't know?"

Seth turned his head and met his boss's stare. Novak's look was direct and full of concern. He seemed to be silently asking if Seth was okay.

Seth nodded. Turned back to Hersh.

"If I hadn't upset her, she wouldn't have gone outside—"

"And the cartel would have snatched her someplace else, maybe somewhere without cameras where we wouldn't know that fucker Arthur was involved or that she'd even been kidnapped."

Seth laughed. "Please don't try to convince me I did her a favor."

Hersh smiled slightly. "I guess not but there is no way this is your fault. Let's concentrate on rescuing Zoe and capturing some of the biggest narco-terrorists this country has even known."

Vehicles from HRT started to arrive, driving straight onto the plane.

Seth stared at the horizon and then he stared at Novak. He strode over to where the man stood impatiently waiting for everyone to load.

"You okay?" Novak asked.

Seth locked down his emotions and nodded. He had to believe Zoe was still alive. That he could save her and, if nothing else, apologize for destroying the best thing that had ever happened to him. And he knew where the cartel was taking her. Knew with the same certainty that he loved her and would always love her, regardless of whether she ever forgave him for being an oversensitive prick.

"Get them to search all vehicles and foot traffic going south to Mexico. Get the Air Force to re-route any unauthorized flights heading across the border."

"Don't you think that might make Santiago nervous? Make him rethink his plans?"

Seth shook his head. "He'd expect it. Anything else will put him on alert. I suspect he has a secret way in and out of the States, somewhere in that desert. We concentrate all our electronic and satellite resources on that part of Arizona and we might not only save Zoe," his priority, "but also find a cartel tunnel and hopefully scoop up some high-level drug lords in the process."

Seth held his boss's gaze. "But they can't know we're coming ahead of time. We can't set up and wait for them—I think they have eyes on the desert—possibly in both human and electronic form. We have to insert silently after dark."

Novak stared thoughtfully at Seth. "It's risky."

Seth knew it was risky. "It's the only way. If they even suspect law enforcement is in the area, they'll kill Zoe and scatter. And we can't alert Border Patrol about this op. Tell them about the abduction and give out a BOLO but do not tell them about our mission. We have no idea who else might be compromised."

Novak nodded and they headed into the back of the plane. It was time to go wheels up.

25

Zoe moaned as her whole body went airborne before smashing back down onto a hard surface covered in a grimy carpet that smelled oily against her cheek.

Her tongue felt thick and wooly. Her body heavy and lethargic.

It took a moment to come back into herself enough to remember exactly what had happened. Then she wished she hadn't. She'd been grabbed outside FBI HQ and her abductors had tranquilized her. She glanced around in fear, but it was so dark she couldn't even see the tip of her own nose.

She reached out her hand only to discover her wrists were tied together with a zip tie. She extended her arms and legs to test the limits of her space. Not big enough to fully stretch out. From the rough ride and stench of exhaust fumes she was traveling at speed in a small sedan.

Was she still in the US? Or had they somehow transported her over the border?

What did they want with her? She didn't know anything.

She recalled suddenly that she should try to signal for help by messing with the rear lights. She inched her way to the nearest corner and pulled away the cardboard covering the light fitting. She pulled on wires and tried to push out the bulb, but she couldn't get her fingers through the small hole to poke it out.

They went over a bump and she wrenched her fingers painfully against the metal. She bit down on a cry.

She needed something long and thin to push through the hole. She searched the entire carpeted area but there was nothing. She tried to lift the mat to get into the well for the spare tire but it was impossible with her bound hands. Even when she managed to lift the carpet the rigid board beneath her denied access.

Dammit.

Defeated, she lay there with her head rattling dully against the filthy floor. How long had she been out?

What had they done to her when she'd been unconscious? Frantically, she ran her cuffed hands over her jeans. The button was still done up and her shirt was tucked in the way she liked to wear it. She didn't feel sore so didn't think she'd been assaulted. But who knew what they planned to do once they stopped.

What time was it?

She had no clue. She didn't even know if it was night or day, but she would have thought some light would have leaked inside had the sun still been up.

They'd removed her watch and cell and the chance of anyone tracking her this time was slim to none. DC traffic was too busy and the kidnappers had probably switched cars almost immediately.

Her teeth chattered but she wasn't sure if it was from cold or fear.

She was assuming the FBI had realized she'd been abducted as opposed to thinking she'd simply left because she didn't want to deal with one particular member of HRT.

Someone, surely, would have witnessed her abduction from outside the FBI building? But what if they hadn't? What if Seth assumed she'd bailed on him because of her bruised feelings?

Once he found out what really happened, he'd blame himself,

but this wasn't his fault. She was the one who hadn't taken the threat seriously. She was the one who'd needed the fresh air. Maybe if she hadn't had such a horrible experience with Colm Jacobs, she would have acted differently, but the panic attack had been real. She was expecting another one at any moment.

It felt silly now.

Not the fact she'd been upset about Seth, but the fact she'd felt as if she needed to keep her feelings a secret. So what if he'd known she thought she might be falling in love with him? She wasn't about to start stalking him or make his life difficult if he didn't feel the same way. And they were hardly likely to bump into one another again, so what did it matter?

Tears dampened her eyes even though she didn't let them fall.

His words came back to her in a rush. About her walking away from him without a backward glance, about her having all the power.

Was he worried that she might stick her mom on any ex in a rush of vindictiveness? In that case why had it taken her so long to tell anyone about Colm?

With sudden clarity she realized he hadn't been talking about politics or careers. He'd been talking about her having the ability to hurt him—and that meant he cared. He cared but he was afraid of taking that first big leap alone. The same way she'd been.

It had been easier for both of them to pretend it was just sex and not…love.

His words had been a cry from the heart. He'd been practically begging her to say that she felt the same way as he did. That she wasn't simply going to walk away and leave him. She'd been too hurt and unsure to comprehend.

She wished she'd recognized that underneath the warrior exterior the man she'd been falling in love with had such a fragile heart.

She might have been braver then.

She wasn't sure if she was going to survive the next twenty-four hours, but if she did, she was going to tell him, gently and calmly, that she thought she might be falling in love with him. And, if he was interested in exploring this thing between them, to come track her down as soon as he had the chance.

She'd play it cool. Walk away with a swing to her hips and a come-get-me smile.

Yeah. That's what she'd do.

She swallowed her tears. She wouldn't cry. She wouldn't give these bastards the satisfaction.

The road got noticeably worse. The noise of the tires on the ground became a deafening roar in her ears.

She hoped her parents and brother weren't freaking out too badly. Did they even know she'd been taken? Would her mom be able to mobilize the troops again, or would Zoe be dead before anyone figured it out?

She froze as the image the man had shown her before grabbing her rushed through her mind. She closed her eyes. Maybe they'd photoshopped it.

The heavy dragging sensation of her thoughts told her she didn't believe that. So much easier for criminals to commit violence rather than to learn a computer program.

The vehicle slowed, although the ride was getting considerably bumpier as if they were driving over a washboard.

She thought she could hear dogs barking. Was this cartel headquarters? Was she in Mexico?

The idea made her stomach clench.

Her mother was not a pacifist. If they killed Zoe, Madeleine Florentine would rain death indiscriminately down on the cartel's heads.

The car came to an abrupt stop and Zoe rolled backwards and bumped her head on the metal of the trunk.

Ouch.

They cut the engine.

Her heart beat faster and she realized it might be better if she pretended to be unconscious. She hurriedly hid the damaged wires beneath the carpeted siding. Then she lay still and tried to regulate her breathing as footsteps approached the trunk.

———

As a former Navy SEAL Seth had made hundreds of parachute jumps, but he was well aware that a distracted mindset could easily get him killed. Worse, it might get his teammates killed and leave Zoe at the mercy of the cartel.

They were inserting into the desert at night via a HAHO jump —High Altitude, High Opening—which, in the absence of time, was the stealthiest approach possible.

Not everyone on Gold team was certified for HAHO so there was a mix of charlie, echo and snipers sitting along the sides of the C-130. Eight jumpers in all. Nash, Birdman, Cruz, Cowboy, Romano, Donnelly, Hersh, and himself.

Nice to have three full-time snipers in the group and the rest of them were all expert marksmen.

Novak and Livingstone were also qualified for HAHO, but currently unavailable. Angeletti was acting as jumpmaster.

Seth had never jumped with Donnelly before but as a former member of the 82nd Airborne Division's "Devil Brigade," she probably had more jumps than he did.

To avoid the risk of hypoxia and decompression sickness Seth and his colleagues sat hooked up to the pre-breather unit where they sucked in 100% oxygen to eliminate as much nitrogen as possible from their blood.

Green infrared lights lit up the cabin. The aircraft was virtually invisible in the night sky.

They were twenty miles from where Zoe had found the body of what was likely Lorenzo Santiago's little sister, and they were running dark. During HAHO, jumpers had the ability to glide for over forty miles. As they weren't yet sure where the cartel members were likely to be—if they came to the desert at all—the plan had a built-in margin for error.

Cowboy smiled at him through his goggles and gave him the thumbs up. Seth smiled back without an ounce of humor. Hersh sat, grim faced. The physiology technician—PT—was paying particular attention to his buddy in case the lingering effects of the rattlesnake's venom had an effect on his heart. Hersh had entered his sniper mindset and looked like a stone-cold killer.

Seth wore a polypropylene base layer and several warm layers beneath a windproof flight suit to combat the near minus fifty temps he and his colleagues were about to endure. He had two pairs of gloves, but he hadn't donned the second pair yet. He'd wait until after the two-minute warning.

The rest of HRT were ready to insert via helo as soon as Novak gave the order to rock 'n roll.

The cargo door opened.

Seth checked his gear again and lowered his NVGs.

His equipment pack was lighter than normal. The load had to be evenly distributed between all eight operators so they all weighed approximately the same and descended at the same rate. Unfortunately for Donnelly, that meant she could barely stand. They'd decided on the parking lot Seth and Hersh were intimately familiar with as the best place to land, assuming the bad guys weren't already there. The backup LZ was up on the plateau above the wash where Zoe had spotted the body.

The decision as to which place to head to was ultimately up to Luke Romano—a former Army Ranger—who would take the lead and navigate the landing. They all had infrared markings on the top of their chutes so they were visible to one another from the air but not from the ground.

They wore comms but Romano was the only one also connected to the Incident Command center the FBI had set up covertly in a warehouse at Fort Huachuca. No one wanted to risk any leaks that might tell the cartel where to aim those assault rifles, and no one trusted the locals right now.

The fact they were once again using tactics of war in their own country was not lost on any of them. But the cartel played to win and right now they believed they had the upper hand. Seth was happy for them to keep thinking that, right up until their last breath.

It was doubtful they'd expect HRT to come silently out of the sky, or to be confronted by DEVGRU, who were conducting the same type of operation south of the border—on orders from the president himself.

More operators and soldiers were stacking up at the border ready to find and block any routes across or go after Zoe, if necessary. The idea she might not be here when he landed would have torn him apart if he'd allowed himself to think about it.

He didn't.

The two-minute warning sounded and Seth's gaze flashed to Romano.

Had HQ spotted Zoe or cartel members in the target area or were HRT deploying now simply to get into position and wait it out? Seth didn't know. He consciously slowed his breathing because it didn't take much to throw off someone's physiology at 35,000 feet. He wasn't screwing this up now.

They all switched over to their personal oxygen bottles, and double- and triple-checked their gear. He pulled on the outer gloves to protect his fingers from frostbite. The light turned green and the jumpmaster indicated they approach the ramp.

Seth checked his helmet, mask, front-mounted pack one more time. The PT examined them all closely for signs of hypoxia or the bends.

Seth gave the guy a nod and purposely wiped his brain of everything except the approaching void.

The jumpmaster counted down with his fingers and then the jumpers unhesitatingly piled out into the inky night, one after the other, in a long string of tightly packed bodies.

The frigid temperature seared Seth's exposed flesh as the rush of air hit him like a sledgehammer. He counted and pulled the chute, his body jerked back by the unfolding canopy. Air whistled by as he sucked on his oxygen, once again forcing himself to slow his breathing and chill the fuck out.

He'd always loved jumping at night. Once the chute opened there was a peace and calmness that was unparalleled by anything he'd ever experienced—anything except holding Zoe in his arms at night as she slept.

It was the landing that had the potential to suck.

They moved into formation, silent now, virtually invisible as the moon had set an hour ago. Romano kept the descent slow, gliding like a vulture riding the thermals, even though Seth wanted nothing except to hurry things along.

But there was no rushing this. Usually, their mantra was speed and aggression but tonight it was strength and guile. He just hoped they weren't already too late.

The trunk opened. Zoe lay without moving and peered through her almost-closed eyelids at the two dark shadows looming over her. Were these the men who'd grabbed her off the street in DC? She thought so.

"Is she awake?" the one man asked.

"Oh, she's awake all right. Come on, Sleeping Beauty," the other man said confidently, shining a flashlight into her eyes.

Zoe squinted and turned away, giving up the pretense of being unconscious.

"Where am I? Why did you kidnap me?"

"Because I told them to."

This voice was new and carried an absolute authority she'd only ever heard from certain high-ranking politicians and five-star generals. People who were used to being obeyed without question. Zoe sat up slowly and one of the men helped her out of the trunk.

She held up her bound hands to shade her eyes from the headlamps from several motorbikes. The wind held a chill as it lifted her hair off her face.

She recognized the place they'd brought her to. It was the parking lot near the head of Brady's Trail.

She laughed suddenly when she realized she was right back where she'd started last Saturday. She and Seth had driven thousands of miles through blizzards, surviving cut brake lines and runaway trucks, and she was right back in the same place as if she'd never left.

And Seth...Seth was back in Washington, DC, probably mad at her for walking out on the meeting.

The men seemed disconcerted by her laughter and muttered to one another like she was crazy. Maybe she was. Who could blame her?

She heard whining and realized a man off to the side held two German Shepherds. A shiver of fear ran through her. Did they intend to make her run and hunt her down like an animal?

"I don't understand what you want with me." Zoe's mouth was dry as parchment and she was desperate for water but, also, she needed to pee. An uncomfortable combination at the best of times, let alone when surrounded by twenty hardened killers in the desert at night.

"What were you doing here last weekend?" the man who was obviously the leader demanded. She couldn't see his face clearly, but she was pretty sure she hadn't met him before.

Zoe went to cross her arms over her chest only to be brought up short by the plastic tie. Dammit. "What I always do in the desert. Look for people who died attempting to cross."

The man took a step forward and she could make out his features now. He was probably in his early forties. Dark hair, pale skin, what looked like blue eyes except it was hard to tell in this light, his face perfectly smooth except for the deep scar slicing one cheekbone.

Her mouth opened in surprise. She'd seen that scar before.

His eyes grew amused. "You recognize me?"

She nodded. "Lorenzo Santiago. I've seen your picture." On Wanted posters.

"You know what I do?"

"I know exactly what you do." A shiver ran up her spine but she decided two could play at that game. "You know who my mother is?"

He nodded.

"She's not a forgiving woman. You should probably know that before you continue."

"Then we are a lot alike, your mother and I."

Her eyes were slowly adjusting to the light, and she thought she recognized the silhouette of the man in black and that of the man who'd dragged her out of her motel room last Saturday night —Luis Ramirez. Someone shoved another person into the ring of light and her heart twinged painfully.

Fred.

She took a step forward only to be jerked back against the body of one of the Americans who'd kidnapped her in DC.

"Why did you bring him here when it's me you obviously want?" Zoe struggled to keep the tremor out of her voice.

"Because I wanted to make sure you came," Lorenzo Santiago said as if it were obvious. "And I want to make sure you tell me the truth. Otherwise I'll kill your boyfriend."

She held Fred's dark gaze. She swallowed, the action dragging slowly down her throat. She wasn't about to say Fred wasn't her boyfriend and risk them deciding he was disposable.

"What do you want to know?" she asked carefully.

"You found something in the desert last week." Santiago walked toward her. He had a pistol in a holster on his waist. Everyone else here seemed to be carrying an automatic rifle.

"I found some remains. Some disarticulated bones which I collected and your men later desecrated in a fire. Then I discovered the body of a young woman that I marked the location of for the medical examiner to collect the next day."

"Is this the woman you found?" Santiago thrust a cell phone toward her.

Zoe looked at the photograph of the vivacious young woman laughing at the camera. Her eyes sparkled, full of life and vitality.

"Who is that?" she asked.

"My sister," Santiago said gruffly. "Gabriella. Was it her?"

Had she been trying to escape life in the cartel? The fact she was related to this drug lord didn't mean his crimes were her fault, no more than Zoe was to blame for whatever policies the current administration implemented. Her heart broke for the young woman.

The missing corpse could be that of this man's sister but, for any scientist, being definitive without all the facts went against the grain. "It's hard to say for sure if that is the same woman I found. It's possible. The face was bloated from decomposition. She's wearing the same sort of necklace I picked up near the body and gave to the FBI for analysis."

The man took a step toward her. "Her *la Santa Muerte* medallion." He touched a similar gold pendant on his chest. "It was a good luck charm. She never took it off."

"*Santa Muerte* medallions are common," put in the man she was now sure was the man in black.

"This one had faint initials engraved on the back of it," Zoe said. "It was hard to tell exactly but..." Realization hit her in the throat as she connected all the dots. "Either CS or GS."

Santiago's face crumpled for a second before he brought himself back under control.

"I'm very sorry."

Under normal circumstances Zoe might have laid a gentle hand on the man's arm in an effort to console him. But Santiago exuded an energy that was malevolent and chaotic. Still, no matter how evil, he was human, and he was grieving.

"I have some photographs in my cloud that I might be able to compare to photographs of her. I can conduct a statistical analysis that will give us a solid indication as to whether or not they are the same person. Or we can compare the DNA off the necklace to your DNA."

"Show me the photos," Lorenzo demanded. "Now."

Zoe shook her head as fear lanced her. "I can't. I hope they are stored in my cloud, but I can't access my account without a security code which went to the cell phone your men destroyed last weekend." She sucked in a gasp as she felt the barrel of a gun poke her ribs. "Once I get a replacement, I should be able to log in." Maybe they'd keep her alive until she could view the photographs. Maybe she'd buy enough time for a rescue.

"Convenient."

Hardly.

"This person you found," Santiago said. "What was she wearing?"

Zoe frowned. "Jeans. Black and pink sneakers. A black t-shirt."

"My sister didn't own running shoes."

"Then maybe it wasn't her." Zoe had the growing feeling that he wasn't going to believe her no matter what she said.

"Did you kill her?" Santiago barked suddenly. He held his gun against Fred's sphenoid bone and Zoe wanted to cry.

"No! The person I found had been dead for several days when I saw her, possibly as long as a week." Zoe spoke quickly, needing to get through to this man that their work wasn't targeted against the cartel. "We spend our spare time searching for victims to bring them home to their families. We don't kill anyone. *You do.*"

Fred's eyes rounded in terror but Lorenzo Santiago was looking at her with a little less madness in his gaze so she jumped on it.

"You can see how important our volunteer work is. Reuniting the dead with their loved ones." She thought about Seth and how DNA didn't work for everyone. She wished she could have helped him find his biological family, give him the information he needed for closure. Right now, it looked like she would never see him again. Her fingernails cut into her palms.

She couldn't believe they'd argued.

Stupid insecurities had made her push him away when she should have just gone for it. Laid on him all the feelings that had exploded over the last few days into something terrifying and glorious.

"My sister isn't dead," Santiago insisted, but without conviction.

"If you truly believe that then why are we here?" Zoe wished she wasn't the one who had to attempt to talk sense into this deranged drug lord.

Rage filled Santiago's bloodshot eyes.

"Maybe she's lying. Maybe this is part of a plot and the Americans have Gabriella. Maybe they snatched her and faked her death," said the man in black.

"The way you snatched me?" Zoe couldn't resist the retort.

Santiago backhanded her across the face. Zoe's head snapped sideways in shock. Her brain shook. Son of a bitch.

"Well, we have someone they'll be happy to swap her for now, don't we?"

"From the pattern of decomposition, the woman I found was likely raped, strangled, then left in the desert like trash." Zoe tasted blood on her tongue.

A few feet away the man in black stiffened. She recognized him now from the images the FBI had shown her. Bruno Ramirez. Luis's brother. No one wore bandanas tonight. She didn't think that was a good sign.

"When whoever killed her realized I'd found the body, they came back and moved her. Then they tried to get rid of me and any evidence I might have collected. But they failed." She stared at Bruno and his brother. "I still had evidence in my jacket pocket that I gave to the FBI for analysis yesterday—including the medallion."

It was a small victory considering she'd probably be dead soon.

Santiago glanced sharply at Bruno.

"Think about it," Zoe pushed. "If I hadn't found her or

photographed the medallion, you would never have thought to look for her here. Not ever."

Santiago's eyes narrowed. "Where did you find this body?"

Zoe pointed west.

"Show me," Santiago ordered.

She didn't miss the look Santiago sent to Luis Ramirez, the man who'd dragged her out of her motel room last Saturday night. Luis sent his boss a slight nod and stepped behind his brother, Bruno.

Luis had told her on that terrifying night that he was good at following orders. Obviously, that included betraying his own brother.

Was Bruno Ramirez responsible for Gabriella's death? He was the one who'd walked out of the desert with a mule and two shovels in the early hours of last Sunday morning. She'd bet money he was the culprit.

Santiago said something to the dog handler who ran ahead with the animals in the direction Zoe indicated. Cadaver dogs, she realized. Fred was dragged to his feet.

Santiago waved his hand to indicate she go ahead as if they were out for a stroll.

After a few minutes walking through the black night lit only by the slowly moving dirt bikes, she said, "You know she's not where I found her anymore, right?"

"We will find her. I will prove this isn't my sister."

If he really believed that he wouldn't be risking everything by being here.

Zoe retraced her steps from last Saturday, certain that this time she wouldn't be returning home alive. She glanced back at Fred and his eyes told her the same story.

They were both going to die, and it wasn't fair. It really wasn't fair.

Dammit. She wanted the chance to tell Seth how she felt about him. That he was worthy. That she was pretty sure she was already deeply in love with him. And that it was okay not to love her back.

Suddenly the sound of barking had everyone lifting their heads.

The dogs had found something.

Something human.

Something dead.

26

Everything went to shit at a thousand feet.

Activity had been spotted at the original landing zone, so they'd aimed for the alternate LZ. Seth had finally allowed hope to seep through him that they might be in the right place and possibly arrive in time to save Zoe.

He turned his attention back to the job at hand.

The chutes they used for these jumps were incredibly responsive and maneuverable, but it also meant they were susceptible to wind conditions. Strong gusts were coming from the north that held a damp edge he didn't usually associate with the desert. It was a lot warmer down here than at high altitude, but his fingers were stiff and he was shivering despite the layers.

Everything seemed to be going well, then suddenly Donnelly was ripped sideways and seemed unable to get her chute under control.

"Donnelly, you okay?" Seth murmured because sound carried in the desert.

"Yeah. Wind caught me." Donnelly was number five in formation. Hersh six. Seth seventh, Cowboy eight.

"Can you get back in the stack?" Seth asked.

He watched her struggle with the lines, but her chute wasn't behaving. There must be a problem with the canopy or the lines had tangled.

"Negative."

The view through the NVGs wasn't promising. The ground was fast approaching, and she was going to crash into the side of the canyon rather than land on top of the plateau. Romano was concentrating on landing which was usually a bitch from high altitude.

"Head into the box canyon. We'll follow you. We'll rendezvous with the others afterwards."

"Roger that," she said.

"Watch out for cacti," Seth warned.

"And rattlesnakes," Hersh added.

Shit. Seth hadn't even thought about snakes in his rush to get here. Not that they mattered. Next to the worry he was feeling for Zoe his fear of snakes had faded into insignificance.

Donnelly struggled with the guidelines and Seth heard the operator's silk brush against the canyon walls, which would throw her farther off course. Hersh was aiming for a gap in the mesquite, dead ahead. Seth was virtually on top of his buddy.

There was a whoosh as Donnelly crashed into the rock. She didn't make a sound and Seth hoped to hell she was okay.

Hersh landed and Seth was only a few feet behind him. He hit the ground hard, a sharp pain stabbing through his foot on impact.

"On your six." Ryan Sullivan landed on top of Seth's chute and bumped into him, knocking him forward on the uneven terrain. "Fuck. Sorry."

Seth ignored the pain in his foot. As long as he could still use it, that was all that mattered.

He unclipped his harness and gathered his chute as Cowboy backed off the slippery material.

Seth stuffed the chute beside a big cactus he was grateful they hadn't smashed into. Before he'd even unclipped his pack,

Cowboy had scrambled up to Donnelly, who was suspended halfway up the cliff face.

Shit.

Seth eyed the rock wall, torn between the need to save Zoe and the need to rescue his potentially injured teammate. He gathered Ryan's parachute and stuffed it with the other two.

"You hurt?" Cowboy asked Donnelly. Everyone spoke in hushed voices that were barely a whisper, but crystal clear on the comms.

She let out a pained breath. "Just winded."

"Happy to hear that," Romano said from the other position. "I took out one of the cartel's watchmen when I landed on the ridge. I doubt he's the only one. We'll work our way down to the east end of the canyon and meet you there."

"Affirmative," Seth replied.

"Can you walk?" Cowboy asked Donnelly.

"Yeah." Donnelly drew in a sharp gasp. "I think so. At least I can feel my toes."

"I'm gonna help you down." Cowboy unclipped her enormous equipment pack and held it out and dropped it to where Seth and Hersh were standing below ready to catch it.

Then Seth watched as Cowboy unclipped Donnelly's harness. She dropped like a stone, but Ryan got a grip on her flight suit and hauled her back against the rock wall.

"Need me to carry you?" he asked her.

"Nope." Donnelly found a foothold and took her own weight. She cautiously turned so she was facing the outcrop.

"Follow my lead," Cowboy told her tersely.

Seth glanced around. At least the howling wind gave them some cover after it had decided to fuck with their landing.

Cowboy and Donnelly worked their way slowly down the rockface to the bottom of the canyon. Seth tapped Cowboy on the back and he moved aside to catch his breath while Seth and Hersh made sure Donnelly's limbs were intact.

Donnelly rolled her shoulders. "I'm good to go. Sorry for screwing up."

"You sure you're okay? You hit pretty hard." Cowboy sounded anxious.

Donnelly sent Cowboy a death glare.

If Seth hadn't been so worried about Zoe he'd have smiled. They quickly redistributed gear from the equipment packs, hid what they didn't need off the trail.

The sound of dogs barking had the hairs on Seth's nape standing on end. *Fuck.*

Donnelly brought up her carbine. "Let's get these mother-fuckers."

Seth prayed they were in time.

———

It took twenty minutes for them all to tramp through the desert in their pathetic caravan driven by death and murder.

Zoe finally figured out where she'd seen the men who abducted her the second time.

"You were at the motel in Gila Bend last week. You guys are with Border Patrol." She tried not to sound accusing but failed.

"Yeah. But it doesn't pay as well as these guys."

"And the benefits aren't as good," quipped the smaller, ferret-faced man behind her.

He meant her, or maybe it was what he hoped to do to her later...

Her stomach turned.

She shivered. The air was damp and cold, the wind making the walk even more miserable than the intense heat had. She was hoping a rattlesnake might pop out and bite a few of these jerks but she doubted it in these conditions.

She tried to look back at Fred but there were too many men with weapons between them, plus one man riding his dirt bike with both feet on the ground. She could hear the dogs whining now.

When they reached the spot that the dogs had marked there wasn't room for everyone. She was thrust into the inner circle where Lorenzo Santiago stood looking at the bare earth. The rain had washed away some of the recently turned dirt and a shallow indent was visible in the headlights.

It was a grave. A new one.

Thankfully, someone had remembered to bring shovels.

Santiago stood for a long moment staring at that small hollow. Then he stood back. "Let us see what the dogs have found."

Zoe half expected them to make her or Fred do the digging. She would have dug as slowly as possible in the hopes of delaying the inevitable.

She exchanged a glance with Fred. She mentally urged him to run if he got the opportunity. Maybe her best hope was turning these men against one another and praying she wasn't caught in the crossfire.

It didn't take long for the men who were digging to hit something that didn't sound like dirt.

A tarpaulin.

It took a while to uncover the rest of the body. Eventually two men lifted either end of the shroud, sand pouring off the rugged material.

"Be careful with her," Zoe warned. It didn't matter whether she was this drug lord's sister or some other unfortunate soul— she was someone, and she mattered. Zoe took a step forward and helped the men gently lay the body on to the ground. Then she carefully eased back the sides of the tarp to reveal the corpse she'd first seen five days ago.

So much had happened since last Saturday but none of it mattered to this poor woman.

Her captors all covered their noses and turned away in disgust. Santiago took a reluctant step forward but seemed bemused.

Zoe stood and stepped back.

Santiago raised his hands. "This can't be my Gabriella. It can't be."

"Did she have any tattoos or a birthmark?" Although the blackening skin might make them hard to distinguish without the help of infrared photography.

"No. How do I tell if this is my baby sister?" His cry was anguished. He looked too scared to approach the body.

"The medical examiner can run her DNA and compare it to yours."

"She's the right height. Her hair is long like that..." Santiago trailed off clearly not listening to Zoe. "What happened to her..."

Zoe eased to her knees beside the dead woman and everyone recoiled when she touched the body. "Let me check her mouth for something."

"What?" Santiago stared at her aghast. "Her mouth?" He looked as if he might vomit.

Zoe felt a certain grim satisfaction showing these men the end results of what they did. They killed people. She hoped the image of this decomposing woman haunted them for the rest of their lives even if she wasn't Gabriella Santiago.

"I found a tooth beside the body. The FBI have it now. But I want to see if Gabriella is missing a molar because otherwise that tooth likely belongs to her killer." Zoe gently eased aside the rotting tissues. "Nope. She has all her teeth."

The implications were obvious.

Santiago strode toward Bruno. "Open your mouth."

"I didn't kill your sister, Lorenzo. This is some trick the Americans are playing on us to make us turn on one another." The man forced out a laugh and looked around the desert as wind swayed a nearby cactus. "I mean, look at us. The FBI are salivating to arrest us both and here we are standing on the wrong side of the border all because of this bitch?"

Zoe narrowed her eyes at Bruno. He was lying. She knew he'd

killed this woman. He was a coward. His words sounded false and desperate.

"What were you doing in the desert last week with a couple of shovels, Mr. Ramirez?" she said loud enough to be heard clearly. "Who killed those two men not far from here? Huh? Because that wasn't the FBI and it wasn't me, either. What are you so desperate to hide?"

———

Bruno narrowed his eyes at the bitch who was ruining his life.

He pointed at the rotting corpse. "That is not Gabriella. And whoever she is, I didn't kill her."

"Open your damn mouth," Lorenzo shouted.

The bitch made herself small on the ground, but her glare didn't waver.

Luis brought his gun up and pointed it at him. Bruno wanted to cry out at the pain of betrayal.

Lorenzo took a few paces toward Bruno.

"Do it, brother. Don't make me force you," Luis said without a flicker of emotion.

Bruno opened his mouth and showed his brother, expecting a bullet for his lies and deceit.

Luis turned back to Lorenzo. "It's not him. He has all his teeth."

Bruno tried not to reveal his surprise or confusion. His brother hadn't betrayed him.

"Let me see." Lorenzo took a step forward and grabbed Bruno's head, tried to force his mouth open.

Bruno pulled away, and he and Lorenzo began struggling with one another while the others looked on in shock.

"You have lost your mind, Lorenzo! You are a crazy person with your paranoia and suspicion. Didn't we grow up together? Didn't my mother feed you at our kitchen table?"

Lorenzo lunged for him again but Bruno side-stepped and shoved him to the ground.

He pulled out his gun and pointed it at the man he'd once loved as deeply as any brother.

He could feel the tension snap taut throughout the men and knew there was no going back from this. You didn't threaten the head of the cartel with a gun and not pull the trigger.

He shook his head slowly. "I'm sorry, my friend. I'm so sorry but you've brought this on yourself."

Bruno pulled the trigger twice and the gunshots reverberated through the night, the sound quickly swallowed by the blustery wind. Lorenzo lay crumpled on the ground, dead.

Bruno looked around at the men who, like him, had followed Lorenzo for so long, but none of them looked surprised or even sorry, suggesting more than one of them had contemplated killing Lorenzo themselves.

He felt a surge of satisfaction and relief. Finally, he was the man in charge, the man who gave the orders.

"What do we do with these two?" Luis asked, his black eyes glittering as he pointed his gun at the meddlesome woman and her boyfriend.

"We kill them and bury them where no one will ever find them." Bruno stared at the blonde woman who'd made his life hell for the last four days. But that was over now and Lorenzo was finally dead.

He could afford to be generous. He glanced around at the others, saw lust in some of the men's gazes. "First, we have a little fun, eh? And make sure the boyfriend gets a good vantage point." He gave an evil little smile. "He might enjoy it."

27

_____

S eth was pretty sure he'd broken a bone on landing because every step he took hurt. Not that it would slow him down. He had no intention of stopping or sitting this one out. Zoe was nearby. And she needed him.

The eight operators had joined up and were now moving stealthily through the desert, past towering cacti. He moved carefully, so as not to trip over any boulders or scuff his boots.

Two gunshots rang through the night and Seth had to force all the fear and dread that they would arrive too late out of his mind.

"I have a visual on both hostages," Romano murmured to the Incident Command.

Relief crashed through Seth but it was short-lived. All it took was one bullet. One fucking bullet and Zoe's life was over.

They spread out and he reached a spot where he could see the small clearing. Two members of the cartel seemed to be arguing with one another and grabbing their crotches. One man lay dead in the dirt.

"Thirteen hostiles. Two hostages. Six dirt bikes. Two dogs and a handler off to one side."

They inched ever closer and Seth spotted Zoe kneeling in the dirt near a freshly excavated grave. A lumpy shape lay on the ground nearby, probably the body she'd been so adamant existed last weekend. Apparently, she was right about the dead woman being important.

A tall, dark-haired man Seth recognized as Bruno Ramirez went over and dragged her to her feet and pushed her into the center of the tiny clearing.

Bruno put a gun to Zoe's head. "Strip."

That son of a bitch.

"We have the green light to engage," Romano said softly.

"I've got the shot," Seth declared, praying Zoe didn't move.

Various clicks of agreement came across his earpiece as everyone picked a target.

Zoe bent as if to undo the kickass boots she was so fond of, although Seth doubted she intended to go meekly to her fate. He sent his bullet straight through Bruno Ramirez's thick skull before she decided to fight back or make a break for it.

The other operators fired, taking out half the members of the cartel in less than a second.

Seth took aim again, moving forward with the others, fighting the urge to rush. Zoe threw herself flat on the ground as bullets flew overhead. Seth spotted Roger Bertrand squatting in the dirt, turning his gun toward Zoe, probably remembering how Seth and Zoe had looked at one another when they'd first met.

Seth put a bullet between the man's ears even as the sound of a motorbike engine filled the night air.

The fact the runner was blindly spraying bullets behind him meant that when Hersh put a bullet in his back it was a clean kill.

That bastard Arthur could no longer betray his colleagues or his oath.

The tangos were either dead or wounded. Those left alive threw down their weapons and held their hands high in the air, begging for mercy.

The unit advanced quickly and four operators cuffed the criminals as two agents stood back to cover them from any unknown threats.

Seth went to Zoe, quickly cutting off her restraints while Cruz checked on Fred.

"I can't believe you're here." She threw her arms around him and held on so tight it almost hurt. He squeezed his eyes shut and banded one arm around her as she clung to him. "Thank you."

He turned off his shared comms because he had things he needed to say to her. He couldn't believe how good it felt to have her in his arms again. The fact she was safe. Whole. Alive.

"I love you," she said. "I know it's crazy and fast and you might not be interested in anything more with me, but I love you and I would love to see if we could make a go of things between us. But if that isn't what you're looking for I understand. No pressure."

Her words came out in a rush and he could barely keep up. But he heard the main words. She loved him. He grinned.

"I love you, too, Dr. Miller. I would love to give this thing between us a try, that is if we can ever get out of Arizona."

He kissed her. Despite the audience. Despite the fact he was supposed to be working. He thought about what a kick his old boss, Kurt Montana, would have gotten out of this scene and that made him smile.

After what seemed like an eternity, they finally let each other go and she wiped her eyes.

"If that's how you say thank you, I'm next," Cowboy deadpanned.

It broke the tension and everyone laughed, except Donnelly who rolled her eyes.

"Thank you. All of you." Zoe looked past the FBI agents and Seth watched her hurry toward Fred.

She paused as she passed Luis Ramirez who was on his knees with his hands cuffed behind his back. His brother was dead. Santiago was dead.

"Well, look at you, *chico*, following orders like a good boy." Zoe's tone was pissed, and Seth couldn't blame her.

Luis's lip curled. Whatever he was about to say was cut off

when Romano jerked him to his feet and led him away to a staging area, under arrest.

Seth limped in the same direction. Romano was taking photos of the dead men and sending them to HQ. Cruz was on the phone coordinating medivacs for the injured and transportation for the detained.

Seth could already hear the sound of approaching helicopters.

The man with the two dogs stood with his hands cuffed. "I usually work for the cops. They made me come out here. Told me they'd kill my wife and kids if I didn't help them find a body."

Cowboy petted the dogs. "Standard procedure to cuff you while we investigate your story and figure things out. I'll have locals go check on your family and make sure your dogs are taken care of."

"Thank you." The man looked shellshocked and Seth suspected he was telling the truth. What the cartel didn't have, they got through threats and violence.

"We need to get you two out of here," Seth told Zoe as she stood there hugging Fred.

The other man watched him over Zoe's head and held out his hand.

"Thank you, again. You've saved my life twice in less than a week. I'm going to need to buy you a beer."

Seth acknowledged the olive branch. "Just doing my job, but a beer sounds good."

A helicopter approached from the south.

Seth caught Zoe's hand. "You and Fred have to get on that flight."

She shook her head. "I'm not going without you."

He smiled at the familiar determined glint in her eye.

"Don't worry, ma'am," Luke Romano stated from behind him. "Hopper and Donnelly need to get checked out at the hospital ASAP."

"You're hurt?" Zoe asked.

Seth shook his head, then decided if he wanted this relationship to work, he'd better go with a little honesty. "Had a rough landing and think I might have fractured something in my foot. It's minor."

"Landing?" She frowned, then looked up into the dark sky and her eyes widened. "You didn't."

He laughed. "We did. I have the aches and pains to prove it."

"Donnelly managed to face-plant into a cliff," Cowboy said with a grin.

"I'm not injured."

"Get checked out anyway," Romano ordered.

Donnelly looked pissed but Seth was grateful for the opportunity to spend more time with Zoe.

Birdman strode over and held out his hand. "Damien Crow, ma'am. We didn't get introduced yesterday."

Zoe shook his hand and whispered, "Nice to meet you with my clothes on."

The operators as one swiveled to face her.

"Wow. My voice must carry, or you all have the ears of bats."

Seth winced and tapped his ear. "Comms. Thankfully, only between us and not to the whole Incident Command room, right Romano?"

Romano slapped his back. "Your secret is safe with us, although the guys are gonna want to know why we call Zoe 'Flash' from now on. I'm going to take extreme pleasure in never telling them."

Zoe groaned and put her arm around Seth's waist despite all his gear. "I want a cute nickname, like Bones."

"Pretty sure Kathy Reichs already took that one."

"Gah. That's not fair."

He realized she was helping to support him as he walked toward the chopper. This petite dynamo assisting him despite the fact she'd been through hell again.

"Are you really okay?" he asked.

She sucked in her bottom lip. "Yes, I am. Or at least I will be now." She squeezed him as if he was the reason why.

It warmed him. Made him realize how lucky he was. He better not blow it.

She hopped a little.

"Are you sure you're okay?"

"I have been dying to pee for about an hour now."

"Go behind that big rock over there."

"Seriously?" She looked around but the others were too far to see anything and Fred had walked on ahead to give them some privacy. "What if there are rattlesnakes?"

"I'll go check and make sure it's clear."

"Really?"

"For you, Doctor Zoe Miller? For you, anything. Anything at all."

EPILOGUE
TWO MONTHS LATER

Meeting the parents of someone you were serious about was never easy, but for some reason Zoe was so nervous her palms were slick with sweat. She wiped them against her thighs.

She'd worn a pretty dress and cardigan. Seth didn't look nervous at all.

"Mrs. Hopper. Mr. Hopper. It's so lovely to meet you." Zoe shook Seth's parents' hands and stood there feeling self-conscious and awkward.

Seth's parents stared at her for a long moment and then broke into wide grins.

Seth's dad gave her a bear hug and lifted her off her feet. Seth's mother smiled like Zoe had brought the sunshine with her.

"We are so happy to meet you, Zoe," said Seth's mom. Then she grabbed her son for a hug for the ages.

"As you might guess I don't often bring women home to meet the family," Seth joked.

"Come in, come in."

Zoe followed Seth's dad inside the beautiful craftsman-style house, through the open plan living room and into a brightly lit kitchen.

"You have a lovely home."

"Zoe's still in the process of decorating her new place."

"Seth's been helping when he has time off."

Her furniture had been released and the evidence suggested Colm Jacobs hadn't had anything to do with the brake sabotage—it had been a chop shop mechanic from Memphis who Luis Ramirez had hired. Jacobs had been given a written warning to stay far away from Zoe, but apart from that wasn't disciplined.

Zoe had installed an alarm system and hoped it was enough. She was thinking of getting a dog as long as Seth's building gave permission that it could stay overnight.

Luis Ramirez was now locked up in a US Federal facility. His brother and the others, including poor Gabriella Santiago, had been repatriated to Mexico for burial.

Zoe was glad it was all over.

She met Seth's gaze as he came to stand beside her. It had been an adjustment, starting a relationship with this man. In all honesty it was proving hard to be in Richmond without him, but it was only a couple of hours and there was an Amtrak three times a day.

She squeezed his fingers. They hadn't only come so she could meet his parents. Seth wanted to tell them something.

He cleared his throat. "Mom, Dad. There's something I wanted to run by you."

They both stood staring at the son they obviously loved. Zoe began to understand why Seth had found this so difficult. The thought of upsetting these people who loved him so completely would have weighed heavily.

"I, er, I've decided to search for my biological parents."

Seth's mom released a big breath. "I thought you would one day."

His father nodded too.

"It's not that I don't love you or appreciate everything you've ever done for me..."

His mom sucked in her lips to contain her emotion and

nodded. "No. We always expected this day to come, honey." She swiped at a tear that escaped.

Seth went to his mother and hugged her and his father rested a large hand on his back.

"I'm just worried you might be hurt by what you find," his mother said.

Seth hugged her tighter. "I won't be. I won't."

They didn't look convinced, and he laughed.

"Maybe if I didn't have you guys and Zoe in my corner, I might be, but I do have you. I need to know where I came from and what happened to my birth mother so I can make plans for my future. I hope she was all right, you know?"

He held out his hand for Zoe to join them and she found herself enveloped in the warmth of this family.

She found herself welling up as emotions rose inside her.

She stepped away and wiped her eyes. "Man, I thought Seth was the one who was going to cry when meeting my family, not the other way around. More from fright than anything else."

Her mother and father had been thrilled to meet him. Within five minutes he'd been regaling her parents with some of his— details redacted—high-octane exploits.

"Well, I'm looking forward to meeting them too," Seth's mom said archly.

"No pressure, son." His father slapped Seth on the back and they all laughed.

"I'm working on it, Mom." Seth sent Zoe a grin that curled her toes. "We've only known one another a couple of months."

"I knew the moment I set eyes on your mother." Seth's dad stared at his wife with all the love he felt clear in his eyes for anyone to see.

Zoe knew too. Had known pretty much from the moment she'd seen Seth.

Seth held her gaze and she knew he felt the same way. It was a whirlwind but it felt right.

"Come on, lemme show you the house."

"Dinner's in thirty minutes," his mom called as Seth took Zoe's hand and climbed the stairs.

He opened the door to his old room, and she smiled to see his trophies still lining the shelves.

"Oh wow. You were quite the sportsman."

Seth shrugged, scratched the back of his neck. "I guess I have a competitive streak."

Zoe wiggled her brows. "I know."

Seth smiled but he looked nervous all of a sudden. He pulled out a CD from the stack and put it on the stereo, chose a song.

He held out a hand. "We haven't gone dancing yet."

She went into his arms and he rocked her gently to the tune.

"We'll get the chance next month at Karina and James's wedding."

She froze when she recognized the song. Springsteen's "I Wanna Marry You."

Seth twirled her around and sang to her sweetly. And then he stepped away before she could catch her breath. He sank to his knees for the chorus and pulled a box out of his jeans pocket.

When he flipped it open, inside was a large square-cut sapphire with diamonds on either side.

"Zoe, would you do me the very great honor of one day becoming my wife?"

Her heart hammered and tears were suddenly streaming down her face and dripping off her chin. She didn't know why she was crying she was so damn happy. "Yes."

He stood and lifted her up in his arms and swung her around. When she slid down his body, she ended up catching her breath as she stared up into his handsome face.

He caught her hand and slid the ring onto her finger.

"It fits," she said in surprise. "Suddenly that trip I took with Coco to that fancy jewelers makes a lot more sense."

"I might have asked for a little help figuring out your size and what style you might like. We can change it though, if you'd prefer something else."

She admired the way it sparkled on her finger like the surface of the ocean. "No. I love this." She looked up at him. "I love you."

She dragged him down for another kiss and only the sound of his mother calling them stopped her from dragging him to bed.

"Do they know?" she asked.

"No." Seth's grin told her how much he loved her and them. "I did tell *your* father I planned to ask his daughter to marry me, and hoped he would support your decision."

"He was okay with that?" She blinked at him, shocked. Not that her parents had a say in her choices, but it was kind of sweet these two important men in her life had gone through that old-fashioned ritual.

Seth nodded, looking smug.

It was so fast and yet felt completely right.

"Let's go break the news to my parents. Be prepared for tears and hugs. Lots of hugs."

Zoe stared at the rock on her finger as they walked out of Seth's childhood bedroom, unable to believe this was happening. Everything suddenly felt so right with her world, everything so perfect.

She thought of Gabriella Santiago.

Life could go wrong so quickly, so unexpectedly. She squeezed Seth's hand tightly in hers, knowing they were lucky they'd found one another whatever the circumstances. She intended to love this man as much as she possibly could for as long as she was able.

"Hey, Mom, Dad. Break out the champagne. We have something to celebrate."

———

Thank you for reading *Cold Deceit*. I hope you enjoyed Seth and Zoe's story. Ready for the next installment of the Cold Justice® - Most Wanted series? Check out Toni's website for release information for *Cold Snap*!

. . .

Have you read the book that started it all? *A Cold Dark Place*, book #1 in the Cold Justice® series.

With over five thousand ⭐⭐⭐⭐⭐ reviews on Goodreads!

When a series of brutal murders links to a cold case that is intensely personal for one FBI agent, she seeks help from a cybercrime expert with a secret identity in the hunt for a vicious killer—in this award-winning Romantic Thriller from *New York Times* bestselling author Toni Anderson.

FBI agent Mallory Rooney spent the last eighteen years searching for her identical twin sister's abductor. With a serial killer carving her sister's initials into the bodies of his victims, Mallory thinks she may finally have found him.

Former soldier Alex Parker is a highly decorated but damaged war hero with a secret—he's a covert government assassin who hunts predators. Now he's looking into the murders too.

When danger starts to circle Mallory, Alex is forced out of the shadows to protect her and they must race against the clock to find the killer. But the lies and betrayals that define Alex's life threaten to destroy them both—especially when the man who stole her sister all those years ago, makes Mallory his next target.

Sign up for Toni Anderson's newsletter to receive new release alerts, bonus scenes, and a free copy of The Killing Game: www.toniandersonauthor.com/newsletter-signup

USEFUL ACRONYM DEFINITIONS FOR TONI'S BOOKS

ADA: Assistant District Attorney
AG: Attorney General
ASAC: Assistant Special Agent in Charge
ASC: Assistant Section Chief
ATF: Alcohol, Tobacco, and Firearms
BAU: Behavioral Analysis Unit
BOLO: Be on the Lookout
BORTAC: US Border Patrol Tactical Unit
BUCAR: Bureau Car
CBP: US Customs and Border Patrol
CBT: Cognitive Behavioral Therapy
CIRG: Critical Incident Response Group
CMU: Crisis Management Unit
CN: Crisis Negotiator
CNU: Crisis Negotiation Unit
CO: Commanding Officer
CODIS: Combined DNA Index System
CP: Command Post
CQB: Close-Quarters Battle

DA: District Attorney
DEA: Drug Enforcement Administration
DEVGRU: Naval Special Warfare Development Group
DIA: Defense Intelligence Agency
DHS: Department of Homeland Security
DOB: Date of Birth
DOD: Department of Defense
DOJ: Department of Justice
DS: Diplomatic Security
DSS: US Diplomatic Security Service
DVI: Disaster Victim Identification
EMDR: Eye Movement Desensitization & Reprocessing
EMT: Emergency Medical Technician
ERT: Evidence Response Team
FOA: First-Office Assignment
FBI: Federal Bureau of Investigation
FNG: Fucking New Guy
FO: Field Office
FWO: Federal Wildlife Officer
IC: Incident Commander
IC: Intelligence Community
ICE: US Immigration and Customs Enforcement
HAHO: High Altitude High Opening (parachute jump)
HRT: Hostage Rescue Team
HT: Hostage-Taker
JEH: J. Edgar Hoover Building (FBI Headquarters)
K&R: Kidnap and Ransom
LAPD: Los Angeles Police Department
LEO: Law Enforcement Officer
LZ: Landing Zone
ME: Medical Examiner
MO: Modus Operandi
NAT: New Agent Trainee
NCAVC: National Center for Analysis of Violent Crime
NCIC: National Crime Information Center

NFT: Non-Fungible Token
NOTS: New Operator Training School
NPS: National Park Service
NYFO: New York Field Office
OC: Organized Crime
OCU: Organized Crime Unit
OPR: Office of Professional Responsibility
POTUS: President of the United States
PT: Physiology Technician
PTSD: Post-Traumatic Stress Disorder
RA: Resident Agency
RCMP: Royal Canadian Mounted Police
RSO: Senior Regional Security Officer from the US Diplomatic Service
SA: Special Agent
SAC: Special Agent-in-Charge
SANE: Sexual Assault Nurse Examiners
SAS: Special Air Squadron (British Special Forces unit)
SD: Secure Digital
SIOC: Strategic Information & Operations
SF: Special Forces
SSA: Supervisory Special Agent
SWAT: Special Weapons and Tactics
TC: Tactical Commander
TDY: Temporary Duty Yonder
TEDAC: Terrorist Explosive Device Analytical Center
TOD: Time of Death
UAF: University of Alaska, Fairbanks
UBC: Undocumented Border Crosser
UNSUB: Unknown Subject
USSS: United States Secret Service
ViCAP: Violent Criminal Apprehension Program
VIN: Vehicle Identification Number
WFO: Washington Field Office

COLD JUSTICE WORLD OVERVIEW
ALL BOOKS CAN BE READ AS STANDALONES

COLD JUSTICE® SERIES

A Cold Dark Place (Book #1)

Cold Pursuit (Book #2)

Cold Light of Day (Book #3)

Cold Fear (Book #4)

Cold in The Shadows (Book #5)

Cold Hearted (Book #6)

Cold Secrets (Book #7)

Cold Malice (Book #8)

A Cold Dark Promise (Book #9~A Wedding Novella)

Cold Blooded (Book #10)

COLD JUSTICE® – THE NEGOTIATORS

Cold & Deadly (Book #1)

Colder Than Sin (Book #2)

Cold Wicked Lies (Book #3)

Cold Cruel Kiss (Book #4)

Cold as Ice (Book #5)

COLD JUSTICE® – MOST WANTED

Cold Silence (Book #1)

Cold Deceit (Book #2)

Cold Snap (Book #3) - Coming soon

The Cold Justice® series books are also available as audiobooks narrated by Eric Dove, and in various box set compilations.

Check out all Toni's books on her website (www.toniandersonauthor.com/books-2)

ACKNOWLEDGMENTS

I can well imagine the stress and uncertainty of not knowing what happened to a loved-one, especially if that loved-one had embarked on a dangerous journey. What must it be like to sit at home and wait for a text message to say someone dear to you is safe? What must it be like if that message never arrives?

The number of deaths and disappearances of people attempting to cross the US–Mexico border is staggering (close to eight thousand known cases since 1998. Data taken from the Colibrí Center website). The Colibrí Center works with the Pima County Office of the Medical Examiner (PCOME) to try to match those who are known to be missing with unidentified remains. Together, in 2006, the Colibrí Center and PCOME instigated the "Missing Migrant Program" using basic anthropological information. In 2017, they progressed to collecting DNA from concerned family members to further aid identification of unknown remains.

Everything in my story is fictitious, but the work these organizations do is real and necessary.

In addition, the International Organization for Migration (IOM)'s Missing Migrants Project is a world wide initiative helping families across the globe find missing relatives. The numbers are again mind-blowing and only liable to get worse during this period of conflict and environmental instability.

I hope you take the time to visit these websites and find out for yourself the great work these organizations do.

In writing the book, my thanks, as always, go to Kathy Altman who sees the wild first draft. Rachel Grant was amazing and always gives me excellent advice. Jodie Griffin was vital for helping me with certain aspects of this story, as was the wonderful Margarita Coale.

My developmental editor, Deb Nemeth, made me rip this story apart and rebuild it, better and stronger. I hope I made her proud.

Thanks to Joan Turner at JRT Editing, and proofreader, Alicia Dean. Your input is much appreciated.

Thanks to my assistant, Jill Glass, who is my rock when chaos flies. Thanks also to my fabulous cover designer, Regina Wamba, for her gorgeous artwork. Eric G. Dove is (still) on his sailboat recording the audiobook right now, living the dream! Thanks for being the voice of the Cold Justice® books and for being such an easy person to work with.

Huge love to my husband and kids for their constant support. And smooches to Fergus, my black Lab. Yes, I'm boring. I'm sorry!

ABOUT THE AUTHOR

Toni Anderson writes gritty, sexy, FBI Romantic Thrillers, and is a *New York Times* and a *USA Today* bestselling author. Her books have won the Daphne du Maurier Award for Excellence in Mystery and Suspense, Readers' Choice, Aspen Gold, Book Buyers' Best, Golden Quill, National Excellence in Story Telling Contest, and National Excellence in Romance Fiction awards. She's been a finalist in both the Vivian Contest and the RITA Award from the Romance Writers of America. Toni's books have been translated into five different languages and over three million copies of her books have been downloaded.

Best known for her Cold Justice® books perhaps it's not surprising to discover Toni lives in one of the most extreme climates on earth—Manitoba, Canada. Formerly a Marine Biologist, Toni still misses the ocean, but is lucky enough to travel for research purposes. In late 2015, she visited FBI Headquarters in Washington DC, including a tour of the Strategic Information and Operations Center. She hopes not to get arrested for her Google searches.

Sign up for Toni Anderson's newsletter:
www.toniandersonauthor.com/newsletter-signup
See Toni Anderson's current book list:
www.toniandersonauthor.com/books-2

facebook.com/toniandersonauthor

twitter.com/toniannanderson

instagram.com/toni_anderson_author

tiktok.com/@toni_anderson_author

9 781990 721052